Fortu

Alex Rutherford lives in London and has travelled extensively in India. Alex is also the author of the Empire of the Moghul sextet of historical novels currently being filmed by Disney Plus/(Hot Star) in India for a six-series, high-budget TV production. The showrunner is Nikhil Advani. The Empire of the Moghul books are also under motion picture development in Hollywood.

Also by Alex Rutherford

The Ballantyne Chronicle

Fortune's Soldier
Fortune's Heir

FORTUNE'S HEIR

ALEX RUTHERFORD

CANELO

First published in the United Kingdom in 2021 by

Canelo
Unit 9, 5th Floor
Cargo Works, 1-2 Hatfields
London, SE1 9PG
United Kingdom

A CIP catalogue record for this book is available from the British Library.

Print ISBN 978 1 80032 587 6
Ebook ISBN 978 1 80032 586 9

Printed and bound in Great Britain by Clays Ltd, Elcograf S.p.A.

'Wars and rumours of wars'

Matthew 24:6

Cast List

Fictional characters are marked with an asterisk. All others are real.

– A. R.

The Ballantynes

*Alexander, son of James and Riti.

*Charles, first cousin of Nicholas.

*Isha, daughter of James and Riti.

*James, laird of Glenmire, Nicholas' uncle and Charles' father.

*James, Nicholas' son by Meena and named for his great-uncle.

*Lizzie and Will, Nicholas' and Lucia's twin daughter and son.

*Lucia, daughter of a Venetian merchant and Nicholas' second wife.

*Meena, Nicholas' first wife and mother of James.

*Nicholas, husband first of Meena, then of Lucia, and father of James, Lizzie and Will.

*Riti, wife of James.

Tuhin Singh's family

*Tuhin Singh, youngest son of the Raja of Nokat and Nicholas' oldest friend.

*Kannika, Tuhin Singh's wife.

*Kaji, Tuhin Singh's and Kannika's son.

*Ravi and Sachin, elder sons of the Raja of Nokat and Tuhin Singh's half-brothers.

The British East India Company

Officials

Richard Barwell, council member.

George Bogle, Hastings' private secretary and leader of the first Company expedition to Tibet.

John Clavering, general and council member.

Robert Clive, former commander of the Company's armies and victor at Plassey.

*Gilbert Cuthbertson, Company envoy to the Moghul court in Delhi.

Philip Francis, council member.

George Grand, aide to Warren Hastings.

Alexander Hamilton, physician and member of Company expedition to Tibet.

Warren Hastings, the Company's first governor-general.

William Hornby, president of the Company in Bombay.

George Monson, council member.

*Septimus Simkin, member of the Revenue Board.

Charles Smith, president of the Company in Madras.

Edward Wheler, council member.

Company army

William Baillie, colonel.

George Brown, lieutenant-colonel.

John Carnac, major.

Eyre Coote, general.

*Vikram Das, army scout.

Charles Egerton, colonel.

Thomas Goddard, lieutenant-colonel.

Leslie, colonel (first name unknown).

Sir Hector Munro, general.

*Anil Roy, army scout.

James Stuart, brigadier.

George Watson, colonel.

Subcontinental rulers and leaders

Begums of Oudh.

Chait Singh, Raja of Benares.

Hafiz Khan, Rohilla leader.

Hyder Ali, Sultan of Mysore.

Kunga Rinchen, Bhutanese paramount leader.

Mahadji Scindia, Maratha leader and ultimately paramount leader of the Maratha Confederacy.

Najaf Khan, Shah Alam's leading general.

Panchen Lama, Tibet.

Phuntsog Namgyal, Chogyal of Sikkim.

Prithvi Singh II, Raja of Amber.

Ragoba, claimant to leadership of Maratha Confederacy (sometimes known as Raghunathrao).

Shah Alam II, Moghul Emperor.

Shuja ud-daulah, Nawab of Oudh.

Tipu Sultan, son of and successor to Hyder Ali of Mysore.

Zabita Khan, Rohilla leader.

Others

∗Aadesh, vizier of Nokat.

∗Anjuli Chastri, Gilbert Cuthbertson's servant.

∗Santem Denzongpa, one of the Chogyal of Sikkim's captains.

∗Asaf Khan, vizier to Shuja ud-daulah, Nawab of Oudh.

Anna Maria Apollonia Chapuset, the former Baroness von Imhoff and Hastings' second wife, called 'Marian' by him.

∗Comte de Tanguy, French military adviser to Mahadji Scindia.

Noel Grand, wife of George Grand, mistress of Philip Francis and later married to Napoleon's foreign minister Talleyrand.

∗Joss Granger, Calcutta silk merchant.

∗Martha Granger, Joss Granger's wife.

Lord North, British prime minister.

Nandakumar, an official of whose judicial murder Hastings is accused.

William Pitt the Younger, British prime minister.

∗Lal Seth, herbalist and Ayurvedic medicine specialist.

Prologue – Land of the Thunderbolt

'These Bhutanese brutes think they can rampage through Sikkim unchecked. They boast they come from the Land of the Thunderbolt and only a thunderbolt can strike them down… Such arrogance…' The Chogyal leaned back in his gilded chair. 'You hear that chanting? That is my priests praying to Guru Rinpoche, our patron saint, for their defeat… They will continue night and day until these bandits are driven out. The Bhutanese believe that because most of my army is far away in the west they have free rein. But they will learn their mistake.'

By the light of oil lamps flickering in niches in the whitewashed octagonal room painted with rows of tiny Buddha images, Nicholas Ballantyne couldn't quite make out the old man's expression but he could hear his determination. Seeing him glance towards the heavy wooden door as if to assure himself it was shut fast, Nicholas exchanged looks with Tuhin Singh, sitting beside him. Why had the Chogyal summoned them so urgently and what had he to say that he didn't want others to hear?

With something of a sigh, the old warrior leaned closer. 'For nearly forty years I, Phuntsog Namgyal, fifth of my line, have occupied the throne of Sikkim. Time and again I have driven intruders out and kept my people safe. You would think they would be grateful… and loyal… Many still are, but I can't be sure of all my counsellors. As I grow older, some scent an opportunity. My heir and only son, Tenzing, is still a child. If I should seem to fail as a ruler they'll see a chance to grab power for themselves before he comes of age. By driving out the Bhutanese, I will show them my time is not over.'

'How far have the raiders advanced into Sikkim?' Nicholas asked.

'At first their bands seemed to be going separate ways, randomly attacking and looting settlements and villages, but the latest reports suggest they are starting to combine. They may, as in the past, attempt to attack Gangtok. If I allow them to sack the sacred city of my ancestors, my people will lose trust in me. But I am too old to repulse them in person, much as I wish to… I need the help of younger men… men that I trust. You and Tuhin Singh. That is why I asked you here. I want you to lead my troops. Will you?'

Again Nicholas glanced at Tuhin Singh. Since he had quit the East India Company, he and his friend had lived with their families on land in the Himalayan foothills granted them by the Chogyal. Until now he had asked little in return beyond advice on how to respond to occasional approaches from the Company. Though this was no small request and a surprise, Nicholas felt honour-bound to accept. Tuhin Singh's briefest of nods told him he agreed. 'Yes,' Nicholas said, 'we will do whatever we can to help you.'

For the first time since they had been shown into his private apartments in his hill-top fortress of Rabdentse, the Chogyal's lined, high-cheekboned face relaxed. 'I thought I could rely on you. The latest information I have is that the Bhutanese are still two weeks' ride from Gangtok… the winter snows are only just thawing in the high passes so I doubt they're hurrying… We know roughly where they are congregating – no more than a few days from here. If you are quick, you can intercept them and catch them off guard…'

'But what about men, Majesty? You said most of your troops have gone to the west?' said Nicholas.

'Yes, to our borders with Nepal – as spring approaches and the passes open the Nepalese sometimes probe our defences. I thought a show of force – "a stitch in time" I think you British say? – would be salutary. But I still have some soldiers here in Rabdentse, including a patrol that only recently returned bringing the news that Bhutanese raiders were crossing into Sikkim. They can guide you. Their captain, Santem Denzongpa, is among my most trusted men and an excellent scout. Otherwise, you must take what you can find. The farmers must forget their spring planting and the herdsmen must leave their sheep and yaks. I will send orders that it is their duty to defend their country. I will also open my treasuries to you – to many money is a more powerful inducement than patriotism.'

Nicholas smiled. How many times while working for the East India Company had he seen the truth of that statement?

'What about horses?' Tuhin Singh asked.

'Take as many as you want from my stables – buy more if you need to. The herds are still here around Rabdentse, waiting to be taken up to pasture when more snow has melted – you should have no problem.'

'And weapons?' Nicholas continued.

'More difficult. My armouries are quite well stocked, though not with the European weaponry you are used to… Again, take anything you wish. I have a few small cannon here… those I purchased in Calcutta on your advice.'

'Yes, to defend the fortress. We'd never get them over the mountains,' Nicholas frowned. 'But we should take gunpowder… The Bhutanese have little experience of it – they keep themselves so isolated except when they go thieving – and still rely on their longbows.'

–

Forty-eight hours later, in the early morning chill, Nicholas and Tuhin Singh inspected the five rows of recruits lined up in the fortress courtyard. Apart from Santem Denzongpa's troop of twenty soldiers, well seasoned and well equipped, too many were either ageing men or callow youths. However, they numbered nearly one hundred in total. Recruits had been easier to find than Nicholas feared and in their hide tunics and woollen leggings some, at least, looked sturdy enough – short, but with muscular, slightly bowed legs. Each had a weapon, though some only barbed spears or long knives. Through the fortress's open iron-studded gates, Nicholas saw their horses, several nervously stamping and snorting, in a roped-off enclosure. In another waited pack mules loaded with tents, provisions and a dozen wooden barrels of gunpowder.

Brass trumpets blared as beneath a yellow canopy supported by four attendants the Chogyal stepped onto the balcony overlooking the courtyard. The recruits drew themselves up as raising both hands he intoned a prayer, then called out, 'Defend our land from these marauders and you will earn not only the gratitude of your king but of all the people of Sikkim. Go with my blessing…'

–

A freezing wind howling off the cloud-shrouded mountains stung into numbness what little skin of Nicholas' face remained exposed between his scarlet facecloth and his well pulled-down felt hat as he turned in the saddle to look back at his column snaking up to the first high pass of their expedition. 'They're keeping up well despite the weather – no stragglers yet. Perhaps some are tougher than they look,' he shouted over the wind to Tuhin Singh, riding easily and elegantly as ever at his side.

'You should know by now how little appearance counts amongst us hill people. Strength of mind and heart are almost as important as of the legs in the mountains.'

'True.' Nicholas nodded before the two lapsed into silence as fine snow began to whirl around them and they approached the top of the pass. At the summit they halted beside a small white Buddhist shrine. A low stone wall into which cylindrical brass prayer wheels had been set surrounded it and strings of triangular red, white, green, yellow and blue prayer flags fluttered from slim flagpoles bending under the wind. 'I'll make sure the men follow Buddhist tradition and go clockwise around the shrine to avoid offending the believers amongst them,' Tuhin Singh told Nicholas. Glancing up at the sky he added, 'It's getting late and the weather looks to be closing in even more. I suggest we find somewhere soon to make camp on the downslope in the lee of the wind.'

'I agree. Ask Santem – he'll know a suitable spot.'

Two hours later they had tethered their steaming horses, unloaded the baggage mules, erected eight felt tents and were cooking stews of rice and lentils spiced with turmeric and cumin. As soon as they had eaten, all retired to sleep, huddling together in the tents under animal skins and rough wool blankets. By morning the sky had cleared and the wind dropped but the cold was intense as Tuhin Singh and Nicholas crouched before a fire sipping hot butter tea from clay cups held in their gloved hands. 'It was so cold,' Nicholas grinned at Tuhin Singh, 'that when I went to piss this morning my urine froze as it hit the ground, building up into a nice little yellow cone.'

'It happens.' Tuhin Singh smiled. 'I'll check none of the men suffered frostbite overnight.' Getting up a little stiffly, he began his round of the tents. He was smiling though still walking awkwardly when he returned ten minutes later. 'Nothing but a frostbitten toe from stupidly going out barefoot. I told you these men were tough.'

'But you're limping. Why?'

'That thigh wound I got when Siraj-ud-daulah and his French allies attacked Calcutta all those years ago. The scar sometimes opens up in the cold. It's nothing…'

'Are you sure?'

By midday they had descended beneath blue skies to a lower level and were traversing a broad almost treeless plateau intersected by fast flowing, jade green streams fed by early spring mountain melt water. They halted beside the ochre walls of a Buddhist temple where the red-robed, shaven-headed monks offered them steaming tea. Before Nicholas could ask they told him they had heard from travellers, passing in the opposite direction and fearful of lingering long, about the ravages of Bhutanese bands no more than twenty or so miles away beyond a further high pass. The monks were already secreting the temple treasure, though the struggles of two young monks trying to hack into the frozen ground with spades showed how difficult it was to bury anything.

As Nicholas ordered his men to remount, the monks chanted blessings and blew rams' horns to summon success to their endeavours. As the booming of the horns reverberated around the valley, Nicholas muttered to Tuhin Singh, 'I hope the sound doesn't create avalanches to block our way.'

–

Next day, after struggling up and over another high pass, Santem, who had been scouting ahead, trotted up to tell Nicholas they were nearing where the Bhutanese were last reported to be. As the column continued across the desolate, icy landscape, the few small thatched dwellings they passed were deserted, as were their animal sheds. Then, in the distance, the sharp-eyed Tuhin Singh spotted smoke rising from a dip in the ground. Getting nearer, they saw it came from an encampment of fifty or sixty people with a herd of yaks. Long experience had taught Nicholas caution. Checking his pair of silver-mounted pistols were primed and loaded, he selected a dozen men to ride with him into the camp. As they entered, a tall man emerged from a tent. Walking rapidly up to the newcomers he asked, tense-faced, 'Who are you?'

'A friend of the Chogyal, riding on his behalf to drive off Bhutanese bandits,' Nicholas replied, using his knowledge of the Sikkimese language acquired over the years.

The headmen, as such he clearly was, visibly relaxed. 'You are welcome. We are fleeing the Bhutanese, forced to leave our winter homes with our yaks for fear of their ravaging, thieving and raping. We don't have enough weapons to defend ourselves against them.' Realising that the newcomers were friendly, more men and some women – several with turquoise and coral headdresses, others with babies strapped to their backs and runny-nosed small children clinging to their long, black skirts – appeared from the tents and gathered round.

'Do you know where the Bhutanese are now?' Nicholas asked.

To his surprise, the headman said, 'Yes. Our young men have been riding out some distance to keep watch. Only this morning one learned from fleeing villagers that two hundred Bhutanese are camped by an ice-clogged lake, a little beyond those hills.' The headman pointed towards hills only four or five miles away. 'They seem to be using the lake as a base from which to raid. More are gathering there each day. We could lead you to them and help you defeat them. Only lack of weapons – not courage – has held us back.'

'We should be honoured to have you with us,' Nicholas replied. 'Let's lose no time in reconnoitring their position.'

Nicholas and Tuhin Singh set out an hour later on foot with Santem, a small escort of their own men and some of the yak herders and their headman – horses might give them away or be unable to follow the most direct route. Their pace was slow and the going tough as, at times gasping for breath in the thin air, they scrambled up and across half-frozen scree slopes and stumbled through deep patches of snow, which overtopped their boots. As they descended from the line of hills Nicholas suddenly lost his footing on loose rock-strewn scree. Only Tuhin Singh's swift, strong grip on his arm prevented a long dangerous fall. 'Saved me again!' Nicholas muttered to his old friend.

'Where would you be without me,' Tuhin Singh replied.

When they reached flatter ground where pale green shoots of grass poked through patches of snow-free ground the headman took the lead. After half a mile he held up his hand and walking quickly back to Nicholas said in a low voice, 'If what we learned is correct, the lake where the Bhutanese are camped is below some more scree just beyond those rocks over there.'

Leaving the rest of the men behind with Santem, moving slowly and quietly Nicholas, Tuhin Singh and the headman neared the lip of what turned out to be a steep scree slope. From the cover of rocks at its edge they looked directly down on a large encampment at its base by the side of a lake on which ice sheets glinted in the late afternoon sun. A number of tents were grouped around fires and the numerous yaks tethered nearby bore testimony to the raiders' success. They appeared to have no fear of attack, since they had neither posted guards nor raised even the most rudimentary of defences around their camp. After a brief word with Tuhin Singh, Nicholas spoke quietly to the headman who quickly returned the short distance to his herders and set off with them and Santem in the direction from which they had come. Meanwhile, Nicholas, Tuhin Singh and their men concealed themselves among the tumbled rocks at the top of the scree and settled down to wait.

He hadn't really expected to see action again, Nicholas thought wrapping his cloak tighter around him against the increasing cold. For a moment, he again heard the deafening boom of the cannon at Plassey and the shrill trumpeting of war elephants as they charged in their glittering armour into the fight… Despite all war's horrors, all its pain and often pointless waste of life, he felt excitement as well as apprehension about the coming fight… That was something Lucia, his Venetian wife of many years, wouldn't understand. But she would accept that he couldn't refuse the Chogyal's request. Before leaving Rabdentse, he had dashed off a letter for a messenger to take to her at their estate, Glenmire, four days' ride to the south, explaining where he was going and why. She would worry – of course she would – but she would want to know…

Nicholas was starting to doze when Tuhin Singh nudged him. 'Look, they're here…' In the fading light a column was descending the scree slope on which Nicholas had slipped. As it drew nearer across the flatter ground, he was pleased to see his instructions had been followed to the letter. Santem and the headman had brought not only the remainder of Nicholas' own troops, but about thirty herders, most armed with weapons fashioned from agricultural implements, such as scythes and pitchforks. Most importantly they had also brought some of their shaggy surefooted yaks whose warm breath was rising into the cold air. Their clanging bells had been removed from around their necks for silence but a dozen had one of Nicholas' barrels of gunpowder strapped securely on their backs.

As the column halted, Nicholas walked across to the headman and Santem. At his whispered command the herders unstrapped the gunpowder barrels from the yaks, removed their coverings and positioned them at the edge of the scree slope immediately above the Bhutanese camp. Nicholas meanwhile carefully unwrapped the dozen tinderboxes he had asked Santem to transport personally in his shoulder pack. As the sun began to set, purpling the western sky and the ice of the lake, and after another word with the headman, Nicholas ordered the herders to lead their yaks forward, then halt with them a short distance behind the gunpowder barrels while keeping a tight grip on the animals' head ropes.

Nicholas then handed a tinderbox to ten of Santem's men and one to Tuhin Singh. Gesturing to them to follow his example, he positioned himself with the remaining tinderbox by one of the barrels all of which already had tapers attached. He then struck the tinder, lit the taper and, when it was fizzing and burning well, pushed the barrel over the edge of the slope with all the force he could muster, sending it rolling and bouncing down towards the still unsuspecting Bhutanese camp. The other eleven barrels followed almost immediately. One exploded before it had covered half the distance to the camp when it hit a rock, sending a shower of scree and stone splinters into the air. As the explosion echoed around the hills, Nicholas ordered the yak herders to lead their animals to the very lip of the slope.

Two more barrels exploded before they reached the camp. The other nine ran into it. One rolled straight through into the lake without detonating. Seven exploded in rapid succession as intended among the tents, creating some injuries and much confusion among the deafened, bewildered Bhutanese. The last barrel ran into a cooking fire and instantly detonated with much greater force, blowing the five raiders squatting round it into the air, together with their food, the pot in which they had been cooking it and blazing logs from the fire. Some of the logs fell onto nearby tents setting them on fire and lighting up the gathering dusk.

Even before the gunpowder barrels exploded, Nicholas shouted orders to the herders to drive their animals down the slope into the growing confusion of the camp and for his own and the headman's men to follow, weapons readied. Sent on their way with shouts and thwacks on the rump, the frightened yaks were soon stampeding, bellowing loudly, throughout the camp, knocking down and trampling raiders, some still staring around, uncertain what was happening and others searching wildly for their weapons. As the racing yaks scattered, ever more panic-stricken, they dislodged guy ropes, bringing down tents, trapping their disorientated occupants inside.

Nicholas, Tuhin Singh and their men were only a little slower, running and sliding down the scree slope, but one young Sikkimese in his eagerness stumbled, lost his balance and fell, tumbling head over heels down the slope until his head smashed into a protruding rock and his skull burst like a ripe watermelon. Nicholas and Tuhin Singh were among the first into the camp. Gesturing to a group of the men to follow him, Tuhin Singh ran towards several Bhutanese, some carrying broadswords and bamboo shields and others with longbows and quivers, emerging from an undamaged tent set slightly apart from the rest, close to the lake edge, and perhaps belonging to one of the Bhutanese leaders. All round Nicholas, his men and the herders were already slashing and hacking at the Bhutanese, some of whom still hadn't located their weapons.

The herders' faces bore grim, set expressions as they fought fiercely and silently, as if intent on avenging not just themselves but their compatriots who had suffered at Bhutanese hands. One thrust his makeshift spear into a tall, axe-swinging Bhutanese with such force that it penetrated the man's chest and the tip emerged from his back. As the raider lay where he had fallen, bright red blood running from his mouth as well as his wound, the herdsman calmly put his foot on the Bhutanese's chest and wrenched out his spear, oblivious to the dying man's cries. Then, still grim-faced, he went in search of more quarry.

Hearing a scream behind him, Nicholas turned to see a grizzled Bhutanese thrusting a burning brand from one of the fires into the face of a young Sikkimese who was scarcely more than a boy and had lost whatever weapon he'd been equipped with. Nicholas quickly raised his pistol, extended his arm, took aim and fired. The ball hit the man in the middle of his forehead and he collapsed onto the frozen ground, arms and legs twitching in his death spasm. Drawing a dagger, Nicholas then hurled himself on to the back of a burly, bearded sheepskin-clad man straddling another of his young soldiers. The man had his hands around the youth's throat and his thumbs on his Adam's apple, attempting to strangle him. Nicholas' first dagger thrust seemed not to harm the Bhutanese. He quickly realised it was because the man's sheepskin jerkin was too thick, so he shifted his attack. Before the man could twist to face him, Nicholas thrust the dagger deep into the side of his neck beneath his ear. Blood spurted and the man collapsed sideways onto one of the cooking fires where his jerkin and beard smouldered as he attempted to struggle to his feet before falling back again onto the fire.

Nicholas leapt up and glanced around. His men seemed to be gaining the better of the fight. Tuhin Singh and his group were advancing in good order, slowly driving their Bhutanese opponents at weapon point into the icy lake. As he watched, Tuhin Singh's sword broke through the guard of one who fell backwards with a splash, arms flailing, into the lake. Everywhere, the few Bhutanese who could were fleeing, most scrambling up the scree, but a few foolishly trying to swim to safety through the freezing lake water, which quickly closed over their heads. The rest were throwing down their weapons and surrendering.

As they did, one of the herders began attacking a disarmed raider, doubling him up with punches to the pit of the stomach and then frenziedly kicking him after he collapsed to the ground.

'That's enough! However much you want to take personal vengeance leave him!' Nicholas yelled. 'Let the Chogyal punish him – as he surely will, and most severely!'

Counting their prisoners, Nicholas and Tuhin found there were over one hundred. They themselves had suffered few casualties – only two others killed in addition to the youth who had smashed his head falling on the descent into the camp. Several, however, were wounded. Tuhin Singh was already placing ice from the lake on the burnt face of the young man attacked by the Bhutanese that Nicholas had killed. He should survive, even if scarred.

Nicholas walked across to Santem who was leaning over one of his men lying on the ground. The soldier had a foot-long slash in his thigh that had gone through the skin and yellow fat, deep into the flesh and sinew. He was biting his lip until it bled to prevent himself crying out as Santem probed and cleansed the wound while consoling him. 'You'll be all right. I'll sew it myself and put some of my mother's healing herbs on it to prevent mortification before I bind it up.'

As the man nodded, Nicholas added, 'We'll have litters made from the poles and fabric of the Bhutanese tents to carry you and the other wounded home.'

After camping for the night by the lake, with sentries posted to guard against any further Bhutanese travelling to their assembly point, Nicholas and Tuhin Singh roused their men early and set off with their prisoners back over the route they had taken, accompanied as far as their own camp by the herdsmen and their yaks, the latter's numbers considerably increased by those seized from the raiders.

–

'I knew you would not fail. I was your friend before but now our bonds are unbreakable. Thanks to you, my authority has been reinforced. None will dare question my rule… at least not for a while,' the Chogyal said as Nicholas and Tuhin Singh again sat with him in his octagonal chamber at Rabdentse. 'Be assured all who fought with you will be well rewarded, and the wounded and the families of the dead will be cared for. As for the prisoners you brought me, they will pay the penalty for their crimes, though I will permit them a more merciful death than they gave their victims.' Rising, the Chogyal went to a small cabinet from which he took two yak-leather pouches. 'I have kept you too long from your homes and families – something for which no thanks, no gifts, can compensate – but please accept these turquoise necklaces for your wives. I wish you a safe journey home.'

As they rode south, Nicholas noticed how quickly spring was coming. The purple buds on the rhododendron trees were well formed. Soon the blue mountain poppies Lucia so loved would appear. Tuhin Singh looked similarly reflective. 'What are you thinking about?' Nicholas asked.

'My horses. When we left I had three mares close to foaling... I'll be glad to see them.'

'Your wife and son too?'

'Of course, that goes without saying...' Tuhin Singh smiled.

–

Three days later, after Tuhin Singh had ridden into the gathering dusk to continue the further five miles to his own home, Nicholas trotted down the wide tree-lined track leading to Glenmire. Knowing a warm stable was not far away, his tired black gelding moved more briskly. Nicholas had constructed the drive to resemble that leading to another Glenmire – the boyhood home in Scotland he had never forgotten – though the house at the far end was very different. This Glenmire was no granite-faced, turreted Highland laird's home but a sprawling bungalow with wide teak verandas on all sides. As it came in view, he urged his horse into a canter, the hoof beats echoing in the cool evening air. Lights appeared on the veranda and a familiar figure came running down the steps towards him.

Reining in, he jumped from the saddle and, all tiredness and stiffness forgotten, swept Lucia into his arms. 'I've been anxious waiting for news. Why didn't you write to me again?' she demanded as he released her.

'*Cara*, I couldn't. We only returned to Rabdentse three days ago – believe me, I rode as fast as any letter could have reached you.'

'You must tell me everything, but first I have something to tell you. You have a visitor.'

'Who?'

'A mysterious young man. He won't say who he is or what he wants. But he claims he's travelled a very long way and insists on speaking only to you… I know you're tired, but it may be important.'

Part One

Old Debts and New Obligations, 1771–1773

1 – *Ghosts from the Past*

The stranger pacing Nicholas' wood-panelled library was a sandy-haired, plainly dressed young man a little shorter than Nicholas and aged about twenty. As Nicholas entered – he'd done no more than pause to take off his riding cloak – the visitor stepped towards him and after a moment's hesitation held out his hand. 'Greetings, cousin.'

'Cousin?' Nicholas ignored the stranger's hand. 'You are mistaken. I have no cousin…'

The visitor flushed. 'I'm sorry. That was clumsy. I wasn't sure how to introduce myself… My name is Charles Ballantyne – my father was James Ballantyne, your uncle—'

'No… that is absolutely impossible,' Nicholas replied. As clearly as if he were in the room now, Nicholas could see his uncle James in his study on that long-ago summer's day in the Scottish Highlands when he told him he was sending him to Hindustan to join the East India Company. Only later had Nicholas discovered why his uncle had been so insistent he must leave Scotland – to avoid becoming embroiled in the coming 1745 Jacobite Rebellion. Out of feelings of ancestral duty and honour – certainly not of conviction – his uncle had joined Bonnie Prince Charlie's army and lost everything. After the prince's defeat at Culloden, the vengeful Hanoverian government in London had confiscated his uncle's estate and put a price on his head. The last Nicholas had heard was that James had fled to France.

He kept the final letter from his uncle to reach him in a sandalwood box in his bureau in this very room. Though the ink had faded he knew every word – *There is nothing for you in*

Scotland – make Hindustan your home and prosper there – and do not think too harshly of your loving uncle… I will write again when I am sure of my safety. But James never had, and for years Nicholas had assumed he was dead…

Recalling himself with difficulty to the present, Nicholas gestured the young man to sit, while he himself stood by the fireplace where a fire Lucia must have had lit smouldered. As he struggled to gather his thoughts, Nicholas noticed that the stranger's anxious grey eyes never left his face.

'If what you say is true, where is my uncle now?' Nicholas asked at last, trying to suppress his conflicting emotions: hope he might finally be about to discover what had happened to the man who had been a father to him mingling with suspicion that this supposed relation might be a fraud of some kind… His accent was like nothing he had ever heard – not Scottish, not English, either.

'He died last year – I'm sorry to say – carried off by an inflammation of the lungs at our farm in Nova Scotia.'

'Nova Scotia? I thought he'd gone to France.'

'He did, for a short while, but in 1747 he crossed the Atlantic and settled near Halifax. Soon after, he married my mother, Shona McPherson – from another family of Jacobite exiles. They met on the voyage to Halifax… I was born a couple of years later…'

Nicholas said nothing, still trying to make sense of it all. Aware of his unease, his visitor looked even more worried and uncertain. 'I don't blame you for doubting my story… But see this! I have some proof of who I am…' With a little difficulty he pulled a ring from the small finger of his left hand and held it out. Nicholas immediately recognised his uncle's gold signet ring engraved with the Ballantyne family crest of a stag's many antlered head and beneath it the family motto, *Amicitia Sine Fraude* – Friendship Without Deceit. The same crest was engraved on the signet ring that his uncle had given Nicholas on his sixteenth birthday. He was wearing it now…

Handing the ring back, Nicholas said quietly, 'Yes, I do recognise it as his... I'm sorry, Charles – I think you said that's your name? Your arrival... what you've told me... has come as a shock. All these years in Hindustan I've not for a moment forgotten my uncle... I even called my house and land here Glenmire in memory of the Ballantynes' Highland estate... I named my eldest son James after him. But as time passed I gave up any hope of ever discovering what happened to him... That's why when you called me "cousin" it seemed so impossible. Now I've seen the ring I need to know more... Everything you can tell me about your life and my uncle's and how you come to be here...'

Without emotion, almost matter-of-factly, Charles described the unremittingly harsh Nova Scotian winters when bitter winds whipped up snowdrifts, sometimes ten feet deep. How his mother, never strong after his birth – he was his parents' only child – had finally died of consumption when he was only seven. The sudden brutal wars between the British settlers, the indigenous Mi'kmaq people fighting to retain their lands and the French, also eager for territory. The packs of savage grey wolves howling around their farmstead and the black bears in the immense dark and trackless forests.

Any joy Nicholas felt that his uncle had started a new life when so many Jacobites were betrayed and executed after the rebellion was tempered by the realisation of how harsh his life must have been – a cultured man in a cultureless wilderness – an exile cut off from everything and everyone he once knew. If only James had contacted him he could have helped... He hadn't grown as wealthy in Hindustan as some Britons but he wasn't a poor man either. He'd have done anything in his power...

By the time Charles finished, the candles had almost burned down and the chief light came from the logs in the hearth, which occasionally shifted as they burned, sending out showers of sparks. 'I still don't understand why my uncle didn't write again as he promised...' Nicholas said, not really expecting a conclusive answer.

But to his surprise, Charles replied, 'It was a deliberate decision. He wanted you to live your own life… not suffer for family obligations that were his, not yours, or so he told me… But towards the end of his life, as time and again our crops failed and his own strength faded, there was something he began to want from you. He'd discovered a little of what you achieved in Hindustan and was proud… Almost his dying wish was that I should find you and ask your help, for his sake, in starting a new life here, just as he once gave you such an opportunity.'

For a moment Nicholas bowed his head. So James had known and approved of what he had made of his chances in Hindustan… Looking up again he said, 'You know – when he first told me he was sending me to Hindustan I wasn't grateful. It was only later that I found out why he was so determined I should go. I came unwillingly to a land I've grown to love and which has given me a home and a family – my eldest son, James, named as I said after your father, is about your age. He left for Calcutta only a couple of months ago to join the Company army as an ensign. His mother, Meena, was a Hindustani… Later I met Lucia, and we have a son, Will, and a daughter, Elizabeth – Lizzie. You'll meet them both in the morning. I owe all this to my uncle. That is why I will do what I can for you. I still have some useful contacts in Calcutta… I'm sure one will help you find a position with the East India Company, if that's what you want. But now, you must be as tired as I am. I've been riding most of the day, as I suspect have you. I'll ask the servants to make up a room for you, if Lucia hasn't already, and bring you food. We'll talk again tomorrow.'

After seeing the new arrival settled for the night, Nicholas made his way down the shadowy corridor and raised the wooden latch on the door to the bedroom where Lucia would be waiting. By light of the candle he was carrying he saw that the thick woollen hangings, usually pulled around the bed to keep out draughts, were undrawn and that Lucia was still awake, lying back against the pillows. She sat up. 'You've been a long time… What was all the mystery? Who is he? What did he want?'

Nicholas put the candle down on a cabinet beside the bed and said nothing for a moment.

'What is it, Nicholas?' she asked again. 'Something wrong? I can always tell…'

'No, nothing's wrong, *cara*, but astonishing news.'

'What? Tell me.'

Lucia sat knees drawn up and arms clasped round them, as Nicholas explained who Charles was and why he had come to Glenmire. When he finished, she said nothing at first, but frowned to herself – an expression he knew well. 'Are you sure he's telling the truth?' she asked at last. 'If he really is your cousin, why didn't he write to you first to explain, instead of just turning up like this? Or why didn't your uncle give him a letter to you, some kind of testament, before he died? And even if what he says about your uncle going to Nova Scotia and marrying and having a son is true, it doesn't necessarily follow that he is that son – he doesn't look much like you. Not half so handsome! He could have stolen that ring and be an… an…' Unable to find the English word she lapsed into her native Italian. '*Un impostore* spinning a story he knows will move you to win your confidence and eventually allow him to get his hands on some of your money!'

'Why would he go to so much trouble, cross half the world and two oceans to find me, if he wasn't genuine? We're not that tempting a mark. You're sometimes too suspicious of people,' Nicholas replied, uncomfortably aware that he'd had exactly the same doubts.

'And you're sometimes too naive, too ready to believe the best of others… to trust them and not doubt their motives! How do you know he's really crossed two oceans? And now this man who could be anyone is here in our home, with us and our children—'

'The way he talked about my uncle… about their existence in Nova Scotia… it was… I can't explain. If you'd heard him, I don't think you'd doubt him. For myself, I'm prepared to believe him until he gives me reason not to – and, for my uncle's sake, to help him. But don't worry, I'll keep a close eye on him and question him further until I'm doubly certain of the truth.'

Recognising the finality in his voice, Lucia sighed and said no more. Instead, raising her arms, she lay back against the feather pillows and smiled up at him. 'What matters most is that you're home again and safe… Now come to bed… you've been away from me for far too long!'

-

'If you fought with him on all those campaigns, you must know Clive well. What is he really like?'

Nicholas poured more whisky into his cousin's glass, then returned to his own seat by the fire in his study. 'Robert Clive?' He half-smiled to himself. 'Where to begin? It's one of the hardest questions you've asked me. Clive's many things – some admirable, some perhaps less so… sometimes so restless, his moods so mercurial. From the moment we met on the ship taking us to Calcutta, his ambition was obvious… He used to say he'd kill himself if he didn't win the fame and fortune he thought his due. But he was a good friend to me. When people accused me of having Jacobite sympathies, even of being a Jacobite spy… he defended me.'

'When did you last see him?'

'About four years ago, shortly before he left Hindustan for the last time.'

'Is it true he took bribes? I read he'd amassed a very great fortune – over four hundred thousand pounds, they say…'

Nicholas hesitated. He'd often argued with Clive about what his friend saw as his natural right to profit from his genius, but that was something he'd only ever discussed with Tuhin Singh, who'd also fought at Clive's side, and with Lucia, of course. Debating it with a newcomer who had never even met Clive seemed somehow disloyal. 'I've heard the allegations against him… that are still being made against him… but his time in Hindustan is past. I think you'd find it more useful if we talked some more about current personalities and policies, that is, so far as I know about them. Like about Warren Hastings, another of my friends

– less flamboyant, a more self-contained character than Clive. It's rumoured he's about to come from Madras to become the new governor of Bengal. But perhaps that's not for now.' Nicholas drained his glass, stood and pulling out his gold pocket watch glanced down at it. 'The day draws on. I've things to attend to on the estate, so if you'll excuse me, we'll meet again at dinner.'

Nicholas wasn't being strictly honest… He had nothing particularly pressing to do but sometimes a little of his cousin's company went a long way. It would be good to get into the fresh air for a while. Since Charles' arrival Nicholas had been conscientious in trying to 'educate' him about the complexities of politics in the sub-continent – the rivalries between competing rulers and factions: the Moghul Emperor Shah Alam, who'd only recently returned to the Red Fort in his capital Delhi after twelve years in exile spent mostly in Allahabad; the Marathas, a warrior confederacy ever-intent on expanding their territories, whose greatest weakness was their internal rivalries; Hyder Ali, the fabulously wealthy ruler of Mysore, whose ambitions were no less dazzling than the diamonds of which he was so fond; the Company's uncertain but ambitious ally the Nawab of Oudh, and the Nawab of Bengal, now reduced to little more than a Company vassal.

Nicholas had also been trying to navigate Charles through the no less complex – though less bloody – intrigues within the great bureaucratic machine of the East India Company, from the officials in Calcutta, Madras and Bombay trading in cargoes of everything from silks and fine cottons to iron and gum, to the Court of Directors and the shareholders in London, demanding ever larger profits and dividends, all of them increasingly looking to the Company's growing army of British and Indian troops to protect and promote the Company's interests. In talking about the Company he was trying hard to be fair, not allowing his own doubts about its activities to intrude. It would be for Charles – if Nicholas could get him the position he seemed so set on – to judge the Company for himself…

As Nicholas set off down the track leading from the house to the fields to inspect a new-planted crop of potatoes, his two dogs – lurchers imported from Britain – running excitedly ahead, he reflected on his new-found relation. Charles was certainly an adept pupil, with an agile mind and remarkable memory for detail, if a little lacking in humour. The Hindustani rulers seemed to interest him less than who was who in the Company hierarchy in Calcutta, their peccadilloes and their rivalries and what these might mean for an ambitious newcomer like himself. Consequently he seemed keen to understand how the Company exercised its control. When Nicholas likened it to a huge spider, spinning an ever larger, more intricate web across Hindustan, anchored in its three centres of Calcutta, Madras on the south-east coast and Bombay on the west, Charles had been admiring, which wasn't quite the reaction Nicholas had intended. Above all, not unlike the young Clive, Charles seemed focused on understanding how the Company could help him succeed, to become wealthy – something that perhaps he should forgive in one whose life had been hard and who had travelled so far to reach Hindustan.

Sometimes, studying Charles' broad features, Nicholas looked in vain for some resemblance to his uncle. Charles must take after his mother. But by now Nicholas had no doubt at all that Charles was exactly who he claimed to be. Everything he'd told Nicholas of James' flight from Scotland with his friend Cameron of Lochiel after the fiasco of Culloden, his period of penury in a Boulogne lodging house before taking ship for Nova Scotia rang true. Charles had been able to describe Glenmire – a place he had never seen – minutely, from the long drive lined with century-old lime trees to Loch Arkaig directly behind the house: 'There's a turf-roofed bothy on its shores, isn't there? My father said he kept a rowing boat and his fishing rods there,' Charles had said. He also knew the story of how Nicholas' sea-captain father and his wife had drowned off the coast of China – details that could only have come from James himself.

Plainly his uncle had never ceased to regret his confiscated estate and Charles seemed to have inherited a vicarious nostalgia for it. One of the few times he'd become really animated – apart from once when Nicholas had taken him trout fishing in the hills with Tuhin Singh – was when he talked of his determination one day to see it – perhaps even to buy it back. 'It's a Ballantyne house. Ballantynes should live there… own it…' he had said, raising his chin.

For an apparently self-contained young man, Charles was getting on well with the two of Nicholas' children who remained at home. The thirteen-year-old twins, Will and Lizzie, enjoying the novelty of having a stranger in the house, pestered him for tales of Nova Scotia and the ferocity of the Mi'kmaq people. Charles, in his turn, relaxed in their company and his storytelling became less painstaking and more imaginative. Last night Nicholas had overheard Charles telling them a tale of a Mi'kmaq master magician – a kind of shaman, Nicholas thought – who could summon the salmon upriver to spawn.

Yet Lucia still had reservations about their guest. Only yesterday, Nicholas had tried to encourage her to be a little less distant with him, but as usual she had an answer ready: 'I agree my earlier suspicions were wrong – I don't think he's an impostor. And I admit there's nothing specific to dislike – he's pleasant and well-mannered enough. But there's something about him… something I feel rather than something I can describe… He reveals so little of himself. For a young man he's too reticent… too reserved… too calculating. Have you noticed how those cool eyes of his are always studying us – as if we're fish in a bowl?'

'Perhaps it's shyness or awkwardness,' Nicholas had replied, stroking her cheek. 'Try to put yourself in his shoes. Imagine how it must feel to come halfway across the world to an alien place to ask relations you've never met to help you. His life has been harsh and uncertain and, for all he knows, might remain so if he doesn't make a good impression on us. Is it any wonder he prefers to be guarded, to think before he speaks, even to keep his real self to himself?'

'If he thinks his life has been hard,' Lucia had said, 'it's been nothing compared to mine before you and Tuhin Singh saved me…' For a moment a shadow had crossed her face. Then she'd continued, with only a slight smile of irony. 'Perhaps Charles will improve under your guidance as I'm sure I have...'

Making his way back to the house as the light began to fade, Nicholas found himself reflecting on Lucia's words. It was remarkable how little the trauma of her early life seemed to have affected her. Strength of spirit, a determined love of life and the will to survive had carried her through. In time he was sure she would come to think more kindly of Charles. As for his cousin, he might start to unbend a little if the opportunities he clearly coveted materialised.

2 – *Land of the Dead*

The eyes of everyone around the breakfast table were on Nicholas as he slid a silver paperknife beneath the heavy wax seal of the letter a servant had just brought in. He'd immediately recognised the two lions rampant, each gripping a banner with the flag of Saint George, and the motto beneath *Auspicio Regis et Senatus Angliae* – Under the Auspices of the King and Parliament of England – impressed into the blood-red wax: the East India Company's coat of arms.

Scanning the lines of copperplate writing, Nicholas smiled. 'This is better than I'd hoped. I suspect we have Hastings to thank, now he's arrived in Calcutta to take up the governorship. Charles, the Company is offering you a post as aide to Septimus Simkin, a member of the Revenue Board, which advises the governor on financial matters… They want you in Calcutta as soon as possible.' Nicholas passed the letter to his cousin, whose face flushed with pleasure as he read it.

'I'd assumed I'd be starting out – if at all – as a clerk, a writer…'

'I'll go with you. With the monsoon ending, it's a good time to travel down to the plains. I've some business there and I'd like to see Hastings again.' Nicholas looked at Lucia. 'Why don't you come? We could take the children?'

'If we could see James of course I'd come, but his regiment won't be back in Calcutta for a while… And you know what I think about Calcutta society. The men boring on endlessly –' for a moment her eyes rested on Charles, still studying the letter '– about their prospects and profits and the cliques of women exchanging sugary words in public while privately appraising and usually disparaging each other's clothes and jewels – and husbands! I've never felt I fitted in… I don't warm to them and they don't warm to me! We'll go as a family another time.'

-

Three days later, Nicholas and Charles mounted up. A wooden box with Charles' few possessions was strapped to one pack mule and Nicholas' water buffalo hide travelling bags to another. Their saddlebags were well stuffed with provisions. 'I don't trust the food they give you along the way – this will be better for you,' Lucia said, patting the bag on Nicholas' horse as he bent from the saddle to kiss her goodbye. Looking up at Charles, seated on a grey gelding that Nicholas had bought for him from Tuhin Singh as a farewell gift, Lucia said, 'Travel safely, Charles.'

'Thank you for taking me into your home,' Charles replied stiffly.

Since moving with his family to Glenmire, Nicholas usually made the journey south to Calcutta twice a year. As the familiar trail descended through the dark alpine forests, a civet cat shot across their path, causing Charles' horse to skitter and Nicholas to grab its bridle to prevent it bolting.

'I'm not usually such a bad horseman,' Charles excused himself, 'the horse is new to me and more mettlesome than I thought.'

'I'm sure,' Nicholas replied, while thinking, just as Lucia had suggested, how self-protective, not to say self-defensive, Charles remained. A simple 'thank you' would have sufficed. He'd made sure Tuhin Singh had provided a quiet mount.

By the third day, the air was growing warmer and stickier and the vegetation thinning. They soon caught their first glimpse of the hazy expanse of the plains below. The closer they got to Calcutta, the quieter the already reserved Charles became. Perhaps it was nerves, Nicholas thought… Hadn't he himself felt apprehensive when he landed in Calcutta from the East Indiaman *Winchester* all those years ago?

On the sixth and last night, as they squatted by the fire of a *chaikhana* – teahouse – sipping cardamom-spiced tea, Charles put down his clay cup and looked at Nicholas. 'By this time tomorrow we'll be in Calcutta and my new life will have begun. Have you any final advice for me?'

'Not really. I suppose if I learned anything during my years with the Company, it was never to let anything surprise me. In some ways the Company's like one of those great juggernauts used in Hindu temple processions – you'll see them in Calcutta, huge seemingly unstoppable chariots. The Company appears so solid, with warehouses piled with goods, ships loading and unloading, all those grand colonnaded offices and mansions and liveried messengers racing through the streets, as if Calcutta were ancient Rome. But it's more fragile than it looks. A sudden event – the death of an important ally, conflict between rival rulers, Britain and France going to war again – can upset the balance overnight. When I first arrived in Calcutta and saw the Company flag flying proudly over Fort William I never thought that just a few years later Calcutta would fall and I'd be among those fighting through the streets to recapture it.'

'So you're warning me to be prepared for anything? That wasn't really what I expected...' Charles said.

'You thought I was going to tell you to work hard, be polite to your seniors, not drink too much and avoid catching the French disease from the whores, didn't you? But you know all that already... I hope...'

–

Reaching Calcutta next day in the early afternoon, Nicholas accompanied Charles to Septimus Simkin's office in Fort William. A clerk explained that Simkin, whom Nicholas had never met, was away upcountry but due to return the following day. In the meantime he would show Charles where he would work and later help settle him into his accommodation. Satisfied his cousin was in good hands, Nicholas made his way to his usual lodgings

– a light, airy hostelry run by a former butler, *khutmagar*, at Government House named Mohammed Aziz. After he'd washed and changed, Nicholas asked for paper, ink and quill and dashed off a note to Hastings, which he gave a houseboy a small coin to deliver. Then he pulled off his boots, took a well-thumbed volume from one of his travel bags – Tobias Smollett's *Adventures of Roderick Random* – and settled down to read.

As the pale light slanted through the woven tattie screens covering the windows the following morning, Mohammed Aziz brought him his *chota hazri* – breakfast – tea, fresh-baked bread and mango preserve. An envelope rested on the brass tray. 'A messenger brought it just now from Government House, Ballantyne Sahib.'

Nicholas recognised Hastings' writing. Good! He hadn't been sure Hastings would be in Calcutta – as the new governor he would have to pay courtesy visits to neighbouring rulers. Inside was a cream-coloured card engraved with the Company crest. Beneath, the message read simply, *Delighted you're here. It's been too long. Come to Government House around seven this evening – it will be good to see you and trade news! W. H.*

The sun was setting, streaking the sky orange and pink as Nicholas set out. The city's dramatic sunsets always enchanted him. If he had Lucia's talent for watercolours – 'Not so surprising, I'm from a city of artists,' she'd reply when he admired her work – he would paint it. The recently built Government House with its long, elaborate facade surmounted by classical urns looked as magnificent as the Company architect no doubt intended as Nicholas walked towards it along Esplanade Row. Arriving at the porticoed entrance, Nicholas handed his card to the liveried, red-turbaned major-domo. After studying it gravely, he returned it and said, 'Thank you, you are expected. The governor is in the gardens but will soon return. This attendant will take you to the terrace to wait in comfort beneath a *punkah*.'

As Nicholas seated himself on a rattan chair in the cooling breeze of the *punkah* swinging back and forth above him like a gigantic butterfly wing, the attendant enquired, 'May I bring you a drink? *Nimbu pani* – lemon water – perhaps?'

Nicholas shook his head. 'No, but thank you.' The minutes passed, no one appeared and he grew restive. He should have brought *Roderick Random*... After twenty minutes he stood up. If Hastings was somewhere in the grounds, why not look for him?

Marble steps led down into the garden. Moths danced in the golden light from scented oil burning in brass saucers set along the gravel path. Somewhere among the trees a late roosting peacock shrieked but of Hastings – or indeed anyone else – there was no sign. Nicholas then noticed a light glimmering at the far end of a side path to his right and headed towards it. As he got nearer he realised the light came from a small Grecian-style pavilion, outside which a marble fountain bubbled. The door was ajar. He pushed it a little wider and stepped inside.

A man and a woman were lying on a couch entwined in a passionate embrace. The woman, looking over her lover's shoulder, saw Nicholas and cried out. As the man twisted to see who was there, Nicholas recognised Hastings' oval, long-nosed face and heard him gasp in surprise. A blushing Hastings got to his feet, catching one buckled shoe in his companion's trailing rose-satin skirts. The woman tucked an exposed pearly white breast into her bodice and adjusted her lace fichu but calmly lay where she was, two diamond clips sparkling in her auburn ringlets. She looked more than a little amused by Nicholas' startled expression.

Recovering from his surprise, Nicholas too was amused. His serious-minded, rather ascetic friend had never struck him as a Lothario. With a muttered, 'I'm sorry... Excuse me...' he turned and set off back towards the house. Moments later, footsteps crunched on the gravel behind him and a voice called, 'Nicholas, wait!' Looking round, he saw the short, spare figure of Hastings tugging on his coat as he ran after him.

'Forgive me. I knew you were coming of course, but I forgot the time,' Hastings said, clapping Nicholas on the back.

'I can understand why...'

'Yes, a fine woman, isn't she.' Hastings gave an almost schoolboy smirk. 'Marian – my mistress, as most of Calcutta knows, and so would you if you didn't live in the wilderness.'

Glancing back over his shoulder Nicholas saw a tall, elegant shadow hastening away in another direction. 'Tell me about her.'

'Marian's my pet name for her. Her proper name is Anna, Baroness von Imhoff. We met on the ship bringing me back out to Madras. She nursed me when I became ill. By then I was already in love with her… But it's hard for Marian to be in such an awkward situation here… Even though I'm governor – or more probably precisely because I am – spiteful tongues wag behind my back and she often has to endure slights and not so *sotto voce* comments from the so-called ladies of "ton" – sour-faced harridans, most of them. But I intend to marry her once her husband gives her a divorce. Come on. Let's get back to the house.'

'Her husband?'

'The baron was on board too. He's a strange fellow without a penny to his name. He tries to make a living painting miniature portraits and – I'm glad to say – he's acquiescent in his own cuckolding. Marian and I became lovers before we reached Madras. When we arrived, they both moved in with me. So long as I pay for his bed and board he turns a blind eye to us… When I was appointed governor here, they came too. But I'm hoping to persuade him to return to Europe to obtain a divorce. I'm confident he'll go if I offer him enough money… You know, when Mary died I never thought I'd take another wife, but that was a long time ago and I don't think nature intended me for a bachelor. There have been others before Marian, but none like her!'

Later as they sat over a bottle of port in Hastings' office – as usual Hastings drank only sparingly – Nicholas said, 'I should thank you for finding my cousin a position in the Company. I assume it *was* you?'

Hastings smiled. 'You know how sorry I was you left the Company – God knows we need people like you. So when you offered me another Ballantyne, how could I refuse?' But then, twirling his port glass in his slim fingers, his expression grew sombre. 'It really *is* good to see you, Nicholas. I'm not saying that out of politeness… or because of our shared past. I have to think about the future now and you're one of the few I trust enough to discuss it openly with.' He glanced up at the large portrait of Clive on the wall as the victor of Plassey, the very personification of power and authority like a Roman Emperor at his Triumph. 'You won't believe the enemies I have already acquired in Calcutta – they never wanted me appointed governor and are willing me to trip up. If I don't, they plan to trip me themselves.'

'But isn't that always the case with important new appointments? The Company's a snake pit of factionalism, backbiting and jealousy – that's one reason I chose to get out of it. You're different – a natural politician, thick-enough skinned and stubborn enough to survive!'

'I'm glad you think so, even if I'm not sure you mean it as a compliment! But listen to this.' Unlocking a bureau, Hastings took out a letter. 'It's from a former colleague in Madras who writes – "I can't tell you my sources but please take this warning seriously and not with your usual sang froid. *Do not employ any cook: let your fair female friend, the baroness, oversee everything you eat!*"'

'What? Don't you think someone's just making a joke at your expense? You can't seriously believe there's a plot to poison you? Even the Company's not that Byzantine, surely…'

Hastings smiled a little wryly. 'I realise it sounds stupidly melodramatic but the truth is I just don't know… I suspect lots of people might like to see me in the next world, though how many would act to put me there might be a different matter… In any case you're right, I am stubborn. I won't be deflected by people who don't care as I do for this country. Destiny has given us a position in Hindustan and we must show ourselves worthy of it.'

Detecting an unexpectedly evangelical note in Hastings' voice, Nicholas leaned forward a little. 'What exactly do you mean?'

'That it is our duty to act with probity and honour. I mean to break the power of corrupt Company men who I have proof are using authority – given in Clive's time – to gather taxes in Bengal to enrich themselves at the expense of the people, and indeed the Company. I will bring them to heel with the help of men like your cousin – new to Bengal and uncorrupted – to enforce my authority and bring prosperity to Britons and Hindustanis alike. Without mutual trust the relationship between us will only founder, to nobody's benefit – least of all the Company's.'

Hastings and Clive were very different, both in temperament and physique, Nicholas reflected, the short, slight Hastings so calm and calculating, the image of officialdom, the much taller, constantly pacing Clive bursting with effervescent if sometimes ill-directed energy and disdainful of convention – an irresistible force of nature. Yet Hastings had the same ability to pursue his aims with unstinting determination… The distinction between them was more of means employed rather than results achieved. If they were dogs, Clive would be a frenetic, dashing, leaping hound and Hastings a persistent little terrier – both well capable of securing their quarry. But which was the more honest about his personal ambitions? Clive had always freely admitted he had come to Hindustan for personal fame and fortune. From what he'd just said, Hastings seemed to believe both he and the Company had a moral purpose in Hindustan beyond mere trade and profit.

The thought prompted Nicholas to ask, 'Something's been puzzling me. Before you returned to England seven years ago, you told me you were leaving Hindustan for ever. Yet it wasn't so long before you were back, in Madras. Why? Was it because you felt you'd more to do here?'

Hastings hesitated a moment, then said, 'Not entirely, if I'm honest. I went back home a wealthy man. I had plans to buy back Daylesford, the Hastings family estate since the Middle Ages, but sold to a Bristol merchant before I was born. However, things didn't work out as I'd anticipated – the fault of my expensive tastes, I fear. I may dress plainly but I like beauty and luxury around me – I've never forgotten how it felt being brought up a near-pauper by my bankrupt grandfather when my mother died and my ne'er-do-well father absconded. I spent lavishly – too lavishly – and without any regard for the value of money and very nearly went bankrupt myself. So when the Company offered me a post in Madras I grabbed at it. Maybe it was fate, otherwise the governorship here would never have come my way… But it's growing late and I've gone on enough about myself. I want to hear what you've been up to in Glenmire… helping the Chogyal, I believe? And I suppose you're still playing that violin of yours? Marian's been teaching me the guitar. Perhaps one day we should play something together…'

–

A sense of contentment and relief flowed through Nicholas as he cantered up the drive after the long ride from Calcutta. As always, Lucia was running out of the house and down the veranda steps to fling herself into his arms as he dismounted. She was quickly followed by Lizzie and Will, all smiles, who immediately began to question him. 'How does the new Fort William look? Is it finished yet? What books have you brought back? Did you get us copies of *The Expedition of Humphrey Clinker* like you promised?'

'And James Cook's account of his circumnavigation, I hope?' Lucia added. 'I want to read about his observation of the transit of Venus from Tahiti. They say such measurements could be key to working out the distance between the Earth and the Sun…' During long voyages with her merchant father she had grown interested in astronomy. At Glenmire she studied the planets through the telescope she had ordered from Calcutta. The first person to point a telescope into the night sky, Galileo, was – she told Nicholas – Italian, like her.

From Lizzie there were further questions about the fashions and dances among Calcutta's young. Everyone, including Lucia, wanted to know more than Nicholas had disclosed in a recent letter about Hastings' love triangle with the Imhoffs. Was the baroness as pretty as some reports said? What was the secret of her allure? To grimaces from her children, hating to think of their parents in any romantic context, Lucia asked, 'She didn't set out to tempt you, did she? Not like that bosomy French *voluptueuse* you once told me about when you were younger in the south?'

'No, no…' Nicholas replied to his children's further discomfort. 'I've saved myself for you as always.'

–

Over the next weeks, his children would have been further embarrassed had they known the passion of their parents' lovemaking. During the day, in the cool tranquillity of Glenmire, Nicholas began to practise more regularly on his violin or travelled across to visit Tuhin Singh, his wife of four years, Kannika, and their young son, and from there went fishing and hunting with Tuhin. Soon letters began to arrive from Charles. He wrote in increasingly tedious detail of the Company's business and his own attempts to ingratiate himself with his seniors whose position and ancestry he respectfully listed. On several occasions when describing men Nicholas knew, his judgements seemed wide of the mark, ascribing wisdom to those Nicholas considered boastful windbags and mistaking modesty for mediocrity. When Nicholas read out to Lucia some of Charles' more extravagantly erroneous opinions, he concluded apologetically in defence of his cousin, 'Time and experience should overcome his naivety.' Lucia's sole response was a raised eyebrow, fully equivalent to an explicit *Do you really think so? Or wasn't I right about him all along?*

James – to Lucia's annoyance – communicated far less, often from remote parts of Bengal where Hastings had launched a campaign against marauding bandit bands – 'dacoits' – plaguing the region. In one of his early letters he related briefly that he was well and settling into military life before proudly recounting how his own quick wits and local knowledge had saved his company's baggage train from a flash flood when crossing a seemingly dried-up river, which the sudden onset of the monsoon turned into a raging torrent. A further letter arrived by *dak* at dusk one evening as the family were finishing their evening meal, the highlight of which had been some trout caught that day by Nicholas with

Tuhin Singh. Nicholas agreed to the pleas from his wife and children to read it out to them as they were finishing their coconut pudding. He broke the seal with the badge of James' regiment stamped into it, cleared his throat and began:

> *You won't believe what happened this afternoon! There we were riding quietly along the road to Jalpur, when ahead of us and a little bit off the track we saw a flock of vultures flapping excitedly about in the branches of some big mango trees. We went to investigate and as we rode closer we heard moaning. Then, in the purple shadows beneath the trees' thick leaves, we saw a dozen wretches suspended by their arms from the branches. They were mostly naked and bleeding. Buzzing green-black flies were crawling over their wounds. Of course, we cut the poor devils down at once. One – an old man with a long white beard – was dead – the vultures had already had one of his eyes out.*
>
> *We thought nearly all the rest were dead as well but after we gave them water, some started to revive. They took a long while – most had dislocated shoulders – to make any sense. They told us they were grain merchants and had been part of a bigger caravan. Fifty or so dacoits with muskets had ambushed them earlier that day. Some of their companions had fled. The dacoits had thrown others for sport to crocodiles in a slow-moving river a little distance away, betting with each other how long they would survive, and aiming to encourage the rest to tell them where their treasure was. The dacoits refused to believe they were just poor men taking a few mule loads of grain to Jalpur. They thought that hiding among them were some gem merchants they'd heard about in the bazaars. So they stripped and searched them, probing their bodies in a way that outraged human dignity, for jewels they thought they might have concealed. When they couldn't find any, they got angry and hung the men from the trees, whipping them and threatening to light fires beneath their feet in a vain attempt*

to make them disclose where their non-existent jewels were, before giving up and riding off with their mules and the grain.

As you can imagine, we patched them up as best we could, although some wounds were so deep and so crawling with flies I doubt they'll survive. Then in late afternoon we set off in pursuit of the dacoits. We soon found that crocodile-infested river with a few mangled and half-consumed limbs and some bloodied scraps of clothing on the muddy banks or floating in the shallows to confirm the merchants' tales. Two dozen or so sated crocodiles were basking in the dying sun, half in and half out of the water. We shot as many of the brutes as we could – apparently they don't lose the taste for human flesh once they've tried it. Once their blood began to flow they set about each other in a truly cannibalistic fashion, thrashing the water into scarlet foam with their scaly tails.

Nicholas paused and looked at Lizzie. 'Are you sure this isn't too much for you? Too gruesome?'

'No, no,' his daughter replied. 'It's exciting. Go on. I want to know everything about James' life.'

Nicholas took a sip of water and continued:

We then rode hard after the dacoits – their tracks weren't difficult to follow. They hadn't gone far – just a few miles into some marshland where they were making camp for the night. Dusk was falling by then so our lieutenant – we call him 'Nervous Nellie' (perhaps you've heard of him, Lieutenant St. John Neville, he says his father knew you?) – wanted to wait till dawn when he could have brought more men up, but I persuaded him that even if we were a little outnumbered we should attack at once when we had the advantage of surprise.

Crouching low, with mosquitoes buzzing round our heads, we crept through the reeds towards the light of their fire – the ground was squelchy and we put the occasional duck in the air, so I thought they'd surely hear us, but several of them were arguing loudly about the division of the grain and then the bullfrogs started croaking fit to burst. The robbers didn't know a thing till we were on them, firing a musket round from the reeds, which dropped a few, and then rushing at them, swords and pistols drawn. When he saw me charging towards him, one burly fellow – he had a blue turban, I remember – who had been stirring a cooking pot over a fire reached for his musket but I was quicker – I had my pistol ready, one of the pair you gave me – and got him bang in the middle of the chest. He tumbled straight back into the fire where his turban and his beard caught alight. You could hear his flesh sizzle. The whole thing didn't take more than ten minutes. Even Nervous Nellie joined in once he realised there was little chance he'd get hurt. A few dacoits fled. Most were killed, but we've got ten prisoners to take back to Calcutta where no doubt they'll be publicly hanged as an example to others. One of our men – a sepoy named Ravi Kohli – got a musket ball in his shoulder but I helped dig it out and bandaged him up. The wound looks clean – he should survive. In any case, not bad for an afternoon's work.

As he finished, in an attempt to undercut the half-appalled, half-reverential hush that had descended upon the table, Nicholas joked, 'Well, whatever else, James seems quite pleased with himself. His letter reminds me a bit of Clive when he was young.'

Displeased, Lucia replied at once, 'Don't liken your son to Clive, even in jest. Clive had little love for others, just for himself and his ambitions from what I saw… James does care and feel, whatever bold veneer he likes to present to us.'

–

James' next letter proved the truth of Lucia's remark. The *dak* messenger rode up the drive one mid morning some weeks later while Nicholas was on the veranda practising on his violin a piece by the young Salzburg prodigy Mozart of which he was fond. Seeing the messenger, Nicholas put down his violin and intercepted him before he could reach the steps of the house. Taking the letter, he smiled to see it was from James, but his expression changed as he began to read.

> *I know I don't write as often as I should – at least I'm sure that's what you both think – but these past weeks, I've had a reason. I've seen horrors I thought only possible in nightmares, though at least you wake up from them. For a while I couldn't think, never mind write about it… didn't know where to begin. But I know I must. I've been in the land of the dead – not that calm subterranean twilight of the Ancient Greeks with its boatman and his two-headed dog that you told me of when I was a boy, but a stinking reality – a struggling despairing mass of the dead and dying.*
>
> *My land of the dead is Bengal. I'd heard about the famine but not seen it till now. These past weeks we've ridden along roads clogged with hollow-eyed skeletal people all grabbing at us with bony hands and begging in croaking, cracked voices for food. Only we can't help them all… and they were the lucky ones because at least they're still on their feet. Lately I've seen children, bright eyes bulging from emaciated faces, sucking dry-mouthed on leaves, dead women clutching dead babies to their withered breasts, corpses of old men with hollow stomachs and skin drawn tight over skulls with not enough flesh on them to rot, pariah dogs gnawing on human bones, ghostly villages where everyone's died or left.*
>
> *Around Murshidabad is the worst. They've sent us here to collect overdue taxes from the townspeople. They've told us to confiscate goods if necessary. But as we rode in it was hard to tell the living from the dead. How can you take from people who have nothing left to give… from people so desperate that they will… I can hardly bring myself to*

write this but I must tell someone... In the compound of one house, I found an old couple sitting around a cooking pot over a crackling fire. They barely looked at me. The pot had all their attention. A dribble of saliva was running down the man's bony chin as he stirred with a wooden stick. Then he dipped in a ladle and took something out. It was a moment before I realised it was a child's arm and hand, complete with tiny fingers. I fell to my knees and retched and retched... I can't get that sight out of my mind. One of the sepoys told me the couple had sworn that the child – their grandson – had died of starvation. They hadn't killed him. But who knows? Tales are rife of cannibalism, of the stronger overcoming the weaker and stealing their last pieces of food. The local rulers do nothing. We do nothing. How in the name of humanity can that be right?

The dark outpourings of his normally cheerful son continued in sickening detail. Putting the letter down and looking out across his peaceful, fertile acres to the green hills beyond, Nicholas tried to get his thoughts – his concern for his son and feelings of impotent distress about the famine – into some semblance of order. He could only hope unburdening himself of what he had seen and his feelings about it had helped James regain some equanimity of mind.

Rumours had been reaching Glenmire of hardship among the peasants of Bengal for some time but nothing like this... What had caused the famine? The monsoon hadn't been all that poor from what he could gather. The harvests should have been good enough to feed a population used to surviving on little. The more he thought about it, the more Nicholas realised he couldn't just stay at Glenmire but must see things for himself, see how he could help. However, before finally making up his mind he must speak to Lucia. He found her in her sitting room, reading a book in her native Italian. As soon as she saw the expression on his face, she snapped the book shut and asked, 'What is it?'

'This letter from James, listen,' Nicholas said, immediately beginning to read it to her. As he finished her expression was as sombre as his. 'You want to go down to the plains, don't you, to see what you can do?' she asked before he could say anything more.

'You know me so well. I can't sit here while this is going on. James' letter isn't many days old and Murshidabad isn't that far. If I ride hard, taking some spare horses with me, I may be in time to see James before he and his company move on. And I want to seek out Amrit Roy, our old cook in Calcutta. When he left us, he retired to where his family come from in the hills around Murshidabad. He'll be in his seventies now. I will try to make sure he and his family have food and, come to that, sufficient protection from looters… Then, well… I'll see if there's anything more I can do. I'm not sure what…'

'You need say no more. Go and go with my blessing.'

–

Nicholas set out down to the famine-stricken Bengal plains early next morning. He soon found the sights in the villages just as terrible as his son had described – pyre after pyre of burning corpses where people still had enough strength to observe funeral rites and, where they didn't, emaciated bodies left to lie where they fell, pecked by the blood-streaked beaks of marauding vultures and chewed by the omnipresent packs of starving dogs, fighting and biting each other and attacking anyone attempting to intervene. Death's sickly sweet stink was sometimes so pervasive as he passed close to huts in hamlets devoid of life that he felt he was choking, and his stomach rising into his throat.

In one village, where some still clung to life, he drove off – with threats to use his pistol – two men attempting to snatch from the grasp of an old woman some small chapattis she had been cooking over a fire. 'They're for my two grandchildren,' she said as she thanked him. 'They're the only family I have left.'

By talking to a group of men armed with makeshift weapons guarding their families' huts and few possessions, then to a Hindu priest offering food to a woman with a small naked child at her side, and in particular to an embittered Company pensioner recently retired from the Company's district office who sought him out to complain that his pension rarely came on time and when it did was insufficient to pay the now inflated prices for food, Nicholas began to piece together the causes of the famine. Some of the blame clearly lay with the Company, which seemed to be manipulating prices in the market to force the farmers to grow opium for export to China instead of their usual food crops, hence the shortage of grain. The Company was also imposing ever higher taxes on land, oblivious to tenants' ability to pay or even to eat. Farmers were being forced to sell seeds they had kept back for next year's planting to buy food for the present, thus worsening their future prospects.

When he reached Murshidabad, itself badly affected by the famine, Nicholas quickly discovered that James' troop was already a hundred miles away. He could only send after him what he hoped was a comforting letter. At least he could include some good news since he had found that Amrit Roy – whose children had played with his own in Calcutta – and his family were alive, having retreated to the farm of a relation who had preserved his stock of grain. Nicholas had given them money and supplies and told them to travel up to Glenmire if things got worse. They had promised to, but Nicholas doubted they would. Amrit Roy, although still strong in body and mind, was too rooted to his homeland to move before it was too late. But Nicholas could hardly blame him… It would take a great deal to move him from his Himalayan Glenmire.

In his lodgings in Murshidabad, Nicholas found sleep difficult. It wasn't only that he was deeply affected by the deprivation, desperation and despair he had seen. It was the realisation that he couldn't simply return to the tranquillity of the mountains and Glenmire. It was his duty to travel on to Calcutta… tell Hastings what he had seen… convince him and any senior officials he still knew that they must take urgent action – action he couldn't understand why they hadn't taken already.

3 – Times of Crisis

As Nicholas rode into the outskirts of Calcutta, the roads became ever more crowded. There were bullock carts, family groups on foot – the young supporting the old – heading into the city probably in search of food or work to pay for it, a platoon of marching red-clad Company infantry led by two officers on horseback who looked even younger than James, and three temple elephants, their brightly coloured surcoats ornamented by pieces of mirror-glass sewn onto them. There were far too many groups of men hurrying along carrying on their shoulders litters bearing white-shrouded corpses to the burning ghats along the Hooghly.

Going further into the city, Nicholas found an even greater gulf than usual between the lives of the better off – whether Bengali merchants or Company officials and officers – and the poor. As he passed the shop fronts of the warehouses belonging to Bengali merchants he noticed two of them, substantial stomachs still straining the buttons of their well-tailored tunics, squatting on low stools at a table. They were drinking sherbets and licking their beringed fingers as they ate sweetmeats, entirely disregarding the elderly man, ribs protruding from his bent frame and leaning on a rough wooden stick, desperately begging for food a few feet away. Nicholas paused and threw the man a few coins. It made him feel better, but he realised it was only a drop in the ocean of need.

Entering the area where European officials and officers had their quarters, he saw in one of the many green spaces a group of young Europeans on horseback. They were laughing and joking at what seemed to be the end of an early evening ride. Two took bread and cheese from their saddlebags. One – after swigging from a bottle of beer – took only a few bites of the food before throwing the rest to the ground to be carried off by scrawny pigeons surging down from neighbouring trees. Such an unthinking public display of waste when so many were starving appalled Nicholas.

Pausing briefly to wash and change out of his dusty, travel-stained clothes at his familiar lodgings with Mohammed Aziz, Nicholas headed through the dusk for Government House and Hastings. As he entered the gardens surrounding the house, birds were already roosting in the trees and beginning to speckle the ground beneath with their droppings while bats swooped low over the ornamental pools in search of insects.

Hastings was in his teak-panelled office, this time with no sign of the baroness in *déshabillé* or otherwise. As a footman ushered Nicholas in, Hastings put down his quill pen, rose from his desk, said, 'Good to see you again, Ballantyne!' and put out his hand, which Nicholas shook. Seeing Nicholas' sombre expression, Hastings dispensed with further formalities and pleasantries and asked, 'What brings you from your mountain idyll to Calcutta? What can I do for you?'

'The famine.'

'The famine? Yes, a truly unfortunate set of circumstances.'

'Unfortunate? It's much more than that. My son James wrote to me about it. I could scarcely believe his account until I set out to see for myself. He hadn't exaggerated… The suffering in the rural areas is beyond anything I've ever witnessed. I came to Calcutta to ask you how the Company plans to alleviate it.'

'I share your concern, Nicholas. Really I do. We're doing the best we can, but the population is increasing and the recent rains have been poor. You must realise that feeding all the starving is entirely beyond the Company's resources. If we favoured some it would only be human if it led to fighting between those who had supplies and those who didn't, would it not?'

After everything that Hastings had said at their previous meeting about duty to those over whom the Company held sway,

Nicholas had expected him to be sympathetic. Instead he found his remarks chilling. 'Isn't that an excuse for inaction? If you saw the suffering with your own eyes you would do more, particularly since from what I hear the Company seems at least partly to blame.'

For a moment, Hastings said nothing, then looking down at his desk in obvious embarrassment, he replied, 'It's not as simple as you may think, Nicholas. You should understand I'm at loggerheads with my council. They are resisting my every reform, it seems often out of sheer bloody-mindedness. The famine – tragic as it most certainly is – cannot be my priority. What matters most is imposing my authority, reclaiming power from corrupt local officials – European and Hindustani alike – and centralising it here in Calcutta to the benefit of the Company and its profits. Before I've succeeded in that, if I attempt to reform the Company's agricultural policies I'll have to fight both the council in Calcutta and the Company's Court of Directors in London and I won't win. I can only fight one battle at a time. If I overcome my enemies within the Company – and at times they seem legion – one day, I'll be powerful enough to prevent such a tragedy as the famine ever happening again.'

Everything Hastings said sounded reasoned and logical but to Nicholas' ears also inhumane and hypocritical. 'You claim to respect the people and to care about them. I've heard you make grand speeches about protecting them as a father would his children. What father would let his children suffer like this when he has the power to prevent it, which you have?'

'Perhaps you should ask Robert Clive who is really to blame,' Hastings replied quietly. 'After he persuaded the Moghul Emperor to confirm the Company's control over Bengal, Clive adopted the policy of growing opium not grain so we could sell it in China to fund the purchase of tea, porcelain and silks to sell both in Britain and here in Hindustan. He was none too choosy about how he encouraged the farmers to follow his wishes. The directors loved him for the profits when he sat in my chair – so did the British government... Now he's a knight of the bath, living like a prince in Berkeley Square in London, the public's darling with a large fortune if the rumours are true… Ask him whether he cares that Bengal's farmers are starving – not that he's likely to.'

Nicholas flushed. Some of Hastings' accusations about his friend were true – Clive was often selfish, as Lucia thought, and always hungered for money, power, position – but had he realised the consequences of his policies on the ordinary people he would surely have acted. It wasn't in his restless, impulsive character to sit coldly back, like Hastings, bloodlessly analysing, calculating and prioritising. 'You belittle yourself by attacking another man who whatever his faults – and he has some, I admit – isn't here to defend himself,' Nicholas retorted. 'Whatever happened in the past, you're the one now with the power… How can you let profit override humanity and your plain Christian duty? Do the lives of thirty million people really weigh so little in your scales and those of the Company? At least reduce the tax on land until this famine is over…'

Staring down at his desk rather than looking at Nicholas, Hastings shook his head. 'I can't, much as I might wish to. Look, I told you before that I trust you. I'm trusting you now by telling you something few others know – at least not here in Hindustan. The Company isn't any more the golden goose everyone seems to think. With Company officials siphoning money off through fraudulent tax gathering and illegal private trading and those venal directors in London voting themselves larger and larger unearned dividends, the Company's almost bankrupt. Unless the home government loans it a million and a half pounds it faces financial ruin. Even now the Prime Minister – still Lord North when last I heard – is trying to muster enough votes in Parliament to get us the money. I won't know for many months whether he's succeeded. Until then my hands are tied… You must see that… We have to pay for our military campaigns which are eroding our profits. Our enemies grow in number and in strength all the time – even the opium profits aren't sufficient.'

'At least open the Company's granaries to the people.'

'I can't. It'd be just the excuse some of my council here are looking for to have me dismissed... Look, you're an idealist – you always have been, like Clive used to tease you – and a better man than me, I'm sure... But you're not responsible for keeping everything together as I am. Part of my holding on to power is making unpalatable compromises. I'm conceited enough to think that I'm the best man to make such compromises and that if I fail the Company fails. And if the Company fails our grip on Hindustan will weaken and we'll be driven out. Think of the bloodbath that will follow for everyone here.'

Hastings was now working his hands, his face a mask, the very image of a place man, a Pontius Pilate even, Nicholas thought. Then Hastings got to his feet – a much smaller figure than Nicholas – and looked, half-embarrassed, half-angry, towards the door. Knowing he had been wordlessly dismissed and with nothing more to say – after all, what would be the point? – Nicholas stood and left without a handshake, a goodbye or even a backward glance. Hastings had disappointed him. Whatever the Company's financial woes, humanity must come first. Hastings should act now and worry about defending his actions later.

It was not late so Nicholas decided to visit Charles in his lodgings no more than a mile away on the banks of the Hooghly. He waved away sedan chair bearers who emerged from the shadows, calling out to him, eager to secure his business. The walk would help him calm himself. When he arrived at the newly built brick bachelors' lodgings where Charles had been allocated spacious quarters overlooking the river, his cousin greeted him warmly and poured him a glass of Madeira. Together they looked out over the river, still busy even at this time of night with ferrymen, fishermen and bargemen, the latter taking out goods to the massive East Indiamen moored in midstream. After some initial polite exchanges about family matters and health – Charles had had gastric problems and was taking what precautions he could, in his own words, 'not to end up in the new but fast-filling Park Road Cemetery and to survive longer than the two monsoons smirking older hands tell me is the average out here' – their talk quickly turned to the famine.

However, as Nicholas began to inveigh against Hastings and the Company's policies, Charles interrupted. 'Some of the Company's policies may have had unfortunate and unforeseen consequences, but it can't be blamed for the famine itself. It's the poor monsoon, the overpopulation.' He was simply parroting some of Hastings' arguments, perhaps learned from Simkin or other officials, Nicholas thought at first. But then Charles went further, 'The real culprits are the farmers, ignorant men determined to cling to tradition at any price – just like those benighted Mi'kmaq natives in Nova Scotia who stubbornly resisted all our attempts to civilise them. If the Bengal peasants would only grow the crops the Company wants – like opium and indigo – they'd earn enough to feed their families. Instead they're obstructing progress.'

'It's profit not progress the farmers are obstructing,' Nicholas retorted. 'Where is your sense of honour? What would your father have thought? He valued his honour – the family's honour – above everything else.'

Charles' face – pale still despite the Indian sun – flushed a deep red. Maybe his cousin was not yet the uncritical disciple of the Company he pretended, Nicholas thought, but Charles' next words disabused him. 'Look where my father's sense of what he called "honour" – "duty" – got him… His real duty was to protect our family and our estate. Instead he hazarded everything through a misplaced, romantic sentimentality… You remember a man you admired. I remember a man who, though I loved him, I did not… I'm sorry if that shocks you, but it's the truth. I'm not like him and I don't want to be. I'm a realist and pragmatist just as the Company has to be realistic and pragmatic – the brain not the heart must rule in our public lives.'

'You can't bury your conscience.'

Charles shrugged. 'My conscience is clear. I've already told you I think the Company is right. And be reasonable, cousin. What would happen if I, just a junior official, questioned the Company's policies? I'll tell you. Septimus Simkin would send me away to scribble accounts in some dusty hell-hole. And what would be the point of that? It wouldn't change anything except to sink my career. I see from your face that you don't understand, but you and I are so different… Simkin told me that after the Battle of Plassey you could have had almost any post you wanted – you could have made your fortune. Instead you turned your back on it all, refusing to make the compromises we all have to make to get on in life, to live in your little utopia in the mountains with a clear conscience but no influence on the world for better or for worse… That's something I could never do… I believe you have to take whatever chances you get in life – and for me there might not be as many as you have had – and make yourself somebody. Then perhaps you might have time for your conscience!'

Nicholas had seldom felt so angry. His voice for once rising beyond his usual calm tones he said, 'Despite what I owe my uncle whose memory you take so lightly, had I known your true character I would not have welcomed you so readily into my home… I won't wish you well in your future career. You won't need it. You will prosper without my good wishes. I'm truly sorry we share the same name – the same family motto.'

Nicholas rose, left the room and strode from his cousin's lodgings out into the warm Indian night where mosquitoes buzzed in the light of the torches in the sconces at the entrance gate. Lucia had been right to sense coldness and detachment in his cousin. How readily, ruthlessly, Charles – like Clive and Hastings – put his own interests first. What had happened to that thoughtful deference with which he had listened to everything Nicholas had told him? Had it all been pretence, or was it that the Company had quickly made him one of its own – not evil, but ambitious, insensitive and selfish, a man capable of causing harm even if that was not his intention?

Yet wasn't Charles just set on doing what so many Company men did – come to India, not out of love for the place but to make their fortunes as fast as they could and then leave? Like Clive, now living in luxury in London. Why condemn his cousin for faults he'd forgiven in others? Because of some foolish idea that the Ballantynes should be better, derived from reading the letters of his great-great-grandfather, the first Ballantyne to go to Hindustan and an idealist if ever there was one? And if he was honest wasn't there at least something in what Charles said about his own behaviour? Perhaps it had been easier for him to get out of Company politics and retreat to Glenmire where, if he wasn't doing any harm, he wasn't doing much good either…

Such thoughts continued to trouble Nicholas as, knowing that his son James was due back from his tour of duty in just a few weeks, he wrote to Lucia telling her of his discussions with Hastings and Charles, confessing she'd been right about the latter all along and explaining he was delaying his departure from Calcutta to see James. It was too good an opportunity to miss.

–

Only a fortnight later, Mohammed Aziz, who had been out early to the market, told Nicholas when he brought him his breakfast that he had heard from a friend – a cook in the barracks – that James' regiment, the 2nd Bengal Horse, were due back that very afternoon, earlier than expected, from their expedition. Nicholas quickly penned a note to his son inviting him to dine with him to celebrate his return, which Mohammed Aziz had one of his houseboys take round to the barracks.

When evening came without a reply Nicholas began to assume Mohammed Aziz and his friend had been mistaken about the regiment's return, but as Mohammed Aziz remained adamant his information was correct, Nicholas wrote again. This time the messenger returned with confirmation from the gatekeeper that the regiment was back but with no accompanying message from James. Nicholas wondered about going to the barracks himself, but would James welcome the appearance of a seemingly over-anxious doting parent at some celebration of the regiment's own of their return?

But then at nearly nine o'clock a messenger from the barracks brought a letter addressed to Nicholas. When he took it, Nicholas saw immediately the writing was not his son's. Worried that something was wrong – perhaps James was ill with one of the prevalent fevers – Nicholas broke the seal. The letter was from one of James' fellow ensigns and only a few lines long. It related simply that James was being held under guard awaiting court martial. It did not say why.

Distressed and desperate, both to know more and to see his son, Nicholas almost ran the mile to the barracks. The luxuriously moustached sergeant, Welsh by his accent, in the gatehouse refused him entry when he demanded to see James. 'No one is allowed in here at this time of night, especially not to see a prisoner. Besides, I'm not sure you're who you claim to be. Ensign Ballantyne has more than a touch of the tar brush about him, which you don't!' Nicholas in his shock and anxiety was about to explode and began to ball his fists, but then realising an outburst was unlikely to do any good forced himself to be polite.

'Although it's none of your business, his mother – my late wife – was Hindustani. Now let me see my son.'

'Really? That explains a bit. But you're still not allowed in. No one is.'

Nicholas then resorted to a stratagem – if that it could be called – he had long despised in others. 'Do you know who I am? I'm a former colonel in the Company army and a good friend of the governor, Warren Hastings.'

A look of disbelief crossed the sergeant's face. Then seeing the cold fury in Nicholas' expression and in his deep blue eyes, he seemed to feel discretion might prove the better part of valour. He turned to one of the two soldiers behind him and shouted, 'Go and see if you can find Captain Collins – I think he's the duty officer tonight. Tell him I've got Ensign Ballantyne's father here demanding to see his son and refusing to take no for an answer!'

Collins, a stout figure only a few years younger than Nicholas, soon appeared, still buttoning his blue uniform jacket. 'Mr

Ballantyne, or should I say Colonel Ballantyne?' he asked, holding out his hand. 'I remember you from your service with General Clive during the Plassey campaign. I'll take you to your son. He's not in a cell but confined to his room. I'm not in his regiment so I don't know too much about his situation. From what little I hear, it doesn't reflect well on anyone. However, I'll let your son tell you about it himself, rather than peddle hearsay.'

They soon reached James' room where a sentry, lounging at the door with his musket, snapped to attention as Captain Collins appeared and at his order stood aside. 'I'll leave you to talk alone,' Collins said.

James was lying half-dressed on his back on his bed, hands behind his head, staring at the ceiling. A single candle was burning. By its flickering light, Nicholas saw his son's lip was cut and swollen, as was his left eye. He had a rough bandage around his right knuckle. On seeing his father, James immediately jumped up and the two embraced. As they pulled apart Nicholas got straight to the point. 'What's happened to your face? What's all this about?'

'If you're worried about my face you should see the other fellow's. His nose is pointing the wrong way. I broke it.'

'Be serious, James. Who did you get into a fight with?'

'Lieutenant Neville – Nervous Nellie.'

'What did you fall out about? Did you question an order?'

'Yes, but that wasn't quite it…' James seemed reluctant to say more and looked away.

'Come on, James. Striking a senior officer is a serious matter – so too is disobeying an order, if that is what you did. For God's sake, tell me what happened!'

'I'm sorry – you're going to find out soon enough… Neville ordered me and my men into a village to evict the families and burn down their huts for refusing – or rather being unable – to pay their land taxes and to confiscate what few goods they had. He wanted to make them an example to others. I said I would rather resign than obey. He laughed and said "Are you going to throw your career away for these peasants?"'

'And you hit him?'

'No, not then. It was what he said next that made me lose control. He said, well this… "No wonder you're disloyal and too craven to do your duty – brown face, yellow liver, that's what I always say". Such words, coming from a coward like Neville, were too much. I lashed out and smashed his nose with my fist. As I aimed a second blow at him, someone knocked me to the ground from behind. I hit a rock as I fell. That's where I got the damage to my face.'

Nicholas said nothing for some moments but then, 'I can understand your anger at both the order and his slur.'

'You'd have hit him too?'

'I fear so though hope not. It alone puts you in the wrong. I can't believe Neville wasn't exceeding his orders when he instructed you to burn the village. No court martial would dare openly sanction such behaviour. Striking a superior is legally another matter, whatever the provocation.'

'I'd do it again, whatever it cost, I can assure you!'

'No doubt.'

After agreeing that extreme provocation was James' only possible defence, Nicholas returned to his lodgings where he spent an almost sleepless night. Recalling James' shuttered face and his initial reluctance to speak, he wondered how many times his son had had to endure taunts and innuendo for being of mixed race – an Anglo-Indian? Why had he himself failed to anticipate this might happen? Because he'd thought the name Ballantyne a sufficient proof of his son's character and courage, whatever his complexion? But what mattered now was considering how best to help him frame his case for mitigating circumstances. James seemed not to appreciate the severity of his situation. He could even be shot if the officers of the court martial were both bigots and disciplinarians – which was not out of the question.

While Nicholas was pacing his room as the dawn broke he heard a knock at the door. Outside was a servant in the gold braided livery of Government House. He handed Nicholas a letter, which to his surprise he found was from Hastings himself.

We parted in anger two weeks ago, which I regret. I write now in token of our long acquaintance – friendship, I would like to call it, though I do not wish to be presumptuous after what has passed between us. I know your son's case. Officially I cannot of course condone his behaviour, though privately, as a man with a heart – though you may not think so – I can understand it. What is intolerable is that he was so shockingly insulted by a fellow officer. I have inquired into the circumstances of his questioning of the order and am perfectly easy in my mind at least that there too your son had some justification. Be assured that I will see the charges against him dropped, though he must pay a price. He has publicly defied orders and struck a senior officer. In those circumstances I see no alternative to requiring him to resign his commission.

I hope I have convinced you that neither I nor the Company are quite the relentless, heartless creatures we must sometimes appear, and I have something to ask of you. If you will again visit me at Government House – any time tomorrow evening I can be at your disposal – I will explain.

Believe me still your friend
Warren Hastings

4 – A Matter of Honour

Not long after Hastings' letter arrived, Nicholas heard another knock at his door. Outside was Captain Collins and, just behind him, James dressed in civilian clothes.

'Colonel Ballantyne,' Collins began, 'I'm releasing your son into your custody on the personal orders of Governor Hastings. All charges against him have been dropped. Bearers will return his chest with his possessions and his equipment in the next day.' Collins saluted, turned on his heel and was quickly away down the corridor, giving every appearance of being only too delighted not to become further involved.

Once inside his room with James, Nicholas, unsure how to begin, asked awkwardly, 'Well… how are you feeling? At least it's over.'

'How d'you think I'm feeling – forced to resign my commission through no fault of my own… Not delighted, Father, I assure you… Not grateful for the small mercy of not facing a court martial. And it's not over, as far as Neville and I are concerned.'

'What do you mean?'

'I'm intending to pay him a visit in his quarters. I will march right up to him, look him in the eye and tell him what a miserable, cowardly bastard he is and see how he reacts.'

'I should have thought he already knows what you think of him. After all, you broke his nose! Think carefully before you do anything else rash. If you go looking for him, isn't there every chance he'll provoke you into some action that will only make your situation worse?' Nicholas paused, and then, speaking very deliberately, said, 'Don't think I don't understand how you feel.

I've never told you before but when I was about your age, fuelled by a similar rage and sense of unfairness and injustice, I challenged a man who'd publicly taunted me about my "traitorous" Jacobite roots to a duel. Robert Clive argued that no one worth his salt would pay any attention to such slanders. I didn't listen and insisted on going through with it. Only after my opponent fired prematurely and missed and then stood a pathetic creature trembling in front of me waiting for me to fire, did I realise that by killing him I would reduce myself to his level and the best way to demonstrate my superiority was to walk away, so I did… I can't expect you to be any more willing to take advice from me than I was from Clive, but at least wait a little until you've got some rest and have thought more about the consequences.'

'You didn't only challenge a man to a duel but actually fought one…?'

'Yes. Don't look quite so surprised. I too was young once. I've never mentioned it until now partly because it was a long time ago, but mainly because it's something I'm not proud of… something that I regret. I'm telling you now in hopes it will make you stop and reflect…'

To Nicholas' surprise and great relief James let his shoulders drop and after some moments said, 'All right, I will think a little more… I don't suppose a few more hours will make much difference to anything.'

'Good. I'm grateful. I'll get Mohammed Aziz to find you a room and bring you some food.'

Nicholas' first instinct was to take his son and head immediately north to Glenmire as soon as James could be persuaded to go, ignoring Hastings' invitation to call on him. But on reflection that appeared childishly petulant. Besides, as both he and Hastings knew, he was indebted to Hastings. He was honour bound to do him the courtesy of a visit and at least hear what he had to say. Therefore, again not long before dusk, he took the familiar route to Government House. Conducted this time by the red-turbaned major-domo himself, he was soon in Hastings' office. After declining Hastings' offer of refreshment, he began very formally, 'I am here to tell you how very grateful I and my family are for your intervention in my son's case.'

'I was glad to help James. He has your determination to speak his mind, whatever the consequences… not the wisest course for a junior officer but to be respected.' After a pause Hastings continued, 'However, I didn't ask you here to discuss your son. To be frank, I pride myself on taking advantage of opportunities as they present themselves and now I want to take advantage of your presence in Calcutta. I need your help and advice about a new threat to the Company's position.'

'From whom?'

'The Rohillas. As I'm sure you know, they're originally Afghans from the mountains around Kandahar but shortly before he died the Moghul Emperor Aurangzeb offered them territory in north-western Hindustan in return for suppressing the Hindu Rajput rulers of the region. They took the bribe, drove out the Rajputs and established themselves in what they call Rohilkhand and have since been a fairly constant irritant to all in Hindustan. However, what you will not know is that Shuja ud-daulah, the Nawab of Oudh, whose lands adjoin Rohilkhand, informed me only a few days ago that after being quiescent for a while, they've begun raiding in force across his borders. He fears they mean to invade Oudh and asks our help to stop them.'

'Is there any reason not to give it to him?'

'Though Shuja ud-daulah is formally our ally I'm not sure how far I trust him. He's a wily schemer who has not always proved all that reliable or trustworthy in the past. What's more, a treaty Clive agreed with him some years ago will expire soon. He's perfectly capable of using his claim of a Rohilla threat to himself – and by implication to us – to extract concessions from the Company in any negotiations about the renewal of the treaty.'

'And if you find the threat is real?'

'Then of course Oudh must be defended. We need it as a friendly buffer against our enemies, especially the Maratha Confederacy – the Marathas remain in some ways unique, not only hungry for land and booty but believing they have some kind of divine mission to drive us and Muslim rulers like the Nawab out and unite Hindustan under their Hindu faith. They will seize any opportunity, like the Rohilla threat, to undermine our position. I'm going to Oudh to assess the Nawab's motives and the real extent of the danger. I want you to come with me. You speak the local languages at least as well as I do, but more than that I want somebody experienced by my side on whose loyalty and advice I can rely totally. Two wise heads will be far better than one.'

Nicholas hesitated. 'I need to think before I give you an answer.'

'I have to talk to the treasurer at some point this evening to go over his report on revenue to tomorrow's council. I could go and speak to him now. I'd be back in half an hour or a little more. Would that give you enough time?'

'I think so,' Nicholas said, reflecting inwardly that nothing could be gained on this occasion by delaying a decision. After Hastings left, he began to pace slowly around the room, head bowed as he went over the arguments. He had deep concerns about Hastings and his attitude to the famine and this increased his reluctance to get sucked back into the Company machine. However, though neither he nor Hastings would ever say so, he would implicitly be repaying his debt to Hastings for his merciful treatment of James – something Hastings was doubtless at least as aware of as he was himself. Such considerations aside, the mission was an interesting one and its aim – to maintain stability in the region – sound. Pertinent too was Charles' jibe that to get things done in ways of which he approved a man couldn't simply stand aside but must become involved. What's more, if he was honest, being engaged once again in the chess game of negotiation was appealing.

When Hastings returned after a bare half hour, Nicholas said without further ado, 'I will accompany you.'

'I'm grateful.'

With little more to say, Nicholas was about to leave when Hastings said quietly, 'Wait. I want to tell you something. I wasn't impervious to what you said about the famine. I'm having granaries built across Bengal to mitigate any future such catastrophe. I know you won't think that's enough, but at least it's something...'

Too late for so many, Nicholas thought, but did not say. As he returned to his lodgings, he pondered the difficult letter he must write to Lucia. She would not welcome his being pulled back into the moral quagmire of the Company's affairs.

On his arrival he found James waiting in his room. 'I've decided ignoring Neville is better than confronting him, Father. All I want now is to go home to Glenmire to get some peace and to think over my future... how to rebuild my life.'

'You cannot know how grateful I am to hear that. I'm sure everyone who loves you will be too.' Nicholas' relief was tempered by the bitterness in his son's voice. He could do little to comfort him... Perhaps some time in the coolness of the hills would help heal his mental scars.

In the couple of days while Nicholas helped James assemble his belongings before he left for Glenmire, his son unbent a little. On the evening before his departure, they sat over a dinner of spicy lentil soup and roasted chicken, washed down by small ale. After going through the final arrangements for James' homeward journey, Nicholas ventured to ask a little more about the prejudices James had encountered on account of his mixed race.

Suddenly a torrent burst from his son's mouth. 'It wasn't that there were many overt insults – in fact probably just two, neither as serious as Neville's and both made in drink, otherwise I would have reacted as I did to Neville. It was rather the constant petty-mindedness that showed in what they chose to call jokes by some – though not all – of my fellow officers... asking me at meal times didn't I prefer to use my fingers to eat, like many Hindustanis, rather than use cutlery? How did I dress at home, in a dhoti? All said with silly smiles and knowing looks. The worst thing I could do, I knew, was to bite back... to show they had got through to me. After all, those idiots also chafed others, in particular Godfrey, an older, slightly deaf fellow who's risen from the ranks and whose manners and behaviour are less polished than theirs. In some ways perhaps the most constant irritation was to be asked, when in civilian clothes, by sentries both British and Hindustani not in my regiment who were on duty at the barracks gates, to prove my identity and state my business before I was admitted – something which rarely happened to my white fellow officers who passed unchallenged. Sometimes I was simply assumed to be a tradesman and waved away to that entrance. It was just totally wearing. Why must some people see superficial differences as cause for at best laughter and at worst hatred?'

'All I can say is that I've found it the way of the world, wherever I've been and whatever I've read of history, that the ignorant, lacking any true sense of self-worth, group themselves into like-minded tribes to disparage and scapegoat those who differ from them in any way, whether in appearance, belief or behaviour.'

'That's one of the bleakest things I've ever heard you say.'

'It would be if I thought it applied to everyone. It doesn't. Those of us who are more enlightened must exert what influence we can, however small. And that is why I've decided to accompany Hastings on his mission to Oudh.'

–

At the end of the two-week voyage upstream from Calcutta the boatmen leapt ashore and, helped by palace attendants, moored the Company riverboat as trumpets sounded from the twin towers of the Ramnagar Palace. Pale sandstone temples and shrines large and small crammed the left bank of the Ganges. Hindu pilgrims stepped down from the ghats into the holy river to bathe and pray, many of the men wearing the sacred white thread of the Brahmin over their left shoulders. Benares was spectrally beautiful, Nicholas thought. He was pleased the Nawab had suggested meeting here in the palace of his vassal the Hindu Raja Chait Singh of Benares, rather than his own more distant capital of Faizabad.

A guard of honour waited on the ghat below the palace. As Hastings, followed by Nicholas, walked down the slightly swaying rail-less gangplank, a tall, thin man dressed in blue and holding a sceptre-like silver staff of office stepped forward and bowed.

'I am Asaf Khan, vizier to the Nawab.'

A young attendant advanced with a tray with garlands of marigolds. 'Please accept these traditional gifts of welcome.' As Hastings and Nicholas bowed their heads, Asaf Khan placed a garland around each of their necks. 'I invite you to follow me. Learning of your boat's approach, the Nawab awaits you in the durbar hall.'

Shuja ud-daulah, Nawab of Oudh, was seated on a silver throne with snarling tiger armrests placed on a white marble dais. Though his face was more lined, he was no less imposing than the last time Nicholas had seen him – a giant of a man, broad chested and nearly seven feet tall and so strong, rumour had it, that in his youth he could grab a soldier in each hand and swing them off the ground, and sweep off a buffalo's head with a single stroke of his scimitar. Even in late middle age, neither seemed out of the question for him still.

The Nawab's scarlet silk tunic embroidered with spread-tailed golden peacocks, waist-long necklace of rubies, emeralds and pearls, large rings flashing on nearly every finger and diamonds glittering on his gold cloth turban confirmed his well-known passion for magnificence and show. Had he had the silver throne brought all the way from Faizabad or had Raja Chait Singh lent it for the occasion, Nicholas wondered.

The Nawab's celebrated well-oiled black moustaches gleamed like ravens' wings as he regarded the new arrivals keenly. 'I am glad to see you again, Governor Hastings, and, of course, Mr Ballantyne. Do sit.' Attendants placed two ivory-inlaid chairs before the dais. Glancing at the assembled courtiers, Nicholas realised he and Hastings were the only ones allowed this privilege. Even though this was his own durbar hall, the young Raja of Benares was standing respectfully to one side of the throne. On the long journey to Benares, Hastings had said, 'The Nawab is the suitor, the Company is the one to be wooed.' A fact their host seemed to recognise.

'Rooms have been prepared for you here in the palace,' the Nawab continued, 'close to my own to enable us to talk whenever we wish. We've a lot to discuss. Nevertheless I have arranged some diversions over the coming days to celebrate the friendship between Oudh and the Company; hunting trips – a pair of tigers has been troubling local villages and should provide good sport – feasts and other entertainments. I hope you'll enjoy them and the spirit of friendship in which they are offered.'

'I am sure we will, Majesty,' Hastings replied in Urdu, the language the Nawab had used.

'But now you must be tired from your journey and want to rest. Attendants will take you to your apartments.'

Four young men in pale green tunics with dark green cummerbunds who, Asaf Khan informed them, were to be their personal servants during their stay led Nicholas and Hastings across interlinked courtyards bounded by tall buildings of apricot-coloured stone from which carved balconies projected. In one courtyard where scented white jasmine was growing, lace-like screens enclosed the balconies – the women's quarters, Nicholas assumed.

Double doors led from Nicholas' room onto a wide terrace overlooking the Ganges. The fast gathering dusk was shrouding the river as he stepped outside and looked down. On a nearby ghat three white-robed Hindu priests were preparing for the *aarti* fire ritual, a ceremony he had witnessed before and knew would begin as soon as darkness fell. As he waited, the fragrant smell of sandalwood burning in brass pots on the ghat rose towards him.

At the blowing of a conch shell, one priest carefully lit wicks in a branched brass *aarti* lamp held by the second priest who, as the wicks burst into flame, passed it to the third, an elderly man, with the white trident of the god Shiva painted on his forehead. As the two other priests rang bells and chanted mantras, he lifted the *aarti* lamp high and approaching the water's edge circled it clockwise, making the symbolic offering of sacred fire to the holy River Ganges and accepting the river's blessing in return. Next, he passed the lamp before the pilgrims gathered on the ghat who, cupping their palms over the flames, raised them to their foreheads to receive the river's blessing. Finally, the priests and the pilgrims placed offerings of flowers, fruit and milk on the ghat and lit wicks in tiny clay saucers of *ghee* – clarified butter – which they lowered into the water to join the hundreds lit by other worshippers all along the riverbank. The current swiftly carried the tiny lamps away into the velvet night.

–

To Hastings' frustration over the following days Shuja ud-daulah seemed in no hurry to talk. Instead good manners meant that Hastings and Nicholas had to attend all the promised entertainments. 'If I have to watch another troupe of contortionists or fire eaters, however skilled, or be asked to admire more ancient manuscripts in the Raja's library, however beautiful, I can't answer for the consequences,' Hastings grumbled to Nicholas as, early on the fourth morning, they strolled along the palace battlements. The riverbank below already teemed with activity while in the distance orange flames and black smoke rose from the burning ghats where the Hindus cremated the bodies of their dead.

'You sound like Clive. I thought you were more patient.'

'I would be if I weren't so far from Calcutta and I hadn't so much else to worry about… Perhaps the Nawab's waiting for me to make the first move. Should I?'

'If nothing happens in the next day or so, probably. But be patient just a little longer… see if he shows his hand first. He may be testing how eager we are.'

'Have you managed to find out anything significant yet from Asaf Khan? I noticed he was glued to your side at the elephant fight yesterday.'

'Yes. He claims that as the Nawab's vizier he wants to learn more about the Company – which of the three centres of

Calcutta, Madras and Bengal is the most profitable, how much trade we do with China – but I'm not sure he's really that interested. He's tried to pump me a few times about your relations with your council. I just changed the subject. But last night at the elephant fight he did say something… He started volubly badmouthing the Rohillas as untrustworthy, unscrupulous, ambitious bandits. I got the impression he and the Nawab are genuinely concerned about the Rohilla threat and it isn't entirely a ruse to extract concessions from the Company. If I'm right, I doubt the Nawab will delay too much longer before raising the issue, maybe at his feast tonight…'

'Ah yes, another interminable banquet made even more indigestible by all those flowery, fulsome meaningless compliments and stupid speeches. I tell you, my face is aching from having to keep smiling… But let's hope you're right.'

'Look down there – the Nawab's clearly preparing something special…' In the internal courtyard beneath the battlements labourers were erecting a large pavilion of heavy, shimmering purple fabric while others leant from bamboo ladders to hang multi-coloured glass lanterns from the jacaranda trees round the courtyard's edge.

'Pity I couldn't bring Marian… She'd have enjoyed all the pageantry, not to mention inspecting the Nawab's jewels – she's a penchant for gems and knows a thing or two about them…'

That night, as he entered the courtyard where the pavilion now stood in all its magnificence, awnings dripping with gold lace, Nicholas smiled. Perhaps the Nawab was indeed approaching the highpoint of his hospitality. Costly amber crystals of frankincense smouldering in brass dishes scented the air. Thick floral carpets covered the courtyard's flagstones. As he neared the tent, attendants flung rose petals over him. Brushing them off he entered, ducking slightly to avoid a swag of lace.

'You are welcome.' Asaf Khan, as usual wielding his silver staff, stepped forward. 'Please follow me.' Eyes adjusting to the subdued light, Nicholas saw Hastings in formal dress already seated at the Nawab's right hand at the centre of a long, low table. He expected

Asaf Khan to lead him to the still empty place on Hastings' other side. Instead he showed him to a seat further along the table, then sat down beside him.

A young man with a long-necked teak sitar and an older one, two hands holding his trumpet-like *shehnai* to his lips, both sitting cross-legged to one side of the table struck up a soulful air. Attendants filed in, each carrying a silver dish piled with food – fragrant vegetable pulaos studded with ruby-bright pomegranate seeds and nuts wrapped in gold and silver leaf, spicy biryanis, stuffed breads, golden samosas and orange tinted saffron rice. Others carried silver pots in which creamy stews still bubbled. As Nicholas well knew this was only the start… later would come sherbets, sweetmeats like the sticky jalebis Lizzie loved and pyramids of mangos, melons and grapes resting on beds of crushed ice…

Glancing along the table as the meal began, Nicholas noticed how the Nawab, and the Raja sitting to his left, touched nothing until a food taster – a man who looked surprisingly thin for one with such a profession – ate a little first. Maybe Hastings should employ a food taster in Calcutta, he thought recalling the warning in the letter from Madras…

'You're not eating. Here…' Asaf Khan drew his dagger from its steel scabbard at his waist and skewering a golden paratha put it on Nicholas' plate. 'Enjoy it while you can – in a few minutes, you may find the entertainment too distracting… Raja Chait Singh's dancing girls are picked for their beauty and famed for their skills…'

As if on cue, the sitar and *shehnai* players stood and withdrew. Their place was taken by four drummers who struck up a slow, rhythmic beat on their *tablas*. Many of the guests began to pound the table with their fists or, like Asaf Khan, the hilts of their daggers. As the noise built to a booming crescendo six dancers, hidden beneath silvery spangled veils, slender ankles tied with bunches of bells, ran into the tent.

They bowed low before the Nawab. Then at a clap and a cry from their leader – a little taller than the rest – they began to whirl, arms above their heads, bodies swaying in time to the drums, which began to pick up speed. As the dancers spun faster, they began casting off their veils, first one, then another, then a third until all they were wearing were tight *cholis* emphasising their breasts and nipples and diaphanous pantaloons showing every curve of buttock and thigh. Their thick-lashed eyes were rimmed with kohl and their lips coloured a deep red. As they tossed their heads their long, lustrous, hennaed hair, interwoven with flowers, flew this way and that.

The pace became so frantic that sweat trickled down the drummers' muscled arms and beaded the near-naked dancers' flesh. At the climax of the dance, the women ran forward towards the table, flung themselves to their knees and leaning back, lips slightly parted, arched their backs, gyrating their sinuous, voluptuous bodies while running their fingers through their hair. Nicholas saw Hastings looking wide-eyed and mesmerised – when he'd said nature hadn't intended him for a bachelor, he'd been right…

'Well, what d'you think?' Asaf Khan nudged him. 'Don't your senses riot and doesn't your blood rise at such a sight? Would you like one of them sent to warm your bed tonight… it could easily be arranged.'

'No!' Nicholas spoke more sharply than he intended.

Asaf Khan, courtier that he was, clearly realised his faux pas and blinked. 'I'm sorry – do your tastes lie elsewhere? In any case, I didn't mean to offend you.'

'Nor I you…' Nicholas took a drink of water. No doubt Asaf Khan thought he was just another European with predictable, hypocritical habits. The dancers had been rousing, but it wasn't only thoughts of Lucia that held him back… Meena's lovely face had flashed before him, a face he'd first seen on just such an occasion when as a court dancer she had been offered to him for the night. But she had given herself to him freely and their love had grown deep and fierce in the short time they had…

Coins went flying through the air, which the women deftly gathered before leaving the tent to roars of appreciation from the guests. As the sitar and *shehnai* players resumed and the raucous hubbub died down, Asaf Khan whispered to Nicholas, 'Tomorrow the Nawab would like to talk to Governor Hastings with just you and I present.'

'I know the governor will welcome it.'

'But before then there is something I should like to ask you… We've already talked a little about the Rohillas – regrettably a problem for all of us in the region. The Nawab has come to believe – albeit reluctantly – that the only sure way to break their power is to expel them from Hindustan.'

'What are you suggesting? Governor Hastings has come here at the Nawab's invitation to discuss how the Company can help him defend his borders against them but that is all…'

'The Nawab's views have hardened. He wishes to have the option to invade Rohilkhand and annex it but needs to know whether the Company would support him.'

'What do you mean by "support"? That the Company should turn a blind eye, or something more?'

'Something more – getting rid of the Rohillas for good would benefit both Oudh and the Company. And think of the powerful message the spectacle of Company troops fighting at the side of the Nawab's would send to our other mutual enemies such as the Marathas. You look startled, but think about it… use your influence with the governor and I promise the Nawab will show you his gratitude… and I'm not talking about a night or two with a dancing girl but enough wealth to change your life… I—'

Nicholas held up his hand. 'Forgive me for interrupting. If the Nawab wishes to discuss such matters, he must do so with Governor Hastings direct… I will advise him on what I consider objectively is in his best interests, uncorrupted by any prospect of personal gain.' Asaf Khan looked as if he wanted to reply but seeing the steel in Nicholas' expression just shrugged. To Nicholas' relief the Nawab summoned his guests outside a few minutes later to watch a display of Chinese fireworks, brought all the way from Kashgar, light up the night sky.

'He wants what?' Hastings said, rubbing his forehead as later that night on the terrace of Nicholas' room Nicholas told him about his conversation with Asaf Khan. 'The Nawab's given no hint of anything like this and I don't like it… A military campaign against the Rohillas would be expensive and almost certainly not in the Company's interests, however much Asaf Khan tries to sugar coat the argument. It's true the Rohillas are a threat to us all, but the Nawab's plan sounds like a grab for land and power for himself. It would risk disturbing the balance of power in the region we've worked hard to create. How would the Marathas react to such an increase in the Nawab's power and territory?'

'Not well is an understatement. And from what you said in Calcutta, your council wouldn't like it.'

'I agree. There'll have to be some plain speaking tomorrow and then I hope we can get back to Calcutta… Now, we'd better get some rest…'

Next morning Hastings still looked tired as they were ushered into a small room in the Nawab's private apartments where he was waiting with Asaf Khan. Shuja ud-daulah, magnificent as ever with a triple strand of pearls around his neck, after inviting Hastings to sit came swiftly to the point.

'We need to talk about the matter that brought you to Benares, Governor Hastings. I have not raised it till now because I was waiting for further reports of the Rohilla incursions into Oudh – three villages burned near Nullabad, the men slaughtered, the girls and women outraged, some even abducted, together with livestock and crops. Every time my men repel them they return somewhere else and in greater force. But I suspect these are just probing raids. As I wrote to you, I believe that before too long they will attempt an invasion.'

'Have you tried to negotiate?'

'They won't. These past weeks, while you were preparing to travel from Calcutta, I tried again. Their leader, Hafiz Khan, returned my emissary, hands tied and facing backwards on a donkey in a gesture of contempt. Anyway, why should I, the Nawab of Oudh, demean myself by negotiating with hill bandits?' Pausing, the Nawab looked down at Hastings, a diminutive figure by comparison with himself and seated on a divan.

'The Company is sympathetic to your situation. Not only are you our valued ally whom we naturally want to support, but the Rohillas are our common enemy. If you wish we will station Company troops in Oudh – that should be enough to deter the Rohillas from any thought of invasion...'

'But what if it isn't?' The Nawab sat down himself on a divan facing Hastings and leaned close, powerful forearms resting on his knees. 'We need a more drastic solution to rid ourselves of these troublesome rats once and for all.'

'What exactly do you mean?'

'I think you know. We are friends and allies as you have said – we don't need to play games with one another. Asaf Khan has already told Ballantyne my thoughts. To ensure the long-term security of Oudh, I want to invade Rohilkhand and drive the Rohillas from Hindustan. The Emperor Aurangzeb made a terrible mistake when he allowed them in – correcting that error is long overdue. I can't look to the present Moghul Emperor to repair the damage done by his forebear – Shah Alam is too weak and anyway has his own concerns... But surely I should be able to look to the Company to assist me...'

'You're right that we need to talk frankly and the truth of the matter is I cannot permit Company troops to cross into Rohilkhand unless you can give me much greater justification...'

'I thought you might say that, but there is perhaps a solution that would suit us both... Believe me, my only concern is to protect my kingdom from these Afghans. I gladly accept your offer to station Company troops in Oudh to safeguard its borders and I will pay for their upkeep. But what if the very worst should happen... that, despite the deterrent of Company soldiers, the Rohillas did invade... Might it not then be necessary – purely in the interests of Oudh's security, of course, to which you have told me the Company is committed – not only to expel them from Oudh but pursue them into their own territory and extinguish their threat for ever…'

'No. As I've just said, I can't permit that.'

'Wait. I've not finished… I appreciate why the Company might be reluctant to allow its troops to participate in such a venture. But shouldn't these decisions be a question of a balance of interests? What if the benefits of invading Rohilkhand were greater to the Company than the disadvantages…? It is of course the great wealth of Oudh that attracts the Rohillas, wealth that I currently have at my sole disposal. If – in the dire circumstances I've described which, let us both hope, might never actually arise – you did permit Company troops to advance with mine into Rohilkhand and we succeeded in cleansing it of the Rohillas I will guarantee to pay the Company forty million rupees as well as all its expenses.'

Nicholas saw Hastings visibly start as he had himself – forty million rupees was an eye-watering sum, equivalent to about four hundred thousand pounds. But it was a naked bribe. The Nawab was saying 'help me to invade and occupy Rohilkhand and I'll reward you'. Nicholas glanced at Asaf Khan, whose own eyes were fixed on Hastings.

'I need to consider,' Hastings said, after a moment.

'Of course. Please take all the time you need.'

As soon as he and Hastings were alone in Hastings' apartment, Nicholas said, 'The Nawab can't seriously believe he can lead you down that path. He's asking you to make mercenaries of Company soldiers! This whole thing is just a ruse to get the Company to help him annex Rohilkhand.'

'Of course it is. But the Nawab was right to talk about a balance of interests—'

'But whose interests? His or the Company's?'

'Nicholas, circumstances change – my policy has to be flexible enough to recognise that. Let's just think about this for a moment… What are the advantages to us? Agreeing to the

Nawab's proposal would strengthen our alliance with him – we can probably write what we want into the treaty when we renew it – and if he actually did go to war against the Rohillas, well, he'd be paying, not us. Also, forty million rupees is nearly a third of the Company's massive debt burden, which is currently dominating my policies and restricting my freedom to act for the benefit of all of Bengal – for example, preparing further for future famines and improving roads and education. No one – not my council in Calcutta nor the Court of Directors in London – could possibly criticise me for accepting the Nawab's offer!'

'Worthy objectives, but aren't you worried about the Nawab becoming too powerful?'

'Yes, it's a risk, but we'll face the problem of the Nawab getting too uppity as and when he does. We're still quite powerful enough to clip his wings,' Hastings replied calmly.

'And the Marathas? What if they object – as we both realise they will – to any increase in the Nawab's power and influence? Doesn't the regional balance outweigh the balance sheet?'

'As I said, circumstances change. What you say is true but I must be realistic. It could anyway be argued that by subduing the Rohillas the Nawab will create more stability and provide a greater bulwark against the Marathas.'

'And the Company will be dragged further into the complex, internecine struggles of Hindustan, further away from its objective of trade. Even if, as you suggest, it might benefit the Company in the short term, it certainly won't in the longer term.'

'As I've told you before, I'm a pragmatist and opportunist, content to change course if I judge the benefit to the Company justifies it.'

'You asked me to come with you to act as your adviser and that's what I'm trying to do – give you the best advice I can. If you won't listen to any other arguments, just answer me this: what serious harm have the Rohillas done the Company?'

'Not much... not directly, yet. But we both know the Rohillas aren't pacific saints, wedded to hearth and home. They are aggressive raiders by nature as they've proved by their attacks on Shah Alam and many others. If unchecked, as the Nawab said, who knows what they might not do in the future? Better perhaps to blunt their threat now.'

Hastings' arguments were sophistry – he was dazzled by the Nawab's offer of money, Nicholas thought. The Nawab and Asaf Khan had judged Hastings correctly, if not himself. Nothing he could say would make any difference. 'I only hope your pragmatism doesn't come back to haunt you, Hastings, as I fear it will.'

'Only time will tell. I honestly believe that by accepting the Nawab's offer – as I intend to do – I'm doing what's best for the Company and that is my responsibility.'

Part Two

An Emperor in Peril, 1774–1777

5 – Departures and Arrivals

'You nearly had me there!' Nicholas said, reining in his sweating horse in the shade of a mango tree.

'I'd have won if that mongoose hadn't suddenly run out and spooked my horse… I almost came off!' Will wiped the sweat and dust from his freckled face with his neck-cloth.

The sun was well above the horizon and farmers were driving their lowing water buffalo down to drink as, at the end of their early morning ride, Nicholas and Will turned to head back along the Hooghly River towards Calcutta. A packed square-sailed barge, a budgerow, sailed past, doubtless delivering passengers to one of the tall-masted East Indiamen moored downstream in the port.

Nicholas glanced across at his son. In just three days Will would board one such East Indiaman, bound for Britain to study Classics at St Andrews University. He was still so young – not yet seventeen – but after talking to Nicholas about his own studies there, he was eager to go. There was no reason why his son shouldn't settle down well at St Andrews, but he found it hard not to feel anxious, and not only about the hazards of the journey… How would the reality of Scotland compare to what he had told Will? Would he ever return to Hindustan? Indeed, would he ever see him again?

From Lucia's sometimes wistful, sometimes distracted expression, Nicholas was sure she was thinking much the same, though she said little. But at least the Jacobite Rebellion was long past and members of the Ballantyne family were free to return to the Highlands that had nurtured them for so many generations.

From what he had heard, Britain was changing, modernising and unifying, with Scots playing an important role. Certainly here in Hindustan there were more Scots than ever in the Company's service.

Though not, of course, James, still justifiably bitter at his treatment by the Company. Nicholas hadn't seen his elder son for some time, during which James, who still hankered for a soldier's life, had raised and trained a small irregular independent cavalry unit. Some of the officers he'd recruited were Anglo-Indian like himself. The last Nicholas had heard was that the unit was heading for far-off Delhi to serve with the forces of the Moghul Emperor Shah Alam.

'I'd have liked to see James before I left,' Will said, as if reading his father's thoughts. 'Tuhin Singh, too – I didn't realise he would be away so long.'

'I suspect he didn't either… but Tibet is remote and the route uncertain not to say hazardous; the expedition will have had to go through Bhutan… But if all's gone well, it shouldn't be too much longer before Tuhin Singh's back.'

'I've heard so many stories – rumours really – about Tibet.'

'I'm as curious as you. Tibet is virtually closed to outsiders. I promise I'll write and tell you everything I can about Tuhin Singh's journey with Bogle. But the main thing we have to think about now is *your* journey. Are you sure you've remembered everything? If anything got left behind at Glenmire there's still time to replace it.' Little of Lucia's strongly practical side seemed to have rubbed off on Will.

'Don't worry. Mother insisted I wrote a list and then checked herself that I'd packed everything on it. People from the ship are coming later today to collect my sea chest.'

'Make sure you keep the money and the banker's drafts I've given you safe during the voyage and on the coach north to St Andrews… Trust no one… That's really important. Now let's get a move on. Your mother and sister will be waiting.'

–

The time before Will's departure passed rapidly, taken up – despite Will's protestations that he had all he needed – in making last-minute purchases. While he was away with his mother and Lizzie at a merchant's, a liveried messenger from Government House arrived at Nicholas' usual lodgings with Mohammed Aziz with a letter from Hastings, which read simply:

> *Come to Government House as soon as you can. There's something you should be among the first to know.*

What could Hastings have to tell him so urgently, and why the mystery? He'd had little contact with Hastings since they had returned from Benares over a year before and Nicholas had gone gratefully home to Glenmire. Several months ago an Act of the British Parliament had created the new post of governor-general to be responsible for the Company's affairs in Madras and Bombay, as well as those in Calcutta. Such powers were unprecedented in the Company's history. Hastings had been appointed to the new role and granted the kingly salary of £25,000 a year. Nicholas had written to congratulate him and received a friendly reply, but there'd been little else. All the more reason why this must be important, Nicholas thought, abandoning plans for a quiet afternoon.

As soon as he arrived at Government House he was taken straight to Hastings' office.

'Nicholas – I'm glad you came. You were the first person I thought of… I'd heard you were in Calcutta,' Hastings said.

'Yes, Lucia and I have come to see Will off to Britain tomorrow. But why the urgent summons?'

'Read this – a confidential despatch from the Company that only reached me this morning, straight off a newly arrived East Indiaman. Its contents aren't public yet, but soon will be. I wanted you to know first.'

Taking the despatch, Nicholas sat down and began to read. Reaching the substance he gasped:

Lord Clive has taken his own life by cutting his throat with a sharp paperknife. After complaining of violent stomach pains, he left the drawing room of his town house in Berkeley Square saying he wished to visit the water closet. When he failed to return, Lady Clive went to look for him. Opening the door to the water closet, she found his blood-soaked body and fainted, but not before her screams had summoned the servants. Fortunately, Lord Clive's secretary, Richard Strachey, was in the house and was able to make suitable arrangements. The body was removed discreetly from Berkeley Square and taken to the village church in his birthplace, Moreton Say, and buried under cover of darkness in an unmarked grave as befits a suicide.

Lord Clive's ignominious end is an embarrassment for the Company. It is already being said he acquired his fortune in Hindustan by such corruption that his own conscience could no longer bear the stain of his crimes. I trust that as governor-general you will do what you can to dampen any unsavoury speculation among our own employees in Hindustan that might undermine our reputation, particularly with the local rulers. This is a most unfortunate and unforeseen event most damaging to the Company and…

Appalled both at the news and the callous, sanctimonious language in which it was conveyed, Nicholas put the paper down, too shocked to speak. What a horrible, despairing end for Clive – and how terrible for his wife, Margaret, to discover him like that…

'I'm sorry, Nicholas, but I knew you'd want to know. It was a shock to me too. I can't understand why he'd do such a thing! I've been going over some of the things I've said about Clive… I may have been too harsh… He had his faults – we all do – but he was an extraordinary man who achieved some extraordinary things. I can only think it was the recent accusations of corruption against him in Parliament that drove him to it… This is the fault of all those politicians who, wanting to attack and discredit the Company, made him their target! His blood is on their hands…'

But hadn't Clive always been a little unstable, Nicholas reflected. Even in their early days together in Hindustan, he'd wondered whether the volatile Clive, bursting with reckless courage and relentless ambition, wasn't even a little mad… What about that night Clive had confessed how, despairing of ever achieving anything that he wanted, he'd contemplated blowing out his brains to free himself from both his anxieties and his tormenting ambitions… even taken his pistol from its case and readied it…

'We should raise a glass to him.' Going to a decanter on a side table, Hastings poured them each a glass of Madeira. Passing one to Nicholas, he raised his own. 'To Robert Clive!'

'To Clive! A good friend in my youth when I had few…' Nicholas responded and after a pause added, 'I think Clive might have envied your new powers as governor-general.'

'Probably but my role isn't that easy. The Presidents of Madras and Bombay are used to taking their own decisions and resent my authority. Also, the new arrangements stipulate I'm to be "assisted" – if that's the right word – by four councillors who in theory can outvote me. They're already being troublesome…'

They sat in silence until, sounding slightly awkward, Hastings said, 'You've heard about the Oudh business, of course? That the Nawab has annexed Rohilkhand?'

'At least that must have been a boost for the Company's treasuries,' Nicholas couldn't help responding.

But Hastings looked more depressed than abashed. 'It would be if he ever pays up, but so far he's sent nothing but excuses. Besides, the money's not the half of it. The Nawab used a raid by the Rohillas on a merchant caravan on the borders between Rohilkhand and Oudh as the pretext for a full-scale invasion with the help we were bound to give – under the treaty I agreed at Benares – of our forces, led by Colonel Champion. The Nawab's troops committed atrocities. Some Company soldiers were at least complicit bystanders and quite likely more. I'm trying to keep it quiet.'

'I don't doubt it… but what happened?'

'I can't be sure of the exact details but it seems whole Rohilla families were massacred – some burned alive in their houses.' Hastings' grey eyes were sombre. 'You were right, you know – I should never have given the Nawab license to go to war, particularly not with the unconditional support of the Company army.'

As he walked slowly back to his lodgings Nicholas thought about Clive and Hastings – such different characters yet each had reached the pinnacle of power within the Company in Hindustan. He'd argued with them both, yet did you always have to agree with a man to call him a friend? How far did Hastings' sensitivity in wanting to tell him, as an individual he knew, about Clive's death before he heard of it elsewhere deserve to be weighed in the balance against his pragmatic unsentimental approach to public policy and the fate in the famine of the faceless, nameless millions of Hindustanis whose very lives and livelihoods depended on his decisions?

–

'I tell you, Nicholas, I'm glad all I have to worry about are my bales of silk…' Joss Granger put down the pamphlet he'd been reading and intermittently chuckling over and shook his head. 'God knows who's writing this stuff but they certainly don't like our friend Hastings. Have a read…'

He and Nicholas were sitting in the library of Granger's handsome colonnaded house in Calcutta's Middleton Street, built with profits from the silk business he had established after leaving the Company's employ. It was spacious enough to house in some luxury his family – his energetic wife, Martha, and three sons, but after a dozen years of marriage and now seven without further offspring, not the daughter Martha still hankered for. That was probably why at dinner with Nicholas and his family after Will's departure, she had taken Lucia's hands and said, 'I know you don't much care for Calcutta society, but do you have to go straight home to Glenmire? Why not stay with us at least for a while. I could take Lizzie about – it's just the season for parties and soirees and I can show her the new fashions.' Lizzie had of course leapt at the idea. Lucia too had been grateful, glad to have a kind and willing chaperon to take Lizzie into society, something she indeed found both stressful and tedious. And so it had been settled they would remain for at least three weeks, extended more recently by common consent to six.

Picking up the pamphlet, Nicholas realised he'd seen copies lying about on hall and library tables around Calcutta. The title – *The Calcutta Spy* – was in large letters next to a silhouette of an elegant young man, hair in a bow and a high-crowned hat on his head, holding a quizzing glass to his eye. The signature on the final page, beneath the columns of dense print broken up by numerous headings, was simply 'Janus'. The two-faced god of antiquity wasn't a bad pseudonym, Nicholas thought, running his eye down a series of gossipy stories about the indiscretions and peccadilloes of such people as 'the beautiful, blue-eyed Mrs X who is said to be rueing a clandestine kiss at Lady Y's recent fête champêtre', 'Sir – still ardent in his pursuit of the ladies despite his recent hunting accident, which might prove an impediment to vigorous activity' and 'the vivacious Mrs Z, recently brought to bed of a child – a remarkable event since her husband only returned from England six months ago'.

However, in the middle of the front page was a virulent denunciation of Hastings with no attempt at concealing identities.

> *But now to the more serious matter of politics and the governance of our beloved Company. New brooms sweep clean, as the saying goes. How fortunate that last November the East Indiaman Ashburnham delivered to our shores three such useful instruments – our councillors sent from Britain to curb the excesses of our newly elevated governor-general. Philip Francis Esquire, Colonel George Monson*

and General John Clavering continue to prove themselves titans in resisting Hastings' attempts to gather all power into his own hands and govern like a tyrant – a veritable Nero. Though their colleague, councillor Richard Barwell, fawns on his master like a whipped puppy, we rejoice that we have three good men and true with the power to bring the governor-general to heel. Would that they had the authority to restrain other aspects of our Nero's behaviour, such as his shameless cavorting with the foreign woman he has installed in a love nest in Alipur. She claims the rank of baroness. Who can say? What we can be sure of is that the bosomy lady has a husband. Yet our wives and daughters must curtsey before a woman whom those more unkind than your humble Janus might consider no better than a common courtesan. O tempora, o mores!

Nicholas smiled and put the pamphlet aside. 'Surely no one takes this stuff seriously...'

'Some will because it's what they want to read. Hastings has many enemies.'

'These councillors... The article makes them sound like avenging angels descending to wrestle with the devil...'

Granger grinned. 'Some angels! I've heard it said that the only things they have in common are hating Hastings and coveting his job.'

'I remember Monson. He fought with Clive and was wounded at Pondicherry. Brave, but not the sharpest of wits.'

'You should meet his wife, Lady Anne. She holds a weekly salon. Martha attended one but said it was one of the stiffest, most tedious evenings she'd ever spent. The prune-faced Lady Anne sat straight-backed throughout and scarcely said a word – odd behaviour for a woman hosting a salon.'

Nicholas laughed. 'I think a friend pointed Francis out to me as his carriage passed – a thin-faced man in his thirties with a long, pointed nose, if I was looking at the right man?'

'Yes, that's him. He's left a wife and six children in England... I've heard he's one for the women and likes to play high at the gaming tables. Lucky he's secured a huge salary.'

'And Clavering? I've not come across him.'

'In his early fifties – about the same age as Monson. He served in the Coldstream Guards without any particular distinction, which makes it odd he's been appointed commander-in-chief of the Company's army as well as one of Hastings' councillors. I've not met him, but he's said to be bad-tempered and a stickler for protocol. Do you know, when he, Francis and Monson arrived last autumn, he complained they were only given a seventeen- not a twenty-one-gun salute! His wife hosts a rival salon to Lady Anne's, which I suspect is equally deadly.'

'Janus mentioned a fourth councillor – Richard Barwell. Not long after I arrived in Hindustan, I recall a William Barwell who was a senior official in Bengal.'

'Yes, and got sent home in disgrace! Richard Barwell's his son and well on the way to becoming one of the richest men in Calcutta. He's apparently the only one of the councillors prepared to support Hastings but that's little help. When Parliament created the new post of governor-general it also legislated that he was to have four councillors to assist him, each with voting rights equal to his own. They can tie his hands as and when they want.'

'He mentioned something about that to me.' Nicholas felt almost sorry for Hastings. His new councillors sounded even worse than those he had complained of while he was governor of Calcutta before he became governor-general.

'Anyway, enough of this. I'm glad neither you nor I have to worry about such things. And it's high time I went to my office – a new shipment of silks arrived yesterday from Canton and I must make sure they're undamaged. Some of the last consignment was stained with salt water.' Granger, a heavily built man, rose a little ponderously but before heading for the door paused and said, 'One thing I can say for Hastings is that he knows a thing or two about silks. Last year he came to my warehouse to choose some lengths for his baroness. When I said I was surprised how much he knew about the silk process, he told me that when he first came to Hindustan he bought silks for the Company in the villages around Murshidabad. Personally I like the fellow. Good luck to him, I say!'

Nicholas remained in the peaceful white-stuccoed library with its high-barrelled ceiling, deep leather chairs and French windows open onto the Grangers' rose-filled gardens. All was quiet – Lucia was resting and Martha had taken Lizzie to a picnic on the banks of the Hooghly – perfect for continuing reading a book newly arrived in Calcutta's bookshops – Samuel Johnson's *A Journey to the Western Isles of Scotland.* Johnson began *I had long desired to visit the Hebrides, or Western Islands of Scotland…* so had Nicholas in his youth. But now, seeing the Isles through Johnson's somewhat acerbic eye was probably the closest he'd ever come… Nicholas was soon so deep in Johnson's trenchant prose that he didn't notice the door open. But then a familiar voice asked, 'Well? Haven't you anything to say to me?'

Looking up Nicholas saw the tall figure of… well he knew the voice was Tuhin Singh's but his friend's face was heavily bearded and deeply weather-beaten. Leaping to his feet, Nicholas embraced him, slapping him on the back. 'When did you get back?'

'A day ago. Since then I've been at Government House with Bogle briefing Hastings. But that's done with – at least for now. I'm lodging with Mohammed Aziz. He told me you were here in Calcutta with the Grangers…'

'Sit down. I want to know everything.'

'I barely know where to start… what do you want to hear about first? The shadowy monasteries barely lit by yak butter oil lamps and honeycombed with smoke-blackened chambers? How the devout crawl beneath the racks of holy texts to pray before Buddha images? The Company's prospects for trade? The Tibetan diet? How polyandry works? Hastings asked us to report on all that and a lot more besides.'

'Polyandry? If I remember my Greek, doesn't that word mean "many men"?'

'Yes. Tibetan women have multiple husbands – like the harem but the other way around... Hastings was particularly interested to know how it works...'

For a moment Nicholas thought that in sharing Marian with the baron Hastings already knew a little about polyandry... 'Why not start at the beginning?'

Settling back in his chair, long legs outstretched, Tuhin Singh began his tale of accompanying Hastings' private secretary, George Bogle, on a mission – the Company's first – to the Panchen Lama in remote Tibet. Hastings had asked Tuhin Singh to go because of his knowledge of mountain peoples and the local languages. Before departing the previous summer, Tuhin Singh had told Nicholas the background to the expedition. Bhutanese war bands had invaded Cooch Behar on Bhutan's southern borders, just as they had Sikkim before being repulsed by Nicholas and Tuhin. But this time they had succeeded in ousting its Raja and installing their own candidate on the throne. The deposed Raja had appealed for help to Hastings who had sent troops, in return, of course, for a handsome payment. Company soldiers had given the Bhutanese a severe drubbing and expelled them from Cooch Behar. As Buddhists, the Bhutanese owed spiritual allegiance to the Dalai Lama in Tibet and looked to him for protection in times of crisis. Since the current Dalai Lama was only a child, they had petitioned the next in the hierarchy, the Panchen Lama, for aid. Subsequently Hastings had received his first ever letter from Tibet. Written in Persian – a language Hastings knew well – it was essentially an appeal:

> *I have been repeatedly informed that you have been engaged in hostilities against the Bhutanese whose conduct in committing outrages on your frontiers has been criminal. They are a rude and ignorant race and have given you provocation to send your army against them. However, they have been defeated, many of their people have been killed*

and they have met with the punishment they deserve. I have admonished them to desist from their evil practices in future, and be submissive to you in all matters. I am persuaded they will conform and now ask you to treat them with compassion and clemency. As to my part, I am but a humble priest, and it is the custom of my sect, with rosary in our hands, to pray for the welfare of mankind and I now, with my head uncovered, entreat that you will cease all hostilities.

Hastings had at once scented an opportunity not only for trade with Tibet – perhaps even establishing a permanent Company trading station in Lhasa, the capital – but of using the Panchen Lama's overture to secure a greater foothold in Tibet's immensely wealthy but foreigner-shunning neighbour, China – source of the tea for which the British had a seemingly insatiable appetite. He had therefore quickly drawn up a peace treaty with the Bhutanese and decided to send an expedition at his personal expense, first to Bhutan, to seal the treaty, but then on to Tibet…

'You'd have laughed to see how we set out from Calcutta,' Tuhin Singh grinned. 'Bogle likes his comforts – he took over sixty servants, everything from palanquin carriers and tent pitchers to torch bearers so we could travel by night. His friend Alexander Hamilton, the expedition physician, was a bit more modest – he only had five servants. But our sepoy guard was quite small. Hastings thought a larger one might alarm the Bhutanese, though, as I told him, I thought that a little risky. Even if the main Bhutanese leaders were ready to make peace, you and I both know there are still renegade bands. But the Panchen Lama clearly has great influence in Bhutan. As we travelled through it we knew we were being watched and our progress tracked, but no one attacked us – no need for exploding barrels of gunpowder and stampeding yaks this time… All the same, conditions were difficult and we sometimes missed our way. But apart from having to plant potatoes at every rest stop as Hastings wanted – he seems to think the potato a great gift to those who don't yet have them – we made good progress.'

'Surely not still travelling in palanquins?'

'No – as soon as we reached the mountains, Bogle sent them back to Calcutta and we continued on ponies. But as we ascended higher the snow deepened. In places it grazed our ponies' bellies so we had to dismount and lead them on foot. Most of our Bengali escort had never seen snow, and till they got used to it some found it difficult to breathe in the thin air. At night the local people gave us shelter in their bamboo houses – built on stilts above where they keep their pigs, so you can imagine the stench. But they were very hospitable, offering us liquor and entertaining us with singing and dancing... All went well, despite having to negotiate iron-chain bridges that sway so crazily only one horse at a time can cross, until we neared the Tashichodzong, the summer residence of the paramount Bhutanese ruler, Kunga Rinchen. Out of the blue, a courier from the Panchen Lama arrived with gifts of gold dust and silks but also a message saying Bogle was not welcome in Tibet and virtually ordering us to return immediately to Hindustan.'

'Why?'

'The message was a bit garbled – something about an outbreak of smallpox in Tibet and something about the Chinese authorities objecting to our mission... Bogle, Hamilton and I decided the best thing was to push on to the Tashichodzong and then think what to do. It's a staggering place – a huge fortress-monastery with high white-washed walls and an inner tower topped by a gilded pavilion housing about three thousand soldiers and red-robed monks. Kunga Rinchen himself wasn't there but arrived next day at the head of a great procession of red-uniformed soldiers, archers, musketeers and cavalry and wearing a scarlet cloak and wide-brimmed yellow hat. Bogle said he looked exactly like a Catholic cardinal he had once seen in Rome!

'Kunga Rinchen's own people treat him like some sort of god but he was cordial enough to Bogle... seemed content with the gifts Hastings had sent and – more importantly – the terms of the proposed peace treaty with the Company. The problems began when Bogle showed him the Panchen Lama's letter. Kunga Rinchen became nervous and tried all sorts of arguments to get us to turn back… the journey into Tibet would be too dangerous… we would perish in the high passes… Bogle gave up on him and appealed direct to the Panchen Lama. I suggested that to allay any suspicions that we were spies or a hostile military expedition, he should offer to bring just a small group with him.'

'How did the Panchen Lama react?'

'He took his time. Nearly three months passed before he finally sent word that we could continue our journey so long as our party numbered less than thirty. You can imagine Bogle's relief, he'd been beside himself with frustration… Kunga Rinchen provided us with guides and we crossed into Tibet over a high pass crowned with prayer flags and close to a sacred mountain, Chomolhari, where the Tibetans lay their dead on the ground to be consumed by birds and animals – sky burials, they call them. Our guides warned us on no account to hunt animals for food or sport within view of the mountain. Travelling on in biting winds across the stony Tibetan plains – my flesh felt as if it was turning to ice and Bogle's nose was quite blue – we saw an even higher mountain, so tall it seemed to touch the sky. The local people call it Kanchenjunga – "the five treasures of the snows". I went ahead with the guides to pick out the best route. Sometimes fresh snow concealed old crevasses – two of our fourteen pack mules tumbled into one. We could hear their desperate braying but couldn't do anything to save them. I didn't even dare shoot them for fear of starting an avalanche.

'As we finally neared the monastery of Dechenrubje, tucked up a narrow valley at the foot of a rock face where the Panchen Lama had told us he was currently residing, he sent envoys to conduct us there. Bogle, Hamilton and I were given rooms with walls painted with writhing fire-breathing dragons and serpents with gilded tongues.'

'How long before you saw the Panchen Lama?'

'He received us the very first afternoon. I'd expected a grave, austere Buddha-like figure. Instead, seated cross-legged on a pile of cushions on a gilded throne was a short, plump, smiling man in his mid-thirties wearing a tall yellow hat with red flaps and a sleeveless yellow jacket and yellow satin shawl over simple monastic robes. On either side of him holding sticks of burning incense stood his chief minister and his physician. He welcomed us in Hindi, a language he had learned from his mother who had for a time been a wife of the King of Ladakh.'

'Did he explain why he'd tried to get the expedition to turn back?'

'He said he'd been warned that the Company was like a great king determined on war and conquest, but that he had since been reassured our intentions were peaceful. He was curious to see his first Europeans and asked Bogle and Hamilton to come closer so he could examine the colour of their skin, eyes and hair… He made it clear he wanted us to stay a long time, which, of course, we did – over five months, waking every morning to the sound of monks chanting. Their customs are certainly fascinating. Bogle and I watched them debate – it's all very stylised… The proposer of an argument stands to present his case, emphasising what he thinks is a good point by clapping, stamping or flicking his rosary beads. When he's finished he sits down while his adversary in turn stands to present his counter arguments, all again accompanied with theatrical gestures. The Panchen Lama told us it's highly valued for marking out those with subtlety of mind…'

'What did he and Bogle discuss? Could they find common ground?'

'They got on well right from the start. The Panchen Lama frequently invited him, sometimes me as well, to his private apartments, strewn with tiger skins and with silk thangkas on the walls. As a mark of special favour he gave Bogle a magnificent purple satin coat lined with fox fur and trimmed with gold lace and a brocade hat and invited him to play chess, at which, like the Chogyal, he excels. What struck me most was the Panchen Lama's huge curiosity – he wanted to know everything about

Hastings and the Company, said he was grateful to Hastings for making peace with the Bhutanese. He also wanted to know about Russia. There've been recent skirmishes between the Russians and the Chinese and he's clearly worried their disputes might spill over into Tibet. He talked about science… showed us a camera obscura he had been sent… and quite a lot about the differences between Buddhism and Christianity. He recalled how Jesuit priests had entered Tibet a few years ago but been expelled for being aggressive, and wanted to know more about the Trinity. He was also interested in the English language and asked Bogle to say something so he could hear how it sounded. Bogle recited a poem – it began with something about a curfew tolling the end of the day…'

'"Gray's Elegy in a Country Churchyard", I think it must have been…'

'In turn Bogle, of course, had a host of questions from Hastings, including that about polyandry. The Panchen Lama explained that the custom in Tibet is for a woman to marry the eldest brother in a family and thereby become the wife of all his brothers too. From what he said it doesn't seem to cause the jealousies and rivalries we might expect. The only real arguments seem to be over the paternity of a child, but even there they have a way of resolving things – either by comparing the child's features to those of the possible fathers or by letting the mother decide! The Tibetan women with their turquoises and coral beads are certainly very handsome – Bogle clearly thought so… While we were still in Dechenrubje, Hamilton told me he was treating Bogle with doses of salts for "a disease of Venus" and that he would need further treatment with mercury once back in Calcutta.'

'Bogle's research into Tibetan customs was clearly thorough…' Nicholas smiled. He had met the affable young Bogle, son of a Glasgow merchant and slight and spry as Hastings himself, but this was a new dimension to him…

'I think Bogle became fascinated with Tibet. He was delighted when the Panchen Lama invited us to accompany him to his main monastery at Tashilhunpo. I wish you could have seen the cortège… At the head rode a single young standard bearer, his huge yellow many-tailed silk banner streaming out in the wind, then mounted drummers and trumpeters, then riders in scarlet coats and yellow sheepskin caps on perfectly matched white horses, then a mass of red-robed monks followed by the Panchen Lama on a white stallion shaded by a huge silk parasol strung with ropes of corals. Behind came his ministers, then Bogle, Hamilton and I – a true place of honour – Bogle wearing his splendid purple fur-lined robe, every inch a Tibetan princeling – and finally more riders on some of the best horses I've ever seen. All along the way, monks and ordinary people jostled for a view, prostrating themselves as we passed. Some had erected shrines along the road where they burned incense. As we neared Tashilhunpo, a great sprawl of a place with tiered gilded roofs – the Chogyal's palace would fit into one of its outbuildings – masked monks came out to meet us, dancing to the clash of cymbals to celebrate his homecoming. As we entered the monastery, several thousand more monks waiting in the courtyard flung themselves to the ground before the Panchen Lama. I've seen many sycophantic courtiers over the years, but these people looked truly adoring… Their veneration of the Panchen Lama is unlike anything I've ever witnessed.'

'What do you think will come out of the mission?'

'Not as much as Hastings hoped. We never got to Lhasa as he wanted us to. The Panchen Lama wouldn't allow that. Neither would he make any specific commitments on trade, however persistently Bogle pressed – and he was persistent. The Panchen Lama is clearly in awe of the Chinese Emperor and reluctant to risk antagonising him by allowing foreigners a foothold in Tibet and hence, perhaps, in western China. But he did request Bogle on his behalf to ask Hastings to build a Buddhist temple on the Ganges in Bengal. In summary I think you could say the door has been opened between the Company and Tibet, though what comes next is anyone's guess… except that I'll get rid of this beard. It's far too hot for Calcutta.'

6 – The Reluctant Ambassador

'We will go, won't we? For one thing, I'm sure the governor's baroness will be there and I really want to see what she looks like.' Lizzie looked eager as Nicholas passed Lucia the card just arrived from Government House – together with one for the Grangers – inviting them to the governor-general's grand ball, a high point of Calcutta's social season. His daughter's appetite for parties and dances hadn't diminished in recent weeks, perhaps unsurprising since all she had previously known was occasional invitations to witness from a discreet distance pageants and religious festivals at the Chogyal of Sikkim's court – very different from the distractions on offer here. Smiling at Lizzie Lucia said, 'Of course you must go.'

'But what about you and Father? I know you don't normally care for such things but this is the last big event before we leave Calcutta.'

Glancing at Nicholas, Lucia said, 'Yes, if you really want us to, we'll come.'

In the days leading up to the ball, Martha Granger – who had already guided Lizzie's purchases of dresses, pelisses and the other paraphernalia essential to the fashionable young woman she was becoming – took her to her husband's warehouses to sift through silks and muslins for material to make up into a ball gown. Nicholas spent his time browsing Calcutta's bookshops for additions to his library at Glenmire, having a leading Calcutta gunsmith check his pistols – one barrel looked as if it might have a crack – and having several violin bows restrung. With Tuhin Singh, also still in Calcutta helping record the Tibet expedition, he inspected some agricultural tools newly arrived from Britain where farming methods seemed to be changing fast. A new design of plough with stronger, better angled blades, which might help his farm workers prepare the ground for some planting experiments he had in mind – like growing tea – caught his eye and he purchased two to be sent to Glenmire.

On the night of the ball, having first delivered the Grangers, their carriage returned to Middleton Street to collect the Ballantynes. Lizzie was wearing a seed pearl and amethyst necklace given her as a parting gift by Martha, while round Lucia's throat was the magnificent silver, coral and turquoise necklace the Chogyal had given Nicholas for her, after he and Tuhin Singh had driven out the Bhutanese raiders. Nearing the entrance gates to Government House the carriage joined a procession of others making their way up the drive. Nicholas remembered what Hastings had often said about his love of magnificence – by the looks of things this ball of his would not disgrace either the Sun King at Versailles or a Moghul Emperor at the height of his wealth and power. Huge flambeaux positioned the length of the drive cast their leaping orange light over bejewelled women, some with feathers or flowers in their elaborately coiffed hair, and men in embroidered coats, lace at throat and wrist and satin knee breeches. Unlike Nicholas, whose hair was tied back with a plain black ribbon, several of the men sweated beneath powdered wigs. As their carriage neared the house, he saw through the deep sashed windows hundreds of candles burning in crystal chandeliers.

As their coachman reined in, Nicholas jumped down, then helped Lucia and Lizzie descend. On entering the wide, marble-floored hall he gave their names to the now especially splendidly turbaned and sashed major-domo who as they approached the grand staircase leading up to the ballroom announced, 'Colonel and Mrs Nicholas Ballantyne and Miss Ballantyne.' Hastings was waiting at the top of the stairs, soberly dressed but with a glittering diamond and ruby starburst on his coat – some kind of decoration, Nicholas wondered. By his side stood the Baroness von Imhoff in a low-cut gown of dark green satin with huge emeralds hanging from her ears and nestling in her cleavage and curling white feathers secured in her auburn ringlets.

As Lucia, a wide-eyed Lizzie and the baroness exchanged curtsies, Hastings shook Nicholas' hand and said simply, 'I'm glad to see you here.' For a fraction of a second Nicholas thought he was about to say more but as he hesitated a white-gloved aide de camp ushered Nicholas and his family on into the ballroom. Beneath the high gilded ceiling the cavernous room, extending the length of one wing of Government House, already reverberated with the voices of guests. Liveried servants offered glasses of chilled champagne, hocks or Moselle, navigating with some difficulty with their silver salvers through so many wide hooped skirts. At the far end of the ballroom, the red-coated military band waited and in a side salon Nicholas saw people – many of them elderly, whose dancing days were over – already seated at card tables.

At the tap of a fan on his dark blue velvet-covered arm, he looked round. 'Here you all are! Joss and I have been looking for you but it's hard to find anyone in this crush.' It was Martha Granger, face dusted with rice powder and a faux beauty spot on her left cheek. Her husband was sweating. After the exchange of a few pleasantries, moping his brow he said to Nicholas, 'Let's leave the women to their gossip for a bit and take a turn on the balcony. I need some air.' As they pushed their way through to one of the sets of double doors opening onto the balcony, Joss said, 'Look! Francis is flirting already...' Following Granger's pointing finger, Nicholas saw the thin-faced councillor – resplendent in gold satin trimmed with silver lace, smiling roguishly at a very young, very pretty woman who, at something he said, giggled, flicked open her fan and hid her face behind it. But then an older man, stout and with a mottled reddish complexion that suggested an over-fondness for port, joined them, to Francis' evident annoyance. 'That's Clavering, another of Hastings' crosses... Come on, Nicholas, I'm suffocating in here.'

A quarter of an hour later, the band striking up for the first dance recalled Nicholas to Lucia and Lizzie's side. They watched

Hastings take the baroness by the hand, lead her to the centre of the floor and, as the music began, take a few stately steps to open the ball, the tall baroness with her plumes towering over him. Before long others joined them in the gavotte, among them Lizzie, partnered by a young officer with hair fair as her own. Lucia's eyes followed them, full of pride. As the dancing continued, Lizzie certainly didn't lack partners, unlike several young women left to stand like drooping flowers beside their mothers, as minuets, cotillions and then less formal country dances followed.

As the band finally paused, put down their instruments and made their way into a side room for well-earned refreshments – many of their red coats, particularly those of the drummers, stained with sweat – Hastings approached, bowed to Lucia and said to Nicholas. 'May I have a word?'

Nicholas nodded. 'Of course.'

'In private, I would prefer,' Hastings said, leading Nicholas from the ballroom through the double doors and along a side corridor to a small ante room where the *punkah* was already in motion, pulled by an unseen servant in an adjacent room, and two glasses and a bottle of port waited on a side table. This was clearly a meeting premeditated by Hastings since he had both the *punkah* and the drink ready, Nicholas realised.

Shutting the door carefully Hastings began, 'Nicholas, I hope you don't mind me drawing you away from the entertainment but I suspect you're little fonder of dancing and chit chat than I am.'

Nicholas smiled. 'You may be right about my indifference to grand entertainments, but is something amiss? Why not just invite me to your office some time?'

'Well, here we're away from the prying eyes and ears of my enemies. What I want to say is sensitive.'

'Perhaps we should come to the point? Even though you're right about my lack of enthusiasm for the dance, my family will want me there. Lucia is uneasy without me in Calcutta society and Lizzie wants to be introduced to everyone...'

'Well in large part the issue I want to discuss stems from the whole Rohilla fiasco. Following their defeat and the death of their leader Hafiz Khan, the Rohillas have been regrouping under a new commander, a charismatic and aggressive firebrand named Zabita Khan.'

'Aggressive…? What d'you think this Zabita Khan intends to do – re-take Rohilkhand?'

'Not yet. My agents suggest he is first planning to attack Moghul territory to re-fill his war chests from the imperial treasuries – perhaps to raid Delhi and even to attempt to topple the Moghul Emperor, Shah Alam.

'I know they've fought before, but don't the Rohillas feel any residual loyalty to the Moghuls? They only came to Hindustan because Aurangzeb invited them.'

Hastings shook his head. 'They came because they're opportunists – a bit like me, I can almost hear you say – and they still are. After Aurangzeb's death they were among the first to stop paying their taxes to the imperial treasuries and to break free… they feel no allegiance to the Moghuls, in fact now it's the very reverse – their present leaders view the Emperor as an ally of the Company whom they blame for colluding with the Nawab of Oudh against them.'

'But surely the Rohillas aren't yet strong enough to attack Delhi?'

'No, of course not on their own, but they are renewing their alliance with some of the Sikh rulers who have what they lack – money, artillery, numbers of infantry as well as cavalry – and good reason to hate the Moghuls. They remember the torture and murder of their Guru Tegh Bahadur at Moghul hands a century ago as if it only happened yesterday. My immediate priority has to be to preserve stability and thus the status quo. This means increasing our support to Shah Alam whom we've neglected in recent years, however weak and ineffective a ruler he may be.'

'I know the Emperor is weak but I thought his power had been reinforced by the successes of his Persian general, Najaf Khan?'

'It has but the latest reports are that although relatively young, Najaf Khan is chronically sick and unable to exert his previous influence over the Emperor who in turn is listening to other counsellors urging him to relax his vigilance and allow them greater freedom – freedom to enrich themselves, of course. The latest is that Shah Alam is again spending his days in a haze of *bhang*, cavorting with his concubines.'

'Forgive me, but what has all this to do with me?'

'I want you to be my envoy to Shah Alam to assess the situation, to put some steel into the Emperor's backbone and to report on Najaf Khan's condition and the character of the Emperor's other advisers, both European and Hindustani. The Company's treasuries are a little fuller than they have been so I will be able to supply you with a substantial sum to use at your discretion to induce adherence to us, as you did so successfully with Mir Jafar before Plassey.'

'But doesn't the Company already have an envoy at the Moghul court?'

'Yes. Gilbert Cuthbertson. He's competent enough, I suppose, at writing reports on trade and revenues but lacks the subtlety – and if I can say it, your intelligence and experience – to understand the often Byzantine Moghul court politics. I don't fully trust his judgement or necessarily his loyalty – he is a friend of Francis – as I do yours.'

As Nicholas hesitated, amused by the blatant flattery, Hastings pushed on, 'Don't I hear James has taken that cavalry unit of his to Delhi? Wouldn't going there allow you an opportunity to see your son?'

Despite himself, Nicholas laughed out loud. 'How could I expect a self-confessed opportunist like you not to be aware of that and throw it into the argument?'

'You know me too well and I you… and that of course is what makes you so valuable to me. You will understand that if the Emperor can't – or won't – turn his armies into an effective bulwark against our common enemies he must be persuaded to accept more of the Company's protection and suzerainty, however unpopular that may be among his nobles and viceroys. I'll give you full authority to make such arrangements. I know it's a lot to ask – especially as the Rohillas would never have allied themselves with the Sikhs if I'd listened to you over the Oudh business as Marian so often reminds me!'

Hastings paused to wipe beads of sweat from his forehead with a linen handkerchief then continued, 'If the Sikhs and Rohillas succeed in overwhelming the Emperor and the remnants of his empire they'll unleash chaos across northern Hindustan with Company settlements overrun and Company employees killed, together with many, many innocent Hindustanis. What's more, any Rohilla success will have an impact on our other adversaries, like the Marathas. They've alternated between being supporters and opponents of the Emperor. At the moment they're spending most of their time fighting each other, but if they ever unite under one leader, then God help us... They'll take any opportunity to profit from chaos. And then to top it all we have the bloody French. They're already plotting against us with anyone they can find – Hyder Ali in Mysore is only one example – seeking to get their foot back in the door. One last thing – although I know that money means less to you than many, I can offer a salary of ten thousand pounds if you will undertake the mission.'

'That's an eye-watering sum. Money has its uses and only those who've never been poor as we both have would deny it. But you ask a lot. I need time to think – more time than we have now when I must return to my wife and family. I promise you an answer within the next two days.'

Re-entering the ballroom, to his astonishment, Nicholas saw Lizzie dancing with a familiar figure – his cousin, Charles. The last he'd heard, Charles had been posted to Madras. He'd also been told by those who assumed, wrongly, that he would be interested in his cousin's progress that Charles was starting to ascend the Company hierarchy. Calcutta was the last place he'd expected to see him but what concerned and surprised him was that he had sought out Lizzie... Back at Lucia's side, Nicholas saw she too was watching the couple and didn't look pleased. 'He came over and asked my permission… what could I say?' Lucia whispered. 'Of course Lizzie knows nothing about the quarrel between you.'

At that moment, the music ceased as the musicians again put down their instruments. The supper interval had arrived. Charles led Lizzie back to them, bowed and said to Nicholas, 'I'm pleased to see you again, cousin.'

Nicholas returned his bow but said nothing. To his relief, at that moment the young officer who had been Lizzie's first partner approached to claim her for supper.

'You must excuse me too,' Lucia said to Charles. 'I need to find our friends the Grangers. They asked us to take supper with them. Don't be too long in joining us, Nicholas.'

'I'm surprised to see you here,' Nicholas said as soon as they were alone. 'I heard you were in Madras.'

'I was but for some reason I've just been recalled to Calcutta. No one's yet told me why.'

'Well, I'm sure you'll soon find out. Now if you'll excuse me, I should join my wife.' Charles' appearance was as unexpected as it was unwelcome, Nicholas thought as he joined the throng in an adjacent salon where tables had been set up and a lavish buffet awaited. Should he have challenged Charles about inviting Lizzie to dance? On reflection he was glad he hadn't. It would have sounded petty. The best thing was simply to forget about it, and it wasn't as if he didn't have other things to think about.

-

Less than forty-eight hours after his meeting with Hastings, Nicholas returned to give him his answer. In truth, he'd almost made up his mind at the time to accept the mission, but it had been prudent to wait a little… talk to Lucia, think over the consequences. 'You should go,' Lucia had said. 'I can tell that you want to… and you can see for yourself how James is… I worry about him… And of course the salary will be useful.'

The thought of reassuring himself about James had certainly weighed with him, as had the salary, as Hastings had known both would. So had Hastings' plea, even if a little exaggerated, about heading off a bloodbath. Though the Rohilla threat to the Moghul Emperor had its origins in Hastings' own ill-advised politicking – as Hastings frankly acknowledged – it could not be undone. What could still be achieved, though it wouldn't be easy, was to prevent an immediate violent break-up of what was left of the Moghul Empire. The likely alternative – just as Hastings had said – would be anarchy and misery for many Hindustanis and Britons.

As Nicholas was shown into his office, Hastings came immediately to the point. 'What have you decided? Will you go?'

'Yes. I can be ready to depart as soon as arrangements have been made.'

'Thank God for that! I can't tell you what a relief that is. I hoped you'd say yes, but I wasn't at all sure…'

'Tuhin Singh should come too. I've talked to him about it and he's willing.'

'Even better. He was every bit as effective and resourceful on the Bogle mission as I'd hoped – you two make a good team.'

'How are we to travel?'

'Unfortunately protocol complicates things. Despite the fact we've rather neglected the Emperor of late – or perhaps precisely because of it – the Court of Directors in London has independently decided to send him some gifts.'

'What kind of gifts?'

'A pair of English mastiffs bred in the royal kennels in Windsor, a solid gold clock and a large telescope – don't ask me why. They are waiting in Bombay, together with some smaller items. I want you to sail first to Bombay to pick them up and then on to Surat where you'll disembark and travel inland across the deserts to Delhi. I know the sea-route takes a little longer but it will keep both you and Shah Alam's gifts safer, not least from the Rohillas and the Marathas. Also, if you were to travel all the way overland, our enemies would soon discover you were bound for the Moghul court. This way, they won't find out until you're nearly in Delhi.'

'What escort will you give us?' Nicholas asked, thinking himself fortunate not to have to take quite such a mass of paraphernalia – mirrors, cutlery, glasses, compasses, microscopes, thermometers, even a so-called 'electrifying machine' capable of administering small electric shocks – that Tuhin Singh said Hastings had sent the Panchen Lama to impress him with British technical ingenuity.

'That's still being discussed – and a host of other details besides. In a few minutes I must attend one of these interminable council meetings but I'll ask you – and Tuhin Singh – to join me in a couple of days to go through the arrangements. I know you'll have your own ideas. But before you go, Nicholas, I've something I want to say… I know we don't always agree but I value your honesty – your frankness – now more than ever. All but one of my council want nothing more than to see me discredited and at least two make no secret they want to replace me as governor-general… Sometimes I think my greatest enemies are in the Company itself and it makes me almost despair… It's good to know I've someone to rely on… Marian calls you my conscience…'

Hastings' unusually pensive expressive stopped Nicholas from smiling at these last words. 'Very flattering, but I've never thought of myself as anyone's conscience but my own…'

Walking slowly back to the Grangers' house, Nicholas pondered Hastings' predicament with his council. Despite their disagreements, he still considered Hastings his friend. He was usually honest about his motives – however dubious – and would at least listen to him. Hastings had honoured his promise to build more granaries to help feed the population in case of further devastating famine. With so much that needed to be done, how frustrating for him to have to keep looking over his shoulder. His situation reminded Nicholas of another powerful man – Nawab Anwaruddin Khan, the ruler of the Carnatic he had served many years ago. He too had tormented himself about the loyalty of those closest to him. Perhaps it was always the fate of those in power to keep looking over their shoulder… 'Throne or coffin,' Anwaruddin Khan used to say, echoing the code of his forebears from the Asian steppes. But didn't that mantra apply equally well to the Company? A stab in the back could be metaphorical as well as literal.

–

As the time for Lucia's and Lizzie's departure approached – Lucia and Nicholas had agreed that, with his own travel plans still uncertain, she and Lizzie would return as planned to Glenmire – Martha Granger filled Lizzie's days with all the gaieties she could muster, including a visit to the recently opened New Playhouse to see Richard Brinsley Sheridan's play *The Rivals.* Preoccupied with his own arrangements, Nicholas paid little attention until from one or two casual remarks he began to realise not only that Charles was quite often by Lizzie's side at these events, but that she liked it. Martha had noticed it too and clearly thought it a budding relationship he would welcome. 'I know Lizzie's still very young but some girls marry even earlier. Charles is how old? In his mid-twenties? A good age for a man to marry and they say he's likely to go far… What could be more suitable if they like each other? But let me give you a piece of advice…' Wishing she wouldn't Nicholas could only listen politely as Martha continued to build her castles in the air. 'Lizzie needs to be quick. I hear the Simkin girl is after him…'

When he talked to Lucia, she didn't seem concerned. 'I didn't like Charles from the start, as you know. But Lizzie's still so young, I doubt such a thing's entered her head – she's certainly said nothing to me – and in any case we'll soon be gone from Calcutta. Once she's home, she'll forget all about him. It's the parties she'll really miss.' Nevertheless, Martha Granger's prattle made Nicholas sufficiently worried to ask Lizzie – as tactfully as he could – what she thought of Charles one evening as they rode on the maidan. After considering for some moments, she said,

'He's… well he's different… I suppose it's because of where he grew up… Most other young men I've met here only want to talk about themselves, their work or their horses… They're noisy and a little… well boring. Charles seems more interested in other people and,' she added to Nicholas' considerable surprise, 'more open minded. He doesn't talk about Hindustanis the way some people do – he said he'd heard what happened to James and how wrong it was… He seems to understand instinctively what other people are thinking or feeling…'

Listening to her, Nicholas realised Martha Granger was right – Lizzie did like Charles… was even perhaps half in love with him, though she didn't realise it yet. Whatever the case, as Lucia had said, Lizzie would soon leave Calcutta and Charles should turn his attentions elsewhere.

7 – *Across Tangerine Sands*

> *You go with all my love, caro. Come back safely to me and keep this note with you as a talisman. Lucia.*

Beneath was a tiny watercolour sketch of Glenmire with two female figures watching from the veranda, one holding up a lantern. The night before Lucia's departure for the cooler air of Glenmire, she and Nicholas had made love with more than usual intensity, knowing it would be many months until they were together again, and she had given him this note to read on the day his own journey began.

A loud knock on the door and Tuhin Singh's voice calling, 'Nicholas? Hurry up… It's time to go,' broke into his thoughts. His travelling bags were already aboard the East Indiaman *The Queen Charlotte* but grabbing his large leather satchel he slipped in Lucia's note and checked for the final time that safe inside were the official letters from Hastings with the governor-general's seal attached proving his bona fides, the banker's drafts Hastings had provided together with a considerable amount of cash, as well as his pistols in their mahogany case.

A short tonga ride brought Nicholas and Tuhin Singh to the docks with its usual forest of swaying masts, but it didn't take long to spot their ship. *The Queen Charlotte*, due to sail on the afternoon tide, was a splendid-looking vessel with a freshly painted figurehead of King George's queen, locks flowing and bosom brimming, and – to judge by the number of gun ports – well armed. Leaning over the rail, smoking clay pipes and shouting down to friends below were some of the thirty blue-coated soldiers from one of the Company's European regiments Nicholas and Hastings had agreed would be sufficient as a military escort. Up in the shrouds, sailors were making last-minute adjustments to the tension of the rigging.

The quayside was a jumble of coils of rope, kegs of supplies and other goods still waiting to be loaded as well as sacks of mail – doubtless Company documents for the officials in Bombay. Nicholas and Tuhin Singh exchanged grins as four sweating sailors – none too concerned about their language or who heard it – struggled to rope an enormous crate to a winch, ready to be hoisted on deck. But Nicholas' smile faded as one of a small group of men also watching the manoeuvrings with the crate glanced round. His cousin, Charles!

'What in God's name is he doing here?' Nicholas muttered to Tuhin Singh as Charles approached, calling out, 'Good morning.'

'What is it? Have you brought a message for me?' Nicholas asked.

Charles looked surprised. 'A message? No…'

'Then why are you here?'

Looking even more surprised, Charles said, 'Waiting for you. I thought you might have some last-minute tasks for me before we sail.'

'What do you mean by "we"?'

'I'm sailing with you. I've been appointed to your mission… Surely you knew…?'

Exchanging a quick glance with Tuhin Singh Nicholas struggled to contain his surprise… and his annoyance. 'Who appointed you?'

'Governor-General Hastings. He said you might find me useful… and that I could learn from you.'

Seeing Nicholas' expression, Tuhin Singh tactfully moved out of earshot.

'Charles, I didn't ask for your participation or agree to it. To be honest, I don't welcome it.'

'I didn't ask to come and was only told a few days ago. I expected you'd contact me. When you didn't, I nearly came to see you but then I thought… well… I thought it wasn't my place. I was surprised at my appointment but I hoped it might mean you'd relented a little towards me…'

'Did you.' Nicholas knew there was no time to ride back into Calcutta, find Hastings and ask for his cousin's removal from the mission. In any case, what reason could he give? As far as he was aware, Hastings knew nothing about their quarrel. He himself had never mentioned it and Charles would have been very unlikely to. But why in heaven's name hadn't Hastings said anything? He'd had ample opportunity at their various meetings. Perhaps it was a last-minute decision to find employment for Charles? Perhaps he'd simply assumed Nicholas would be pleased to have his cousin with him? Perhaps he'd just forgotten he'd not mentioned it… Hastings had certainly seemed distracted these past days, fulminating about what he called Francis' and Clavering's 'obstructive posturings'… Or maybe he'd intended it as a pleasant surprise.

'It seems I've little choice in the matter,' Nicholas replied. 'But don't assume this alters things between us. I will treat you as I would any other Company official. Please do not presume on our family relationship. Is that clear?'

'Don't you think that we—'

'Is that clear?'

'Yes.'

That afternoon as *The Queen Charlotte* began her stately passage down the Hooghly, the warm breeze tautening her sails, Nicholas stood at the rail watching Calcutta slowly recede. At least if Charles was with him he couldn't be sneaking up to Glenmire to woo Lizzie – if that had ever been his intention, not that Lucia would allow it. But the weeks and months ahead would inevitably throw them together. He must find a way of co-existing with his cousin and already regretted being quite so brusque, churlish even. The fact that Charles had impressed others with his ability should mean there must be something useful he could find for him to do. Once back in Calcutta they could again go their separate ways. Till then he would maintain a polite but distant working relationship with him and regard it as a return on his debt to his uncle James… The thought mollified him and in a better frame of mind he went to find Lieutenant Tom Cathcart, the young commander of his military escort.

–

The ten-day voyage to Bombay passed uneventfully with good weather and calm seas. Sometimes dolphins leapt in the wake and flying fish, tiny silvery daggers capable of propelling themselves out of the water for extraordinary distances, darted out of the ship's path. Nicholas spent his days reading or sometimes with Tuhin Singh attempting to fish over the ship's side, albeit without much success. Charles, who seemed to have made friends with Cathcart – Nicholas saw them playing whist with two others on deck – wisely kept out of his way.

When *The Queen Charlotte* anchored in Bombay's wide harbour, Company officials brought the gifts for the Emperor out to the ship. The telescope – according to the manual given to Nicholas for safe keeping, of a power and sophistication Lucia would covet – and clock were well protected in stout wooden boxes wrapped in lengths of oiled cloth to protect against seawater. A collection of smaller items included a brass-bound mahogany box filled with packets of different types of seeds – a gift to the Emperor chosen particularly by King George III himself in the misguided conviction that the Moghul Emperor must share his own passion for farming and gardening. Taking personal charge of the box Nicholas thought himself lucky that 'Farmer George' hadn't saddled him with the veritable farmyard of animals that he had apparently given Captain Cook to carry to the South Seas! The two mastiffs, tongues lolling, looked in fine condition despite their recent journey from England and should be more to the Emperor's taste. Tuhin Singh who had a way with all animals offered to take charge of them.

The voyage northwards up the coast to Surat where, in James I's reign, the Company first established a foothold in Hindustan, took a further thirty-six hours. Although it felt good to disembark and have firm ground beneath his feet, Nicholas knew the most arduous part of the journey awaited – on horseback, baggage loaded onto the string of hardy mules selected by Tuhin Singh at a Surat horse dealer's.

With the two mastiffs running behind Tuhin Singh's horse, the embassy set out across the tangerine sands of the Rajasthani desert north-east towards distant Delhi. Just as Hastings had predicted, now they were travelling overland, news that a Company embassy was on its way to the Great Moghul spread rapidly. Local rulers sent gifts – incense, boxes of fragrant melons and sweet yellow-fleshed mangos wrapped in soft cotton to protect them from bruising, lavishly embroidered horse cloths, even an ornate saddle for Nicholas.

Most pressing of all in his hospitality was the Raja of Amber, a leading Rajasthani ruler to whom Nicholas had sent a courier bearing a courteous letter from Hastings requesting safe passage through his kingdom. The courier returned with two of the Raja's retainers and an invitation for Nicholas' party to overnight in the Raja's Amber Fort. Nicholas had heard of the magnificence of the great hilltop sandstone fort but had never seen it. The sun was dropping, the desert turning pewter in the growing shadows as his little column reached the fort and passed through a tall gate, above which were carved two words, *Suraj Pol* – 'Gate of the Sun'. In the *Jaleb Chowk*, the main courtyard, the Raja's orange-turbaned steward, flanked by attendants, waited to greet them.

While his companions were taken to their accommodation, the steward conducted Nicholas to where Raja Prithvi Singh – a tall slender man with large gold earrings – waited, seated cross-legged on a low throne beneath a jewelled canopy fashioned, Nicholas realised, to resemble the rising sun.

'You are welcome,' the Raja began. 'When I received the governor-general's letter seeking permission for his ambassador to pass through my lands on his way to the court of Shah Alam I wished to receive you here, as is fitting.'

'On behalf of the Company I thank you, Highness.'

'But I also invited you because there was something I wished to say. My clan claims descent from the sun through Kush, son of Lord Rama, just as some of my brother Rajput rulers trace their descent from the moon. We are a warrior people who once fought the Moghul invaders, as I'm sure you know. Much of our blood and of theirs was spilled and many of our women committed *jauhar*, burning themselves alive to avoid being taken captive. But then in the reign of the Emperor Akbar came a golden time. Akbar took wives from the royal houses of Rajasthan and allowed them to practise their Hindu faith. He appointed Rajputs to be his generals, Rajputs as his advisers. The close bonds he fostered between Rajput and Moghul endured for over a hundred years until the reign of the Emperor Aurangzeb who, unprovoked by us, tore down our temples and attacked us. We survived Aurangzeb by retreating to our desert fortresses until the times calmed. However, I believe we are now again living in a turbulent world with the Marathas, the Sikhs, not to mention the Rohillas in expansionary mood and the Moghul Empire weak. I hope your mission, whatever it is and it would be discourteous of me to ask, does not signal yet further uncertainty for the Rajput clans.'

Prithvi Singh's fine dark eyes scrutinised Nicholas closely as he replied, 'I assure you, Highness, the Company's intentions are to promote peace and security in the region. To maintain stability for the benefit of all is the purpose of my embassy to Shah Alam. As you say, you are a warrior people. The Company, however, are traders, and for trade to flourish what the Company seeks is peace. I assure you my purpose is neither to stir up old rivalries nor to create new ones. Any hostilities will not be of the Company's making.'

'Then I repeat that you are indeed welcome.'

Making his way to the feast Prithvi Singh had arranged for his guests in the main courtyard that evening, Nicholas reflected that he'd answered the Raja like a true Company man – the smooth words of reassurance had flowed so easily from his lips… But he hoped Prithvi Singh had believed him because he'd spoken the truth. He wanted to prevent widespread bloodshed and so, he believed, did Hastings.

'You look pensive,' Tuhin Singh said as Nicholas took a seat beside him at the long table laid out beneath the stars.

'Do I? I'm just tired. I'll be glad to reach Delhi and get on with what we came for.'

Attendants brought succulent game stews, roasted chickens and fresh-baked bread while for their amusement acrobats tumbled across the courtyard and fire-eaters swallowed fiery brands, but Nicholas was still mulling over his conversation with Prithvi Singh, whose religious beliefs prevented him from dining with them. The Raja had reminded him how much depended on the days ahead.

–

Eager to push on, Nicholas kept up the pace, travelling until the light began to fade and setting off again at dawn. Charles, he noticed, didn't shrink from physical work, helping the escort set up the tents, joining parties going out to look for brushwood and volunteering to inspect the pickets posted around the camp perimeter each night. For company he sought out Tom Cathcart and sometimes Tuhin Singh while continuing to keep out of Nicholas' way. However, one evening, when they were only at most ten days from Delhi, as Nicholas sat alone after dinner beside the blazing campfire, his cousin joined him. After a moment's hesitation Charles asked, 'Nicholas, can we speak about our quarrel over the famine? I can sense the distance you feel it still places between us.'

'If we must but I'm not quite sure what the point might be.'

'This. I know I disappointed you—'

'You're right about that but go on.'

'I realise I expressed myself badly and I was mistaken to blame the farmers for their fate. I was not being insensitive to their suffering. I know how hard life can be. In the last winters in Nova Scotia we often went to bed hungry while eking out the few root vegetables from our increasingly meagre harvests. As a junior official I simply wanted to demonstrate to you that I saw it as my duty to be loyal to the Company as my employer.'

'Even if they were in the wrong?'

'But it wasn't only they who were selfish. The local landowners hoarded food and merchants of whatever race sold to the highest bidder and not the most needy.'

'Agreed. But because others do something, it doesn't make it right or acceptable to do it oneself.'

'Yes, but I wanted... I still want to succeed, to get to the very top of the Company. If – or I hope when – I achieve that, I'll have the freedom and the power to do what I, not others, consider is right.'

To Nicholas this seemed remarkably like Hastings' comments to him during the famine – '*Once I am in full command it will be different*.' He replied, 'So the fulfilment of your own ambitions would allow you to do the good deeds you postponed out of fear of offending your seniors? In fact, your ends would justify the means – an age-old defence for misdeeds and inaction.'

'No. I just mean that compromise and consensus have their place in human affairs, just as does conscience.'

'Perhaps, but I know which of the three I place first. However, in fairness I must admit that one of your other arguments that evening – that to bring about change you must remain engaged – was key to some of my recent decisions to become involved in Company affairs again—'

Suddenly a loud shout of warning from one of the pickets Nicholas and Tuhin Singh had posted broke into their conversation, quickly followed by the crack of several shots. Staring into the darkness, with eyes adjusting from the bright campfire light, Nicholas made out little for some moments but grabbed his musket and threw his pistol to Charles. Experience had taught him always to have his weapons to hand and primed when in unknown territory.

As he did, several riders on camels emerged from the darkness, racing yelling into the camp. Most were heading for the baggage lines where some quickly dismounted and began slashing at the tethers of the pack animals with their scimitars ready to carry them off. One raider, however, dressed entirely in black, seeing Nicholas level his musket, swerved his snorting camel to charge directly at him and his cousin. Nicholas took steady aim and squeezed the trigger. Nothing happened.

The rider still bore down on them, getting closer… so close that Nicholas could smell the camel's foul breath. Then he heard the crack of Charles' pistol. The camel came crashing down in a sprawl of splaying kicking legs, knocking Nicholas backwards to the ground. As the camel collapsed, his black-clad rider jumped free. Drawing his dagger, he threw himself onto Charles who, although pinned to the earth, succeeded in seizing his attacker's dagger hand. Nevertheless he was slowly losing the struggle to keep its tip from his throat. Staggering winded to his feet Nicholas saw his musket lying nearby, grabbed it, reversed it, swung it and hit the raider on the side of his head with the butt. The blow knocked him off Charles, made him drop his dagger, but did not stun him. The man quickly scrambled up and began to run.

As Nicholas followed, still grasping for breath, a musket ball grazed his temple. Turning his head he saw a second black-clad figure attempting to reload his long-barrelled musket. Before he could even get the powder in, Nicholas heard another shot and the man dropped his weapon and fell forward, clutching his chest. Charles must have had one of his own pistols with him.

Nicholas was slowly gaining on the first – and seemingly now unarmed – raider who, turning to see how close his pursuer was, stumbled. Throwing himself full length Nicholas seized the man's legs and brought him crashing to the sandy earth. There they rolled over and over, struggling for their lives. Despite the attacker's powerful physique, Nicholas was getting the advantage when the man's body went limp and Nicholas felt warm liquid seep onto him. Pushing the attacker aside, he looked up to see Charles with a large cooking skewer in his hand. It was dripping blood. He had used it to stab the intruder in the middle of his back, almost certainly penetrating his heart since the man now lay quite still in a growing pool of blood already glinting in the moonlight.

As Charles dropped the skewer and pulled Nicholas, who had blood running into his left eye from the wound on his forehead, to his feet, they heard more shots but further off. The surviving raiders were fleeing on their camels, pursued though only on foot by the pickets led by Tuhin Singh. As they watched, Tuhin Singh dropped to one knee, levelled his musket and fired. A cry of pain from the darkness suggested he had hit his target. However, the raiders were soon out of sight and the danger was over as quickly as it had arisen.

When they had dusted themselves down and Charles had used his neck cloth as a makeshift bandage for the wound in Nicholas' forehead, he and Nicholas made a tour of the camp by the light of the moon and stars. Two of the pickets had been wounded in the first onslaught, both by scimitar slashes, but neither badly. Tuhin Singh was already tending to their injuries. However, the telescope intended as a gift for Shah Alam which had been left in its large packing case by the baggage lines, ready to be reloaded on its pack animal next morning, was missing, together with several bales of Chinese silk destined for the Emperor's women.

As they returned to the tents together, Nicholas, whose head was beginning to throb, said, 'Thank you, Charles. You probably saved my life when my musket misfired. That was a cool, calm shot with which you brought down the camel. It would have been so easy to panic and to miss.'

'I did learn something, you know, among the bears and wolves in the Nova Scotian forests. But in turn I must thank you for knocking that raider off me. He was a powerful fellow. A minute or so more and he would have finished me.'

As he retired to his tent to sleep soon afterwards, Nicholas had to acknowledge that at least his cousin's bravery and calmness as the camel and its rider bore down on him didn't shame the name of Ballantyne.

As soon as the light came up the next morning, Nicholas and Charles, together with Tuhin Singh, rode out in the direction the raiders had fled. They quickly came upon two bales of the stolen silk lying on the sandy ground. From one, which had split, a stream of bottle green material was fluttering in the early morning breeze. Half a mile further on the keen-eyed Tuhin Singh spotted from a distance a camel on the ground ahead. As they got closer they found it was wounded and that its blue and bloody intestines were protruding from a gash in its stomach. As Nicholas dismounted, it tried to stand but its rear legs crumpled under it and it fell back, bellowing piteously. Nicholas at once put his pistol to its head and despatched it from its misery. After riding a few miles more and finding no further sign of the raiders, they returned to camp.

As they resumed their journey later that morning, villagers confirmed Tuhin Singh's assessment that the raiders had been Jats, members of a renegade band that had become increasingly bold over recent months in raids on caravans. 'With the disintegration of the Moghul empire the Jats have long been a menace in this area,' Tuhin Singh said to Nicholas. 'A few years ago they even stole the silver doors from the Taj Mahal, such is their disregard for Moghul power.'

'Perhaps if we persuade Shah Alam to exert greater control over his territories and people it will give some respite from raids like this.'

–

Over the next few days as they continued towards Delhi, Nicholas, impressed by Charles' behaviour during the Jat raid, decided he should perhaps make a greater effort to understand his cousin and his attitudes. One morning as they rode together in the rearguard – it being Tuhin Singh's turn at the head of the column – Nicholas began by asking Charles what tasks he had undertaken in Madras. He fully anticipated a reply describing hours at a high desk in a stuffy office bent over ledgers, quill pen in hand, calculating profits and writing dull papers on land taxes – a life enlivened only by attempts to ingratiate himself with his colleagues and seniors – in a word everything Nicholas detested. To his great surprise Charles, after describing the expected few months of boring training with other 'griffins', as the newcomers were known, said, 'I was chosen to join an embassy to Hyder Ali of Mysore, aiming to encourage him to become an ally of the Company or at least not to hinder its operations.'

'What did you make of him?'

'On this first visit – and on the two others I made – I found him astute and highly intelligent, always reluctant to be more forthcoming than he judged essential, preferring to keep his options open and his intentions veiled, rather than commit himself unnecessarily. He was quite willing to play the Company off against the French who are once more expanding their trading missions from Pondicherry and, being in a weaker position than the Company, are prepared to offer rulers like him greater concessions, greater payments, than ourselves. Nevertheless, on the third mission we succeeded in securing his neutrality between us Europeans for the present, basically because we agreed to support him if the ever-threatening Marathas should attack him.'

'He's quite old, isn't he?'

'Nearly sixty, but he doesn't look it. I got the impression of a man still massively ambitious, as to be expected of someone who clawed his way to power from being a mere junior officer, a nobody.'

'Is it true he's illiterate?'

'He makes great play of being so, claiming script just jumbles before his eyes, but I'm not sure that's not just a ruse to make others underrate him in negotiations. He has certainly secured the loyalty of his courtiers and officers – none were prepared to take up our hints of Company payments for information or assistance.'

'Did you see anything of the batteries of rockets he's rumoured to have?'

'Yes, they exist and became a special interest of mine. Both out of personal curiosity – and because I doubted how reliable an ally Hyder Ali and his firebrand of a son, Tipu Sultan, really are

– I set out to learn everything I could about the rockets. Hyder Ali's making more all the time. He's created special units to launch them and – so his batteries can be moved quickly – he's equipped them with the best of the draught oxen Mysore's so famous for.'

'What are the rockets like?'

'The big difference with previous types – I've read up about them – is that Hyder Ali's use hammered iron casings to hold the black powder that propels them a mile or more. Previous less-sturdy designs apparently went only half that distance.'

'How accurate are they?'

'Not very, even though Hyder Ali's fitted them with bamboo tails several feet long to help guide them. But that's not really the point… The black powder inside the casings is to make the rockets fly – there's usually too little left for any explosion on impact. Their purpose seems to be to spread terror. The rocketeers practise firing salvo after salvo in quick succession from special metal stands. You can imagine the effect of hundreds of them whooshing like shooting stars over or into raw or ill-disciplined troops…'

Nicholas nodded. 'Yes – I can see it could cause chaos and confusion – even put them to flight…'

'Exactly what I thought, even though I'm no military expert. So I managed to sneak in and steal a rocket from a store left unattended by a sentry when he went to a nearby ditch to shit and took it back undetected to my quarters. I made some drawings of it. I didn't think I could smuggle the whole rocket back to Madras with me, so I broke the bamboo tail off and concealed the iron casing for the black powder propellant – it's less than a foot long and only an inch in circumference – in my baggage after emptying out the powder, I didn't want to have my baggage explode! When I got back to Madras, I handed the casing and a copy of my drawing over to an officer in one of the Company's engineer regiments, but he didn't appear very interested.'

'That's quite something you did,' Nicholas said. 'I hope you're wrong in your suspicion the Company engineers won't make use of your acquisition, but experience teaches you may be right.'

They relapsed into silence. Soon afterwards Tuhin Singh rode back to replace Nicholas in the rear-guard and Nicholas pushed his horse into a canter to reach the head of the column. As he then jogged along through what was becoming greener and more populous countryside, he realised that there might be more to Charles than the conventional, compromising, conscience-free man he had assumed after their argument. Perhaps he had judged him over hastily.

8 – A Family Reunion

'I hope you'll be comfortable here. As the Salimgarh overlooks the Jumna it's more airy than palaces in the city. There's plenty of room for your escort and stabling for your animals. The staff are from the imperial household so they're well trained. Now if you'll excuse me, I'll leave you to settle in.'

Gilbert Cuthbertson, the Company's envoy to the Moghul court, was already halfway to the door when Nicholas said, 'Wait a minute, if you will. I've a few questions…'

A flicker of annoyance briefly crossed Cuthbertson's handsome, rather languid face. 'I'd be grateful if they could wait until tomorrow. To be honest, I've a lot to attend to and I've already spent much of the day waiting for you to arrive. The messenger you sent ahead told me to expect you by mid-morning.'

'I'm sorry to have inconvenienced you,' Nicholas replied, an edge to his voice. 'One of my escort was bitten by a viper in our camp early this morning. We had to find a *hakim*, a doctor, to treat him before moving on…' The man was still in agony – the snake, hiding in a pile of horse blankets, had struck as he went to saddle his horse – and the *hakim* was uncertain he would survive.

'Forgive me, I'm truly sorry to hear that. I intended no criticism. What would you like to know?'

'How quickly you can arrange an audience for me with the Emperor?'

The condescension of Cuthbertson's smile as he shook his head irritated Nicholas more than his earlier brusqueness. 'It won't be easy or quick. The Emperor's no fool. He will know that if the Company has sent you all this way, it's because it wants something that will probably require him to make decisions, which he can be reluctant to do. Even if Shah Alam were more energetic, Moghul court etiquette is complex and not to be rushed. Let me explain how it works. I will of course inform His Majesty at once of your arrival but it is for him to make the first move. I would expect him to send you a message of welcome and some small tokens – a basket of fruit, a ceremonial dagger perhaps. Then, when His Majesty feels the time has come, he will receive you formally in his Hall of Public Audience in the Red Fort where you may present your credentials and the gifts you told me you have brought. Finally – and it is again for the Emperor to take the lead – I would expect him to invite you for a more intimate meeting, to which I will accompany you. There you may raise the issues that have brought you from Calcutta. And may I suggest—'

Tiring of Cuthbertson's catalogue of reasons for why he couldn't see the Emperor at once, Nicholas broke in, 'Do please impress on the Emperor I would be grateful for a meeting as early as possible. I have come here with the authority of Governor-General Hastings. My business with the Emperor is both important and urgent.'

'But may I ask what this urgent business is? All the governor-general said in his letter to me was that you are undertaking a mission to the Emperor on his behalf and that I was to assist you. If you'd explain why you are here, it would help… I must admit I'm puzzled why Hastings didn't ask me to deal with whatever it is… Is it something to do with the Company's trading rights?'

'Until I've spoken to the Emperor I'm afraid my business with him must remain confidential. Since I have travelled nearly two thousand miles to be here, I really would welcome anything you could do to obtain an early audience for me despite the difficulties.'

'I'll certainly do my best, though I can't promise anything. Shah Alam is not a man to be easily hurried.'

Neither was Gilbert Cuthbertson, Nicholas thought as, after Cuthbertson had left, he went outside onto the sandstone balcony overlooking the Jumna where in the muddy shallows water buffalo were wallowing. The apartments Cuthbertson had found for him in the ancient Salimgarh were luxurious with thick Persian rugs on the floors and silk hangings on the walls, as there were in Tuhin Singh's and Charles' adjacent quarters. The palace itself was close to the Red Fort, just a little further along the Jumna – he could see its battlements from here. It would have been even more convenient to be in the Red Fort itself where Cuthbertson had his own lodgings, but at least he was here in Delhi and, he comforted himself, would soon see his son. Returning inside, he sat at a table, opened his travelling writing slope and penned a short letter to Hastings reporting the embassy had reached Delhi safely, then a quick note to James telling him he hoped to visit him later that day.

Shortly before sunset, guided by a groom from the Salimgarh, Nicholas rode southwards along the Jumna to the house where James was quartered, about three miles beyond the Red Fort. As a pair of sarus cranes took flight, silhouetted against the pinkening sky, long legs trailing, the groom pointed to a rambling, ancient-looking red sandstone building enclosed by low walls ahead. 'That's where your son lives, sir.' Dismounting at the gate, Nicholas gave his reins to the elderly watchman and walked through into a courtyard in front of the house where marigolds grew in clay pots and a small fountain, carved like a lotus flower, bubbled.

'Father.'

At first Nicholas scarcely recognised the young man in the long indigo tunic, dark hair falling to his shoulders, hurrying towards him, but as he got nearer it was unmistakably James.

'It's good to see you!' Nicholas said, embracing him.

'And you, Father! Is everyone well? Will must be settled in Scotland by now… But Lizzie? Lucia? Tuhin Singh?'

'All well and Tuhin Singh's with me.'

'But what's brought you here? Your note from Calcutta was quite mysterious.'

'All in good time. I want to hear what you've been doing since you've been in Delhi.' Nicholas suddenly sensed they weren't alone – turning his head he saw a woman watching from the shadows near the house. 'Who's that?' he asked.

James hesitated then called out, 'Riti? Won't you join us and meet my father.'

A tall, slender young woman, long hair secured with a jewelled pin and wearing a yellow embroidered tunic and trousers came towards them. Joining her palms, she bowed her head and gave Nicholas the traditional Hindi greeting, '*Namaste*.' Then raising her head again, she looked into Nicholas eyes as she said slowly and carefully in English, 'I am so happy to meet you at last.'

'Father – Riti is my wife. We married five months ago in Rishikesh.'

'Your wife?' Nicholas struggled to register what he had just heard.

Riti touched James lightly on the arm and in Hindi said, 'We have taken your father by surprise… I will go and oversee the preparations for our meal and leave the two of you to talk…' To Nicholas, also in Hindi, she said, 'We are both so glad you are here.'

As she went inside, father and son sat down side by side on a stone bench by the fountain. 'I'm sorry,' James said awkwardly. 'I know I should have written to you – more than once Riti told me I should – but I didn't know quite what to say… Then, when I heard you were coming to Delhi, I put it off so I could tell you face to face… You know I've never been much of a letter writer…'

'No, that's what Lucia always says… But tell me now about Riti – where you met, how long you've been together. If I don't write tonight to Lucia and Lizzie with all the details they'll never forgive either of us.'

'It's an odd story… We met by chance… literally by accident you might say… After the commander of the Emperor's cavalry agreed to take my unit into the imperial service, I gave my men a few days' leave before we took up our new posts – some have families close enough to Delhi to visit. I decided to use the time to go hunting in the hills around Rishikesh – just as you and I used to do around Glenmire, though this time I was alone. One afternoon, having shot nothing that day except a pair of pigeons and feeling impatient with myself I was about to ride back to my lodgings when a deer suddenly shot through the dense foliage fifty or so feet ahead of me. I fired, missing the deer, but almost instantly heard what sounded like a woman cry out… Pushing into the undergrowth, I found Riti lying on the ground, her pony grazing close by. At first I thought I must have hit her but she didn't seem to be bleeding. Then I guessed what must have happened… that my shot had spooked her pony which had reared and thrown her, knocking her unconscious… As I splashed water from my bottle on her face, she began to come round… You can imagine my relief… Her first words were to call me an idiot… She had been out hunting too – it was her approach that had startled the deer and flushed it across my path. My shot must have passed within inches of her.'

'I entirely understand her reaction! And then?'

'She refused any further help from me and remounted her pony, but she still looked dazed and though she kept telling me to go away, I insisted on accompanying her to her home which wasn't far. Her father owns land in the hills above Rishikesh. She's his only child. I thought he'd be angry and blame me – as Riti did. Instead he thanked me for seeing her safely back and told her it was her fault… that he'd warned her to take more care in the forest, not least because of tigers… Then he invited me to be his guest for the rest of my stay… Of course I soon had to return to Delhi and my men, but I couldn't get her out of my mind. Whenever I could get leave, I went back to Rishikesh – it's only two days' ride.'

'I gather Riti eventually forgave you for nearly killing her?'

James grinned. 'Of course. It wasn't long before I knew I wanted her for my wife and found she felt the same… Her father gave his blessing to our marriage. He's an unusual man – unconventional in his thinking – and so is she! We had just a simple ceremony… I never met a woman like her, so independent… so free spirited… She rides as well as me – don't be fooled by her fall from her pony in the woods – and she's teaching me archery… She's like one of those Amazons you told us about when we were young.'

'I don't need to ask whether Riti makes you happy. I can already see she does. To be frank, I'd worried that after what happened with the Company you'd struggle to find equilibrium again…'

'It's odd how things work out. When Neville called me a half-caste, it was a shock… for a while I felt bitter… but in some ways it was good for me… it made me think about who I am… and more importantly who and what I want to become… You and Lucia sheltered me from so much, treated me no differently to Laura and Will. But all the time in the eyes of the world I *was* different. I needed to go out into that world to discover that for myself. Because of it I'm stronger, less naive, more realistic about people's prejudices and perceptions and thus more able to forestall or counter them…' James broke off for a moment, then said, 'But enough of my introspection, I've something else to tell you, Father – Riti agreed I could…'

'What's that?' Nicholas asked, though he thought he already knew.

'It's still early days but she thinks she's pregnant… If so, in a few months you'll be a grandfather…'

Nicholas put his hand on his son's shoulder. 'That's wonderful news… I'm very glad for you both… as your mother would have been…'

For some moments neither spoke, each wrapped in his own thoughts, then James said, 'I've no further surprises for you. Now, it's your turn. Tell me why Hastings has sent you. I've heard gossip about your mission and plenty of theories, but none I suspect anywhere near the truth…'

'I couldn't say too much when I wrote in case my letter fell into the wrong hands, but now I'll tell you more and I'd welcome your opinion.'

As a thin sliver of moon rose and bats darted through the warm night air, James listened as Nicholas outlined his mission. After he'd finished his son reflected for some moments, then said, 'From everything I know, Hastings was right to send you. Shah Alam's position *is* precarious and not only because of the serious external threat you described. The Emperor has problems much closer to home – he's surrounded by scheming and ambitious relations and courtiers, all eager to prosper at his expense. Though he must surely realise that, he hesitates to impose his authority, avoiding confrontation whenever he can...'

Nicholas nodded. 'What you say confirms everything Hastings thinks, but where did you hear all this?'

'It's common talk among some Moghul officers – and some of the foreign mercenaries. They say the Emperor's commander-in-chief, Najaf Khan – I've met him when he's inspected us but exchanged only a few words with him – is deeply frustrated. He believes that if Shah Alam won't rouse himself to action he should at least delegate power to those he could trust to enforce his authority for him.'

'Like Najaf Khan himself, I presume?'

'No, I don't think so. For one thing he's not well enough.'

'Hastings said he'd heard Najaf Khan wasn't in the best of health... so that's true is it...?'

'Yes. Whatever it is, it's an odd illness. Sometimes he's full of vigour, then a sudden debilitating bout of sickness strikes him down, on occasion leaving him too weak even to walk. The last time he inspected my unit he had to be carried in a palanquin. Of course when he's ill he can't maintain his remaining influence over the Emperor. I've seen some of the problems with my own eyes. My unit's first assignment was as part of an expedition to retake a small fort commanding an important river crossing that the Rohillas had recently seized. We succeeded – if I say so myself, we did our job well – but not long after we returned to Delhi, the Rohillas re-occupied it. Do you know why? Because the corrupt Moghul governor of the province had failed to re-garrison the fort properly and strengthen its defences as he'd been paid to do. Instead he kept the money for himself. They say Najaf Khan was furious when he found out... hobbled from his sickbed to see Shah Alam.'

'I don't understand why the Emperor won't listen. Surely he realises the danger he's exposing himself to? He must want to keep his throne.'

'Of course he does but he almost wilfully refuses to acknowledge that there are problems. Although Najaf Khan and some of his officers have been urging him to modernise his army and root out corruption, another faction at court has been soothing his fears... telling him precisely what he wants to hear... that his forces are adequate, that he has no reason to spend more money from his already depleted treasuries and that he has no need to trouble himself.'

So, the situation appeared even more complex and the need for some straight talking with Shah Alam was perhaps even more critical than Hastings believed, Nicholas thought, frowning a little. The days ahead would be difficult... how could he make an Emperor who refused to listen hear what he had come to say... and how could he hurry a man who refused to be rushed to act in time to save himself?

'Come inside. The meal is ready,' Nicholas heard Riti call. Looking round he saw her in the doorway, a lamp in one hand and beckoning with the other – a reminder that this was a time for family celebration. Worrying about complex Moghul politics must wait. Nicholas put his arm around his son's shoulder and they walked slowly inside.

–

In fact, despite repeated messages from Nicholas to Cuthbertson who seemed to be avoiding him, nearly three days passed before an invitation to an audience with the Emperor arrived. Shah Alam would see him that very afternoon. 'Finally! I'd hoped Shah Alam would at least be more curious to know why we're here,'

Nicholas said to Tuhin Singh and Charles, with whom he was strolling in the Salimgarh's gardens, accompanied by the mastiffs.

'Well, it just confirms everything we know about him – that he prefers poetry to business and politics…' Charles said, bending to tickle one of the dogs behind the ears.

'Put like that it makes him sound rather more likeable than some potentates. But I must make him understand how fragile his position is – I'm sure he'd rather continue to write his verses in the Red Fort than go back into exile or be killed or rot in some Rohilla dungeon… And it's not only himself he should be worrying about but the thousands whose lives depend on him. Anyway, I'd better go and prepare, and you –' Nicholas smiled at Tuhin Singh '– had better say goodbye to your two canine friends. They're about to acquire a new master.'

Four hours later, Nicholas, with Gilbert Cuthbertson seated beside him, swayed in a *howdah* atop the imperial elephant sent to the Salimgarh to carry him to the Red Fort. Behind followed a wagon with the gifts for the Emperor including the mastiffs, secure but doleful in a large iron cage The *mahout*, seated cross-legged on the elephant's neck, used his metal *anka* to guide it through the tall Lahore Gate into the fort. The sudden booming of drums made Nicholas start, but the elephant, which had doubtless trodden this path many times, continued on its stately way, turning at a tap from the *mahout* down a surprisingly narrow twisting passage – a reminder that the labyrinthine Red Fort had been designed to keep out attacking enemies. As the elephant emerged into a large square, at a cry from its *mahout*, it lowered itself to its knees. Attendants brought wooden steps and helped Nicholas and Cuthbertson down.

'That's the *Diwan-i-Am*, the Hall of Public Audience, over there.' Cuthbertson pointed towards a colonnaded pavilion beyond some rose beds. 'And here comes Hassan Bakhsh, the Emperor's chamberlain – nice enough old boy, if a bit forgetful.'

The chamberlain, supporting himself on a carved rosewood stick and with a heavy jewelled gold chain of office around his neck, bowed, exchanged a few words with Cuthbertson, then said, 'Please follow me. Bearers will bring the gifts.'

The many pillared Hall of Public Audience was so full of courtiers and officers that at first Nicholas could not see the Emperor. But as the crowd parted to allow him through, he made out a slim, fine-featured man of about fifty sitting very upright on a golden throne, a white egret plume nodding in his silver cloth turban. Attendants on either side were slowly fanning him with giant peacock's feather fans. 'Welcome to my court, Nicholas Ballantyne,' Shah Alam said as Nicholas, with Cuthbertson a little behind him, made their bows.

'Thank you, Majesty. May I present this letter from Governor-General Hastings.' From his leather satchel, Nicholas extracted the folded-document bearing the heavy Company seal and placed it on a silver tray, which, at a sign from Hassan Bakhsh, a green-clad *qorchi* – page – held out to him.

But as the *qorchi* approached the Emperor, he waved the boy away. 'I will read the letter later, but what is that I can hear?'

It was the excited barking of the mastiffs who were being led into the hall by two servants. 'His Majesty King George III of Britain hopes that you will accept these mastiff dogs, bred in his own kennels, as his personal gift to you. They are hunting dogs, well known for their strength, speed and loyalty.'

Shah Alam leant forward to take a closer look and smiled. King George had chosen well – good hunting dogs were prized in Hindustan. Who knew, the Emperor might also like the collection of seeds, which Nicholas had arranged with Cuthbertson would be sent with the other smaller gifts to the imperial apartments later… A pity the raiders had stolen the telescope. Shah Alam was known to have an interest in the stars and to consult his court astrologers regularly. However, Nicholas still had the golden clock to present.

The mastiffs were led away and two further attendants approached, carefully carrying the clock on its stand of finely polished granite resting on gilt wooden feet carved in the form of elephants. Two kneeling cherubs, sturdy arms aloft, supported a round white enamel clock face edged with diamonds and painted with elegant black numerals, the whole surmounted by an entire heavenly host of golden angels. Looking at the magnificent confection, Nicholas only hoped the clock would keep reasonable time. After its lengthy journey, first by sea, then bumping on mule-back across the desert, he somehow doubted it.

'I shall examine the clock later,' Shah Alam said. 'It appears most… intriguing. But now I would like you to join me in my private apartments to talk in more comfort. My chamberlain will show you the way.' So saying, the Emperor rose and walked quickly through a tall arch directly behind the throne.

'That's a surprise,' Cuthbertson muttered, tapping Nicholas on the shoulder. 'It usually takes far longer to obtain a private audience. Let's see what he has to say.'

'I'd prefer to see the Emperor on my own, if you don't mind.'

'But as the Company representative to the Moghul court I should accompany you—'

'As the governor-general's personal envoy, I can absolve you of that duty… Besides, you told me the other day how busy you are.'

Cuthbertson seemed about to object but Nicholas' expression dissuaded him. 'Of course. But I hope you will brief me on your conversation with His Majesty.' With a shrug, Cuthbertson turned and joined the courtiers streaming from the hall into the sunlit courtyard beyond.

'Colonel Ballantyne? Follow me, please.' Hassan Bakhsh led Nicholas from the audience hall along a wide corridor. At the far end were double doors of solid silver inlaid with jewelled peacocks, preening tails outspread. As Nicholas and the chamberlain approached, the two soldiers standing sentry on either side opened them wide. Hassan Bakhsh courteously stood back to allow Nicholas to enter the large chamber where Shah Alam was already reclining on a yellow silk divan. Close by him was a sitar. Pointing to another divan he said to Nicholas, 'Do sit. Hassan Bakhsh, you may leave us.'

Surprised by this apparent lack of formality after Cuthbertson's lecture about Moghul protocol, Nicholas settled himself. However, the Emperor's next words confirmed some things Cuthbertson had said about Shah Alam's personality. 'I haven't, of course, yet read the governor-general's letter so let's not discuss business today. I've been curious to meet you. I know from reading the chronicles written by my ancestors that you aren't the first Nicholas Ballantyne to visit a Moghul Emperor...'

Nicholas blinked in surprise. 'Yes. My great-great-grandfather came to the court of the Emperor Jahangir as page to the English ambassador Sir Thomas Roe and stayed many years after Roe departed...'

'Your family's enduring relationship with Hindustan intrigues me and in due course you must tell me more... Your son and his cavalry unit recently entered my service. My cavalry commander tells me he's a promising young man.'

'As his father, I have always thought so, but I am glad others share that opinion.'

Shah Alam smiled. 'You speak as a proud father, which is how it should be. But I wonder why he is here in Delhi, not with the Company? If I have been informed correctly, you fought at Plassey.'

'Yes, Majesty,' Nicholas replied, wondering where this was leading.

'And yet your son has not followed your course.'

'I left the Company many years ago. Governor-General Hastings asked me to be his envoy to your court not as a Company employee, but as a trusted friend. As for my son, he did once serve with the Company but it proved not to be to his taste.'

'Well, you must be glad to be reunited with him while you are here. You may tell him the Emperor values his service. Now, I am a little fatigued so please leave me, but we will talk again soon.'

'I hope so, Majesty. When you read the letter from Governor-General Hastings you will see that urgent and important matters have brought me here.'

‘Urgent and important? To whom? The Company?’

‘Certainly, Majesty, but perhaps above all to you…’ Nicholas said, standing up. He’d have liked to say more but all his instincts warned him against it. He must be patient…

As Hassan Bakhsh, who had been waiting outside, led him back down the corridor he heard behind him the haunting strains of a sitar.

9 – *A Throne in the Balance*

'Stop here, help me get down, then leave us,' Najaf Khan ordered the four bearers carrying his palanquin as they reached a quiet section of the battlements of the Red Fort overlooking the pearl-drop domes of the Jama Masjid built, like the fort, by the Emperor Shah Jahan. Najaf Khan had suggested to Nicholas this tour of the fort's defences at an imperial *durbar* a few days before. There, anticipating from what James had said that Najaf Khan would be a likely ally, Nicholas had hinted at the concerns that had brought him to Delhi. The tall, powerfully built general had seemed in better health at the *durbar* but his debilitating illness had since reoccurred. 'Today I can walk only a few steps without tiring,' Najaf Khan had said when they met earlier, 'I must use my palanquin.'

Two bearers helped Najaf Khan to one of the low sandstone benches placed for use by sentries. Settling himself he said to Nicholas, 'Look down over the battlements for a moment and you'll see a bastion pockmarked by cannon balls and crumbling round the base. It's never been properly repaired since Nadir Shah captured Delhi forty years ago… If I felt better I could show you several other weak points around the fort. The city walls also need reinforcing.'

As Nicholas – after briefly inspecting the bastion, which was indeed in poor condition – sat beside him, Najaf Khan continued. 'Following his return from exile, Shah Alam approved without question my plans to refortify the fort and city and re-equip his armies… didn't even want to discuss the details… Some work was done but these days whenever I ask for money to repair obvious weaknesses, he smiles and says, "Be patient!" You are a soldier, Ballantyne, so you'll understand my frustration, I'm sure.'

'It's many years since I called myself a soldier, but yes, I do understand.'

'To be honest, Shah Alam seems to be losing what resolve he possessed and that was never a great deal on military affairs such as these. In my worst moments I think the only thing that would penetrate the haze of *bhang* into which he so often retreats would be the sound of enemy cannon, but by then, of course, it would be too late…'

Nicholas understood exactly what Najaf Khan meant. By now he had had several further meetings with Shah Alam. As soon as he tried to turn the conversation to serious matters the Emperor deflected him – inviting him to listen to him play his sitar, quizzing him about European violins, reading verses of his own poetry, offering him *bhang* or opium – '*So much preferable to the affairs of the world.*' Nicholas had once or twice accepted *bhang*, enjoying its pleasant languor, but with memories of its destructive effect on Clive he refused the opium, which the Emperor enjoyed drinking dissolved in wine.

'Why won't the Emperor listen to you, his commander-in-chief?' Nicholas asked.

'A clique at court has his ear at present – courtiers who understand the Emperor's temperament and how to exploit it – Malik Khan, his vizier, and Imran Hazin, his treasurer, to name but two. They reassure him that all is well, telling him what he wants to hear – to leave everything to them. They've prospered mightily as a result. If they were in the pay of Zabita Khan himself their advice to Shah Alam could not be more damaging to our security here. If it weren't for this cursed illness of mine I could perhaps make him listen, but every time I think I'm getting better, able to play a fuller part in imperial affairs, I relapse, as I have today…'

'I will keep trying to convince the Emperor of the difficulties he faces… That's why I am here.'

'Why does Shah Alam's fate matter so much to the Company?'

'To continue to trade and to prosper the Company needs stability above all. If the Moghul Empire were overrun there would be chaos and chaos is bad for business. But it's not only that – hundreds of thousands would die.'

'That's really of concern to Hastings, a foreigner?'

'Yes, I believe so – as I'm sure it is to you, even though as a Persian you could be said to be a foreigner by those of ill will.'

'*Touché*, as I think European swordsmen say. But some words of warning. Though he would be too courteous to say so to your face, Shah Alam has long been sceptical about the Company's intentions towards him. Many years ago, after he was forced to flee Delhi, he raised his imperial standard at Allahabad. Thirty thousand of his own people rallied to him but he knew it wasn't enough so he wrote an appeal to your King George – as a fellow sovereign – for help. He even offered to acknowledge your king's overlordship and sent him rich gifts. But Shah Alam later discovered that Robert Clive intercepted both his letter and his gifts, which never left Hindustan... Shah Alam regained his throne with no help from the Company, which he hasn't forgotten... But now, forgive me. I'm feeling so unwell I should probably return to my quarters.'

–

Back at the Salimgarh that evening, Nicholas mulled over his conversation with Najaf Khan. What he had told him about Clive – though new to him – wasn't really surprising. Clive had often acted high-handedly, doing what he alone thought best, when he thought best – and he certainly was not above enriching himself at others' expense. As for what the general had said about the Emperor, it confirmed much that Nicholas had gleaned since arriving, including from conversations with some officer friends of James who'd volunteered both himself and Riti to keep their ears to the ground on his behalf.

The exception to the worries expressed by most was Gilbert Cuthbertson to whom Nicholas had now explained why Hastings had sent him but who seemed puzzled by Hastings' concern. 'The Emperor sees no need for alarm, nor do his closest and wisest advisers. I think they're correct. After all, who are the Rohillas? Just hit-and-run raiders… Shah Alam knows he has a large army and, even though Najaf Khan's a sick man, plenty of competent officers. If you want my advice, you should return to Hastings and tell him not to worry. If the situation should worsen – which I honestly doubt – I'll of course send word.'

Was Cuthbertson relying for his opinions solely on a single self-interested – or at least misguided – faction at court? Now that Nicholas thought about it, he realised that the few senior courtiers Cuthbertson had introduced him to had included both Malik Khan and Imran Hazin… Was he indebted to them in some way? Cuthbertson certainly was not encouraging him in wider investigations but kept suggesting distractions – a tiger hunt, a cruise down the Jumna… Yesterday with a smile he had said, 'Before you leave Delhi you must let me arrange a little entertainment for you in my lodgings… I can provide some willing women. They have certain skills that will surprise and relax you.'

As Nicholas and Tuhin Singh later stood on the terrace overlooking the Jumna, Nicholas vented his frustrations about his failure to engage Shah Alam in discussion of serious matters for more than a minute or two.

'You must be more patient,' Tuhin Singh said. 'I remember that's what you used to tell Clive when he couldn't make things happen the way he wanted, when he wanted.'

Before Nicholas could reply, an attendant appeared. 'Mr Ballantyne, sir,' he said. 'A messenger brought this letter – he says it's urgent.' Recognising James' writing, Nicholas opened it to find a short note.

> *Father, half an hour ago two Moghul scouts arrived with news that an advance force of Sikhs and Rohillas has overrun a Moghul fort near Sirhind, massacring some of its garrison, and appears to be advancing south in the direction*

of Delhi. That is all I know but I'll be in touch when I can get further information.

Nicholas handed the message to Tuhin Singh who scanned it quickly, then said, 'In a way this is good news for you, isn't it? It's proof at last of the danger the Emperor's been trying to ignore.'

'You would think so... but knowing Shah Alam as I think I now do, he'll need more specific information than this before he'll act decisively...'

–

The following day brought no further news. Nicholas tried to arrange to see Najaf Khan only to be told by Gilbert Cuthbertson that the *hakims* said he was too ill to receive visitors that day. He debated seeking a further meeting with Shah Alam, but decided that until he knew more, or had more support, it would probably be pointless. He must take Tuhin Singh's advice and be patient a little longer.

Another day passed before more news started trickling in from Moghul territories north of Delhi, but it was vague and contradictory. Despatches from two provincial Moghul governors described recent small Rohilla and Sikh raids on farms and settlements. Another from the commander of a remote Moghul fort about a hundred and fifty miles from Delhi reported simply that his scouts had seen what appeared to be an advance party of Rohilla and Sikh forces passing close by. However, other neighbouring commanders in their weekly despatches reported everything calm.

'With Najaf Khan still ill, no one is going to do anything significant until the enemy is literally at the gates...!' Nicholas complained to Tuhin Singh as they returned from yet another visit to the Red Fort to attempt to glean more information.

Tuhin Singh nodded. 'To convince the Emperor we need firm information on the actual size, quality and equipment of the Rohillan and Sikh forces.'

'Agreed, but how can we obtain better information without going to see for ourselves?'

'And is that so out of the question? The Rohillas' most advanced unit is apparently under a hundred miles from here. We made expeditions to spy on our adversaries in the days of our youth with Clive and we're not in our dotage yet!'

'It's an idea,' Nicholas replied. 'I suppose we'd have to leave in secret as well as travel in disguise. I wouldn't trust some of the Moghul officers or European mercenaries not to have a foot in both camps, so to speak. And then there's the always inquisitive, interfering Cuthbertson.'

'Well, we could depart at dawn and get Charles to occupy Cuthbertson that day with detailed questions about the specific trading arrangements between the Company and the Moghul Empire on the pretext of having to write a report for Hastings. We could be back in a day and a half.'

'That could work. What about our disguise and cover story? The ones we used to use of being a pair of Kashmiri or Persian merchants? We could quickly get together a few Persian carpets and claim, if challenged, that they're the remnants of a successful trading expedition to Delhi.'

'Of course.'

'Well that's settled, then. All we need to do is to prepare. If we get a move on we can leave the morning after tomorrow.'

-

Despite the obvious hazards of the mission, Nicholas felt a lightness of heart as he and Tuhin Singh successfully made their preparations without attracting untoward attention. The dawn light was scarcely up as less than thirty-six hours after their conversation the two made their way on horseback out of the city, leading two spare horses and three pack mules on which the carpets, the supposed remnants of their trading venture, were carefully strapped. They passed easily through the cursory checks by lounging Moghul soldiers at the gates of Delhi and at various checkpoints along the road.

The pair made good progress through the morning and the heat of the midday – such good progress that by afternoon they were approaching a small town on the dust-blown plain. Some Moghul officials hastening back to Delhi in fear of their lives had told them all Moghul forces had withdrawn from there the previous day, following rumours that the Rohillas were approaching fast. Nearing the town, a collection of mainly modest dwellings enclosed by a mud wall and clustered round a small brick fort set on a low hill in the centre of the town, they saw that just beyond was an encampment with tents, baggage wagons, horse lines and all the usual paraphernalia of a military force on the move.

'How many men d'you think, Tuhin Singh?'

'From those I can see and by the number of tents, horses and so forth, perhaps four hundred fighting men.'

'I don't see any cannon – do you?'

'No. So perhaps it's a reconnaissance in force?'

'Maybe, but let's investigate. No reason for us as merchants not to enter along the road.'

Nicholas had not shaved and now pulled his woollen Kashmiri cap a little lower over his brow to show less of his face, but his heart was beating fast as they approached the two burly Rohillas at the town gates.

'What's your business?'

'Merchants returning to Kashmir, looking for a bed for the night.'

'There should be plenty – many of the townspeople have gone and not many people on the road… I can't think why…' The sentry grinned as he waved them through.

Only a little way into the town, peering down a side street, they noticed a small *serai* that still had its gate open and headed towards it. Dismounting and going inside, they found an elderly man – the owner they presumed – squatting with his back against a wall and an ancient musket across his lap. Seeing them he stood. 'What d'you want? I'm a poor man. There's no money or valuables here.'

'We want to give you money, not to take it,' Tuhin Singh replied. 'We're merchants in search of a quiet room for ourselves and stabling for our animals.'

'It will cost you eighty-four rupees – I know it's more than usual but, being away from the centre of the town and the fort, it is quieter and safer here in – how should I describe them? – these difficult times. I've been careful to do what I can to placate the few Rohillas who've passed this way.'

'I'm glad to hear it. We'll take the accommodation.'

'I don't want any trouble so once you're inside please don't go further into town, particularly since – from what I hear – Zabita Khan himself is to address his officers in the square in front of the fort sometime in the hour before sunset.'

Nicholas and Tuhin Singh exchanged glances. 'No more do we want trouble. We understand and will stay safely within the *serai*,' Nicholas replied.

Within ten minutes, Nicholas and Tuhin Singh were installed in a small room with two rough *charpoys* to sleep on but no other furniture. A small unglazed window gave onto a malodorous side alley – the determining factor in their choice when invited to take any room they wished.

After resting until it seemed that the hour for Zabita Khan's address was approaching, first Nicholas and then Tuhin Singh squeezed through the window and dropped into the side alley. Keeping to the deepening shadows they began quietly navigating their way towards the square through deserted streets along which the wind was whipping up puffs of dust. Suddenly a snarling, barking dog, its ears flat against its head, flung itself out of nowhere at Nicholas, only to be pulled back when its teeth were inches from his thigh by a thick rope around its neck, attached to the gate post of its owner's house. As it continued to bark and growl, Nicholas and Tuhin Singh quickened their pace.

When they reached the last corner before the square, they could see troops gathering there. They ducked into the rear courtyard of a large *haweli*, which they thought must front onto the square. One of its double gates now lay splintered on the ground and a door into the main dwelling was off its hinges, but it must have been a prosperous establishment before being deserted by its owners and looted. Pistols in hand, Nicholas and Tuhin Singh climbed some creaking external stairs to the second floor. There they cautiously pushed their way through some remaining curtaining into what were clearly the women's quarters. They retained a scent of patchouli oil. Several large painted wooden chests were open and some flimsy garments discarded by looters as not worth their trouble were scattered across the wooden floors. Investigating further, Nicholas discovered to his great satisfaction that the suite of rooms had a pale sandstone *jali*-screened balcony overlooking the square, presumably designed for the women to observe goings on without themselves being seen. 'Ideal for our purpose. I think,' he said to Tuhin Singh. 'We can watch events from here.'

Moving quietly onto the balcony, they waited. The standard of the Rohillas – two yellow scimitars on a green background – fluttered from the fort's meagre battlements. A large four-wheeled cart was positioned in the centre of the small square. At each of its corners stood a tall straight-backed sentry, equipped with what looked like a modern flintlock musket. The sentries' eyes constantly scanned the crowd grouped around the cart. It consisted of about fifty men, nearly all with daggers and scimitars in scabbards at their side. Most had pistols tucked into their leather belts and powder horns hanging from them. In the front row a group of five tall, well-built bearded men were standing together dressed, from turbans to pantaloons, in orange – Sikhs of course.

After about ten minutes, the iron-studded wooden gates of the fort opened and a tall man aged about thirty with a neatly trimmed beard emerged, flanked by two guards again carrying modern muskets. The crowd stood respectfully back to afford him a path to the cart, which he sprang nimbly onto. As he raised both hands in the air an immediate and loud cry of '*Zindabad* – long live – Zabita Khan' broke from those assembled and reverberated around the square to be followed by frenzied cheering. Motioning for a moment's calm, Zabita Khan – it was undoubtedly he – began to speak in Pushtu, the Afghan language of which both Nicholas and Tuhin Singh had an imperfect but sufficient knowledge.

'Look around you,' Zabita Khan shouted. 'How easily have we – only a relatively small band – got this far? How many of the so-called soldiers of Shah Alam have fled in fear, putting up no resistance? How many have died beneath our avenging weapons? How many have abjectly surrendered? Tell me, my loyal officers. Isn't one of us worth fifty of these cowardly curs?'

'Yes! Yes! *Zindabad* Zabita Khan!' the crowd chorused in unison, raising their fists in the air.

'Tell me, my brave officers, when more of our forces – already on the move – have arrived and when –' he paused to gesture at the orange-clad Sikhs '– our Sikh allies have joined us with their cannon, newly purchased from the Persians, and their promised regiments of proud warriors, won't we find it easy to brush aside Shah Alam's main forces and enter Delhi in triumph as did Nadir Shah forty years ago?'

'Yes! Yes! *Zindabad* Zabita Khan,' thundered the crowd.

'And, my deserving officers, won't our booty be as great as his? Gold, slaves, women… we and our brave soldiers will enjoy them all, will we not?'

'Yes! Yes! *Zindabad* Zabita Khan,' came the chorus in growing ecstasy.

'After we have conquered Delhi and made the Rohillas great again, revenging ourselves for once and for all on the pusillanimous Moghuls, won't we move against the Nawab of Oudh and his treacherous allies the infidel British and crush their heads like ripe pomegranates beneath a stone?' Zabita Khan cried, his voice rising to a crescendo.

'Yes! Yes! *Zindabad* Zabita Khan! Death to all our enemies.'

At a gesture from Nicholas, Tuhin Singh followed him down the staircase. 'We've seen enough. Let's move before the crowd breaks up,' Nicholas whispered. They slipped out of the back of the *haweli*, forcing themselves to walk quietly rather than risk rousing suspicion by moving too quickly, and made their way back towards the *serai*, avoiding the street in which the guard dog had attacked Nicholas. Reaching the *serai*, they climbed back into their room through the unglazed window. There they quietly agreed that what they had seen – in particular the quality of the muskets and the availability of both them and the pistols, the presence of the Sikh officers and the promise of Sikh reinforcements – were sufficient to confirm that the Rohilla threat was real. Pre-emptive action was essential to crush it before it reached full force.

After spending a night of fitful sleep, drawing their garments around them in a mostly vain attempt to protect their exposed flesh from the mosquitoes buzzing around the room, they rose at dawn. As Tuhin Singh handed payment to the elderly owner of the *serai*, the man said, 'Be grateful I am no friend to the Rohillas. I found your room empty last evening when I came to offer you food and you at least –' he said pointing to Nicholas '– are no more a Kashmiri than I am. Now go, before you bring trouble on yourselves or more importantly on me!'

–

Safely back that same evening in his airy quarters in the Salimgarh in Delhi, Nicholas agreed with Tuhin Singh that his friend should ride to the border of Shah Alam's territory with that of Oudh to locate the Company forces Hastings had promised Nicholas before leaving Calcutta he would have stationed there, ready to intervene if required. Using the authority granted to Nicholas by Hastings, Tuhin Singh should ask the commander of the Company forces to despatch two regiments – one of cavalry, one of infantry – to Delhi at once. Ten members of Nicholas' escort would accompany Tuhin Singh to Oudh. Half would then ride on as fast as they could, exchanging tired horses for fresh ones, to

Calcutta with a despatch to Hastings, carefully crafted by Nicholas in Latin in case it fell into the wrong hands, reporting on progress. Tuhin Singh would leave early the next morning.

Nicholas himself submitted an urgent request that evening for a private audience with the Emperor. A reply came back quickly that Shah Alam would see him the following afternoon. At the appointed hour, accompanied by Charles who had successfully kept Gilbert Cuthbertson occupied and in ignorance of Nicholas' reconnaissance mission, Nicholas made his way to Shah Alam's Hall of Private Audience – a magnificent vaulted room of carved sandstone decorated with marble inlay portraying irises and other flowers.

Ushered in by a green-clad servant, Charles and Nicholas bowed before Shah Alam who was reclining on a low upholstered divan. Seeing their expressions, he sat up. 'What is the matter? Why the serious faces, my friends? Is there a problem?'

'Exactly that,' Nicholas replied. 'You and Delhi are in serious danger from the Rohillas and Sikhs unless you act immediately.'

'How can you sound so certain? Many of my counsellors advise any danger is much exaggerated.'

'I am sure of it because I heard it myself from the very mouth of the Rohilla leader Zabita Khan. My friend Tuhin Singh and I made an expedition in disguise to where he is leading some of his forces in an exploratory raid less than a hundred miles from here. All he is waiting for, I heard him tell a crowd of his officers, is more reinforcements – in particular from his well-equipped Sikh allies who will bring cannon and more horsemen. Then he will act and I assure you—'

The mother of pearl inlaid entrance doors behind Nicholas suddenly swung open and despite the efforts of the green-clad usher to hold him back, in strode Gilbert Cuthbertson. Bowing low before Shah Alam, he said, 'Forgive my intrusion, Your Majesty, but I heard from one of your courtiers that Ballantyne had requested an urgent audience. I thought you would wish me to be present too as the Company's appointed representative at your court, in case I could be of any assistance to your Majesty. May I ask what is the matter under discussion?'

'Ballantyne tells me we are in danger of imminent attack by Rohillas and Sikhs.'

'This cannot be,' a clearly agitated Cuthbertson responded.

'I assure you it can,' Nicholas said quietly. 'If the Emperor wishes to keep his throne he must take immediate action. I am here on behalf of Governor-General Hastings to offer him the Company's support in doing so.'

'At a price, I am sure.'

'There's always a price, but I believe His Majesty Shah Alam will find it acceptable. Before you interrupted us I was about to make the offer of support and outline the terms, which would basically consist of His Majesty granting further trading concessions and tax-raising abilities to the Company in areas beneath the Emperor's titular control where we have an interest.'

'Your Majesty, Ballantyne has no authority to make such an offer,' Cuthbertson spluttered. 'He's not even formally a Company official.'

'I can assure you I have the authority, Your Majesty. It is spelled out here in a confidential document from the governor-general.' Nicholas extracted from a white leather pouch at his belt a folded parchment with the Company seal hanging from it.

'Even if he has the authority, Majesty – and that document could well be a forgery – you should not accept his offer. Your own commanders are competent and your forces sufficient to repel any attack should it occur, which I doubt. Ballantyne is being alarmist. You should listen to me and disregard his exaggerations. I have much greater experience here.'

'Cuthbertson, if you persist in attempting to undermine my judgement and the authority given to me on account of it by Hastings, I will be forced to tell the Emperor of the bribes you have so regularly taken.'

'Bribes? What bribes, and who from?'

'From certain of His Majesty's senior counsellors to use your influence in the name of the Company on their behalf to allow them to continue their exploitation of His Majesty's people to the benefit of their purses and yours. In particular at their behest you have sought to undermine the standing and good influence of His Majesty's leading general, Najaf Khan, who is now so unfortunately ill.'

'You are lying, Ballantyne! You yourself must be in league with and paid by warmongers such as Najaf Khan. Some think his current illness may be divine retribution on him!'

'Majesty, I have undoubted proof of Cuthbertson's guilt.' Nicholas paused and, to a look of horror on Cuthbertson's now flushed face, produced another document from the pouch at his belt. 'This is a letter from your vassal Nasir Khan whose lands most directly abut Oudh. It confirms his agreement to give Cuthbertson a *lakh* of rupees for influencing you to allow him to raise ten times that amount in taxation on the pretext of the need to make never-to-be-undertaken improvements to the navigability of the Ganges.'

'It's a forgery, Majesty, it must be,' Cuthbertson interrupted.

Nicholas stepped forward and handed the letter to Shah Alam. 'It has the signature and seal of Nasir Khan, both of which I am sure you recognise. It reached me from a member of Gilbert Cuthbertson's own household.' In fact, James' wife Riti had obtained it during Nicholas' expedition with Tuhin Singh by befriending a woman, Anjuli Shastri. Though highborn she had been forced by poverty to become a servant and Cuthbertson had compelled her to share his bed together with two of her fellows. 'He robbed me of all that remained to me – my honour,' she had told Riti. 'I hope this letter will dishonour him and free me from his unnatural vices.'

As Cuthbertson continued to protest and bluster, Nicholas walked across to him, looked him in the eye and said quietly, 'I advise you, Cuthbertson, to pack your bags and leave not only this court but Hindustan immediately.'

Cuthbertson glared back. 'You and your master Hastings will discover what powerful friends I have – Philip Francis, for one

– and what secrets I know. Majesty, if you accept Ballantyne's advice you will regret this day and so will he, whether you accept his advice or not.' With that Cuthbertson left the room with as much dignity as his agitation would allow.

During these exchanges the Emperor who had remained silent had a wide-eyed look combining astonishment with amusement and a degree of unease. After a short silence following Cuthbertson's exit, Shah Alam said with a slight smile on his face, 'I had no idea that the Company was nearly as riven with division and corruption as my court…'

'Don't people the world over have the same potential for good and bad? In my view it is how we nurture our good and control our worst instincts that defines us.' From the corner of his eye Nicholas saw a smile cross Charles' face at his admittedly sanctimonious response and continued, 'Leaving such metaphysical thoughts aside, Majesty, may we talk about the details of Governor-General Hastings' offer to you?'

The discussion that followed was neither long nor difficult. Shah Alam quickly agreed to Hastings' terms, which were indeed not onerous, given the threat. The Emperor was seemingly pleased to shed more of the responsibilities and authority he appeared to find so burdensome.

That evening Nicholas sent four more of his escort with another despatch to Hastings, this time in Greek, asking for a formal treaty to be drafted on the terms he'd agreed with Shah Alam and also warning him about Cuthbertson. Nicholas could only hope Hastings' obstreperous council would not object to his proposed treaty terms.

Gilbert Cuthbertson left Delhi three days later, bound – according to what he told Shah Alam's courtiers – not for Calcutta but for Bombay, perhaps, Nicholas hoped, taking his advice to leave not only Delhi, but Hindustan. Cuthbertson departed without paying or making any arrangements for his staff and servants. Nicholas used some of Hastings' money to pay them – feeling it was a matter of honour to do so on the Company's behalf. Sympathising with Anjuli Chastri's position, Riti asked her to join her household. With Riti's advancing pregnancy, she needed more help on which she could rely. Anjuli moved her few possessions to Riti's home immediately.

Within three weeks, one of Nicholas' escort who had ridden with Tuhin Singh to Oudh returned with news that the two Company regiments Nicholas had requested would be on the move from the border with Oudh to Delhi in the next two days. Tuhin Singh would ride with them.

–

As the three Ballantynes were dining together in the cool of the evening on the balcony of Nicholas' quarters in the Salimgarh a few days later, a messenger brought him a letter that had just arrived bearing the Company seal. Putting aside his napkin, Nicholas broke the seal to find Hastings' reply to his first despatch.

> *You have done well, as I knew you would. As you suggested, I agree you should remain to take part in any defence of Delhi but I want your cousin, Charles, to return quickly to Calcutta to brief me in person. I may need the more detailed information he will bring and the questions he will be able to answer to carry my council with me – never the easiest of matters.*

After reading the letter to his companions, Nicholas raised a glass in toast. 'To Charles in thanks for all his help during the expedition delivered like a true Ballantyne.' Charles' smile of pleasure told Nicholas his remark and the softening of his attitude to him that it implied had been appreciated.

10 – The Empire Fights Back

All too aware that time was neither on his nor the Emperor's side, Nicholas – assisted by James and Tuhin Singh – hurriedly reviewed the strength of Delhi's defences. Sometimes Nicholas used Hastings' money to buy equipment, funds for which had been provided by the Emperor but diverted by corrupt officers and officials for their own benefit. As the days passed he had increasing help from Najaf Khan who seemed to be growing ever stronger and no longer needed to be carried by palanquin on his tours of inspection. His comments were daily more acute and penetrating as he suggested positions suitable for enfilading fire or the positioning of cannon batteries. 'I'm feeling back to myself,' he told Nicholas. 'I'll soon be ready for anything. You cannot believe how happy I am to be free of that dreadful listless torpor that afflicted me for so long. It was almost as if I had been drugged…'

Nicholas forbore to reply that that was only too possible. He had suspected it for some time and a recent conversation with Anjuli had strengthened his suspicions. She had told him how Cuthbertson used regularly to send Najaf Khan what he called 'an English tonic', which he himself prepared. She had recovered a near-empty bottle of it after Cuthbertson's precipitate departure. Tasting it and smelling it, she suspected it contained opium. 'Very likely,' Nicholas told her. 'It's like the *pousta* mixture the Emperor Aurangzeb used to subdue and eventually kill his nephew when they were rivals for the throne…'

With repairs to the fortifications in hand, including to the crumbling bastion in the Red Fort that Najaf Khan had complained about, the question was what next. From his experience, including with Clive, Nicholas believed that sometimes the best option was not to wait to be attacked but to carry the fight to the enemy – a view he was pleased to find the reinvigorated Najaf Khan shared. 'We'll need the Emperor's approval, of course, but somehow I doubt this will be a problem, particularly following his agreement to accept Company support. I'll request an audience.'

In fact, the Emperor received them the very next day in his Hall of Private Audience. 'Your Majesty,' Najaf Khan began, 'Ballantyne and I have been working together over the past weeks to strengthen the defences of Delhi against the Rohillas and Sikhs—'

'I know and I am grateful…' Shah Alam broke in.

'However, Majesty,' Najaf Khan continued, 'we both believe that our best policy is not to remain behind the city's defences. Delhi is too large and too populous to protect fully. We think it better to confront our enemies before they can fully assemble. We plan to advance to give battle to them along the great road into Delhi, perhaps fifty or so miles north of here. Our purpose in coming to you is to seek your agreement to our following this strategy and making the necessary final preparations.'

Shah Alam looked almost surprised to have been asked to take such a decision. 'I am sure that you both know best. I agree to your advice. Nevertheless, explain to me a little more about your plan and the thinking behind it.'

'I will be in overall command, of course, Majesty, but Ballantyne and I will discuss strategy. He will command the two regiments of Company troops that he now has here at his disposal. In addition he will be responsible for our artillery. We seem to have an advantage in that department. Our spies report that as yet not all the cannon promised by the Sikhs have arrived, if they are ever going to, and the Rohillas have few of their own. That's right, isn't it, Ballantyne?' Najaf Khan seemed anxious to bring Nicholas into the conversation.

Nicholas nodded. 'Yes, of course. Najaf Khan and I are as one, Majesty. Now we have your consent we intend to march within a day or two. Our force will total around fifteen thousand – infantry, cavalry and artillery, cooks, labourers and so forth… Only a few final preparations remain – in particular to check that our cannon limbers are strong, that sufficient gunpowder and ball for them are safely stowed beneath oiled cloth covers on the ammunition wagons and that we have more than sufficient bullocks to haul both limbers and wagons. Experience has taught us to leave as little to chance as possible.'

'Well so be it,' Shah Alam replied. 'You go with my blessing.'

As they walked across the courtyard away from their audience with Shah Alam, Nicholas said to Najaf Khan, 'Although I've found the Emperor an intelligent man, knowledgeable about the world, and a fine musician and poet, as we've talked about before he always appears happy to have responsibility lifted from his shoulders, particularly in military matters. Why is it, do you think?'

'It's more than indolence. He's endured great swings of fortune during his life and reign and has learned to resign himself to them. As you know, he was kept in semi-confinement in this fort during his childhood, and later his father, the second Emperor Alamgir, was assassinated. While he is indeed content to leave military matters to others, when he has to he has an acute nose for politics and character. He's only survived on the throne so long by knowing when to compromise and when to concede, even sometimes humiliatingly to remain alive to make a comeback another day.'

Nicholas nodded. 'Survival is a strong instinct amongst us all.'

–

Two days later, Najaf Khan led Shah Alam's forces in great ceremony out of Delhi through the grand arched sandstone northern gatehouse of the city. He was riding in a silver *howdah* on a large elephant with a gold cloth surcoat, waving to the cheering bystanders. Shah Alam himself, wearing his most opulent and formal imperial robes, saluted his departing troops from a balcony above the gates. A band of twenty mounted trumpeters and drummers, all wearing Moghul green and riding matched grey horses, followed, playing as they went, augmenting the booming of kettledrums from the watchtowers along the city walls. A regiment of Moghul cavalry – the elite of the army, according to Najaf Khan – came next, harnesses jingling and green pennants fluttering from the tips of the lances each rider held vertical as he rose and fell in his saddle.

Four regiments of marching Moghul infantry followed, mainly succeeding in keeping in time to the beat of their own drummers, scarcely audible above the general hubbub. The second of these regiments had two European officers riding next to its commander, a luxuriantly moustached, ramrod-straight-backed Moghul prince, Asaf Husain, a friend of Najaf Khan. Najaf Khan had previously pointed out to Nicholas the two muscled shaven-headed men, each wearing a single pearl earring, as French former pirates – 'Inseparable and hard to control before and after the battle, but great fighters in it,' he had said. 'Asaf Husain recruited rather than hanged them after he captured them smuggling a large quantity of rubies.'

James' small cavalry unit came next, James riding proudly at its head on his favourite black horse and, like his officers, wearing a purple turban and military jacket of the same colour. Two Hindustani troopers rode just behind him playing bagpipes. James had told Nicholas that he had bought the pipes many months before at the sale of the effects of a Scottish merchant captain who had died with half his crew on his fever-stricken ship in the Hooghly. After learning to play them himself from an impecunious, often drunk Scot – a janitor at a Company warehouse – he had taught two of his men to play. One was Ravi Kohli, the sepoy whose wound James had sewn after his skirmish with the dacoits while still a Company ensign and had subsequently recruited to his unit. According to James the skirl of the bagpipes was proving popular, perhaps surprisingly, with the members of his unit, whatever their race.

Amid the rising heat and dust, the water bearers – *bishtis* – were already moving among the troops. Nicholas himself came next, riding at the head of the Company regiment of blue-uniformed cavalry. Tuhin Singh, who had personally inspected the regiment's horses to ensure they were sound and that sufficient re-mounts were available, rode as usual at Nicholas' side. The regiment was in turn followed by the artillery, cannons on their six-wheeled wooden limbers pulled by teams of eight bullocks and with some of the artillerymen sitting astride the cannon barrels to save themselves the trouble of marching. Nicholas and Najaf Khan had decided that twenty smaller-bore cannon – mostly fifteen-pounders – provided the best compromise between firepower and mobility.

After the cannon marched the Company infantry, European officers on horseback and the sepoys, mainly from Bengal but some from Madras, all well equipped with muskets, with packs on their backs and cartridge pouches hanging from their white webbing crossbelts. More and more regiments of Shah Alam's troops followed, two-thirds of them infantry. Most were also well equipped but some of the final units had few if any gunpowder weapons. Nevertheless, Najaf Khan and Nicholas believed their troops were overall better drilled and organised than their opponents and at least as well armed.

After the troops themselves and amid what were now great clouds of choking dust, came the columns of creaking baggage wagons and snorting, skittering pack animals carrying the provisions and stores no army could operate without for long. Beside them walked their drivers, many of them barefoot but with cloths over their mouths and noses to keep out the dust.

–

In the evening of the third day Najaf Khan called a council of war in his large red command tent, swiftly erected at the centre of that night's camp. Since leaving Delhi the column had covered about forty-eight miles, mostly following the Jumna River north, slowed as both Najaf Khan and Nicholas knew it would be by the need to keep close contact with the baggage train to prevent any enemy attempt to cut it off from the fighting troops. Earlier that afternoon, scouts riding ahead of the main column had brought back news that the Rohillan and Sikh forces were themselves advancing towards them and were no more than six or seven miles distant.

Najaf Khan and Nicholas had immediately consulted and decided to halt for the night so that their troops could put themselves into battle order for the likely engagement the next morning. They had positioned their forces so that their right – eastern – flank was protected by the nearby Jumna whose water was still too deep and fast flowing after the monsoon for opposing troops to cross easily, and their left flank rested on one of the rare low hills of the plain. Najaf Khan had quickly despatched a strong screen of pickets to keep watch at two miles from the camp in the northerly direction from which the enemy force would be most likely to appear to forewarn of any attack, either during the evening or the night.

Najaf Khan opened the council of war. 'May I ask, my commanders, have you made sure our troops will get a good meal tonight? Something essential, I always think, as battle approaches.' There was a general nod of agreement. 'And are you making arrangements for their weapons to be checked and where necessary powder and ball distributed?' Again a nodding of heads and some affirmative murmurs but Nicholas noticed at least two officers slip quietly from the tent, presumably to rectify their failure in this regard.

'Ballantyne and I,' Najaf Khan continued, 'have already had some initial discussions about our strategy to engage the enemy tomorrow. We propose that we should tempt our opponents into attacking our strong position here rather than meet them on the open plain in a more unpredictable battle of movement. The Rohillas, although warlike, do not have the reputation of being disciplined fighters and so may need no temptation, but their Sikh allies may persuade them to be less rash. What do you all think?' He looked around the assembled officers.

The leader of the scouts, a slight, fine-featured young man named Vihrat Sunak who had brought the news of the enemy advance earlier that afternoon, spoke first. 'From what my men and I saw, about three quarters of the enemy – their numbers in total look about the same as ours – are Rohillas, so Zabita Khan will undoubtedly be in undisputed command. Like you, I believe he would need little persuasion to attack.'

'Thank you,' Najaf Khan said, before Nicholas spoke for the first time.

'You may well be right, but we still need to work out how to induce the enemy to attack us here in the event they don't do so of their own accord. I suggest we launch a cavalry attack but then, a little after it comes under fire, our men should suddenly retreat in feigned panic and disarray, drawing the Rohillas forward in pursuit, intent on completing their rout by overwhelming our position here, whereupon we can destroy them.'

'A feigned attack is certainly a good idea,' Najaf Khan said to cries of agreement, 'but to make it sufficiently credible we need to send some infantry as well as cavalry forward, perhaps two or three regiments.'

'Let my men be among the infantry,' Asaf Husain broke in.

'Why not?' Najaf Khan replied. 'I myself will head the feint with two of our Moghul cavalry regiments. You, Ballantyne, if you agree, should remain in command here.'

'It will be an honour, but should any Company troops join the attack? They're steady men with good morale.'

'I think not. It would do more for Moghul prestige if the burden of tomorrow's fighting falls mostly on the Emperor's own troops rather than on what many consider outsiders.'

Nicholas noticed Tuhin Singh nodding vigorously in agreement. While he had agreed with Nicholas about the need for stability, he had argued to him while they were in Delhi that it was better for Hindustanis to sort out their own problems rather than permit European outsiders – whether British or French – to take a central role. Nicholas simply replied to Najaf Khan, 'I understand.' With the major decisions taken, the council of war broke up soon afterwards.

Nicholas with Tuhin Singh inspected some of the units that would remain under his command in their present position the next day. He first visited the Moghul artillery, which was led by a squat, pock-marked veteran called Hanif Mohammed – 'A good man,' Najaf Khan had said, 'of few words but great experience and stubbornness who would never desert his post.' Hanif Mohammed quickly satisfied Nicholas that he had had sufficient powder and cannon balls brought up to the guns, together with spare ramrods, sponges and such like and that the guns were well sited and maintained. Recognising that Hanif Mohammed neither needed nor would welcome any further guidance, Nicholas moved swiftly on. He found the commanders of the two Company regiments similarly calm and prepared. Their men were already eating and the European cavalrymen had been issued a tot of rum to steady any nerves.

Nicholas and Tuhin Singh next crossed to the large tent where the *hakims* and their orderlies were making preparations to deal with the morrow's inevitable casualties. Knives, saws and axes were being sharpened, washed and laid out for use together with the surgeons' sets of needles, bandages and tourniquets. Just outside the tent, firewood was being heaped up which Nicholas recognised with an involuntary shudder would be used to make a fierce fire to bring to red heat instruments to cauterise wounds and stumps of amputated limbs.

Nicholas then inspected some of the less well-equipped Moghul infantry units. There he urged the commanders – at least one was as young as James – to remind their men of the necessity of keeping close formation and maintaining discipline under fire. 'In battle it's always safer to fight as a unit, rather than as individuals who can soon become isolated. Allow no wild attacks if your enemy appears to be retreating. Be resolute and don't panic if they appear to be gaining temporary advantage.'

'I think that's all we can do,' Nicholas said to Tuhin Singh as they returned to their quarters. 'We have too little experience of these men to be certain that their morale and discipline will hold under fire.'

'True,' Tuhin Singh replied. 'We can only wait and see.'

That evening Nicholas and Tuhin Singh ate their simple meal with James who was unusually quiet. Remembering his own feelings before his first major battle – a combination of foreboding and excitement – Nicholas said little to interrupt his son's reverie. As James left early to rejoin his unit, which Najaf Khan had suggested join the Company cavalry for the coming battle, he silently and briefly embraced his father. After he departed, reading Nicholas' thoughts Tuhin Singh said, 'He knows his duty and will do it just as you will.'

'I trust so and I trust too that God will preserve him. I don't know how I could tell Riti, or Lucia and Lizzie for that matter, if anything should happen to him.'

Nicholas woke early the next morning to find as he ducked out of his tent a low, dawn mist rising from the Jumna and enveloping the camp. However, cooking fires were already burning and troopers were cleaning their weapons and talking quietly in small groups as they waited for their final orders. Grabbing some bread and a piece of cold chicken left over from the previous evening, Nicholas strode across to Najaf Khan's tent. 'Will you wait a little for the mist to clear before you make your move?' Nicholas asked.

'I think not. The mist will give us some cover as we approach the enemy and as we retreat into it in pretended panic it will give us protection.'

'It will require good discipline to manoeuvre within it.'

'The regiments I've chosen are steady and experienced – and so am I. Trust me!'

'Of course,' Nicholas replied, thinking both how different the strong-minded, vigorous commander before him was from the invalid he had first met – and how difficult maintaining cohesion in the mist might prove.

The low white mist still shrouded the camp as first a group of forty scouts headed north in the direction of the Rohillas and Sikhs and, about ten minutes later, Najaf Khan on his chestnut horse, surrounded by his steel breast-plated personal bodyguard of about a dozen, led out his two regiments of Moghul cavalry. The regiment of foot soldiers followed, muskets on their shoulders, their drummers silent for the moment. Their officers, including Asaf Husain and the two French pirates, rode quietly at their regiments' head with drawn swords.

After they had been gone about a quarter of an hour, the mist began to rise just a little. Nicholas ordered an empty baggage wagon to be pulled to the top of the low hill on the flank of the camp and then climbed on it to get the best view he could through his telescope. But the mist was still too prevalent for him to see much. After half an hour Tuhin Singh joined him. 'Najaf Khan can only have gone about three miles in this time, I think, if his horsemen are to keep in close touch with the infantry.'

Nicholas nodded. Ten minutes later Tuhin Singh pointed towards the misty horizon. 'Aren't those horsemen coming this way?'

Nicholas could see nothing, either through his telescope or straining his eyes. 'Where?'

'The mists have covered them again.' Then all of a sudden a group of riders emerged, galloping fast towards the camp. 'Some of our scouts, I think,' Tuhin Singh shouted.

'I agree.' Nicholas turned to Lieutenant Cathcart sitting patiently on his horse beside the cart, ready to act as his aide de camp and ordered, 'Have the men stand to action stations.' Tom Cathcart immediately galloped down the hill to relay the order and almost at once drums began to beat and trumpets to sound the call to arms.

By now Nicholas could clearly see that the approaching riders were indeed the Moghul scouts led by Vihrat Sunak. Each man had his head bent to his horse's neck, urging it on with hands and feet. Suddenly the rearmost rider collapsed slowly sideways from his saddle, fell to the ground, rolled over twice and lay still. His riderless horse continued towards the Moghul lines while three of his comrades, pulling hard on their reins, turned and rode back to their companion. One held the reins of the other two's horses while they dismounted, lifted the fallen scout and laid him carefully across the back of one of their horses. Both remounted and all three continued back towards the Moghul lines.

Within minutes of the scouts regaining the camp, a *hakim* was bending over the wounded man and a sweating, dust-streaked Vihrat Sunak was standing slightly breathless in front of Nicholas who had quickly returned to the centre of the line. He was now sitting on his horse outside Najaf Khan's scarlet command tent, just behind where Hanif Mohammed's artillery were positioned and where at his command gunners were already ramming powder and ball down the cannon barrels.

'Give me your report, Vihrat Sunak.'

'We were moving cautiously through the mist – thicker there than here – about three miles away from this camp and only a few hundred yards ahead of Najaf Khan's troops when we encountered the Rohillas. They were advancing but not directly towards this position. Instead, they were circling a little west perhaps to attack our left flank here. Immediately we saw them we rode back to warn Najaf Khan, with the vanguard of the Rohillan cavalry – which had seen us at the same time as we had seen them – hard on our heels. The Rohillas crashed into the side of our leading cavalry units just as we reached Najaf Khan. Through the mists we could see several of our men had been unhorsed under the weight of the impact. Najaf Khan quickly ordered me to ride back with my men to alert you that the enemy were taking the bait and inform you that he would restore order on his left and then fall back on this camp making the best time he could. As we galloped back through the mist we came upon a small party of Rohillas – presumably scouts like us. Their leader pulled out his pistol and shot and wounded my comrade whom the *hakim* is treating. We in turn brought down one of the Rohillas before they disappeared back into the mist and we resumed our return here.'

'You and your men did well. How far do you think Najaf Khan will be behind you?'

'He'll take time to reorganise to fight the threat on his left. It was a serious incursion. Then of course the speed of the foot soldiers and how far he can disengage from the enemy will dictate his progress. I think it will be an hour at least before he appears.'

'And the Rohillas?'

'That depends if Zabita Khan decides to take the risk of sending his cavalry ahead of the infantry. If so, it could be only a matter of minutes…'

The mist was rapidly dispersing and the sun rising through its translucent remnants, an orange ball, when Tuhin Singh, back at Nicholas' side, spotted Rohillan cavalry emerge through the wisps of mist to the left of the front line only about a mile away. They were moving slowly and after a minute or two they halted and their officers appeared to be consulting.

'Quickly, Tuhin Singh, can you ride to the Company infantry and order them to move to the left flank to protect against an attack from that quarter.'

'Of course.' Tuhin Singh was in the saddle in an instant and in less than five minutes Nicholas saw the Company sepoys marching in parade ground order to take up their new position. It was a good job they did since suddenly the unit of Rohillan cavalry – perhaps three hundred riders in all – began to move forward again, quickly gathering speed and levelling their lances for the attack. They were charging towards the position the Company infantry were taking up. Immediately the Company's sepoys formed two ranks, the front rank knelt and both ranks levelled their muskets. When the Rohillas were within range – no more than a hundred yards – Nicholas saw almost simultaneous puffs of white smoke from the muskets of the kneeling rank then immediately afterwards from those standing behind.

Several Rohillan riders collapsed dead or wounded from their saddles. Others were pitched out of them over their horses' heads as their mounts, hit by musket balls, crashed, legs splaying and kicking, onto the ground. Some riderless horses continued with the charge. Others swerved away across the path of the Rohillan cavalry following, slowing their advance. Nevertheless the Rohillas pressed on and were onto the sepoys before all but a few had a chance to reload. Several sepoys and at least two of their officers fell, transfixed by lances. Others closed ranks, stood their ground and fought back with swords or the bayonets fixed to their muskets, thrusting the blades into the bellies of the attackers' horses or the legs of their riders. Yet others simply dragged cavalrymen from the saddle and grappled with them on the hard earth.

Regiments to the right of the sepoys opened fire and, almost as quickly as they had attacked, the Rohillan riders withdrew as if they had simply been a reconnaissance in force testing out the strength and commitment of the Moghul forces. Immediately bearers ran forward from the lines with stretchers and litters to carry the Moghul wounded to the *hakims'* tent.

As the noise from that fighting died away the sound of musketry and shouting became louder from the direction in which Vihrat Sunak's scouts had first come. Some of Najaf Khan's retreating troops began to appear. Many were horsemen who had taken a foot soldier up behind them. 'A good idea,' Nicholas shouted to Tuhin Singh who had returned. Other Moghul foot soldiers were running in groups between the horses. What looked like orange-clad Sikh cavalry were swooping into the Moghul ranks to cut down stragglers and then veering away again.

Nicholas quickly recognised Najaf Khan still surrounded by his bodyguard, their breastplates now glinting in the rising sun, riding near the back of his retreating column. Nicholas ordered Tom Cathcart, once more at his side, to ride to order the infantry officers holding the front line to form gaps to allow Najaf Khan's troops in through the defences but, once they were inside, to close ranks quickly to prevent any enemy infiltration of the lines. His orders were quickly implemented. As the first Moghul troops approached the camp defences, officers had the lines opened to allow them in. Najaf Khan and his bodyguard were among the last to enter. The very last was Asaf Husain's infantry regiment with the two French pirates bringing up the rear. Both had lost their horses and one had his arm around the other, supporting him as he was clearly wounded.

A large group of yelling, scimitar-wielding Rohillan and Sikh cavalry were hard on their heels. The impetus of their charge carried them through the front line of Moghul infantry who had had little time to reform their ranks or to reload. The riders were followed by a rush of Rohillan foot soldiers who in hand-to-hand fighting began to enlarge the breach in the Moghul lines, pushing resolutely towards Hanif Mohammed's artillery, which was firing over the heads of the melee into the later waves of attackers.

Acrid smoke from the guns was beginning to get into Nicholas' nose and throat and obscuring his vision, but through it he saw the squat figure of Hanif Mohammed, who had been standing on an ammunition wagon better to direct the fire of his cannon, fall to the ground to be pulled away by some of his men who left their posts to help him. Consequently the cannon fire began to falter, allowing the Rohillas to make further progress towards their position.

By now Najaf Khan had ridden up to the command tent on his chestnut horse whose neck and flanks were flecked with sweat and foam. 'I'll take command here, Ballantyne, while, if you please, you take over the artillery. At all costs we must not let our guns be overrun.'

Immediately Nicholas, with Tuhin Singh, rode the two hundred yards to the cannon positions. There he urged the gunners to resume their precision-firing rhythm – 'Swab the barrel, load powder then ball, fire, reposition if the recoil has moved the cannon, prepare to fire again.' Suddenly Nicholas saw four large war elephants towering over the other Rohillan attackers – elephants were now much rarer in warfare than in his youth, but these beasts had swivel cannon in their *howdahs*. A ball from one hit a Moghul cannon position, sending up a shower of dirt, propelling two gunners into the air and dislodging the cannon barrel from its limber.

'Concentrate on maintaining your own speed of fire,' Nicholas shouted to the gunners. As he did so, he saw from the corner of his eye the Company cavalry regiment, together with James' unit, enter the fight scarcely two hundred yards to his left. James was at the head of his men, yelling and waving his sword, bending from his saddle to slash at some Rohillan infantry. Moving forward against a group of mounted troopers, he beheaded a young Rohillan banner-bearer with a single swing of his sword. Blood spurted from the man's neck as for a moment his body swayed back and forth in his saddle as if he were still living and then he fell. His banner became entangled with the legs of another horse, which in turn crumpled, catapulting its rider over its head.

Only a short distance from James a Company trooper succeeded in thrusting his lance into the belly of one of the war elephants which – trumpeting in pain and with the lance still dangling from the wound in its stomach – turned away from the attack and ran towards the rear, trampling some of the infantry beneath its great feet. After a short distance its *howdah* and the men and the cannon within were dislodged and fell to the ground. At the same time, some mounted Sikh troopers charged forward, keeping close formation as they avoided the wounded elephant and attacked two of the less well-equipped regiments of Moghul infantry, some of whom began to turn and run, only to be cut down with sword slashes to their fleeing backs. Most, however, held position but were clearly being hard pressed, including by grapeshot from the swivel gun in the *howdah* of the largest of the war elephants.

'Elevate your cannon by pushing timber under the front wheels. Use water buckets, even spare ramrods, anything... we must bring that elephant down!' Nicholas yelled to the sub-officer commanding the cannon nearest the elephant. The sweating gun crew, most of whom were stripped to the waist, rushed to obey his instructions only for one to spin round as he was bringing forward some wood, hit by a musket ball in the middle of his forehead. His comrades stuck to their task and in less than five minutes the cannon fired. Its ball hit the elephant just beneath its head, partially shredding its ear and killing both the elephant and the *mahout* riding on its neck instantly. As the elephant collapsed sideways it crushed two or three Rohillan infantry who could not get out of the way in time.

Looking along the defences Nicholas realised the Moghul troops were maintaining discipline and now seemed to be stabilising the line and slowly getting the better of the fight. The third war elephant had swerved away in uncontrolled panic towards the Jumna. The *mahout* of the fourth now began to guide it from the fight, both he and the occupants of its *howdah* unwilling to face the fate that had overtaken the other three.

Then to his horror Nicholas saw James' black horse rear and his son tumble backwards into the heaving mass of fighting men. With a shouted order to Tuhin Singh to take over command of the cannon, Nicholas mounted his own horse and charged towards his son with some dozen members of his escort whom he had kept by him to act as messengers following closely at his horse's hooves. As he rode, crouched low over his horse's neck and spurring the animal forward, he saw James was on his feet fighting back to back with a few of his men who had also been de-horsed against a much more numerous group of Sikhs and Rohillas surrounding them.

With the sounds of battle – the clash of steel on steel, the shouts, the cries of pain or victory rising all around him – Nicholas pushed his horse into the heaving, sweating melee around his son. Bending from his saddle he slashed a bearded Rohillan across his face with his sword, exposing his bloodied teeth before thrusting the sword deep into the guts of another wielding an axe. A Sikh stood his ground and swung at Nicholas with his scimitar. Nicholas raised his bloodied sword quickly enough to half deflect the heavy blow, taking away some of its power but nevertheless felt a numbing then searing pain as the sharp steel blade sliced into his left thigh just above his knee.

An enemy musket ball hit a young member of Nicholas' escort riding directly behind him in the neck. Dropping his sword he fell to be trampled under the hooves of those following. His riderless horse swerved away from the action, reins dangling, impeding others. Nicholas was almost up to James, who had only three comrades remaining at his side. Heart thumping in his chest and hacking almost frenziedly at the Sikhs surrounding his son, Nicholas reached James and extending his arm dragged him up behind him on to his saddle. Three of his escort did the same for James' companions but as the last of them was mounting, a Rohillan spear pierced him through the belly spitting him like a chicken and he fell back mortally wounded. Turning, Nicholas forced his horse, weakening under the weight of two riders, back towards the Moghul lines as a pistol ball grazed his cheek. Reaching them safely, the horse crumpled to the ground just as Nicholas and James jumped clear. The whole action had lasted no more than a quarter of an hour.

Blood from his leg wound was now seeping into Nicholas' knee-high boot. He allowed one of his escort to bandage roughly the cut in his thigh with his neck cloth, but then waved away any further assistance and resumed the direction of the artillery from Tuhin Singh. He heard Najaf Khan shout an order for the elite regiment of green-clad Moghul cavalry who had been among the leaders in the parade out of Delhi and whom he had held in reserve, concealed behind the hill, to attack the Sikhs and Rohillas in the flank. Soon they were riding into the action, their banners flying, their horses' hooves drumming the earth. They took the enemy by surprise and, living up to their reputation, began to push them back from the left flank. After another few minutes of fierce hand-to-hand fighting, the Rohillas and Sikhs finally began to disengage all along the line and to retreat in some semblance of order while they were still able and thus to avoid a defeat turning into an irretrievable rout.

The fighting was now swimming before Nicholas' eyes. He was feeling faint from loss of blood – the welling crimson blood from his wound had soaked through his makeshift bandage and was running freely down his leg again. His knees began to buckle. Then everything went dark. He regained consciousness lying on a bloodstained trestle table in the tent of the Moghul *hakims* at the moment one of them pierced the skin of his thigh with his needle to begin the process of stitching up what, when Nicholas raised his head, he saw was a deep seven-inch-long gash. A sudden anguished cry in English of 'mother' caused him to twist round, only to smell burnt flesh and to see another *hakim* holding a red-hot sword, hilt protected by a cloth, to the lower arm of Tom Cathcart who had clearly lost his hand at some later point in the fighting.

When his own wound was stitched and bandaged with clean white cloth, Nicholas limped over to Cathcart who was now slipping in and out of consciousness. He held the young man's remaining hand, telling him he would survive to see his mother again – something Nicholas was grateful to hear later from the *hakim* who had treated Cathcart was likely since his wound, although severe, had been clean and no dirt or cloth had got into it.

Soon afterwards an anxious-faced James pushed his way towards his father. After checking that his wound was not too serious, to Nicholas' surprise he burst out, 'How could you neglect your duty and leave your position as deputy commander and the direction of the cannon at such a critical moment to ride to help me?'

Nicholas replied simply, 'You will know when your child is born.'

The next morning, the scouts – mainly fresh men but led by Vihrat Sunak despite his exhaustion – reported to Najaf Khan and Nicholas, still weak from loss of blood and using a crutch to help him move around, that the enemy were already fifteen miles away and showing no signs of halting to make a stand any time soon. Given the number of bodies of their enemy and of animals lying in front of the Moghul defences, cloaked in buzzing, iridescent green-black flies, being pecked at by screeching, querulous vultures and the large amount of equipment the Rohillas and

Sikhs had abandoned in their flight, the threat to Delhi looked to have been blunted. Because of the number of their own dead and wounded, Najaf Khan and Nicholas decided not to attempt a pursuit but to return to Delhi as soon as they had buried or cremated their own dead in accordance with their religion.

As the Moghul column began its return, Tuhin Singh, riding at Nicholas' side, asked, 'What do you think this victory means?'

'Well, the threat to Shah Alam from the Rohillas and Sikhs is ended. From what some of the prisoners said their alliance was already beginning to disintegrate before the battle.'

'You'll need to make sure Shah Alam signs the treaty you agreed with him on Hastings' behalf while he's still grateful and before he changes his mind.'

'Of course,' Nicholas smiled. 'Shah Alam will always remain susceptible to the arguments and blandishments of others – it is in his character and his experiences have ingrained it further – but he will remain loyal to the Company... for the present at least.'

'You're probably right, particularly if Najaf Khan retains his health as there's every sign he will. The other question though is who will be the greatest threat to the Emperor in future?'

'A resurgent united Maratha attempt to influence or even usurp him, perhaps, although at the moment the Marathas remain divided. My nagging fear is how the Company acts next... Hastings will be content with maintaining stability but will others of his council? I'm not so sure... Whatever the case, we've done all we can here.'

–

'I give you a toast – two men without whom Shah Alam would not tonight sleep so comfortably in his bed in the Red Fort, my good friends Nicholas Ballantyne and Tuhin Singh!' As Hastings stood and raised his glass, the assembled company seated at the long mahogany table spread with fine china, silver and glittering crystal in the governor-general's private dining room in Government House also rose and, as with one voice, repeated,

'Nicholas Ballantyne and Tuhin Singh.' Nicholas and Tuhin Singh exchanged slightly rueful glances. They had arrived back in Calcutta only a week before, after travelling overland from Delhi with the surviving members of Nicholas' escort including Tom Cathcart who, though recovered from his wound, complained he could feel his amputated hand as if it were still there. They had both tried to convince a jubilant Hastings that there was no need for any formal celebration but he would not be deterred. 'Even if you don't, I want to see the prune faces of Francis, Clavering and Monson – not even they can deny the success of my policy towards Shah Alam!'

Presiding over the dinner – her fine bosom ablaze with diamonds – was Hastings' baroness, Marian, whom, during Nicholas' absence in Delhi, he had finally been able to marry, following confirmation of her divorce from Baron von Imhoff, now back in Europe. Taking Nicholas aside earlier that evening, she had gripped his hands and told him how obligated Hastings felt to him. 'He knows how much he owes to you and your friend. He is truly grateful he can trust you completely – unlike that unruly council of his. However, my husband will never let them get the better of him.' Had he detected a particular celebratory emphasis on the word 'husband' in her little speech, Nicholas had wondered, or was it merely her accent?

Hastings had pressed Nicholas to remain in Calcutta a while longer – 'I've a number of things I'd welcome discussing with you…' – but Nicholas had stood firm. The day before a message had arrived at Mohammed Aziz's boarding house for him from James who had remained in Shah Alam's service in Delhi. It announced that Riti had given birth to a son – his first grandchild. Both mother and child were doing well. The proud parents had named the baby Alexander, just as much a hero in the north-west Hindustan hills, where he was known as 'Sikunder', as in Europe. With such good news as well as himself to take home to Glenmire and Lucia, nothing would stop him leaving with Tuhin Singh for the hills in the next few days.

Part Three

A Dangerous Alliance, 1778–1781

11 – *Enemies at the Gates*

'You take the shot – with your sharp eyes you won't miss,' Nicholas whispered to Tuhin Singh as they crouched side by side in a clump of ferns in the hills near Glenmire. Upwind of them a male barking deer nibbled moss beneath an oak tree. They had been stalking it all morning – an excellent candidate for the pot. Now they had their reward. Tuhin Singh soundlessly levelled his musket and with an expert shot hit the deer in mid-forehead, causing it to crumple instantly. Leaping up, hunting knives in hand, they ran towards it. The deer was indeed quite dead.

With the skill born of long experience, they eviscerated the animal, then found and trimmed leaves and twigs from a strong branch and tied the carcass to it. 'Kannika will be pleased – she was complaining I've been spending too much time with my horses and not enough hunting for the table…' Tuhin Singh grinned.

As they came back through the forest towards Glenmire carrying their burden, Nicholas felt a pleasant lethargy after his exertions – just like in his youth when he and his uncle James had returned from a successful day's stalking in the Scottish Highlands. Reaching the house, while Tuhin Singh instructed the servants about the division of the carcass – they too would have their share – Nicholas went indoors to look for Lucia.

His wife was in her sitting room where she and Sunita, the family's capable if somewhat dour housekeeper of many years, were inspecting a roll of bright red woollen cloth Lucia had ordered from Joss Granger in Calcutta. 'I can tell by your expression – and the mud on your clothes – that you've had a good day, Nicholas, so I shan't enquire,' Lucia smiled at him. Turning back to Sunita she asked, 'So what do you think? Will it do?'

'It would be better if it were thicker, ma'am, but lined with cotton wadding it should make heavy enough door and window hangings to keep out the winter draughts. I'll see what I can manage.' As Sunita picked up the roll and left the room, Lucia came over to Nicholas and kissed his cheek. 'I'm forgetting… you have a letter with the Company seal. The *dak* messenger brought it just after you left. It's on your desk.'

Going to his study, Nicholas saw the letter was addressed in Hastings' neat hand. Over the eighteen months since his return to Glenmire, Hastings had written several times – short, friendly missives reporting some piece of Calcutta news like the sudden death of council member Colonel Monson or spicy gossip he thought Nicholas might enjoy or venting his frustrations about some issue or person. Sometimes Hastings sent copies of books he had sponsored, including a new grammar of the Bengali language and an English version of the classic Hindi epic *The Bhagavad-Gita* – the first translation into any European language. Once Hastings told him how well his cousin, Charles, was doing since his posting back to Madras – he had been promoted twice within nine months, though admittedly one promotion had been to fill a dead man's shoes after a particularly virulent outbreak of cholera.

However, opening this letter Nicholas saw it was several pages long, the lines densely packed, and immediately sensed its contents were entirely different – a suspicion Hastings' opening words confirmed.

> *My dear Ballantyne,*
>
> *I wish I had better tidings but the truth is we are facing the greatest threat to Company power in Hindustan since Siraj–ud-daulah captured Calcutta. Despatches newly arrived from the Court of Directors in London – and sent on the fastest East Indiaman they could find – inform me that Britain is again at war with France. Not content with supporting the rebels in the American colonies, as they've done these past three years, Britain's old enemy has now formally recognised the so-called United States of America*

as a sovereign nation and signed a military alliance with the colonists.

Most dangerous of all for us, France is clearly planning to exploit Britain's present preoccupation with restoring order in the colonies as an opportunity to re-open hostilities in Hindustan in a blatant attempt to snatch back what she lost – I don't need to remind you of all people how much blood we spilled to extinguish French influence in Hindustan. I have indisputable evidence not only that the French are providing weapons – the latest designs of artillery and new, more efficient muskets – but also officers and soldiers to the Marathas and that their first target is likely to be Bombay.

I suspect you have already guessed what I am about to ask. I know you want nothing more than to live quietly at Glenmire. I also know that you have sometimes doubted both the Company and – if we are honest with one another as friends should be – myself. But this is a matter of survival not only for the Company, but for British interests here and just perhaps, if things go badly, for Britain itself. That is why I am asking you, please, to come to Calcutta as soon as you can to lend me your assistance. My council is more hindrance than help – they neither agree with me or each other. Neither can I look to the government nor to the Company in London for guidance. It would take too long to obtain and anyway I doubt I'd have any confidence in their views! I find a certain irony that a factor in the American colonies' revolt was the cheap Company tea sent to Boston from the Company's London warehouses where we had a surplus. In their naivety and stupidity, Lord North and the British government thought selling the colonists tea at such a low price it appeared untaxed would divert them from their demand for no taxation without representation. Instead they dumped it in Boston harbour. And God help me, I answer to these same politicians for how I manage affairs here.

If we are to lose our American colonies – as may be inevitable if the latest reports I hear are true – to prosper we must at least retain our presence in Hindustan and the trade routes to the east. I am already taking what military precautions I can. I have ordered the recruitment of further Bengali sepoys as well as the raising of a volunteer militia of a thousand Europeans. I have instructed Company forces in Madras to seize the French enclave at Pondicherry in an attempt to forestall the French making common cause with Hyder Ali of Mysore against us. To help defend Bombay in case of French and Maratha attack, I am despatching six thousand troops and a small artillery train overland to Bombay under the command of Colonel Leslie. But in the coming storm such measures may not be enough. The situation we face is not just a question of brute strength but of understanding Hindustani politics, personalities and alliances. That is why I would so particularly value your advice in these precarious days.

Please do not delay your answer. If it is yes, as I hope, come down to Calcutta as soon as you can.

Your friend,
Warren Hastings

P.S. If he is willing, bring Tuhin Singh.

Nicholas put the letter down and sat for some minutes deep in thought, elbows resting on his desk and chin on his interlinked hands. He had been following reports of the war in the American colonies from the first skirmishes at Lexington and Concord and the British victory at Bunker Hill to other later confrontations. His interest in the progress of the war had been heightened by the implications for the Jacobite families who, after Bonnie Prince Charlie's failed bid for the British throne, had like his uncle James fled Scotland for North America. James had chosen Nova Scotia, but many others had settled in the Carolinas or Virginia only to find themselves swept up in this fresh internal conflict. Some had chosen to fight for the British government rather than on the revolutionary side, which struck him as odd. Why should those who had suffered so brutally under the Hanoverian regime – albeit thirty years ago – now risk their lives to support it? More explicable was why the French, though ruled by an absolute monarch, King Louis XVI, unfettered by any parliament and convinced he was divinely appointed, should support freedoms for the American colonists the French authorities would never grant their own people. Purely self-interest, as Hastings suggested, of course. France saw any defeat for Britain as France's gain, whether in Europe, the American colonies or here in Hindustan.

'Lucia told me you were in your study. Why the serious face?' Looking up, Nicholas saw Tuhin Singh.

'Read this, then you'll understand.'

Settling in a chair opposite Nicholas, Tuhin Singh quickly scanned the letter. 'It sounds panicky… most unlike Hastings.'

'I know. He's worried about everything – the French, the Marathas, his council and his home government. I think he feels in need of allies. That's why he wants us in Calcutta.'

'He wants you – I'm only an afterthought in the postscript,' Tuhin Singh said wryly. 'Will you go?'

'I'm reluctant, but I feel I've little choice. He's appealed to me as a patriot and a friend…'

'Tell me something. Is he more worried about the Company's position or his own?'

'Both. Obviously he wants to preserve himself as governor-general, but I believe he really does care about the Company and, by his own lights, Hindustan. When he was first appointed governor of Bengal, he assured me he wanted the Company to be a force for good…'

'But good for whom? The Europeans who skim off Hindustan's wealth? The local rulers happy to sell their people short for their own benefit? Surely not the often starving common people!'

'A good question. But on the conflict with France and the stability of Hindustan I'm prepared again to give him the benefit of the doubt. But you clearly don't share my view. Why?'

'As I've often said, I think it's for the Hindustani people to make their own decisions, control their own destinies… Yet how can they when the Company denies them the means to do that? Hastings rails against the American colonists for resisting taxation without representation in decision-making but their objections seem to me entirely reasonable and would be seen as such by the ruling classes in Britain if they themselves were denied them. I believe you told me that was one of the causes of the English civil war. Equally, I don't understand why people in Bengal – who have no voice either – are expected meekly to accept the taxes the Company imposes on them. I think some Hindustanis might see what is happening in the American colonies and wonder whether they too shouldn't resist the policies of the Company or indeed of autocratic Hindustani rulers every bit as despotic as that French king Hastings writes about…'

'You sound quite a revolutionary…'

'Not entirely. Don't forget I'm a son of a ruler who ruled well. It's rulers who don't I take issue with. There are advantages in a wise single ruler. Revolution causes chaos and bloodshed. It's usually the ordinary people who suffer while the rich and influential find their way through and often profit from it. It's just that I don't see Hastings as such a promoter of the common good as he – or perhaps you – seem to think he is!'

'Does that mean you won't come with me?'

'No – as far as the Company goes Hastings is the best of a bad lot and perhaps for the present the best hope for stability in Hindustan. I'll come, though Kannika won't like it.'

'Nor will Lucia!'

After Tuhin Singh had departed home with his share of the day's kill, Nicholas went in search of his wife. She was still in her sitting room, tidying up her sewing box, but alone. 'There's something we need to discuss,' Nicholas said, bending to kiss his wife's forehead and wishing he could turn back the hours and regain the lightness of heart he'd felt as he returned from hunting.

Lucia's green eyes regarded him steadily as she said, 'It's that letter, isn't it? What does Hastings want this time?' She listened in silence, sitting, head bowed, in her chair as he told her about Hastings' appeal. When he had finished, she said, 'What is there to discuss? You've already decided, haven't you.'

'To be honest, I don't feel I've much choice. But if you really don't want me to, I won't go…'

'No, *caro*.' Putting her box aside, Lucia stood up and took his face between her hands. 'I would never try to stop you doing what you feel is right. If I'm angry with anyone it's with Hastings – he's so confident of himself, feels such a great man until things go wrong and then his thoughts fly to you…'

'If what he says is true – and I've no reason to doubt it – these are more dangerous times than we've known for many years. They could even threaten our life in Hindustan…'

'I have one condition, however – that Lizzie and I come with you…'

'I'm very glad. Whatever's coming, I'd be happier knowing you were both in Calcutta.'

–

Three weeks later, comfortably settled with his family in the Grangers' mansion – Tuhin Singh was to follow in a few days after taking Kannika and their son to her family in the hills – Nicholas made his way along Esplanade Row to Government House. Since his arrival, he and Hastings had had several private meetings at which Hastings had confessed he had despatched the six thousand troops on their twelve-hundred-mile march across Hindustan to Bombay without the authority of his fellow council members. 'Each of them has an equal vote with me though, in the event of a tie, as governor-general mine is the deciding voice. But I can't afford that nonsense – I knew they'd object that we couldn't spare the troops from Bengal. In times like these and with a council like that my strategy has to be act now, tell later.'

However, late the previous evening Hastings had sent Nicholas a note telling him he had received serious news from Bombay and asking him to attend a council meeting next morning. In the few minutes they had in private before making their way to the council chamber, he told Nicholas quite enough for him to understand the reason for Hastings' new alarm.

The other councillors were already seated at the round table in the grand, colonnaded room, documents secured with brass paperweights to prevent them blowing about in the breeze created by the huge *punkah* swinging back and forth above their heads. The tall, thin, pinch-nosed Philip Francis had changed little since Nicholas had last seen him but he looked at him with fresh interest – Martha Granger had told him Francis had recently been caught *in flagrante delicto* with a blonde French beauty when her husband, George Grand, one of Hastings' aides, unexpectedly returned home. Grand had challenged Francis to a duel – a challenge which he had disdainfully ignored on the grounds that Grand was too junior. 'They say Grand is going to sue him for "alienation of affection". As for that young French hussy, Francis has set her up as his mistress in a house along the Hooghly... and him the son of a clergyman and with a wife and six children back in Britain!' Martha had added, face crinkling with laughter.

As Hastings introduced Nicholas as his adviser, Francis visibly bridled while an ill-looking General Clavering, even stouter than Nicholas recalled and with several unsightly boils on his mottled face, gave an indeterminate grunt. Edward Wheler, a recent addition to the council sent out from England, shook Nicholas' hand, saying simply, 'Glad to meet you.' The fourth member, Richard Barwell – a man whose plain dress gave no clue that he was one of the wealthiest men in Calcutta – nodded politely.

'Well, gentlemen, to work,' Hasting said, settling himself in a chair more elaborately carved than the rest, with Nicholas to his right. A clerk, seated at a high desk a few feet away – the minute taker – dipped his quill in his inkpot and waited expectantly.

'I've called this meeting because I've serious news. Yesterday evening I received a despatch – already seven weeks old – from President Hornby in Bombay informing me that his administration has formed an alliance with Ragoba, the chief who as you know claims to be the rightful paramount Maratha leader. He has convinced Hornby that the ordinary Marathas will rise for him and that in return for the Company's support he will be a faithful friend to it. The fact that Hornby has committed the Company to this alliance unsanctioned by me is bad enough. But what's even worse is that he is planning to launch an invasion into Maratha territory with Company troops fighting alongside Ragoba's to capture the stronghold of Poona and install Ragoba on the Maratha throne. This insane scheme has been hatched entirely without my knowledge or consent even though I am ultimately responsible for what happens in Bombay. Hornby is meddling in the snake pit of Maratha affairs of which he knows little and understands less. Bombay is already dangerously under-defended. If he sends a column into Maratha lands it will make the situation far worse.'

'Well,' Francis said, 'it would seem history does repeat itself. Hornby is forming alliances and contemplating despatching troops from Bombay without authority just as you despatched six thousand of our soldiers from here to Bombay without the agreement of this council. Small wonder that the Court of Directors in London are nervous about how you are controlling – or should I say failing to control – the Company, whether here in Calcutta or indeed elsewhere in Hindustan.'

Hastings flushed. 'If they are, it's with your encouragement! This is not the time for sneering and personal animosities. Our priority now must be to retrieve the situation. Two things matter: making sure that Bombay is as well defended as we can make it in case it comes under attack – which was why I despatched Leslie – and stopping Hornby's mad scheme.'

'Where's Colonel Leslie now? He's been gone over a month… At our last meeting you said the monsoon was holding him up and that he was only making ten miles a day, if that! What more can you tell us?' Wheler asked.

'From the last message I received, with the weather improving he's making better progress but that was over a week ago. I've heard nothing since.'

'So in other words we don't know where he is... That's a great deal of help,' Francis said, sitting back in his chair. 'If we were going to send troops to Bombay we should have sent them by sea...'

As the discussion continued, Francis and Clavering, occasionally supported by Wheler – 'No friend to me either,' Hastings had told Nicholas – seemed more concerned with inveighing against Hastings' decision to despatch troops overland to Bombay than in discussing what to do. Several times to emphasise a point Clavering thumped the table with his heavy fist as if lecturing a group of callow young officers. Although they seemed united in their opposition to Hastings, from their frequent jibes at each other Nicholas could tell that, just as Jos Granger had said, little love was lost between them. He wondered what the young clerk, quietly scribbling away, made of it all, and whether – when he made his fair copy – he would massage the language to sound more statesmanlike. Richard Barwell spoke calmly and reasonably enough – when Francis and Clavering allowed him the opportunity – but even he seemed to have no real solutions to deal with the crisis.

Hastings was growing ever more exasperated, twisting in his carved chair and running his hand across his face. Listening to the ragged and ill-tempered discussion an idea formed in Nicholas' mind. As the blusterers finally ran out of bluster and the testy exchanges slowed, he saw his chance. 'Might I suggest, gentlemen, that we can all agree the real problem here is one of intelligence... We simply don't know how far Leslie's relief force is from Bombay nor when Hornby intends to launch his invasion with Ragoba – or even if that's still his intention. I am prepared to ride with only a small escort to make contact with Leslie's forces. Though the terrain is difficult, as I know from experience, travelling light on good horses we should be able to move at least four or five times faster than a column burdened with artillery and a baggage train – perhaps more. A force of six thousand troops shouldn't be hard to locate and when I do catch up with it I can pass on fresh orders to Leslie, alerting him to Bombay's perilous position and ordering him to speed his advance. I can then continue on to Bombay, with orders to the president to abandon any thought of an expedition into Maratha territory and to concentrate on defending Bombay.'

Some moments' silence followed before Francis said, 'For God's sake, that's frankly ridiculous... What would happen if you're captured or fall ill? We can't rely on just one man!' Clavering nodded vigorously. Before Nicholas could reply that he would have with him Tuhin Singh who, following his service with Bogle, had acquired some reputation, albeit grudging, among the Calcutta officials, independent of his work with Nicholas, and who could continue the mission if anything happened to himself, Hastings cut in.

'I've known Ballantyne a long time and I trust his judgement more than that of any man around this table! But if any of you has a better idea, let's hear it!'

Francis though was silent. So too were Clavering and Wheler. But Barwell – 'My only ally,' Hastings had told Nicholas – said firmly, 'I think we should be grateful to Ballantyne for his offer. It's no small task that he's offering to undertake. I support it.' To Nicholas' surprise so too, after some moments, did Wheler.

'Frankly, I can't think what else we can do. We can despatch more troops from Bengal to Bombay by sea as back-up, but if other Hindustani rulers such as Hyder Ali go into alliance with the French – as seems only too likely – we may soon have to defend both Calcutta and Madras. Sending Ballantyne seems a reasonable first step. And what do we lose by it?'

'Well then, gentlemen, shall we take a vote?' Hastings asked.

As the council approved Nicholas' scheme by three votes to two – Francis and Clavering, were the dissenting voices – a relieved-looking Hastings clapped him on the back and whispered in his ear, 'Well done. If that suggestion had come from me not you, Wheler would never have backed it and we'd have lost the vote…'

12 – *A Ride Against Time*

The sun was scarcely above the eastern horizon as Nicholas and Tuhin Singh disembarked from the riverboat that had brought them overnight to a small Company settlement on the muddy banks of the Hooghly, not far from Burdwan. Already waiting ashore was their escort of twelve Bengali troopers and two of the scouts who had brought the most recent messages from Leslie's column. They would guide Nicholas along the route the troops had taken. One, a tall, well-built man, saluted as Nicholas came down the gangplank. 'Mr Ballantyne, sir. I am Vikram Das, assigned to help you locate Colonel Leslie's force. Your other scout is Anil Roy, waiting over there with the escort.' He pointed to a smaller figure on a chestnut mare. Like Vikram Das, Anil Roy and the escort were dressed as Nicholas had requested in dull-coloured everyday clothes to avoid attracting undue attention. Nicholas knew, however, each man would have weapons within easy reach.

'Pleased to meet you, Vikram. This is my colleague Tuhin Singh. I'm glad to see you have horses ready. How many spare mounts will we take?'

'Through Bengal and Oudh, one spare mount per rider. We have sent messages ahead to ensure changes of horses are available at our planned nightly halts. When we leave Oudh and are less certain of the route and of our daily progress we may need to take more spare horses with us to maintain the sixty miles a day you wish.'

'Excellent. How long do you think we will take to catch up with Colonel Leslie?'

'Not an easy question… When I left the column three weeks ago they were only making fifteen miles a day and had covered about three hundred miles. If they maintained that speed they would now be five hundred or so miles ahead. We might reach them in just over a fortnight. However, there is a big proviso – how far we can be certain of their route. When I left, Colonel Leslie was thinking about saving some miles by going across country.'

'Well, we can only do our best. Now let's lose no more time in mounting up. Every journey, however long, has to have a beginning…'

-

The first days passed without incident as the group made Nicholas' desired daily mileage along roads still muddy from the recent monsoon. On the sixth day, two of the escort began to feel ill, alternately sweating and shivering, their eyeballs bloodshot and their limbs shaking as they struggled to stay in their saddles and keep up with their companions. That night their condition worsened. Their clothes and bedding became soaked with their sweet-smelling, sticky sweat. Next morning Nicholas asked the keeper of the lodgings where they had stayed to summon a *hakim*. His verdict was that the men were far too ill to continue. In a conversation with Nicholas outside the men's hearing he agreed in return for a small payment to care for them. If they recovered he would help them return to Calcutta. If not he would arrange suitable funerals. Thereupon, with consoling words to the sufferers, the rest of the group mounted and departed.

Three nights later, they prepared to spend their first night under canvas. With dusk falling they halted in a roadside jungle clearing. After shooing away a troop of marauding monkeys, the group quickly put up two tents and collected wood to make a small fire to cook their simple meal of dal and rice. After eating, Anil Roy took the first hours of sentry duty and everyone else retired to the tents to sleep, wrapped in their horse blankets.

Nicholas found getting to sleep on the ground difficult. He must be getting old, he thought as he heard Tuhin Singh start to snore loudly at his side.

As he finally began to doze after what seemed an age, a sudden animal scream jerked him back to full wakefulness. Other screams and a shout of alarm from Anil Roy followed. Nicholas and Tuhin Singh were quickly outside the tent, pistols at the ready. Anil Roy, holding a brand from the fire in one hand and his musket in the other, was running towards where the horses were tethered. Nicholas and Tuhin Singh quickly followed when suddenly Tuhin Singh stopped, pointed and whispered, 'What's that?' Following his outstretched arm Nicholas made out in the shadows of the trees two amber eyes glinting in the light of Anil Ray's brand. A shape emerged sinuously and slowly from the gloom towards them – a tiger. The great beast halted, crouched and began to snarl, pulling back its lips to expose its long incisors. But then – even before Nicholas and Tuhin Singh could raise their pistols – it decided flight was the better part of valour, turned tail and vanished back into the jungle.

Going cautiously forward to the horse lines, Nicholas and Tuhin Singh found one of their mounts – a dapple grey – lying on the ground, its head pulled back in an unnatural position and a great bite torn from its throat. The other horses were pulling at their tethers, neighing and bucking in fear.

'We should build up the fire, Nicholas,' Tuhin Singh said, 'and move the horses closer to it.'

Nicholas gave the necessary orders to the now fully wakened camp. Everyone worked in pairs by the light of the rising moon to gather more wood and to calm and move the horses, one man doing the work and the other guarding him with his musket.

'I think I'll climb into one of those trees near the corpse of the grey in case the tiger returns to its kill,' Tuhin Singh said.

'No need, unless you're determined to relive our first hunt all those years ago in Calcutta… If the tiger was really hungry or resolute it would have stood its ground when we disturbed it.

Besides, the horses are now nearer the fire and the two watchmen we've designated.'

'All the same, perhaps I'll climb up there with my musket for an hour or two. It might be good sport.'

'As you wish, but I'm going back to sleep. Take care, won't you.'

When Nicholas woke the next morning Tuhin Singh was again snoring loudly at his side. Ducking out of the tent, Nicholas found the two sentries on duty quietly making chapattis and boiling water over the fire ready for breakfast. The tiger had not returned and, as Tuhin Singh later admitted, he'd only lasted three quarters of an hour in the tree before cramp and pain in his old leg wound had forced him trophy-less back to the tent.

Travelling on, constructing a makeshift raft from logs to cross a tributary of the Ganges, fast flowing after the monsoon, and passing through a forest of pinky-orange jungle flowers, they soon began to find evidence of an army on the march. Roads were rutted by the passage of cannon limbers and heavy carts. Pieces of broken equipment, the ashes of cooking fires, piles of dung, both human and animal, discarded tent pegs and all kinds of rubbish blowing about marked the column's overnight campsites.

One afternoon sixteen days after setting out, the group came upon the corpse of a dead bullock with vultures pecking at it. Part of the traces from which the animal had been cut when it dropped was still around its neck. Dismounting and scaring away the vultures, Nicholas carefully scrutinised the remains, then shouted across to Tuhin Singh, 'These traces have the Company's mark on them and it looks to me from the state of the bullock that it died no more than a day ago. That means Leslie and his men can only be twenty miles or so away. If we ride hard, we should reach their camp tonight.'

Nicholas was right. After three hours' cantering, they rounded a bend in the road to see about two or three miles away the column encamped at the base of a low hill with smoke from cooking fires already rising. Pushing their tired mounts into a gallop, Nicholas and Tuhin Singh quickly reached the screen of pickets around the camp. 'Halt! State your business,' ordered an elderly sergeant – an Irishman by his accent – manning a checkpoint across the road.

'My name is Ballantyne. My colleague Tuhin Singh and I have important and urgent despatches for Colonel Leslie from Governor-General Hastings. We must see him straight away.'

'You'll have a problem there then,' the sergeant replied, expression deadpan. 'He's dead and buried this past week.'

'Who's commanding in his place?'

'Leslie's deputy – Lieutenant-Colonel Thomas Goddard. Show me evidence of your identity and I'll have you conducted to his tent.'

Nicholas and Tuhin Singh were soon sitting with Goddard, a muscular man in his late thirties, outside his large tent at the centre of the camp. 'I'm glad we've not been forgotten in Calcutta,' Goddard said, 'We haven't made the best speed – late monsoon rains delayed us near Chatterpore – but we're in good shape and there's been remarkably little disease, apart from poor Leslie of course.'

'What happened to him?' Nicholas asked.

'He fell ill a month after we left Calcutta, suffering acute diarrhoea and growing weaker all the time, but insisted on continuing in command and riding his horse each day, instead of being carried in a palanquin. Ten days ago he collapsed completely. The surgeon who had been giving him opium to calm his bowels could do nothing further for him. He was dead within twenty-four hours.'

'I'm sorry.'

'A reminder death can come quickly here, however seasoned one is… For myself, I'm grateful to have reconfirmation of the orders to continue to Bombay. Nevertheless, I'm not clear how I can increase our speed of advance as Hastings wants without the column becoming strung out along the road, eventually splitting in two. That would be dangerous, especially when we are passing through the territories of the Marathas, many of whose princes are ill-disposed to the Company or indeed any other forces entering their territory.'

'Could some of this problem be forestalled if you reorganised and deliberately split your forces, rather than allowed it to happen gradually?'

'Dividing forces and pressing on incautiously goes against all my military instincts. So many catastrophes have resulted from such decisions. In Classical times alone, wouldn't both Crassus' and Mark Antony's disastrous expeditions into Parthia and Varus' loss of three legions to the German Arminius in Augustus' time be examples? And what about Saladin's victory over the Crusaders at Hattin?'

'I'm no student of warfare but your examples are many centuries ago. Perhaps you might think about it as a decision to create a separate, more mobile, faster advance force of the type Clive so often deployed successfully here in Hindustan, while leaving a still well-protected slower artillery and supply column to follow?'

'I could perhaps consider sending an advance party of cavalry without diminishing the defensibility of the main column and its guns.'

'I'd be grateful – and more importantly, so would Hastings – for whatever you can do. However, I recognise that the orders I've brought go no further than confirming that you should continue to Bombay at the best speed that you can but do not instruct you to split the force...'

'I'll think further overnight, but what are your own intentions? Will you travel on with us or return to Calcutta?'

'Neither. I have urgent despatches for William Hornby, the president of Bombay. If you can furnish us with a change of horses and some spare mounts we will leave tomorrow morning.'

'That I can do.'

'I'd also be grateful if you could provide four or five reliable messengers to take a despatch from me back to Hastings in Calcutta telling him I have found you and reconfirmed your orders, as well as about your assumption of command following Leslie's death.'

'Of course. I'll go and make the arrangements for everything.'

After Goddard had left, Tuhin Singh said to Nicholas, 'Your discussions with Goddard – a good officer, I thought – showed you're developing into a politician! He now knows what he is expected to do, but that if it goes wrong it will be his responsibility, not yours or Hastings'.'

'You may be right but it's part of his burden of command. Besides, if he succeeds it will redound to his credit, just as failure would to his detriment.'

'But there's a difference – many will claim a share in any success but none in any failure of his.'

'You're becoming a cynic in your old age. I must write to Hastings. Then it's time for sleep if we're to start early tomorrow.'

Goddard was as good as his word. Next morning replacement horses and some supplies awaited them. As he wished them Godspeed, Goddard said, 'I'll think hard with my senior officers about how to get at least some advance support quickly to Bombay.'

'That's all I can ask on Hastings' behalf,' Nicholas replied as he swung himself into the saddle.

-

Nicholas and Tuhin Singh's onward journey through central India proved uneventful. Each day after breakfasting at dawn they set off, rode for five hours, rested themselves and their horses in the shade somewhere away from the worst of the heat till around three, then rode on again until dusk when it was time to camp or find lodgings – usually the former to keep themselves away from prying eyes. After bypassing Nagpur and its rulers – the powerful Bhonsles clan of Marathas – the fourteen men continued directly west on the remaining five hundred miles of their journey before turning south, crossing the Tapti River and heading for the city of

Nasik on the banks of the Godavari River. Nasik – Tuhin Singh told Nicholas – was one of the most celebrated pilgrimage places for Hindu people in the whole of India. Rama, the hero of the epic *Ramayana*, was said to have lived there with his wife, Sita, and his brother, Lakshmana, who nearby had sliced off the nose of the demon enchantress Surpanakha.

Nicholas and his men crossed the broad river, again using makeshift rafts, a few miles to the west of Nasik to avoid the crowds of the devout. These included, as Tuhin Singh pointed out, some ash-daubed but otherwise entirely naked long-haired *fakirs* – holy men heading for the city as part of their ceaseless pilgrimages during which they relied on local people for their only sustenance.

Leaving the Godavari they pressed on towards Bombay over dusty, orange hills sculpted into strange shapes by the wind. Some days the heat of the sun was so intense that Nicholas felt himself swaying in the saddle but forced himself to ride on towards the shimmering horizon. Being without a change of horses for a few days, their pace slackened as they zigzagged up some of the steeper hills, pausing frequently for their weary mounts to catch their breath. At last they reached the coast where the wind blowing off the sparkling, mirror-like sea provided refreshing relief to both body and soul. They spent one more night under canvas on the palm-fringed seashore with the sound of breaking waves in their ears. The next day, after nearly six weeks on the road, their eyes red from the heat, glare and dust, their limbs aching, they at last saw Bombay before them.

A fortified wall – two miles in circumference, Nicholas had been told on his way to visit Shah Alam – surrounded the settlement. Passing through the arched gates, the weary riders headed for Bombay Castle, the centre of the settlement's government. Constructed from blue-greyish stone, it overlooked the esplanade and the broad harbour. Its origins were Portuguese before the small enclave was gifted to King Charles II of England as part of the dowry of his Portuguese bride, Catherine of Braganza. There had, however, been many improvements and additions over the succeeding century.

Dismounting in the sun-drenched parade ground in front of the castle in the late afternoon, Nicholas crossed to the guard post where, on hearing of his mission to the president, the presiding sergeant major, a stout elderly man, the empty right sleeve of his jacket testifying to his frontline service, immediately sent a message to the president's aide de camp. A few minutes later, a well-groomed young man, immaculate in the uniform of a lieutenant in the Company's army, appeared and held out his hand to Nicholas. 'I'm John Steele, the president's aide. Was I told correctly that you had ridden all the way from Calcutta?'

'That's right. I have important despatches from Governor-General Hastings to President Hornby. I would like to see him as soon as possible.'

'It can't be today, I'm afraid. He's been struck down by one of the recurrent bouts of fever he's suffered for some years, but if the fever follows its usual pattern of abating after a day or two he should be well enough to receive you tomorrow.'

Nicholas wondered whether to insist on an immediate audience but knew that would be bound to get his relations with Hornby off on the wrong foot. So he replied, 'Tomorrow it must be then. But my business is both urgent and important. If he is still unwell tomorrow, I must see his deputy.'

'Of course. I realise it wouldn't be for a trifle you've ridden from Calcutta. I'll have rooms found immediately for you and your men and food prepared.'

Within half an hour Nicholas was installed in an airy room overlooking the sea. Within an hour he was eating chicken and potatoes, washed down by pale ale on his balcony with Tuhin Singh. An hour later he was sprawled asleep on a comfortable feather mattress.

He was still asleep next morning when an attendant brought him tea, bread and fruit preserve and more importantly a note from Steele saying the president was well enough to see him at ten o'clock. Nicholas shaved more carefully than he had in weeks and dressed in the slightly rumpled formal clothes he had brought with him. Then with Tuhin Singh he made his way to Hornby's apartment on the third floor of the castle.

When Steele ushered them in Hornby was sitting in a rattan chair. His bony face was pale, his eyes bloodshot and his sparse hair sweat-streaked but he rose to greet them. 'I'm sorry I couldn't receive you yesterday but as Steele doubtless told you this fever plagues me. I've tried all the supposed remedies – chewing rhubarb, blocking my nostrils with linen dipped in camphor and vinegar when I go outside, swallowing a disgusting concoction of bark, garlic and rhubarb in brandy, everything... God knows whether any of them actually do any good. Still, I suppose I should be grateful I seem to recover each time. But enough of me. What is this important business that brings you from Calcutta?'

'The full message is here,' said Nicholas, passing the envelope with Hastings' seal to Hornby who immediately opened it. 'But the gist is that Hastings wishes you not to send Company forces in support of Ragoba's claim to the paramount leadership of the Marathas.'

'Hastings' wishes are not relevant.'

'I was being politely euphemistic. It is an order – as the despatch makes clear – from him as the governor-general responsible to the Court of Directors in London not only for Calcutta but also for Bombay and Madras.'

'Yes, I can read. Governor-general or not and titularly responsible or not, Hastings should not meddle in what I consider local matters. It takes weeks – months even – to get orders from Calcutta. I can't wait for that, any more than Hastings can wait for London to tell him what to do. I must be free to use my initiative. What's more I've already done so. Company troops under Colonel Egerton left with Ragoba's men ten days ago.'

Taken aback, Nicholas glanced at Tuhin Singh. They had been too exhausted to make further enquiries the previous evening and in any case Nicholas had wished to speak first to Hornby.

After a few moments he said, 'In that case as you will also see in the despatch, Hastings orders you to recall the Company troops at once and prepare to defend Bombay against the all too likely consequences of your action.'

'Hastings is plain wrong, God dammit. As the man on the ground I disagree profoundly. I've been president here since 1771, longer than high and mighty Hastings has been in his post. During that time to the best of my knowledge he's never visited Bombay and knows nothing first-hand of local conditions. I am convinced Ragoba is a good man worthy of our full support. With him on the throne and grateful to us our trade will prosper.'

'Not in Hastings' view. He believes that Ragoba is now unpopular with his people, that his time is past – if it ever came – that he will be defeated and in four months Bombay will be under siege by French-backed Marathas. That is why, as you know, he ordered Colonel Leslie to march his column to reinforce you and why following Leslie's death I, on Hastings' behalf, have instructed his deputy Goddard to make all possible haste here.'

By now Hornby's face was flushed and beaded with sweat. 'This is beyond tolerance. You can bloody well tell Hastings I refuse to comply. I will defend my conduct before the council in Calcutta, even the Court of Directors in London if necessary. If Hastings wants Egerton and his troops brought back, you'll have to go and get them yourself and on Hastings' and your head be it!'

'Is that your final word on the matter?'

'Yes, I believe Bombay has greater potential than either Madras or Calcutta and to help the settlement achieve that greater potential I must be free to act as I think fit.'

'Very well, I will convey that message to Hastings.'

'As you wish. It will be four months before his response reaches me. By then a grateful Ragoba will rule the Marathas and I will have been proved right in my judgement.'

'Again not in Hastings' opinion, but it is not for me to argue further with you but simply to repeat as clearly as I can the governor-general's orders.'

Hornby wiped the sweat from his face with a silk handkerchief and took a drink of water from his glass, then continued more calmly, 'I think, Ballantyne, both you and I have made our positions entirely clear and we both have competent witnesses – Steele here and your colleague Tuhin Singh – that we have done so in case of future dispute. I regret if weakness from my fever has meant I've expressed myself more forthrightly than I might otherwise have done but my mind is clear and made up. I shall have the support of my council here in Bombay in any dispute with Calcutta or London about my actions and, from what I hear, his council in Calcutta may not even agree with Hastings. Steele here will make whatever transport arrangements you require and indeed, if you wish, for messengers to take despatches from you swiftly back to Hastings in Calcutta. I have no wish to conceal my actions from him. You have my admiration for the determination and speed with which you pursued your mission, however wrongheaded I think it. Now I feel my fever returning so please do excuse me.'

'You have indeed made your position admirably clear, president.'

–

'I've spent the time since we left Hornby turning over in my mind what our next steps should be,' Nicholas said that afternoon as he and Tuhin Singh were sitting in Nicholas' room drinking *nimbu pani*. 'It would be futile to argue further with Hornby. He is determined to continue with his own policy and to disregard Hastings' instructions, which on this occasion I think are the right ones.'

'So?'

'As I see it, I'm left with only two alternatives. Return to Hastings and confess my failure or attempt to locate Ragoba's army and issue Hastings' order to withdraw direct to Colonel Egerton commanding the Company forces accompanying him.'

'If you go after the column you'd certainly be following Hastings' orders but wouldn't you also be becoming increasingly drawn into Company politics – a mire you've always told me you want to avoid?'

'My cousin Charles once told me you can't make a difference without getting your hands dirty. On this issue, at least, I'm already deeply involved, however I may feel about it and I do consider Hastings' policy of preserving the status quo is the correct one, rather than Hornby's aggressive and expansionist views…'

'I think you've probably already made up your mind to go after Ragoba and Egerton. It's never been in your nature to accept defeat when you believe yourself to be in the right. You want to fulfil your mission and see to it that the Company army withdraws and are simply looking to me to reassure you that you're acting both responsibly and reasonably, aren't you?'

'You know me too well. Yes, I want to find the column.'

'Then there's no more to be said. I'll find Vikram Das and order him and Anil Roy quietly to assemble fresh horses and supplies. Then I'll do my best to find out discreetly what I can of the precise route the troops took. I suggest you do the same – Steele might prove a useful source for you.'

13 – An Inquisition

The next morning Nicholas and Tuhin Singh rode quietly out of Bombay with Vikram Das and Anil Roy and eight members of their original escort – Vikram Das had judged two men who had reached Bombay too exhausted to continue. Each man had a spare horse on whose back was strapped some of their small amount of supplies and equipment. The guards at the settlement's gates made no attempt to question their destination or identity, let alone to detain them. As they turned south, Nicholas and Tuhin Singh outlined their plans and what they knew of Ragoba's army's movements to the rest of their party.

Tuhin Singh began. 'Between us we've discovered that Ragoba has around seven thousand men of his own, mostly horsemen. In addition, Colonel Egerton and his deputy, Major John Carnac – both in their sixties, by the way – have about two thousand sepoys, a few hundred mostly European cavalry and a small number of cannon. They've also taken an enormous baggage train – using nearly twenty thousand bullocks to haul it, I was told.'

'What on earth they need that for is beyond me,' Nicholas added.

'That will slow them considerably. They won't make more than ten miles a day in this hilly country,' Vikram Das said, then asked, 'Where are they headed? Towards Poona?'

'Yes, we understand Ragoba believes that the people there will welcome him – although even in Bombay quite a few Company officials doubt that.'

'That was the impression we gained in the barracks too,' Anil Roy put in.

'Well, we must aim to catch up with the troops before they reach Poona or any decisive engagement takes place,' Nicholas said. 'I intend that once we get further into Maratha territory we should travel mainly at night to avoid attention and rest up in seclusion during the day. Today we'll follow a route Tuhin Singh has been told of over the hills, which should serve as a short cut to the Poona road the army will almost certainly have taken.'

–

On the moonlit evening of the second day, after descending to the Poona road just before dusk, Nicholas decided to ride on until near midnight, snatch a few hours' rest, and then travel until dawn before finding shelter for the day. After two or three hours of darkness Anil Roy, who was riding in advance of the rest to warn of possible dangers or difficulties – whether groups of Marathas, rivers or precipices – cantered back to Nicholas and reported, 'About a mile or two on, there is the remains of an overnight army camping place. In the moonlight it's difficult to judge how recent.'

'Thank you. We've made excellent progress. We'll get to the site and wait there until dawn to examine it and then look for somewhere to hide out during the day.'

Their exploration of the camp site early the next morning showed that the fires were long out and that the copious quantities of animal dung were hardened by several days' sun. Ragoba and Egerton had clearly departed some days before. After resting most of the day, the group rode hard through the next night, passing through two more of the army's camps before spending the next day in a large hillside cave. That evening and night they made further good progress through the hills, following the clear rutted tracks of the army and its trail of rubbish and passing through three more camp sites.

As a pink dawn was rising and they were thinking of halting, they emerged from a rocky defile into a wide valley to see vultures circling ahead, dark against the lightening sky. Drawing nearer they found the vultures were feasting on thousands of bodies of animals and men. A major engagement had clearly taken place. Looking at the uniforms and clothing of the dead it soon became clear that Ragoba's and Egerton's men had had much the worst of it, presumably after coming under attack by a rival Maratha army. Discarded equipment and clothing littered the ground.

As they picked their way, neck cloths bound around their noses and mouths to keep out as much of the sickly sweet stench of death and putrefaction as possible, they sometimes bent to check a body in the remote chance that any life might linger. It never did. Here three drummers seemed to have been killed together, their drums lying at their sides. There, several sepoys had probably fought hard to the last, their mangled bodies lying close together among blood-stained tussocks of dry grass. A little further on a group of Ragoba's red-turbaned horsemen had died together, two trapped beneath the fast decaying bodies of their mounts.

Nicholas paused by the corpse of a blond-haired young man dressed in the uniform of a Company ensign lying on a banner bearing the Company's striped flag. Vultures had pecked out his eyes, creamy maggots were crawling in and around his mouth and nose and a lance protruded from his abdomen. Nicholas put his hand into the pocket of the ensign's jacket in case there was any letter or other paper to identify the youth or keepsake to return to his relations. Looters had stripped all the corpses of any obviously valuable items such as watches, rings and chains and even in some cases boots and clothing. Nicholas pulled out a folded piece of paper blood-stained around the edges. Unfolding and reading it, he discovered it was from the ensign's mother, sending her only son greetings from herself and her daughters in Shropshire on his nineteenth birthday.

Although he had seen many deaths and many corpses, the letter brought a tear to Nicholas' eye as he thought of his own sons. He refolded the paper and put it into his pocket. He would write to the mother, although he knew that would prove little consolation. He then carried on towards the remnants of part of the baggage train. There the stench was even worse from the bodies of many bullocks, some of whose stomachs were bloated with gases and others covered in black, buzzing flies and maggots where the bellies had already burst and the putrefaction was more advanced.

He continued over to Tuhin Singh who looked as distressed as he felt at the waste of war. After a moment or two Tuhin Singh said, 'This appears to have been carnage for Ragoba's and Egerton's men. They must have been taken by surprise and completely overwhelmed. Did you notice that the cannon and nearly all the muskets and pistols have been removed?'

'Yes, together with many of that host of bullocks and baggage wagons – a fine haul for the victors. The battle must have been a few days ago.' Suddenly Nicholas noticed a *fleur-de-lys* on a tricorn hat, which had fallen from the shattered head of one of the corpses. Turning the body over, he saw that it was wearing a blue French uniform. 'The attackers clearly had some French help,' he said to Tuhin Singh.

'Yes, I found another body in French uniform. But what I don't see are enough corpses to account by any means for a combined force nearly ten thousand strong. It strikes me that a good number of Ragoba's and Egerton's men either escaped or surrendered.'

'Probably mostly surrendered and taken prisoner to Poona by Ragoba's opponents among the Maratha clans. If they'd escaped we'd have surely encountered some.'

'I think so. I noticed in particular few bodies of Company officers – certainly not of elderly men like Egerton and Carnac – or of what look like senior commanders among Ragoba's troops, though it's sometimes hard to tell given the state of decay. Senior people would make the most valuable prisoners – or hostages if you prefer that term.'

'Whatever the case, whether dead or captured, so much for Ragoba, Egerton and their army. Lives have been pointlessly lost and the Company's prestige has suffered a heavy blow thanks to Hornby's lack of judgment and misplaced trust in Ragoba. An attack on Bombay is now only too likely and the settlement will have to defend itself without their aid. We've arrived too late. All we can do now is get ourselves and our men back to safety behind Bombay's walls with the news of the defeat. Our luck has held till now. Let's hope it will last that far. Tired as we may be from our overnight ride, we must turn back immediately and risk riding during the day.'

'Do you think it's really worth the risk of daytime travel? As you say, we've been lucky so far but we can't necessarily expect that to last. No one's luck lasts forever. If we're captured, Bombay will get no warning. Will gaining a day or two really make such a difference?'

Nicholas hesitated but only for a moment. 'I hear what you're saying but a day or two might make all the difference. I'll take the chance… Let's gather our men together.'

Tuhin Singh nodded and said no more.

Leaving the battlefield behind them, even before the sun was high in the sky, Nicholas, Tuhin Singh and the rest of their group were already retracing their tracks back through the defile and up into the hills. After they had been travelling nearly three hours, a figure suddenly appeared from the shelter of some jagged rocks high on the hillside above the trail and ran down towards them, waving his arms and yelling for them to stop. Once he stumbled over some loose rocks and fell but was quickly back on his feet, running and shouting again. When he got closer, Nicholas reined in on seeing he was dressed in the uniform of a *risaldar* in the Company cavalry much coated in dust. His right hand had a bloodstained piece of torn cloth bound roughly around it, his hair was matted with dirt and sweat, his face bruised and his lips blistered. 'I think you must be Company men?' he said as he halted before Nicholas, gasping for breath.

'We are,' Nicholas replied, 'but who are you?'

'*Risaldar* Kumar – I was one of the chief scouts for Colonel Egerton's force.' His voice was dry and cracking.

'Here, take some water,' Nicholas said, passing his water bottle, 'and then tell me what happened as far as you can…'

The *risaldar* immediately put the bottle to his parched lips and gulped greedily. Then he began. 'I don't know the full story of course. Our troops and Ragoba's made slow progress from Bombay mainly because of the speed of the many bullocks. Not far beyond here, I and several other scouts were sent ahead to find out what we could of the mood of the local people, even – if we could – in Poona itself, at the time no more than twenty-five miles away.' He paused to take another swallow of water. 'I myself rode to the outskirts of Poona where I saw that the Maratha chiefs were assembling a large force. Entering their camp in the disguise of a seller of sweetmeats I learned that the Marathas had heard of our slow advance several days before and – rather than preparing to welcome Ragoba – the inhabitants of Poona had rallied to the support of their existing leaders, in particular Mahadji Scindia who was preparing to lead his troops against us. I returned quickly to Colonel Egerton to report, as did several other scouts with similar information.

'From what I learned – either while standing outside the command tent or from the orders issued a little later – Ragoba and his commanders seemed to have begun to lose confidence, while Colonel Egerton – as you know an elderly man and in increasingly poor health – decided with Major Carnac that their best option was to turn back to Bombay. Subsequently Ragoba agreed that his force would follow. To increase their speed they abandoned some of the larger cannon and heaviest baggage wagons, pushing them into a lake. The combined force then swung around – a cumbersome procedure – after which we rested for the night. The next morning both we and Ragoba's men began our retreat. I was sent ahead with two of my men to check that the route back through the defile and beyond was clear. This we did as far as two of our previous campsites before turning to rejoin the column and to report. When we emerged through the defile into the valley we saw our troops were under heavy attack from all sides. I could see no way to rejoin our commanders so I and my companions hid among the rocks. After about only an hour or so, the sounds of battle ceased. Peering from our hiding place, it seemed that both our troops and Ragoba's were surrendering. While we watched, during the rest of the day, the attackers – clearly Scindia's Marathas and we guessed five times more numerous than our men and Ragoba's put together – began leading off long lines of their captives towards Poona. They took with them our remaining cannon and the intact portion of that vast baggage train.

'The next morning, when I thought all the victors had departed we rode towards the battlefield but a small group of what may have been deserters who were looting the bodies attacked us. Both of my companions were shot from their horses. I escaped but my horse was wounded. I only got a mile or two further before it collapsed, throwing me onto the rocky ground. Bruised and winded I staggered into the hills. No one followed.'

'What have you been doing since then?' Tuhin Singh asked.

'After hiding for a day or two – the battle happened nearly a week ago – I began walking back towards Bombay. I found some water at one or two springs in the hills but have eaten only a few wild fruits since then.'

'We'll find you some food,' Nicholas said, 'but from what you could see, did any organised body of our men escape?'

'Certainly not in this direction. I've seen no one before you, either friend or enemy.'

Turning to Tuhin Singh, Nicholas said, 'That he's seen no Marathas is at least some comfort. It supports our assumption that after the battle they returned towards Poona with their prisoners and booty, rather than pressing on to attack Bombay immediately. This is the only viable route they could have taken.'

'That gives Bombay some time to prepare and to have some chance of reinforcement by Goddard and any troops Hastings sends by sea.'

'We must still get the news of the defeat back to Bombay as soon as we can,' Nicholas said before addressing the *risaldar.* 'We can give you one of our spare horses and you can ride with us to tell your story to the authorities.'

The *risaldar* smiled, 'It'll be good not to be alone.'

-

As the following day they picked their way over a pass between two high, wind-eroded hills, Tuhin Singh, keen eyes scanning the horizon, said, 'Look down there – that must be the Koli River...'

Shading his eyes against the midday glare Nicholas saw a silvery ribbon fringed in green winding through the plain below them. 'Good, once we cross that and the next range of hills, we'll be over halfway back to Bombay and can slow down a little, which is just as well – most of the horses are exhausted.'

An hour later, they were making good progress over the sandy plain dotted with scrubby lantana bushes. Scenting water ahead, the thirsty horses picked up speed of their own volition but suddenly Nicholas heard a cry of warning from Vikram Das, riding in the rear of the group. Twisting in his saddle he saw a troop of about fifty or sixty riders galloping at a furious pace towards them, their horses kicking up clouds of pale red dust. 'Ride for the river! Fast as you can!' Nicholas yelled, drawing his pistol and urging his horse to one last great effort.

The ground flew beneath them as, keeping low in their saddles, he and his men galloped towards the river. But it was no good. Glancing over his shoulder, Nicholas saw the pursuers gaining. Moments later a pistol shot cut the air close to his face. Swerving his horse and holding his reins in one hand, he turned and discharged his own pistol at the fast-closing attackers, mostly turbaned Marathas but with at least two blue-jacketed Europeans riding with them. A pistol shot knocked one of the leading riders from his saddle – whether it was his shot or Tuhin Singh's riding close beside him who had also turned and fired, Nicholas had no idea.

The attackers were fanning out now, some racing past to the right and left, determined to get between Nicholas and his men and the river. A few minutes more and they had completely surrounded them, leaving them no option but to rein in their sweat-scummed horses. A voice called, 'Throw down your arms.' Thoughts of the corpse-filled valley and of the body of the young ensign came into Nicholas' mind. For a second he wondered whether, even now, they should try to fight their way out rather than surrender. He exchanged a quick look with Tuhin Singh. Reading his mind as ever his friend gave a little shake of the head, confirming what Nicholas already knew – that there would be no point. Instead he signalled his men to obey. They dropped their weapons to the ground to be quickly gathered by two young Maratha soldiers.

A lavishly bearded Maratha officer – presumably the troop's commander – trotted closer and after briefly scrutinising the group addressed Nicholas. 'Who are you? Company men?'

Nicholas nodded.

'Your name?'

'Nicholas Ballantyne.'

'What are you doing here?'

'We were trying to locate a Company column accompanying Ragoba's troops to Poona. We were too late. All we found was the site of their defeat.'

A blue-jacketed European – a French officer Nicholas realised by the uniform – trotted close to the commander and whispered something in his ear. For a moment the Maratha hesitated as if weighing his options. Was he about to have them all killed, Nicholas wondered. His mouth, already clotted with dust, felt even drier as the moments passed. Why hadn't he listened to Tuhin Singh and travelled by night…? Then the commander ordered, 'Tie their hands, hood them and take their reins. We'll bring them with us.'

As the troop cantered back over the uneven ground of the plain – without his reins to steady him it took all Nicholas' concentration not to topple from the saddle – from overheard snatches of conversation he realised they were being taken to Poona. Did the Marathas intend using them as hostages? They spent that night under close guard in a village hut with only a few mouthfuls of water and some stale chapattis before the troop set off again at dawn, the captives again hooded. *Why?*

Nicholas wondered. Was it to prevent them seeing Maratha troop dispositions and armaments? Once, he guessed from the sound of men's voices, the neighing, braying and lowing of animals and the creaking of wagons that they might be passing a large military column. Ominously – if his bearings were correct – it seemed to be heading north-westwards in the direction of Bombay.

When the Maratha commander finally ordered their hoods to be removed, Nicholas – blinking after so many hours of darkness – saw by the sun's position that it was nearly midday and that they were riding along the banks of a river towards a walled settlement. Poona? As they entered – the captives bringing up the rear – Nicholas realised why the commander had taken off their hoods. It was to give the population, pouring from their houses into the narrow streets, the chance to see the captives' faces. Laughing and jeering, they threw refuse, rotting vegetables, sometimes even rocks. A stone sliced the skin above Nicholas' right eye. Hands still bound, he could do nothing about the warm bright red blood trickling down the side of his nose into his mouth where it tasted oddly metallic.

They emerged onto a wide parade ground on one side of which was a squat fortress. On the thick walls flew the swallow-tailed saffron flags of the Maratha Confederacy. 'So this is where they're taking us,' muttered a grim-faced Tuhin Singh as they passed through the tall, spiked gates into a central courtyard. Maratha soldiers ran forward, pulled the prisoners from their horses and bundled them towards a narrow doorway. Nicholas was the first to reach it and as a man shoved him in the small of his back, he stumbled. Further jabs – this time with what felt like a sword hilt – propelled him forward into a darkness so intense after the bright daylight that he couldn't see the narrow stone steps in front of him and tumbled bruisingly down. Others crashed down behind him – somewhere in the noise and confusion he heard Tuhin Singh's voice. Scrambling up, he felt his way cautiously forward in the gloom.

From somewhere ahead he heard a man say, 'What's this then…?' Footsteps echoed and an orange light approached out of the semi-darkness. As Nicholas' eyes adjusted he saw he was in a long corridor lined with narrow metal doors and that the light came from a flaming torch grasped by a stocky Maratha. Round the man's waist was a broad, metal-studded belt from which dangled a variety of keys. Behind him were several guards who, from crumbs on their clothes and food stains around their mouths, looked as if they'd been interrupted eating. Nicholas just had time to glance round to see Tuhin Singh and *Risaldar* Kumar – whose already battered face was, like his own, cut and bleeding – before the Maratha said to the guards, 'Put them in the cells.' Nicholas tried to resist but with his hands still bound it was useless. Grabbing him by the shoulder a guard shoved him into a tiny cell. Just before the door clanged shut he called out Tuhin Singh's name and thought he caught a muffled response. Then all was silence.

The guards must have lit torches in the corridor outside because a little light at least filtered through the grille in the door. Dropping to the dank stone floor, Nicholas set to work with his teeth to try to loosen the rope cutting into his wrists. It was useless but then he had an idea. Crawling around the cell and running his fingers along the walls, he found a place in one corner where the mortar between the stones was crumbling. Scraping away at the mortar he at last managed to expose a sharp stone edge. Crouching close, he placed his wrists against it and began to saw at the rope. Slowly… very slowly… he started to cut through the tough fibres, wincing as sometimes his hands slipped and he cut his skin. But after about twenty minutes his hands were free. They tingled as he rubbed them together to get the circulation going. Then, tearing a strip from his shirt, he wiped away the semi-congealed blood from the cut over his eye. That felt better but he was still a prisoner in this humid cell smelling of sweat, piss and worse… Closing his eyes, he tried to conjure the cool pure air of Glenmire… the rolling hills and tall, silent mountains…

As time passed – propped up against the wall in the half-light it was impossible to tell how much as one of the Marathas had taken his pocket watch soon after his capture – Nicholas wondered whether anyone would ever come. He was so thirsty his tongue felt stuck to the roof of his mouth. Again he cursed himself for not heeding Tuhin Singh's warning to travel only by night. His overconfidence in his abilities and invulnerability, built up over so many years – 'hubris' the ancient Greeks called it – was to blame for what had happened. Now others as well as him were paying the price... Certainly Tuhin Singh and his men, and perhaps the whole settlement of Bombay.

Hearing a key finally turn in the lock he got up, hoping someone was bringing food and water. The man standing in the doorway was holding a flaring torch, which for a moment blinded Nicholas so he couldn't see him but he heard him say to someone in the corridor behind him, '*Oui, c'est lui, c'est l'Anglais*' – 'Yes, it's him, the Englishman'. Nicholas couldn't catch the muffled reply but the next moment, the man with the torch – a French soldier – entered the cell, seized him and though he tried to resist half-dragged him into the corridor.

Waiting was a tall young French officer – quite senior or at least a wealthy one judging by the *fleurs-de-lys* worked in thick gold thread on his high collar, the fine lace at his throat and wrists and the ruby ring glinting on his finger. 'Who are you? What do you want with me? And I'm not English, I'm a Scot,' Nicholas said in English, then – as the officer regarded him steadily but said nothing, repeated in French, '*Qui êtes vous? Que voulez-vous avec moi? Et je ne suis pas anglais – je suis ecossais!*'

'You are in no position to ask questions. But since you do, I am the Comte de Tanguy, military adviser to the Maratha leader Mahadji Scindia whose stronghold this is,' the young officer said in faultless English. Not waiting for Nicholas to reply he ordered the soldier, '*Vous, l'amenez*,' – 'Bring him'.

De Tanguy led the way back along the corridor – Nicholas wondered which doors Tuhin Singh and the others were behind – back up the narrow stairs and out into the courtyard. Dusk was falling and green parakeets were swooping down to drink from a fountain in the centre of the courtyard. Nicholas pulled out of the soldier's grip, ran to the fountain, flung himself on his knees and drank. He felt a kick but paid no attention and continued gulping down what he could. There was another kick but then de Tanguy called out, '*Non. Laissez-le boire.*'

With Nicholas again in the soldier's grasp and watched by two orange-turbaned Marathas leaning down from a balcony to see what was going on, they continued across the courtyard, through an arch, up a wide shallow flight of stairs and into a large room, the door guarded by two more French soldiers in high-polished boots – de Tanguy's private apartments, Nicholas guessed. With night approaching, candles already burned in silver sticks around the room.

Pointing to a stool placed in the middle of the floor, de Tanguy said to Nicholas, 'Sit! I know your name is Ballantyne. You are a Company man?'

'No… an envoy of the Company…'

De Tanguy shrugged. 'No need to split hairs, as I understand the British say. What were you doing in Maratha territory?'

'I might ask you – a French army officer – the same.'

'I and my men are here because Mahadji Scindia invited us. You're the trespasser, which can be dangerous… Let me tell you a cautionary tale. When your foolish president in Bombay sent an army into Maratha lands supporting the pretender Ragoba, I encouraged Scindia to hold back… to lure them on until they entered a valley from which they had little chance of escaping. Then Scindia's men attacked, killing many invaders and taking others prisoner.'

'What have you done with them?'

'The Company prisoners including Egerton and Carnac – do you really think it wise to send such old men to war? – are in the Sinhagad fortress just a few miles away. Ragoba himself is here in the dungeons – he was just a few doors away from your cell – and will soon answer to Scindia for his crimes. But I'm much more interested in you and what you can tell me. I repeat, what were you doing in Maratha territory?'

'Trying to locate Egerton's force so that I could order them to withdraw. As we both know, I was too late… What do you intend to do with me and my men?'

'That depends on you. You see I'm not sure I believe you. Why should your President Hornby despatch a force with Ragoba then change his mind? I think the Company sent you to spy on Scindia and in particular to find out how much French support he has.'

'I'm no spy.'

'I have to be sure of that.' Going to the door, de Tanguy opened it and said something to one of the soldiers posted outside who set off down the corridor – Nicholas could hear his fast receding footsteps. Then adjusting a gold-buttoned cuff, de Tanguy wandered back across the room to the window at the far end to contemplate the purpling sky in silence.

After about ten minutes the door opened. Turning his head, Nicholas saw a youngish man with thinning sandy-red hair and wearing a leather apron over breeches and a dun-coloured shirt enter. He was holding a number of long metal rods with thickly wadded ends. Behind him came two French soldiers struggling beneath the weight of a brazier of the type used in army camps to burn charcoal for light or heat. Three more followed, each carrying two large buckets of burning charcoals, hands protected from the heat by padded gloves. Once the brazier had been placed on the stone flags near the window, they tipped the charcoals in. When the brazier was full – glowing a deep, orange-red at its heart – the man in the apron plunged the metal rods in.

'Bind him and bare his back!' de Tanguy ordered. Before Nicholas, who had been watching all this with dawning comprehension, could react, one of the soldiers grabbed his arms and forced them behind his back to be tied tightly by another with cord. A third soldier bound his ankles, while a fourth ripped open the back of his shirt with a dagger.

'Monsieur Ballantyne, the brands will take some minutes to heat up. I hope that before then you and I will have concluded our conversation in a civilised way and that I won't need the services of Corporal Chapoutier here – an army blacksmith by trade but with other skills… So let's start. I ask you yet again what was the true purpose of your mission?'

'I've already told you. If you don't believe me, then you're a fool.'

'The fool is the man who suffers pain unnecessarily. While we wait for Corporal Chapoutier to tell us he is ready, I suggest you reflect on my words.'

As the temperature rose in the room Nicholas felt sweat pour from him and hoped de Tanguy – observing him closely – wouldn't take it for fear. But he was afraid. He'd been wounded in battle but the knowledge he was about to be tortured was very different. Looking down at the floor, he tried to gather his strength.

After a few minutes, de Tanguy said, 'Anything to say yet?'

'No.'

Chapoutier and de Tanguy exchanged a few words then de Tanguy ordered, 'Hold him! One on each side!' and two soldiers seized Nicholas. Chapoutier slowly approached across the room holding by its wadded end a rapier-thin rod glowing red-hot at its tip, then paused a few feet in front of him.

'Spare yourself this,' de Tanguy said. 'If you won't talk about your mission tell me something else.'

'Like what?'

'The whereabouts and strength of the force sent to Bombay from Bengal? Whether more forces are coming from Calcutta by sea? Surely you can tell me something about that?'

As Nicholas shook his head, de Tanguy gave Chapoutier a quick nod. As the two men holding him tightened their grip, Nicholas braced. Chapoutier moved behind him and for several seconds applied the glowing metal tip to his bare back just beneath his right shoulder blade. His body arched in agony, and he couldn't help crying out.

'We can stop this now. It's all up to you,' he heard de Tanguy say. 'This rod will cool in a few moments but other thicker ones are waiting. Chapoutier's already selecting one. Let's try some other questions… Tell me about the state of Bombay's defences? How many cannon are there in the castle and of what calibre?'

Biting his lip to control the pain, Nicholas again just shook his head. A few moments later, he once more felt an atrocious pain as Chapoutier seared his skin… The questions went on and on. 'What is the strength and disposition of the Company's other armies? Tell me about the defences of Calcutta and Madras. What do you know of French plans in Hindustan? The strength of our forces? The whereabouts of our fleet?' Through the haze of pain as another burning tip singed his skin Nicholas wasn't quite sure what he was hearing – his own half-suppressed cries of agony… Chapoutier's measured tread as he returned to the brazier… de Tanguy's soft but relentless voice – 'Why subject yourself to this? We already have most of the information. I just want you to confirm it… You're not betraying anyone… We can stop this as soon as you give me a sign… What man wants to smell his own flesh burning?'

Teeth clenched, he still refused to speak. Then he heard de Tanguy, for the first time sounding impatient, say, 'Chapoutier – take a fresh iron and see what happens if you apply it to his tongue rather than his back… Perhaps that will encourage him to use it!' Chapoutier seized Nicholas' hair and wrenched back his head with one hand and with the other brought the white-hot point of a brand closer and closer to his face. With a last desperate effort that took the two soldiers holding him by surprise, Nicholas flung himself sideways with such force that the stool toppled over, taking him with it. Hands grabbed him, dragging him up again, when behind him he heard the door open and a deep voice shout 'What are you doing, de Tanguy? He's my prisoner, not yours! You have no authority for this!' Then as he passed out all was darkness.

–

A bright light was trying to penetrate his eyelids. Very slowly he opened his eyes… His head felt muzzy and he was lying on his stomach, but where was he? As memories of what had happened began to return, he saw he was not back in his dark cell or in de Tanguy's apartment but in a high-ceilinged room with pale muslin hangings stirring in the breeze blowing through an open casement. As he tried to raise himself, a stab of pain shot across his back and he heard a voice say, 'Lie still and drink this.' A neatly turbaned man in dark clothing and wearing spectacles bent over him and held a brass bowl to his lips – 'I am a *hakim*, this is opium dissolved in rose water. It will ease the pain. I have applied a balm of oil, camphor and sandalwood to the burns and blisters on your back and bandaged you. But now it is time for me to change the dressings again, so please lie still.'

It was two days before the *hakim* – very stern in his instructions to Nicholas – would allow him to get up and dress in the loose cotton tunic and trousers he had brought for him. His back still felt stiff and raw but he was now trying not to drink too much of the opium infusion. Though it helped the pain, it clouded his mind just at a time when he needed to be able to think. There were so many unanswered questions… Who had stopped his torture? Where were Tuhin Singh and the others and had any been subjected to the same maltreatment? What was happening to Egerton and Carnac and their men? What a mess it all was, he thought. Bombay was in imminent danger of attack and there was nothing he could do about it. Whatever way he tried to look at what had happened, he had failed… In all his past adventurings with Clive and Tuhin Singh things had always worked out in the end. But they'd been young, so full of confidence…

As more time passed, broken only by visits from the *hakim* and servants bringing food, and with his wounds fast healing, Nicholas' frustration mounted. The door to his room was firmly locked and on the rare occasions it opened he saw two well-armed Marathas guarding it. The window was at least thirty feet above the ground, the walls beneath falling smooth and sheer to the courtyard below. He tried to distract himself by reading a book of Marathi verse he had found lying on a table – though he spoke Marathi, deciphering the intricate script was another matter. On the seventh evening, as he sat reading, he heard the door open but didn't look round.

'Nicholas Ballantyne?' a voice said. Turning, he saw an imposing man dressed in saffron yellow.

Getting to his feet, he replied, 'Yes. Who are you?'

The man gave half a smile. 'You are one of the very few in Poona not to know that – I am Mahadji Scindia.'

So this was the Maratha leader who had made such short work of Ragoba and Egerton! He looked to be in his mid-forties, powerfully built, with thick moustaches and a thin white scar running across his left cheek and into his upper lip. From the steel-link belt around his waist hung a broad-bladed scimitar with a diamond and emerald hilt. Scindia seated himself on a chair and after hesitating a moment Nicholas sat down again and waited to see what his visitor had come to say.

'What were you reading?'

'Some poetry by Tukaram.'

Scindia's brow arched. 'Remarkable. Few of you foreigners bother to learn our languages. My French advisers certainly don't and I thought the same was true of you British.'

'It usually is.'

'I have something important to say to you. First, that I regret the way you were treated. Sometimes in war such methods are necessary but on this occasion one of my French allies over estimating – as they sometimes do – his authority and importance did not consult me. As soon as I was told what was happening I stopped it and sent one of my own *hakims* to attend you. He tells me you are recovering well.'

What did Scindia expect, his gratitude? Nicholas replied, 'I'm anxious about my men. Where are they and are they unharmed?'

'Yes. I had them removed from the cells and given more comfortable lodgings here in the fortress. Egerton, Carnac and their men are confined in another of my strongholds not far from here – under guard but also well-treated. It is partly on account of all these Company prisoners that I have come to see you. Their fate may depend on you. I understand that you are an envoy from Governor-General Hastings and also that you have a reputation among some of my fellow Hindustani rulers for plain speaking.'

Was this another attempt to get information out of him? Nicholas wondered – a cool, soft-tongued approach after the torturer's hot irons? 'I hope I am a plain speaker but as Hastings' envoy I have allegiances… If you have the same questions as de Tanguy, let me tell you now that I can't and won't answer—'

'No, no. You entirely misunderstand me. What I have to say goes beyond short-term military considerations and certainly does not concern the extraction of information. It is a matter of some delicacy… I would not wish the other Maratha leaders to know of this conversation and certainly not my self-important French advisers for reasons that will soon become clear. What I have to say is for your and Hastings' ears only and it is this… Though many of the Maratha confederacy want to drive the British back into the sea from whence they came – together with all foreign invaders from the Moghuls onward – I have started to wonder whether the Company might not at least in the interim prove a good ally. We Marathas have many enemies in Hindustan – some of them also the Company's enemies. Why should we dissipate our strength and energy confronting each other when for the present we could make common cause? President Hornby in Bombay may have been thinking along similar lines when he decided to support Ragoba. The fact that he backed the wrong man does not mean my basic suggestion is wrong.'

'What exactly are you saying?'

'That now I have demonstrated my power by defeating Ragoba and the Company army, I am a rising power among the Marathas. I believe – in fact I am certain – that very soon I will be proclaimed the paramount leader. As such it is surely in Hastings' interests to make a friend of me rather than an enemy.'

'You mean an alliance of some sort?'

'No, not yet at least. Perhaps Hastings and I could agree to co-exist for the present, even to guard each other's backs.'

'I've known Hastings for many years. He will certainly listen but he will also want proof you mean what you say and that this isn't just a delaying tactic while you increase your military strength.'

'Don't believe I don't have good sources in the Company – surprising ones you might think, if I named them – which of course I won't. Through them I know of your unique position beginning with your mission to Mir Jafar before Plassey and now your closeness to Hastings individually, while retaining your distance from the squabbling Company hierarchy and politics. Of course I know Hastings will require some tangible sign of my good faith. To show I am in earnest, I will release you and your men. I will also allow Egerton, Carnac and their men to return to Bombay and undertake not to attack your settlement there unless the Company give me new cause. I can put nothing in writing in case any such letter was used against me but I will trust you to be my messenger, if you are willing. Will you do it?'

'Yes. I would be happy to report to Hastings what you have said. It will be for him to decide how the Company responds.'

'Of course, but I've heard he's a pragmatic man, just as I am…'

'And your French advisers?'

'As soon as I am assured the Company has no hostile intentions towards me, I will distance myself from them and of course not allow myself to be influenced by them. Thereafter – and depending on how our own relations progress – I will slowly dispense with them. Their greatest and almost sole benefit to me has been in the supply of modern weapons of which I now have sufficient.'

'In that case, I would like to leave with my men as soon as possible.'

'Certainly. You may depart tomorrow. I will supply you with fresh horses and an escort to the borders of the Maratha territories. The rest of the Company prisoners will follow in subsequent days once I have made arrangements – some are wounded and will need to be transported in wagons.'

–

Next day, reunited with Tuhin Singh, Vikram Das, Anil Roy, *Risaldar* Kumar and the rest of his men – Scindia had been telling the truth, none had been harmed – Nicholas could scarcely believe the change in the fortune of his mission. He apologised at once to Tuhin Singh for ignoring his warning about travelling in daytime. 'You were right and I was wrong – in fact I was a fool!'

'It proves you're only human like everyone else – as I believe you once told me triumphant Roman Emperors needed to be reminded,' Tuhin Singh replied with a wry smile.

Riding back towards the Maratha border, Nicholas wondered about Mahadji Scindia. Would he really prove a man with whom the Company could do business? Instinct told him he might well be, though it was possible he was engaged in some deeper game, playing the Europeans off against each other. Even now he might be putting out further feelers to King Louis of France… But for the moment just to feel the breeze on his face and have his liberty again was enough to restore his spirits.

Reaching Bombay three days later, Nicholas at once went to Hornby, taking *Risaldar* Kumar to recount the story of the Company army's defeat. Shocked and chastened, the president immediately ordered further strengthening of the settlement's defences including mounting more cannon on the walls, doubling the watch and having rows of wide pits, lined with sharpened wooden spikes and then concealed beneath a thatch of leaves, dug to frustrate attack from the landward side.

In any case, as Nicholas was glad to discover, during his absence Goddard had managed to march his advance party all the way to the coast, covering the last three hundred miles through difficult mountainous territory in just seventeen days. Bombay – and the settlement of Surat further up the coast – were already far better defended than they had been and soon the rest of Goddard's men would arrive, as would further troops sent by Hastings by sea. Had Scindia already known some of this when he made his magnanimous pledge not to attack Bombay, Nicholas wondered. Perhaps. By his own admission he was a pragmatist – just like Hastings!

14 – *Pistols at Dawn*

As he and Tuhin Singh stepped from the wobbling gangplank of the budgerow that had brought passengers from the newly arrived *Bengal Queen* to the quayside in Calcutta, Nicholas said to his friend, 'Won't you come with me to the Grangers? Lucia and Lizzie will be disappointed if you don't.'

Tuhin Singh shook his head. 'No. I don't want to get in the way of family reunions. I'll take a tonga to Mohammed Aziz's and come to the house tomorrow.'

'Be sure you do!'

Twenty minutes later Nicholas' own tonga drew up outside the Grangers' mansion, the doors opened and servants hurried out to take his bags. Lucia, who must have heard the commotion, appeared in the doorway and within moments was in his arms. 'From your last message we'd expected you days ago… I was worried something had happened!'

Nicholas bent and kissed her lips. 'Our ship was delayed. We hit bad weather rounding Cape Cormorin.'

'These long absences… they don't get any easier… Come inside – I want to know everything.'

As Nicholas followed Lucia into the large hall with its white and black marble flooring and classical busts on plinths – Joss was an enthusiastic admirer of ancient Rome – Lizzie emerged from the drawing room. As Nicholas hugged her, another figure appeared – his cousin. 'I'm glad you've returned safely,' Charles said. 'Since Hastings recalled me once more from Madras – he's appointed me to the Revenue Board – he's done nothing but sing your praises about your mission to Bombay.'

'You can talk about all that later,' Lucia said firmly. 'I want my husband to myself after so many months. We'll all meet again at dinner.' To Nicholas she said, 'Come to our rooms, *caro*, and I'll ask the servants to bring you some tea...'

As soon as they were alone, Nicholas took her face in his hands and gave her a kiss very different from the decorous peck in front of the servants outside the house. 'This is what I want... not tea! I've thought of you every day... You were right when you said absence doesn't get easier...'

As they began to make love, Lucia exclaimed in horror at the livid burn scars on his back. 'I knew you were hiding something in your letters... What happened? Who did this?'

He stopped her questions. 'Hush... It looks worse than it was. I came back to you just as I promised, didn't I?'

Later as they lay still entwined, Nicholas told her everything including about de Tanguy and Chapoutier's torture and how Scindia had intervened. When he had finished, she asked no more questions but gently stroked his cheek. After a while she said, 'You know that I think Hastings uses you – I don't mean that he doesn't value you, clearly he does... but like so many so-called "great men" he can be thoughtless. Well, his baroness certainly thinks so too. While you were away, she called several times. I was surprised – but I realised, as I think she does, that we have something in common. We're both outsiders, she a French woman, me a Venetian. Neither of us accepted by nor comfortable among the British matrons here who openly disparage foreigners and give themselves unmerited airs... Marian told me her defence is to rouse their envy with ever finer gems and opulent clothes... But beneath all that dazzle she's a shrewd judge of character. She loves her husband but knows his faults. She told me she's warned him several times neither to take you for granted nor to ignore your advice as he did over the Rohillas.'

'And what did you tell her about me?' Nicholas smiled as he tried to imagine the conversation.

'That you don't regard the missions Hastings asks you to undertake as a burden so long as you see sense in them... that you thrive on an element of risk… Tuhin Singh as well… Sometimes you're like schoolboys.' But then, disentangling herself from Nicholas, Lucia sat up, clasping her arms around her bare legs. 'What I didn't tell her was that I don't want these adventurings of yours to go on forever. You're not growing any younger, *caro*. The quiet life we thought we'd have when we built Glenmire – it's never lasted very long, has it?'

'I know. I promise you one day soon we will go home and we will stay there. I'll play my violin, read and perhaps write a few memoirs. You'll paint and sketch and star gaze. We'll grow old together in the peace of the mountains…'

'But when?'

'Soon, but not quite yet… The Maratha threat has receded, but I know from letters from Hastings that reached me in Bombay that other dangers are increasing. The French are redoubling their efforts to stir up trouble wherever and whenever they can… Until Britain's war with France ends – or we expel the French from Hindustan for good this time – the situation will remain precarious and the Company needs to act decisively.'

'And you wish to be involved?'

'Yes… I feel I must – unless you are set against it.'

'As I've told you before, I'd never stop you. I can be patient a little longer.' Lucia lay back again and smiled somewhat wistfully. 'In any case Lizzie enjoys life here in Calcutta. She's certainly in no hurry to go back to Glenmire, which reminds me… There's something you should know.'

'What?'

'About your cousin, Charles. He called here almost as soon as he arrived back in Calcutta and has been here many times since…'

'I assume to see Lizzie?'

'Yes. From something Charles said, I realised they'd been writing to each other while he was in Madras. Martha thinks it's only a matter of time before he proposes, but you know what she's like – she sees romance and wedding bells everywhere…'

Nicholas frowned. 'How do you feel about this? You disliked Charles from the moment he turned up at Glenmire.'

'I did but I know that when you travelled together to Delhi, even though you'd argued with him about the famine, you started to see some good in him… He's still too reserved for my tastes – perhaps it's my Italian nature – but it's not my feelings that matter, only Lizzie's.'

'Has she said anything to you?'

'No. I can see that she likes him, but Charles is not the only young man to call. Martha says Lizzie seldom lacks partners at the balls and dances she takes her to.'

'All we can do is wait – see whether their relationship grows and – if it does and Charles proposes, trust Lizzie's judgment as to whether she wants him. I can't doubt he'd make a satisfactory husband – better a man who's a bit stolid than one of the wild young rakes Calcutta has aplenty.'

'I suppose you're right but I sometimes think how strangely things work out. James is very like you. He always has been, ever since I first met him when he was what? About six? But our two children are quite different from us – Will so immersed in his studies at St Andrews that – as far as I can tell from his letters – little interests him beyond them… Lizzie equally absorbed in parties, picnics, new pelisses and all the gaieties Calcutta can offer. They both seem content with more conventional lives than either of us has led, either by choice or by fate… But there's no harm in that, is there?'

'Of course not – so long as they're as happy as we are and always have been.' Leaning over, Nicholas kissed Lucia again, then drew her back into his arms.

-

Over the days that followed Hastings invited Nicholas quite frequently to Government House, often just to vent his frustrations. Though Clavering's recent death, a few months after Monson's, had removed another critic from his council, Francis, often backed by Wheler, was continuing to block him at every turn. 'Again and again I've tried to convince him that in this crisis for the Company in Hindustan we must put personal animosities aside but he refuses to listen… How can I govern properly when I have to waste so much of my time dealing with his tantrums? To top it all, the intelligence reports coming in are either confused or contradictory, often both! All I can be sure of is that the French authorities are pouring ever more troops, equipment and money into Hindustan in particular in support of Hyder Ali of Mysore – I wish I knew precisely what he's up to…'

–

Hastings soon had his answer. Returning from his customary early morning ride along the Hooghly, Nicholas found a message from Hastings asking him to come at once. Looking as if he'd dressed hurriedly – unusually for him his neck cloth was awry – Hastings was waiting, pacing the terrace of Government House clutching what looked like an official despatch. Seeing Nicholas approach, he hurried towards him, flourishing it. 'This has just come from Madras. Hyder Ali has marched eighty thousand men – apparently trained by French officers and including some French troops – all the way to the coast south of Madras, ravaging and burning everything in his path. Even worse, at Pollilur a force of Hyder Ali's cavalry – led by his son, Tipu Sultan, and supported by some of those rocket units of his – overwhelmed a column of Company soldiers commanded by Colonel William Baillie sent from Madras to confront them. The Mysoreans killed over two thousand of our men including two thirds of the officers and carried off a large number of prisoners – Baillie included – to Hyder Ali's stronghold of Seringapatam. The few Company soldiers who could fled, abandoning their guns and equipment.'

Nicholas struggled to take in what he had just heard. If the report was accurate, this was the most devastating military defeat Company forces had ever suffered – worse even than Mahadji Scindia's victory over Egerton. 'What d'you think Hyder Ali will do next? Attack Madras itself?'

'Probably, and I doubt he'll waste much time. The French admirals have despatched a fleet from Mauritius in his support, presumably to blockade Madras. And if Madras falls, Calcutta will be next… You and I remember what happened when Siraj-ud-daulah – also with French help – captured Calcutta. But that was different – then we could call on support from elsewhere in Hindustan… It's not like that now… We can't rely on the Company in Bombay for help. As you know only too well, with the Marathas on their doorstep they've their own problems… The Company's position is like a house of cards – one puff of wind and everything will come tumbling down…'

'You're being over pessimistic. We still have Hindustani allies in the south like the Nawab of the Carnatic and the Raja of Tanjore – friends for many years who would far rather deal with the Company for all its faults than Hyder Ali and the French…'

'Would they? Some might prefer short-term gain to long-term advantage. I've evidence French agents are doing their damndest to bribe several of our allies to change their allegiance. Only a week ago the Rana of Venkat showed me a letter promising him money and increased territory to break his treaty with us. I begin to fear we could be driven out of Hindustan completely… Despite all my efforts I will become the scapegoat, the target of unmerited odium, unable to hold up my head either in Britain or Hindustan.'

By this time Hastings' composure had all but deserted him. His voice had risen and he was waving his hands in agitation. For a moment he reminded Nicholas of Clive in a similar crisis when, seeing no way forward, he too had despaired – almost suicidally. Yet once Nicholas had persuaded him to calm down they'd agreed a plan which had led to the victory of Arcot that had secured Clive's military reputation as – in Prime Minister Pitt's words – 'a heaven-sent general'. Solutions could usually be found if only one kept a cool head.

Picking his words carefully Nicholas said, 'You're shocked by the news about Pollilur. So am I… A terrible defeat… unprecedented… there's no getting away from that. But the Company still has weapons in its armoury, actual and figurative. You need to decide how best to use them. If you think Madras will be the first place Hyder Ali will attack, perhaps that's where you should concentrate your effort. But whatever you decide, the one thing you mustn't do – either within or outside the Company – is to allow people to suspect you've lost confidence.'

Hastings gave him a thin smile. 'You're right, of course. Marian's away visiting friends at Chinsura but if she'd been here I know she'd have said something similar… *Nil desperandum!* It's my tactics not my strategy that must change. Let's go to my study and consider our options. If we can put together something concrete enough, I'll call a council meeting for tomorrow.' As they walked back to the house he added, 'By the way, you'll meet an old acquaintance there, Eyre Coote, if you've not run into him already since you got back. He's just returned to Hindustan as commander-in-chief of all Company forces.'

–

Next morning after little sleep – he and Hastings had spent the rest of the day and evening until nearly midnight considering strategies, consulting maps and calculating logistics, pausing only briefly to eat the food brought to them – and hoping he didn't look as tired as he felt, Nicholas entered the council chamber. Hastings, by contrast, looked infused with new life, neatly dressed – no dishevelled neck cloth now – and calm as he sorted through his papers. Only a slight purpling beneath the eyes as he looked up to nod at Nicholas betrayed his lack of sleep. To Francis, Wheler and Barwell, like him already seated at the table, Hastings said, 'As on some other occasions, I've asked Ballantyne to join us. We may need his expertise again, just as we did with the Bombay business. As soon as Eyre Coote gets here we can begin.'

As if Hastings' words had conjured him, Nicholas heard a loud tread outside and Lieutenant-General Eyre Coote entered. 'Morning,' he said gruffly to Hastings and the other councillors, but seeing Nicholas seated on Hastings' right, he started. 'Great God, is that you, Ballantyne? I thought you'd disappeared up some mountain to become a hermit…' Before Nicholas could reply, Eyre Coote sat heavily down and without drawing breath addressed Hastings, 'Well, let's get on with it! From everything I hear Pollilur was a complete fiasco…!'

Nicholas smiled to himself. Eyre Coote was just as querulous and direct as he remembered from Plassey. Hastings also understood Eyre Coote's peppery personality and allowed him to finish before turning the discussion to the business in hand. 'Pollilur *was* a shambles, both literally and metaphorically – and a serious blow to our prestige. But it happened. It's in the past. We must move on. What matters now is we act decisively to restore the Company's position and our reputation.'

'And how do you suggest we do that?' Francis asked.

'Hear me out, if you would. It's obvious Hyder Ali's objective is Madras – Pollilur will have given him confidence. He may not even wait for the French fleet we believe's coming from Mauritius. Our priority must be to act immediately to defend Madras.'

'No! Our priority – as always – must be to protect Calcutta, the Company's foremost possession… the jewel in the crown. Thanks to you we've already dangerously compromised our defences here by sending Leslie's force to Bombay and yet more soldiers by sea. You know I still believe that was a dangerous error of judgment!' Francis said.

Before Hastings could reply, Eyre Coote cut in, glaring across the table at Francis, sitting opposite. 'What do you know about such things, Francis? You're a civilian! I very much doubt you've ever shot anything larger than a pheasant. The Company has put me – not you – in charge of our armies in Hindustan and I'll thank you to let me take the lead on military matters!'

Francis gave Eyre Coote what he doubtless thought was a withering look, but Coote continued unperturbed, 'I've only been back in Calcutta a short while but I've already been reviewing our troop dispositions. What I've seen so far – and what Hastings tells me about the political situation – convinces me that as he proposes we despatch a large force south as soon as we can make the arrangements. If we do nothing we'll look spineless and craven, not only to Hyder Ali and the French but to all the other on-looking Hindustani rulers, uncertain which way to jump. Acts that proclaim confidence and determination are the only way to overcome danger. Everything else is defeatism!'

As Coote continued to press for military action, Nicholas realised some of his arguments resembled his own to Hastings the previous evening. Taken aback by Coote's verbal onslaught, Francis said little more, Wheler even less – not that it was easy for anyone to interrupt Eyre Coote in full flow.

'Well, gentlemen, shall we take a vote?' Hastings asked when Eyre Coote finally finished.

'This is not a decision to be rushed. I think we need more time to consider,' Francis said, avoiding Coote's eye.

'Time is precisely what we don't have...' Hastings began, then continued more emolliently, 'But very well. After all, Eyre Coote needs to consider the detailed implementation of his strategy – I suggest we meet again tomorrow. Does that give you time enough, General?'

'Ample!'

Back in his study with Nicholas, some of Hastings' apparent ebullience left him. He looked drained as he poured them both a midday glass of sherry. 'Well that didn't go too badly. I think I'll win the vote when it comes. Eyre Coote's a pretty irresistible force – though an annoyingly provocative one if not on your side...'

'You talked to him before the meeting, didn't you?'

'Of course! I had breakfast with him.' An almost schoolboy grin lit Hastings' tired face. 'I'd have been a fool not to get him on board.'

In fact, matters went even more smoothly than Hastings anticipated. To his surprise Francis and Wheler told him privately they would, after all, support an expedition south, so with council members unanimous there was no need for a vote. 'For once, the Court of Directors will see that we can act together and perhaps stop their carping and give me the support I need,' Hastings told Nicholas with evident satisfaction.

With Hastings busy on so many fronts, Nicholas saw relatively little of him in the next few days until one evening, while he was practising some Mozart pieces on his violin, a messenger arrived to ask him to come to Government House urgently. Entering Hastings' study half an hour later Nicholas saw him sprinkling sand to soak up surplus ink on a letter he had clearly just written. His expression was so grim that Nicholas wondered whether it was his resignation. He waited in silence while Hastings warmed a stick of red sealing wax over a candle flame then sealed the letter. When he'd finished, he handed it to Nicholas. 'If anything happens to me, will you see Marian gets this, please?'

'Of course. But what is all this? What could possibly be going to happen to you?'

'It's Philip Francis. He's pushed my patience too far this time. Despite promising to support sending troops to Madras, today at a council meeting he announced he'd changed his mind and that he had written an open letter to the Court of Directors in London accusing me of corruption, incompetence and goodness knows what else. He's launching a naked attempt to undermine me and grab my power for himself. But if he thinks he's going to get me to resign or rush to London to plead my case he's mistaken his man.'

'So what will you do?'

'I've already done it! I've circulated a public minute denouncing Francis as the liar and charlatan that he is. Look, here's a copy.'

As Nicholas read, some sentences in particular leapt out:

> *...In truth, I do not trust to Mr Francis's promise of candour, convinced that he is incapable of it, and that his sole purpose and wish are to embarrass and defeat every measure which I may undertake, or which may tend even to promote the public interest, if my credit is connected with them. Such has been the tendency and such the manifest spirit of all his actions from the beginning... I judge of his*

public conduct by my experience of his private, which I have found to be void of truth and honour.

For a moment Nicholas thought of Francis's scandalous seduction of the youthful Mrs Grand still ensconced by him as his mistress in a love nest up the Hooghly. Hastings' note continued in similar vein:

> *This is a severe charge against Mr Francis, but temperately and deliberately made from the firm persuasion that I owe this justice to the public and to myself as the only redress to both, for artifices of which I have been a victim… The only redress for a fraud for which the law has made no provision is the exposure of it…*

'I wanted to provoke him and I succeeded. Here's what he sent me this evening.'

As he took Francis' note from Hastings, Nicholas already knew what it contained – No man could tolerate such damning and public slurs on his reputation without seeking redress. It read:

> *Hastings,*
>
> *The dishonour you publicly inflicted on me earlier today has left me no alternative but to demand personal satisfaction of you for the affront you have offered me. Name your place, time and choice of weapon.*

'Nicholas, I've accepted his challenge. We meet in two days' time at five thirty a.m. in the grounds of the Belvedere, my house at Alipur – and we fight with pistols. Of course Francis and I must keep it all very quiet – you know the Company's views on duelling and that it's illegal. As well as the letter to Marian, who I am very glad to say is still away and knows nothing of this, I've written my will and a summary of government business for whoever succeeds me if I die. If I *am* killed, I at least have the satisfaction of knowing Francis can never be my successor – how could he be made governor-general after killing the previous one? I am locking those documents in my desk. If anything happens to me, tell my secretary where to find them. But the real reason I wanted to see you was to ask you to be my second.'

'You know I will… though I wish it hadn't come to this.'

'No. I'm glad it has. It will end my dispute with that blaggard once and for all.'

'Have you fought a duel before?'

'No – but neither, I suspect, has he!'

After promising Hastings he would do everything a second should, including calling on Francis' second, Colonel Watson, Fort William's chief engineer, Nicholas walked slowly back to the Grangers' house. Hastings had no idea how it felt to fight a duel… How long was it since he himself had fought his one and only duel on the beach near Madras with Clive as his second? About thirty years. Even so, he'd never forgotten his opponent, George Braddock, who had fired prematurely and missed, standing shivering with fear before him. He had fired his own pistol into the ground and just walked away. 'That was generous of you. I only hope it wasn't a mistake. Debts of gratitude don't always sit well with the likes of him. You should have killed him,' Clive had said. As things later turned out, Clive had probably been right…

–

Hastings and Nicholas spent the night before the duel at the Belvedere. The house, with wide terraces and high arched windows, had been a gift to Hastings from Mir Jafar, Nawab of Bengal. Finding it almost impossible to sleep himself, Nicholas wondered how Hastings was faring. At 4.30 a.m. when the *khutmagar* – butler – tapped on his door to rouse him he was already up and dressed. Going downstairs, he found Hastings on the terrace where breakfast had been laid, cup of coffee in hand and watching the pale apricot glow as the sun came up. He looked the image of tranquillity as if duelling was a daily occurrence.

'I've told the servants to leave us in peace. Help yourself to coffee.' Hastings gestured to a full-bellied silver pot on a table. 'I've just been wondering whether Francis will actually come… I wouldn't put it past him to play sick.'

'No. He'll come. If he doesn't, after what passed between you he'd have to leave Calcutta for good…'

Nicholas was proved right. At about 5.15 a.m. they heard the thud of hooves as Francis and Colonel Watson cantered up the drive. When they had dismounted and handed their reins to two grooms, the *khutmagar* led them over. Nicholas and Watson shook hands but Hastings and Francis merely exchanged nods. Then Hastings said, 'Well, there's no point waiting. The spot I've chosen is over there near those neem trees, unless you've any objection, Francis?'

After they'd walked over and inspected it Watson said to Francis, 'I see no problem, do you?' Francis shook his head. Moving out of earshot of their principals, Nicholas and Watson checked the pair of duelling pistols the colonel had procured for the occasion. 'God help Francis,' Watson muttered. 'He's never fired a pistol before… I was giving him lessons till midnight last night.' Glancing over at Francis, who had already removed his coat, Nicholas saw how pale he looked. Once Watson and Nicholas were satisfied the pistols were functioning properly and each had primed and loaded one of them, Watson replaced them in their mahogany case. Walking across to Hastings he gave him – as customary for the man who had been challenged – first choice. Then he took the other pistol to Francis who picked it up a little gingerly.

'Gentlemen,' Watson said in his loud, deep voice, 'Ballantyne and I will now measure and mark the fourteen paces you must maintain between you.' Carefully calculating the distance along a north–south axis so neither duellist would have the disadvantage of the sun in his eyes, Nicholas and Watson stuck their swords in the ground as markers. Then Watson said, 'Hastings, you may select your end.'

As Hastings took up his chosen position to the north, Nicholas gave him an encouraging nod. When Francis too was in place, Nicholas standing to one side with Watson called out, 'Gentlemen. You see this white handkerchief in my hand? When I let it drop you may fire.'

It was still so early that all was very quiet except for the distant barking of a dog and the squawking of a flock of white parakeets that must have been roosting in the neem trees but chose this moment to take flight. With the eyes of both adversaries fixed on him, Nicholas waited for the raucous noise to die away. Feeling his heart beating faster, he raised his right hand with the handkerchief. Then he let it fall.

Francis, hand shaking wildly, squeezed the trigger. His pistol misfired. Hastings just stood there. Why hadn't he fired at the same moment, Nicholas wondered. And why in God's name didn't he fire now, as he had every right to? Watson, looking as puzzled as Nicholas, took Francis' weapon from him, reprimed and reloaded it. And so it began again. Nicholas once more raised his arm and dropped the handkerchief. Now sweating visibly, Francis took aim. For a second time his pistol misfired. The powder must be damp, thought Nicholas, hoping the same wasn't also true of Hastings' powder, though the two pistols had been primed from different cartridges. To his astonishment Hastings remained standing motionless. Shaking his head, Watson took powder from a fresh cartridge and again primed Francis' pistol. For the third time the two men confronted one another. A crack split the air as this time Francis succeeded in discharging his weapon. Hastings – seemingly finally galvanised into action – fired at almost exactly the same moment. Francis screamed. Then, the shoulder of his white shirt crimsoning with blood, he collapsed to the ground crying, 'I'm dead!'

Nicholas, who had seen many men wounded on the battlefield, somehow doubted it. To his practised eye, Francis had merely been winged in the right shoulder – serious enough, but unlikely to be fatal if treated properly and promptly. However, ashen-faced but uninjured – Francis' ball had missed – Hastings dropped his pistol, ran to his adversary, knelt beside him and said, 'Good God, I hope not. Do not say so!'

Francis extended his left hand and said weakly, 'Take it, Hastings, please. I offer it in friendship and farewell.' And Hastings did.

After a quick word with Watson, Nicholas leant over them both and said bracingly, 'From what I can see, it's only your shoulder, Francis. The ball needs to be taken out and the wound cleaned. Servants will carry you into the house and Watson will stay with you while Hastings and I ride back to Calcutta to fetch a doctor.'

'I'll send you my personal physician, Francis. He's a good man, I promise,' Hastings said, a little colour returning to his face. Francis lay back, closed his eyes and said nothing more.

As they waited for their horses to be saddled and brought round from the stables, Nicholas dug in his pocket for Hastings' farewell letter addressed to 'My Beloved Marian' and handed it to him. 'You'd better have this back. I'm very glad it's not needed.'

'I'll still tell her about it, though. If not, she'll only find out anyway and be even angrier with me...'

'Hastings, what possessed you to just stand there at first and not fire back?'

'I don't know... until he finally fired I felt as if in some kind of trance... as if what was happening wasn't real... What I do know is that I'm heartily glad it's all over. Look, here come the horses. We must ride as fast as we can for Calcutta and the surgeon!'

15 – Delicate Negotiations

'So we are agreed! We'll at once requisition as many ships as necessary – trade for once must wait – to transport Eyre Coote and the four thousand troops he has asked for to Madras with a further five thousand men under Colonel Pearse to follow overland?' Hastings looked around at his fellow council members. A pale, subdued-looking Francis nodded, as did Wheler and Barwell. 'Excellent. Now, Coote, perhaps you'd be so good as to outline your plans to the council, as you have to me.'

Watching from his place beside Hastings, Nicholas wondered how much the others knew – or had deduced – about the duel just five days before. It was too succulent a piece of gossip to suppress in a place like Calcutta. Doubtless Janus would quip about it in the poison pages of *The Calcutta Spy*. As for the apparently chastened Francis, once his wound healed – the ball had chipped his collarbone but as Nicholas had thought it wasn't serious – and memories of his reconciliation with Hastings faded, would his grievances resurface? But for the moment he would have to allow Hastings and Coote their heads over Hyder Ali which, given the present perilous situation, was fortunate.

'I've already started selecting troops and suitable artillery but it will take time,' Eyre Coote was saying.

'How long do you need, General?' Barwell asked.

'Four to six weeks… I can't be certain yet. A new regiment from Britain – mostly Highlanders – is expected here within the month. If it does arrive that will help, but Hyder Ali's hardly going to wait for our convenience…! If the reports are true, all that's apparently holding him back from attacking Madras immediately is an attempt to form an alliance with the Marathas to protect his flanks and rear. It seems he doesn't trust them not to invade Mysore while he's away fighting elsewhere. Of course, his negotiations may not succeed. It's not as if they're natural allies. The Marathas distrust Hyder Ali's territorial ambitions while he sees them as volatile, unpredictable raiders, every bit as expansionist as himself.'

'Do we know which Maratha leaders Hyder Ali has approached?' Nicholas asked.

'I understand what you're getting at,' Hastings answered. 'As we know to our cost, the Maratha Confederacy can be like a multi-headed hydra. So many contending factions make it impossible to know whom to deal with. But from everything we hear, Mahadji Scindia's star has continued to rise following his humiliation of the Company and capture of Ragoba. A large number of Maratha chiefs have accepted him as paramount leader and sworn allegiance to him.'

'So if Hyder Ali's chasing a deal with the Marathas it's likely to be with Scindia. Is that what you're saying, Hastings?' Francis asked as he shifted a little in his chair in apparent discomfort and took a sip from a glass of cloudy liquid. Nicholas guessed it contained pain-dulling laudanum.

'Yes – after all, what would be the point of Hyder Ali approaching any other chief?' Hastings replied.

'And that could be to our advantage,' Nicholas cut in. Though he had reported everything that had passed between himself and Scindia to Hastings, he wasn't sure how much Hastings had told his council so he picked his words carefully. 'When I was held captive in Poona, Scindia himself intervened to stop my interrogation and torture. Later he made a point of coming to see me. He told me he believed he would soon be paramount leader of the Marathas but – more importantly – hinted that one day it might be in both the Marathas' and the Company's interests to reach an accommodation.'

'A treaty, you mean?' Francis asked.

'No, not so specific – more an informal understanding. Translated, the phrase he used was something like "mutually beneficial co-existence".'

'Did he, by God! He's confident enough of himself, this Scindia. But I don't follow his reasoning,' Wheler said, leaning forward to take a pinch of snuff from his wrist, then giving a little sneeze. 'Are you sure he wasn't just playing you along?'

'His basic argument was that since the Company and the Marathas share a number of common enemies it makes more sense – for the present at least – for them to tolerate rather than fight each other. As a token of his good faith he promised to release me and the other Company prisoners and pull back from Bombay. He honoured those promises.'

'Poppycock! He didn't attack Bombay because he knew we'd just reinforced it and he'd be beaten!' Francis said testily.

'Perhaps, but he also promised to get rid of his French advisers—'

'Which he mostly has, from what I've heard!' Eyre Coote put in. 'Though a fat lot of good that's done us, Ballantyne. Some of his erstwhile French artillery experts are now advising Hyder Ali in Mysore.'

'But all this does show he was serious,' Nicholas persisted.

'So what are you suggesting?' Hastings asked.

'That we beat Hyder Ali at his own game – if we can, strike a deal with the Marathas before he does.'

'But that means trusting Scindia – a man who slaughtered hundreds of our soldiers,' Francis objected.

'If Mahadji Scindia himself was here, I think he'd say he was defending Maratha territory against an unwanted incursion by an alien power seeking to install their own candidate as leader of the Marathas – a candidate most Marathas didn't want. It's all a matter of perception,' Nicholas replied, trying not to think of the young ensign's maggoty corpse lying on the battlefield. 'Now, having demonstrated his strength to the Company and established his reputation among his own people, it's possible Scindia's perception of things has moved on. He may genuinely believe it's not in the best interests of the Marathas to fight the Company – at least not at present – and that could buy us a breathing space. Perhaps I'm wrong, but I'm willing to go and find out from him.'

The ensuing silence showed Nicholas he'd taken the others by surprise, just as he'd surprised himself. Hastings and Eyre Coote were looking thoughtful. Francis was frowning. Wheler's eyes were fixed on Francis. Barwell pushed back his chair, put his hands behind his head and stared up at the *punkah* swinging slowly back and forth above their heads.

'Well, where's the harm in trying?' Hastings said at last. 'The Marathas have fought against Hyder Ali at least as often as they've fought against us – why shouldn't Scindia prefer us as an ally of convenience? At least he knows we're not after territory for ourselves.'

'I agree. But Ballantyne will have to get a move on if his scheme's going to work,' Eyre Coote said.

'What do you think?' Hastings asked the others.

'As you say, what do we have to lose, though personally I doubt much will come of it and – even if it does – we shouldn't take Scindia's promises at face value,' Francis said. Wheler and Barwell nodded agreement.

'Good!' Hastings turned to Coote. 'You're right that Ballantyne will need to be quick if this is to work. What do we know about Scindia's whereabouts?'

'The last news from army scouts – they've been tracking him since he left Poona several weeks ago – is that he's moving with a large force south-east along the Bhima River.'

'Towards Mysore, then?'

'Exactly. That's what confirmed my belief he's agreed to meet Hyder Ali or perhaps his son, Tipu Sultan, somewhere near the Mysorean borders. But from what I also hear, Scindia doesn't appear to be in any hurry.'

Nicholas thought quickly. 'If Scindia is advancing down the Bhima that puts him at least eight hundred miles from here. Finding him could take me some weeks… It'll depend on the terrain, how easy it is to get fresh horses and of course how quickly I can actually locate him… But I'll do my best.'

'We'll give you whatever resources you ask for – an escort, good horses, plenty of money to buy fresh ones,' Hastings said. 'And I should add that you go with the council's thanks.'

Eyre Coote nodded. 'Good luck, Ballantyne… You'll probably need it!'

Preoccupied with everything he needed to organise before he could leave, as he made his way back to the Grangers', Nicholas nearly collided with a palanquin. Its skilful bearers managed to swerve out of his way but for some moments the palanquin resting on their shoulders swayed precariously. The curtains parted and its elderly male occupant peered dyspeptically out. Nicholas smiled but at the thought that soon – very soon – he must part yet again from Lucia, his smile faded. He had made a promise that before too long they would return to Glenmire and stay there and he must honour it, both for her sake and his own. But at least during his absence she and Lizzie would be comfortable with the Grangers. Though he'd suggested months ago that he and his family had imposed on them long enough and would rent their own house, Jos and Martha had refused to hear of it.

–

Nicholas was ready to depart within three days with an escort of twenty soldiers, all travelling light and with spare mounts. Tuhin Singh was also with him as Nicholas had hoped he would be. As they headed south-west out of Calcutta, slung across Nicholas' chest was his old leather satchel with the rupees Hastings had given him and an official letter from the governor-general to Scindia offering inducements to make a pact with the Company.

Though they rode as hard and fast as they could, six weeks passed without news of Scindia's whereabouts. Since some of the journey took them through or close to lands controlled by rulers hostile to the Company, they could not always take the most direct route but had to skirt towns and villages and sometimes travel by night. Finally reaching the Bhima River close to its confluence with the Krishna River and well into Maratha territory, they followed the Bhima upstream looking for any signs along the muddy banks, much trampled by water buffalo, of a large force passing that way. Finding nothing, Nicholas began to worry that Scindia might have withdrawn back towards Poona or that he had missed him and Scindia had already crossed into Mysore.

Then one evening towards sunset – just as Nicholas and Tuhin Singh were discussing halting for the night at a spot where dense clumps of palms should conceal their modest campfire from prying eyes – Saugata Bannerjee, a Bengali sepoy Nicholas had sent to scout ahead, reappeared. He was riding fast towards them, head bent low and earth flying from his horse's hooves, against the backdrop of the reddening western sky. Realising he must have something important to communicate, Nicholas and Tuhin Singh exchanged glances.

'I've found them!' Bannerjee shouted triumphantly. 'They're camped about eight miles ahead, just beyond a bend in the river. By the look of the camp they've been there a while.'

'You're certain it's Scindia?'

'Yes – his banner's flying over the camp and as I crept through some long grass, I overheard pickets saying he'd gone hunting but would soon be back. They were joking it would be more than their lives were worth to challenge him if he returned from their direction.'

'I wonder what's Scindia doing?' Nicholas said to Tuhin Singh when they were alone. 'What's he waiting for?'

'Maybe the question is who's he waiting for? Perhaps he's expecting an envoy from Hyder Ali – or maybe the Nizam of Hyderabad whose borders are also close.'

'Perhaps he's waiting for us? His spies and agents may have picked up that we're coming. He told me he had more and higher-placed sources of information in the Company than I'd ever imagine. Whatever the case, we'll find out tomorrow. The question is how best to approach him. From what I saw of him – or at least from the image he chose to present – it may be best if I ride into his camp alone.'

'Without the escort?'

'Yes. It will demonstrate trust in him as an honourable man and if things go badly, what use would a few men be anyway? I'd only be risking their lives.'

'And me?'

'I want you to stay with our men at a safe distance from Scindia's camp. If I don't return or send word within twenty-four hours of setting out, get them well away from here – then split the group. Send half to Eyre Coote in Madras to tell him I've failed and take the others back to Calcutta. But I'm certain it won't come to that. Even if Scindia's changed his mind about making a deal with the Company, the worst that will probably happen is that he'll dismiss me with an unpalatable message for Hastings.'

'When will you go?'

'Not now – I don't want to be shot at by an overzealous Maratha picket in the fading light – but tomorrow morning.'

–

The sun was well up as next day Nicholas rode slowly northwards along the riverbank. His pistols were in his belt and his sword at his side, while in his old leather satchel was Hastings' message to Scindia. White egrets picked delicately in the shallows and dragonflies whirred amongst the reeds but apart from some distant figures at work in the fields, nothing stirred. However, rounding the bend the scout had described, Nicholas saw pale smoke from what must be campfires, curling up into the air. After a further mile, he thought he caught what sounded like shouted orders – troops being drilled?

Halting for a moment, Nicholas took off his tricorn hat and wiped his face with his neck cloth. Despite his confident assertions to Tuhin Singh, now that he was nearing Scindia's camp his heart was thumping. Kicking his horse on he looked around, surprised his approach had not yet been spotted. Only as Scindia's camp came into full view did he hear a shout of 'Halt!' as a Maratha soldier, who'd been lying concealed among some scrubby bushes, rose with levelled musket to confront him. Nicholas reined in and waited as the soldier, soon joined by three others, came closer and demanded, 'Who are you?'

'My name is Nicholas Ballantyne. I am bringing a message from the governor-general of the East India Company in Calcutta for Mahadji Scindia.'

'Why are you alone?' The soldiers looked suspiciously around as if at any moment Company soldiers might suddenly burst from the bushes.

'Knowing Mahadji Scindia is an honourable man I decided I did not need an escort. Now please take me to him. My business is urgent.'

'Very well, but first throw down your weapons and show us what's in that satchel of yours.'

Unbuckling his sword, Nicholas surrendered it and his pistols, then opened his satchel and held it out. 'All that's inside – as you can see – is a letter I must deliver to Mahadji Scindia, and which is for his eyes alone.'

Twenty minutes later, after one of the pickets had hurried into the camp to report Nicholas' arrival and returned with a message that Scindia would see him and after a further search by a guard stationed outside, Nicholas was admitted to Scindia's tent. As he entered, the Maratha leader, who was alone, looked up from the table where he had been studying a map. 'Ah, Colonel Ballantyne. I'm glad to see you again. This must mean Hastings has thought about my idea. I also assume he hasn't sent you with empty hands?'

'He's sent you this letter.' Approaching the table Nicholas handed it to Scindia. 'As you'll see when you read it, if you will agree to stand aside in the coming conflict with Hyder Ali of Mysore, the Company will restore certain territories taken from the Marathas in earlier years.'

As Scindia gave him an appraising look, Nicholas again noticed the thin white scar on his upper lip. 'I'm sure your governor-general considers he's being very generous, but answer me this. Why should I be content to be given what I could take back for myself?'

'Because – as I believe you yourself recognise – by holding back from conflict with the Company, you will avoid an uncertain outcome and save a great deal of bloodshed. The Company will never yield Madras and Calcutta without a fight – any more than they would relinquish Bombay or you Poona. Even if you did finally defeat the Company – perhaps in alliance with others – strong though you are, the struggle would weaken you and leave you vulnerable. As you said when we talked in Poona, you have many rivals… many potential enemies. Take Hyder Ali of Mysore, for example. Whatever promises he might be offering you at present to combine with him against us, once the Company was out of the way wouldn't he try to extend his hegemony over your lands? The fighting and the carnage would be relentless until much of Hindustan was laid waste and you very probably crushed?'

'That's not quite how Hyder Ali's envoy presented matters to me.' Scindia smiled somewhat archly. 'He only left my camp three days ago – a pity you missed him. I would have enjoyed listening to your competing offers… But to return to your fine words, am I right that what you are actually saying is that if I make a pact with the Company I'll prosper and grow strong, but if I turn against it, those I thought my allies will ultimately turn against me? Curiously, you don't say anything about the great advantage it would be to the Company to have me as a friend.'

'No, because I know you understand perfectly well that Hastings hasn't made this offer out of the generosity of his heart. And you also know that this alliance… arrangement… call it whatever you like… wasn't originally his idea but yours, even though you now choose to ask me to justify it.'

Scindia's smile broadened. 'Well said! I see I chose well when I selected you as my emissary to Hastings!'

'There's something else I want to say. In Poona you predicted your people would soon acknowledge you as paramount leader and you were right. The fact that Hastings sent me to you and not to any other Maratha leader is proof that he acknowledges your status. That's useful to you personally.'

'Go on...'

'In recent years your people have spent almost as much time fighting each other as their external enemies. These rivalries have been your greatest weakness and have not gone away. But conclude this agreement with the Company and you yourself will become more secure... It will show your people that so great is the Company's respect and esteem for you that it is even prepared to restore lost lands – something it doesn't often do! It will establish you in their eyes as a great leader. They already know you as a soldier but now they will understand you are something far more rare – a statesman who can bring unity, strength and security!'

Scindia was silent for some moments before saying, 'Seductive words. Perhaps I should have let that Frenchman burn your tongue as he did your back! But now I would like to be alone to read Hastings' letter and think for a while. My steward will find you food and somewhere to rest. You are my guest and I promise no one will harm you. Whatever my decision I will inform you before sunset and you will be free to leave unmolested.'

Nicholas, who had spent some of his time watching Scindia's men drilling and practising musketry, was summoned back to the Maratha leader's tent just after midday.

'You talked about the nature of leadership,' Scindia said. 'What is it that distinguishes the truly great leader from the rest? What is it that made Shivaji such a hero to my people that we still revere him a century after his death? I will tell you. It is the ability successfully to balance benefit and risk. That is what I have been pondering these past hours and I have now made my decision. Clearly it's not in my people's interests for Hyder Ali to become too powerful. He is less predictable, less trustworthy even than the Company... In the past he imposed savage taxes – the *chauth* amounting to a quarter of their revenues – on Maratha leaders whom he forced to accept his suzerainty. I will never permit him the chance to humiliate me or those who look to me for protection like that.'

'So you agree to Hastings' terms?'

'Yes. That is where I have decided the balance of advantage lies. If he honours his commitments to me, I will pull my men back and not intervene in any coming struggles in the south between the Company and Hyder Ali.'

Concealing his jubilation, Nicholas said quietly, 'It will take a little time for me to get the news to Hastings, but I give you my personal assurance that he will honour every word in his letter to you.'

'And as a token of my word I give you this for your governor-general.' Scindia twisted a ring from the third finger of his right hand and passed it to Nicholas. Looking down at the heavy golden ring, Nicholas saw it was engraved with an elephant's head, a symbol in Hindustan of strength, determination and honesty.

Having reclaimed his pistols and sword, with *laissez-passer* letters from Scindia to smooth his and his companions' paths out of Maratha territories and escorted by two of Scindia's men on the first mile of his return journey, Nicholas pondered the results of his diplomacy. As Tuhin Singh would doubtless tell him, in persuading Mahadji Scindia to keep out of the conflict between the Company and Hyder Ali, he had followed the Company's favoured policy of divide and rule – the cynical tactics for which he had once criticised Clive. In this case, though, the ends did justify the means, didn't they? Hyder Ali and his French backers threatened not only British interests in Hindustan, but the wellbeing of hundreds of thousands – perhaps millions – of ordinary Hindustanis who would be engulfed if Hyder Ali was not stopped. Inducing Scindia and his Marathas to stand back would help contain the conflict… And Mahadji Scindia was no naive local ruler dazzled and cajoled into making concessions to the Company… Yet he couldn't stifle the thought that he had become more like Clive – and indeed Hastings – than he might like to think…

Next day at first light, Nicholas, Tuhin Singh and their twenty men set off back along the Bhima. Just beyond its confluence with the Krishna River, as Nicholas and Tuhin Singh had agreed the night before, they parted. Tuhin Singh and half the escort would head north-east back to Calcutta to report to Hastings. He was also taking a letter from Nicholas to Lucia telling her he was safe and well and – as always – thinking of her. Nicholas, with the remainder of the soldiers, would hurry south to Madras to tell Eyre Coote he need no longer fear Maratha intervention as he laid his plans to confront Hyder Ali.

16 – Into Battle

Once safely arrived in Madras, Nicholas lost no time in going to the Company headquarters in Fort St George. Inside he made for Eyre Coote's apartment on the second floor. While he was still crossing the courtyard he heard Coote's familiar belligerent roar echoing through the building and out of the windows.

'Look here, Smith, you've failed me in every possible way a man can. You and your predecessor, Whitehill, allowed Colonel Baillie – a half-wit in my view – to lose an entire Company army at Pollilur. You failed to do anything about removing Hector Munro from his command, even though he didn't move an inch to support Baillie despite being only a few miles away. Now you quote all kinds of rules and regulations requiring documents in triplicate – requests for financial appropriations counter-signed by God knows how many officials – before you will grant me funds and the authorisation to spend them on defending Madras.'

'You must realise the Revenue Board in Calcutta will require such documentation,' a less strident, slightly quavering voice responded, clearly that of Charles Smith, the Company president of Madras.

'By the time you've pushed enough paper, Hyder Ali and the French will not just be at the gates of Madras, not even at the gates of Fort St George, but banging on this door, or your door. They won't submit forms. They'll just take what they want.'

'I'll do my best,' Smith protested.

'Doing your best is an incompetent's excuse. It simply means you're not up to the job.'

'Be reasonable, Coote, as the president here I must respect the formalities. We're all on the same side, aren't we?'

'If so – and you continue to obfuscate – it won't be the winning side, will it?' Eyre Coote roared. Then Nicholas heard his familiar gruff laugh as he continued, 'Well! Enough! I think I've made my position clear. Now off you go and, as you say, do your best. If you need me to kick any backsides, let me know and I'll put my heaviest military boots on.'

A minute or two later a balding, slight figure – obviously Charles Smith – a sheaf of documents under his arm and his face flushed pink, descended the flight of steps from Eyre Coote's apartment into the courtyard as quickly as his dignity as president of Madras allowed and walked swiftly away. After waiting a few moments to allow Eyre Coote to regain any lost equilibrium, Nicholas went up the staircase, introduced himself to Coote's aide de camp and was immediately ushered into the general's presence. Eyre Coote – even stouter than when Nicholas had last seen him – was staring out of the window towards the harbour, but on hearing Nicholas' name announced turned, a smile on his rubicund countenance. 'Ah, Ballantyne! Glad to see you've survived at least. But what news? Did you succeed in your mission to Mahadji Scindia?'

'Yes. I'm fresh from a meeting and agreement with him. He will keep the Maratha Confederacy neutral in our war with Hyder Ali and the French.'

'That is indeed excellent news. Now tell me in more detail. You met and talked to Scindia yourself – as you did Mir Jafar before Plassey, I remember? You think he is in any way trustworthy?'

Coote listened in silence as Nicholas told his story concluding, 'I do think we can trust Scindia – for the present our interests and his coincide. And so you will at least be free of the possibility of Maratha attack on your flank and rear as you march against Hyder Ali.'

'You've done well, Ballantyne, even if you were a friend of that braggart Clive,' Eyre Coote responded with a smile.

'I'm glad you think so since Hastings told me after my visit to Scindia I should report to you to offer my services as a political and military adviser.'

'I'll be pleased to have you, provided you don't interfere where you're not wanted – I've enough people doing that already!'

'I'll try to judge where my advice may be wanted and where not…' Nicholas replied, smiling.

'Well, if you're going to advise me I'd better fill you in on a few things… On the political front, just as you've seemingly secured Scindia's neutrality, the Company has persuaded the Nizam of Hyderabad to stand aside from the conflict. Militarily, the good news is that Hyder Ali seems reluctant to move against Madras, preferring to attack and loot smaller settlements. That at least gives us some time to prepare our response. However, the problem is the number and morale of our troops both European and local. Hyder Ali's brutal treatment of the prisoners after Pollilur is a constant topic of talk in the barracks. He is said to have had hundreds of young British soldiers – many of them Scots – forcibly circumcised and turned some of the circumcised drummer boys into a dancing troupe. His cruelty to other prisoners is beyond doubt, building piles of severed heads, beating, torturing and humiliating captives in front of their comrades – undoubted truths exaggerated and re-exaggerated with each telling. Whereas I can do only a little to hasten the arrival of reinforcements, it is my task to put some heart into the soldiery… get them proper food and decent equipment rather than have commissariat funds siphoned off by corrupt officials or wasted by incompetent ones… get them disciplined and drilled rigorously to re-establish their confidence and *esprit de corps*. I'll be grateful for any and all the help I can get in that.'

–

Over the next few weeks, Eyre Coote had his officers institute daily drills in which the infantry practised firing their muskets in volleys, reloading quickly and then firing again, giving a cash bounty to the unit that completed the process the quickest. He had sandbags hung from trees for the foot soldiers to practise bayonet attacks and watermelons placed on the parade ground for the cavalry to attempt to spear with their lances while galloping at full tilt.

Coote himself, stout and sometimes wheezing as he was, went from regiment to regiment. Often accompanied by Nicholas, he would first give a simple speech – 'Believe in yourselves! Believe in the man next to you! Be loyal to yourself and to your regiment! We're strong in our unity – together we will be victorious! Have no doubt of that!' He would then dismiss the officers and go amongst the men. He would ask the sepoys in their own languages – albeit sometimes haltingly – about the adequacy of their rations and whether they met their religious needs. He would ask whether they had enough powder and ball, how often they drilled and practised firing volleys in unison.

While with the artillery he enquired about precautions to keep powder dry, how often the cannon limbers were inspected and their wheels greased and whether there were sufficient spare ramrods and sponges. When visiting one of the European cavalry units, although struggling to bend he inspected some of the horses' feet himself and found them infected and imperfectly shod. Questioning the troops he found this was a common and long-standing problem. He therefore ordered the sergeant-farrier – a burly, sandy-haired Yorkshireman – before him, berated him, demoted him to the ranks and ordered him to receive twenty lashes before the whole regiment.

When Coote learned that a handsome young lieutenant in the infantry regularly paid another, newly promoted from the ranks, to stand his watch for him while he went hunting or played cards, he cashiered him, himself ripping the gold epaulettes from his uniform despite him being the son of a senior official in Bombay. 'Privileged brats have never had any place in my army!' he told Nicholas, 'whatever the consequences for myself… and I'm now senior enough for there not to be any!' For such efforts his men

– whether European or local – admired and trusted him, joining together to salute him as Coote *Bahadur*, 'Great Coote'.

After some weeks – time during which his measures had taken their effect – Coote received reports that Hyder Ali had moved to attack the territory of the Company's ally the Raja of Tanjore. 'Ballantyne,' the general told Nicholas, 'the moment has come to march to challenge him. Let's call my senior officers together and put the plans in hand for the campaign.'

The council of war took place the following morning in Coote's rooms in Fort St George. With the breeze from the sea and the flapping *punkahs* overhead Nicholas found it pleasantly cool as he took his seat, compared with the intense heat outside. In addition to Coote, his deputy Brigadier James Stuart and some other army officers, Charles Smith, the president, was seated at one end of the table trying – it seemed to Nicholas – to look inconspicuous. Next to him, a tall, gaunt figure in blue naval uniform introduced himself as Admiral Hughes.

Coote began in his usual no-nonsense manner. 'I don't think anyone here will dispute that if Hyder Ali and his French allies had been braver after the defeat of Baillie and Munro, they would have overrun Madras. Hyder Ali would have subjected our allies in Tanjore and elsewhere to his hegemony and the French would have supplanted us as the chief European trading power on the Coromandel Coast. I, for one, am determined that we should never be put in that perilous position again. Does everyone agree?'

Nods followed before Coote continued. 'I have now trained and reinforced our armies to feel confident in confronting Hyder Ali in the field and intend to set out west soon to do so. Let me be clear –' he turned to the army officers '– our advantage is in our equipment. We have more and better cannon, muskets and other weapons than Hyder Ali, even though his more mobile forces outnumber ours. Our aim must be to bring him to pitched battle where our advantage in firepower and materiel will count most. What we must never do is act rashly, however courageous we think we are being in doing so. In other words, no headlong cavalry charges, no detaching troops to rush off after reports of vulnerable enemy detachments nearby! Hyder Ali is quite clever enough to draw us into ambushes and inconsequential engagements to fritter away our troops, equipment and stores. I'll be hard on any of you who allow yourselves to be deceived by him. Is that clear?'

Again vigorous nods of agreement from the army officers.

'I knew it would be! But in itself, the army may not be enough to win a complete victory. Admiral Hughes, can you explain what part your ships will play?'

A slightly startled-looking Hughes began, 'Well, obviously protecting Madras from the French fleet reported to be gathering in Mauritius under Admiral Suffren and preparing to attack us here or to land troops to our south.' Hughes stopped, and then seeing Coote's eyes still on him continued, 'And of course we'll mount coastal patrols to limit supplies reaching Hyder Ali by sea and to support you by bombardment or by landing our marines.'

'That's what I wanted to hear!' Coote said, then turned to Charles Smith who shrank back into his chair under his gaze. 'And you, president, don't think you haven't a part to play – and an important one too.'

'As I've told you before, anything I can do,' Smith replied.

'Well, first make sure that we receive regular and good-quality supplies – no trusting to dubious middlemen. Then there's communications. I will report regularly to you by messenger and you should equally inform me of what is happening on the coast and at sea when I am inland. Keep Hastings and Calcutta off my back by sending them regular reports without giving them enough detail to allow them to interfere.'

After a pause, Coote continued, 'That's my strategy and my requirements. Anybody got anything to add?'

No one had until as the meeting broke up Nicholas heard Admiral Hughes whisper to Charles Smith, 'That's us told! But at least there's no doubt whom we can blame if it goes wrong, which of course, pray to God, it doesn't.'

'Quite,' Smith replied.

Ten days later Eyre Coote led his reinforced and now well disciplined and well supplied army from Madras, flags flying, drums beating and trumpets sounding, and headed south-west towards Hyder Ali's last reported position. However, any optimism either Nicholas or Coote nurtured about an early or easy victory was quickly dissipated. Hyder Ali's Mysorean troops – mostly well-mounted cavalry – proved impossible to bring to the desired pitched battle. Instead, Hyder Ali succeeded in hit-and-run raids on Coote's less mobile column, carrying off considerable quantities of their supplies, all the time wearying and wearing down the Company troops forced to remain constantly on the alert. Despite Coote's strictures against rash sallies, a young captain named Jameson led his cavalry squadron in chase of a party of enemy horsemen whom he believed to be fleeing in panic, only for them to turn and be joined by reinforcements to cut down a good part of the Company squadron, including the young captain himself, shot from his saddle as he tried to rally his men.

However, by early summer, the dogged persistence of Eyre Coote and his forces was at last bringing them closer to Hyder Ali's army, led by himself and his son, Tipu Sultan. Both armies were moving through country familiar to Nicholas from his campaigns with Clive. One humid evening, riding with some of the large group of scouts Coote routinely deployed ahead of his main column for fear of ambush, Nicholas recognised a track branching off the main one as a shortcut Clive had used during his Arcot campaign. Returning to the main body, which had made camp for the night, he went immediately to Eyre Coote. The general was sitting in front of his tent, legs widespread and his large belly resting between them, drinking whisky from a metal tumbler. 'I found a track Clive and I used – it's rough and through rocky hills but I believe passable to the army,' Nicholas reported. 'If we take it, we could well get ahead of Hyder Ali and have a greater chance of forcing him into battle.'

'Good man as you are,' Eyre Coote replied, slapping at one of the mosquitoes buzzing around his face, 'I've nothing to learn from the tactics of that vainglorious braggart Clive.' Nicholas – knowing that argument with Eyre Coote was futile, only serving to harden him in his position – didn't push the point and returned to his tent shortly afterwards.

Next morning, as he walked to the general's headquarters Nicholas was both surprised and amused to find preparations being made to follow the very route he'd advised. 'I'd heard of that side-route and was thinking of following it all the time,' Eyre Coote smiled. 'I didn't want you to get above yourself.' Nicholas could only likewise smile.

Although the route he had pointed out indeed proved difficult – several bullocks broke their legs in potholes and had to be shot – it was passable and put the Company forces ahead of Hyder Ali. Perhaps increasingly uncertain of the position of the Company troops and the speed of their movement, Hyder Ali turned his army east. With Eyre Coote's forces struggling to maintain contact but succeeding through their widespread and excellent scouts, Hyder Ali made swift progress towards the Coromandel Coast. By the end of June, both armies were near the sea, marching and counter marching across a series of small rivers and indulging in a number of indecisive skirmishes from which Hyder Ali and his men always broke away quickly after inflicting initial casualties at little cost to themselves.

On the last evening of June, Coote's men were camped not far from the village of Porto Novo on the north bank of the Vallor River where it joined the sea – an easily defensible position, as Coote told Nicholas. While they were talking, a group of scouts rode up. 'Sir,' their leader reported, 'my men and I have discovered that Hyder Ali's main army – still numbering around forty thousand and mostly horsemen – is camped for the night about three miles north from here next to the shore with his left wing resting against the sand dunes.'

Turning to Nicholas, Coote said, 'Ballantyne, for once we can be certain of Hyder Ali's position. If he is indeed camped for the night, we could advance and attack him in the morning.' Nicholas nodded but before he could say anything, Coote continued, 'Call a council of war for me, will you.'

The council convened around a long trestle table in Eyre Coote's tent. The general began, as was his wont, without any preamble. 'I believe that tomorrow we have a great chance to win a decisive victory and put an end to Hyder Ali's marauding. Even though he outnumbers us by perhaps five to one we remain better equipped and in particular better armed and certainly better disciplined. From the very fact he outnumbers us, he will expect us to sit on the defensive rather than attack, and so if we advance – as I propose – at first light we will have at least some small advantage of surprise.' He looked belligerently around the table. 'Does anyone disagree that we should attack tomorrow?' No one spoke, although one or two middle-ranking officers looked doubtful, an elderly major of artillery in particular. However, Coote forestalled any discussion by continuing almost immediately, 'Good! That's the strategy settled. Now to the detail. Make sure your men are fed and their equipment and horses inspected tonight. Rouse them at around four a.m. Have them breakfasted, the cannon yoked to the bullock teams, the cavalry mounted and the infantry in battle order ready to march just after six a.m.'

Turning to his deputy, Brigadier Stuart, he said, 'Stuart, I want you to command the infantry and for them to make their advance along the coast. The cannon will follow you, with the cavalry protecting your left flank. You will have the sea on your right. We'll signal to any of Hughes' ships that hove in sight to support you with their guns.'

Stuart – a tall, thick-set man – simply replied, 'I understand. We'll be ready!'

To Nicholas the whole meeting, which lasted less than half an hour, underlined Eyre Coote's total command of his men and their respect for him. They had no doubt who was in command and that he was happy to shoulder that lonely responsibility.

After the council of war broke up Nicholas accompanied Coote as he rode amongst his troops, speaking to them in small groups. What he said varied little. 'Tomorrow will be a great day for us – a day about which you will tell your children and grandchildren. Be of stout heart. Trust in me and your officers as I trust in you. Tomorrow will be the day we take our revenge on Hyder Ali and his troops who have tortured and killed so many of our comrades and have laid waste the lands and carried off the few possessions of the poor farmers and labourers.' Everywhere, as he finished, a familiar cry of 'Coote *Bahadur*!' rose, together with protestations of confidence and loyalty.

–

Next morning, Nicolas was one of the first to duck out of his tent. It was still moonlight and by the additional light of fires and of flaming torches he saw soldiers were already eating breakfast, others cleaning their weapons or smoking clay pipes. He rode down to inspect the artillery as Coote had asked him to do the previous evening. The gunners had the most difficult preparations to make, ensuring that the bullocks were yoked to the cannon limbers and that the bullock wagons with powder and ball were ready to follow close behind them. Noticing a major peering beneath the oiled cloth cover of an ammunition wagon, Nicholas asked, 'Any problems?'

The reply came: 'None – or at least nothing serious. We've drilled often enough for just such an occasion as this. Everyone will be as glad as Coote to get the battle over and won.'

By 6.30 a.m., with the sun rising – a golden ball over a glistening sea – Eyre Coote, now stationed on a low hill on his large black horse, was satisfied that all was ready and gave the order to advance. Stuart's infantry moved first, officers with drawn swords in the lead, young drummer boys keeping up a steady tattoo, and after them the foot soldiers. Whether Hindustani or European – Hessians and Hanoverians as well as Britons – they all saluted as they passed the statuesque figure of Coote on his hill. Shortly afterwards the whole army was underway, bullocks straining to get the cannon and creaking ammunition wagons into motion, cavalrymen trying not to let their nervousness convey itself to their mounts, some of whom were already restlessly skittering and tossing their heads.

After about ten minutes a scout on a sweat-scummed pony galloped up to Coote, whom Nicholas had joined. Reining in, he reported, 'As instructed, sir, we made a raid at first light on the enemy's outlying pickets and captured a few. Once out of earshot of his comrades and with the added promise of money, one was happy to volunteer that Hyder Ali commands his right wing and his son, Tipu Sultan, his left against the sand dunes. Whether true or not, he said that the heaviest defences were on the right of Hyder Ali's line since Hyder Ali did not think we would attempt to attack so close to the sea shore and certainly not through the dunes bordering it.'

'Well that's where he's wrong!' Coote said, continuing, 'Ballantyne, be so good as to ride to Stuart and tell him to hasten his men. Surely he can go faster. And you –' he turned to the scout '– ride to the artillery and tell them once they judge themselves in range to unyoke and go into action as soon as they can.'

Nicholas cantered along the shore, his horse's hooves kicking up the sand and within a few minutes had reached Stuart and delivered his order.

'Does Coote think I'm not advancing as quickly as I can already?' Stuart replied tersely. 'But yes, of course, I'll see what more I can do to push the men along. We can't be more than a mile or so from the enemy positions.'

As if in confirmation of this proximity, some of Hyder Ali's celebrated rockets whooshed over their heads. Hyder Ali was now clearly aware of Coote's advance and responding. A little later, Nicholas heard the boom and crash of the Company cannon opening fire, followed by the answering salvos from Hyder Ali's much less numerous batteries. Eye-stinging, acrid white smoke began to drift across the two armies, which were now closing fast.

Returning to join Eyre Coote, now in a more advanced position but again on raised ground to give him a better view of the battlefield, Nicholas saw another salvo of Hyder Ali's rockets flying towards the Company's lines. His cousin Charles had been right when on their journey to Shah Alam he had told him the rockets were inaccurate. Several, trailing white smoke, were heading towards the sea. More, however, began to land amongst the Company infantry.

Through his telescope Nicholas saw one hit a Hessian soldier full in the stomach, propelling him backwards and, he assumed, killing him instantly. Having been counselled in advance that the rockets were more sound and fury than anything else, the Company infantry continued to advance stoically despite several more men falling. The only waverers Nicholas could make out were three young drummer boys who after one of their companions had been hit, began to run back from their exposed positions only to be stopped and encouraged to return to their posts by their older comrades advancing behind them.

By now the leading infantrymen were scrambling up through the dunes. Some stumbled in the sand, others were shot and collapsed, but gradually the regiments seemed to be inserting themselves in an expanding wedge between Tipu Sultan's men defending the line in that area and his father's troops on the right. Once through the front line, the Company infantry began to turn west to attack their enemy in the rear.

After only a few minutes more Nicholas heard trumpets ring out all along the enemy line. Hyder Ali and his son appeared to have realised the danger and ordered an all-out cavalry attack on Stuart's infantry and their flanking horsemen. More rockets erupted from Hyder Ali's artillery, many as wildly off target as previously, some blown west by the wind coming off the sea. One by chance, however, falling in flames hit a Company ammunition wagon, which exploded with a bang and a flash of fire, throwing the waggon into the air and dismembering at least two of the gunners beside it as well as the bullocks pulling it. Others landing among a squadron of Company cavalry caused the horses to buck and rear, several throwing their riders, and disrupting the squadron's advance. Rockets clearly had potential, Nicholas thought, even if they needed refinement.

Lifting his telescope to his eye again, Nicholas saw sprays of sand rising among the far-off dunes where some of the reserve enemy infantry were readying themselves to join the action against Stuart's infantry who were breaking through their front line. Some of these men began to fall even though the area was out of range of the Company artillery. Turning his telescope towards the sea, Nicholas discovered a small British naval schooner had closed in to the shore. Smoke from the broadsides its cannon were firing into the enemy troops almost concealed the white ensign it was flying. 'Coote!' he shouted, 'one of Hughes' ships is getting into action.'

'About time, but welcome,' Coote replied. 'The crisis of the battle is coming. Time for us all to get involved. Ballantyne, order the rear units of our cavalry to charge their Mysorean counterparts now attacking our infantry! I'll do the same for our more advanced cavalry.' With that he dug his spurs into his black horse and was off. Nicholas lost no time in following Coote's instructions and was soon charging with the cavalry, the smell of powder in his nostrils and in his ears the sound of trumpets, battle cries and horses' hooves thudding into the sandy ground.

A musket ball hit one of the colour bearers riding in front of Nicholas and he plunged sideways. As he fell he dropped his blue and white striped banner. It caught in the hooves of the horse galloping next to him, bringing it crashing down. Its flailing legs caused Nicholas to pull hard on his reins and swerve sharply away, losing a good deal of his momentum. Calming his now bucking horse he pushed quickly on, succeeding in rejoining the leading units just as they crashed into Hyder Ali's cavalry attempting to overwhelm Stuart's infantry who – having had no time to reload their muskets – were now fighting with the steel of their bayonets and swords.

The fighting quickly became hand-to-hand, specks of blood and sweat flying through the air. Nicholas found himself confronted by a green-turbaned enemy officer on a grey horse who, turning from his attack on an already wounded Company sepoy struggling to defend himself on the ground, charged towards him. Nicholas succeeded in deflecting his onrushing attacker's sword away from himself with his own sword but not from his horse. His enemy's blade penetrated deep into the animal's rump, dislodging the sword from the man's grasp but causing Nicholas' horse to rear and throw him backwards on to the ground, momentarily stunning him.

As he struggled to his feet, dazed, ears ringing and seeing double, he just made out the Mysorean officer wheel his mount, grab a lance embedded in the ground and spur back towards him. Gathering his scrambled wits, Nicholas reached for the pistol in his belt as the rider bore down on him. Steadying his hand as best he could, he fired, knocking his attacker from his saddle and causing his horse to career away riderless. Less dazed than Nicholas but bleeding from a shoulder wound, the officer was quickly on his feet. Rushing towards Nicholas he threw himself on him, grappling for his throat. Nicholas twisted from his grip and, reversing his pistol, hit the man twice in the face with its bulbous butt, smashing his nose and knocking out some of his front teeth. Another blow to the side of the head and the Mysorean was stretched out on the ground, unconscious at least.

With his senses and his sight now fully restored Nicholas looked around and seeing another riderless horse grasped for the reins, pulled himself into its saddle and headed forward again. After only a few hundred yards he saw Coote still on his black horse, a bloodied sword in his hand. As Nicholas rode up to him, the breathless and purple-faced Coote gasped, 'We've got 'em on the run! They're breaking off the action!'

Pulling his telescope from the leather satchel which had remained slung across his chest throughout the battle, Nicholas saw several Mysorean officers galloping up and down their lines, waving their men to follow them in an ordered retreat. In response to an officer in what looked like blue French uniform, some of the artillerymen seemed to be spiking their bigger guns prior to abandoning them.

'Ballantyne, order the cavalry to pursue the enemy but ride with them yourself to make sure they don't get too far ahead of the rest of the army in their excitement and leave themselves vulnerable to counter-attack.'

Nicholas rode away immediately to join the Company cavalry who were already beginning their pursuit. Galloping with one of their regiments, he turned frequently to check how far ahead they were of the remainder of the advancing Company army. The Company cavalrymen instinctively began to increase their speed and gallop after the enemy cavalry as they turned inland to protect the flank of Hyder Ali's retreating forces. Nicholas kicked his willing mount on to join a young red-haired captain heading the Company charge who was spurring on, head low to his horse's neck and yelling to his men to follow. Seeing a coppice in a fold in the sandy ground about half a mile ahead, Nicholas shouted to the captain to rein in to avoid any prospect of an ambush by enemies hiding among the trees and bushes. The captain didn't appear to hear so Nicholas – using every ounce of his horse's strength – drew level with him. Reaching across he grabbed his reins with his right hand, bringing him and his squadron to a halt.

'What are you doing? Are you mad?' the captain yelled. Just as he did so, a large group of Mysorean horsemen appeared from the rear of the coppice and galloped away, thwarted of the possibility of an ambush.

'Mad or not, as you can see saving you and your men from yourselves! Listen to an old campaigner – don't allow yourself to be carried away by your hot blood and the excitement of the moment… always keep thinking and looking around you. Use your brain before your spurs as Captain Jameson did not, to his cost. Headlong pursuit is more often madness than a route to victory!'

After only two or three miles the Mysoreans began to outdistance their pursuers apart from some stragglers among them, several either wounded themselves or riding wounded horses and others slowed by taking up an infantryman behind them. A few tried futilely to put up a fight and were killed. Most wisely threw down their weapons and surrendered. Within ninety minutes Nicholas and the rest of the cavalry were riding back to the main body of the Company army. The only exception were a few of the freshest and best-mounted riders whom Nicholas had ordered to follow Hyder Ali's army at a distance as scouts to be sure of the direction it was taking and in particular to guard against any inclination of the enemy – unlikely as it might be – to circle back to re-open the action.

That evening as the officers sat over dinner, Eyre Coote, who had just returned from a visit to the surgeons' tent to comfort the wounded, proposed a toast. 'To our victory – the first on our path to Hyder Ali's defeat!' To this his officers enthusiastically raised their motley collection of glasses and shouted 'Coote *Bahadur*', just like their men. Coote smiled. 'Celebrate well tonight. But the war is not over. We follow Hyder Ali tomorrow.'

17 – *Blood and Rockets*

The victorious Company army did not begin its pursuit of Hyder Ali the next day as Coote's rhetoric suggested, but only after three days. They used the interim to recuperate, tend the wounded, clean and repair their weapons and sort through Hyder Ali's abandoned camp for anything of use or value. During this time Company troops counted nearly ten thousand bodies of Hyder Ali's men on the battlefield and collected a few smaller undamaged cannon. Coote himself sent messages to Calcutta and to Madras reporting his victory and asking for reinforcements and resupply to make up for his losses and more.

Scouts reported that Hyder Ali and his army had only travelled about fifteen miles before themselves halting to lick their wounds and reorganise, the better to be able to defend against pursuers. When he began to move again, now with a strengthened rear-guard, Hyder Ali headed north-west – perhaps, as Coote said to Nicholas, looking to obtain reinforcements of both men and equipment from Mysore.

Over the next eight weeks Coote and his army, soon joined by reinforcements including troops who had marched overland from Calcutta under the command of Colonel Pearse, followed Hyder Ali's army as it travelled somewhat more slowly than before Porto Novo. The reduced speed owed much to the now daily rainstorms of the monsoon, which turned some of the route into liquid mud. Cases of fever increased in the Company army and diseases like foot rot grew among the baggage animals. By the fourth week of August, Hyder Ali was approaching Pollilur, the site of his defeat and capture of Colonel Baillie's force the year before. The nearer they got to Pollilur, the slower their pace became. 'Do you think Hyder Ali's contemplating making a stand against us on the old battleground?' Nicholas asked Coote as they rode together towards the humid end of one day.

Coote, his face red and running with perspiration and his uniform darkened by sweat, shrugged. 'Perhaps Hyder Ali's sufficiently superstitious or believes in his astrologers to such an extent that he considers Pollilur well omened enough to want to fight there again. Let's hope so! However, less fancifully perhaps his slower speed is simply the result of the rains and of weariness and indecision about his next move.'

'Maybe. It's true we've succeeded in thwarting most of his recent initiatives, in particular his attempts to rendezvous with reinforcements. That may be taking a toll.'

The following afternoon returning scouts confirmed that Hyder Ali had halted and was drawing up his troops on the old battlefield, seemingly ready to engage the Company army in the morning. Coote's council of war that evening, again round the trestle table in his tent, was once more brief. 'Hyder Ali has chosen this site for a battle and thus tomorrow we should let him initiate the action. After a short bombardment from his cannon and rockets he is bound to begin with an attack by his cavalry who still far outnumber his infantry. We should assemble our foot soldiers on the rising ground in two lines, one close behind the other, one firing while the other reloads – simple in theory but more difficult in practice, I know. Brigadier Stuart, you'll command the infantry again.'

'Certainly. And I'll instil in the commissariat officers the need to have enough powder and ball at hand close to the lines.'

'I would expect as much from you. We'll station units of cavalry at regular intervals behind the infantry ready to repulse any enemy who breaches our front line and to exploit an advantage if we get the enemy on the run, as I know we will! Anything to add, anybody?'

'Presumably we should deploy our cannon to give us the widest field of fire possible, shouldn't we, Coote?' one grizzled artillery commander asked. 'And do we have your authority to open fire at will?'

'Yes, both go without saying,' Coote replied, brushing away some mosquitoes buzzing around his head and neck. 'Now, everyone, go and prepare. God speed and good luck to us all on the morrow, of course, but don't forget both God and fortune help those who prepare the best.'

That evening as large raindrops beat on the canvas roof of his tent Nicholas wrote by the light of a single candle a letter to Lucia expressing his love, his desire to be back with her and promising that this would indeed be his last campaign. He awoke before dawn and leaving his tent found the rain had stopped, although sheet lightning was still flashing along the horizon. The camp, as usual on the day of battle, was already awake around him and preparing. Walking to Coote's tent he found the general sitting on his folding campaign chair, the personification of calm, eating bread and cheese and drinking tea. 'Morning, Ballantyne. As usual I'll make a round of the lines shortly to encourage the men and check that everything is ready. I know it will be. But then it is up to Hyder Ali to make the first move.'

As good as his word after – accompanied by Nicholas – he undertook his tour of the lines, Eyre Coote returned to his tent and seated himself again. Nicholas – unable to contain his nervous energy – began to pace around the tent. 'Ballantyne, do stop that. It reminds me far too much of Clive,' Eyre Coote snapped, perhaps more on edge himself than his outward demeanour suggested.

Nicholas stood still. After just a few minutes a series of loud booms came from the direction of Hyder Ali's position, louder even than the now ceased rolling thunder of the previous evening. Hyder Ali was opening his attack. Moments later Nicholas heard the whoosh of some of his rockets, followed by a blaze of light. Going outside, he saw that a rocket had hit a nearby tent, which was now on fire. Cooks and orderlies were rushing to throw water on the flames. Fortunately plenty had been collected overnight in the rains and the fire was soon put out. The tracks of other rockets criss-crossed the sky, at least half, as previously, seeming to deviate wildly from their planned course. Soon afterwards a young infantry officer rode up and saluted Coote. 'I'm sorry to report, sir, a cannon ball has taken Brigadier Stuart's leg off below the knee. He's conscious and we're carrying him to the rear, to the surgeons' tent. His deputy, Colonel Brooks, has assumed command and wishes to assure you, sir, that everything is calm and as it should be.'

'Tell Brooks I've every confidence in him to hold the line – my single order to him.'

As the officer rode away, Coote said, 'Ballantyne, I hope Brooks behaves sensibly. I've no problems with his bravery – only with his brains. He's not always the quickest to respond to events. When Hyder Ali's attacks begin in earnest I want you to take yourself down to his position to keep an eye on him. From what I know of your time with your headstrong friend Clive, I believe you'll find ways to guide him discreetly and tactfully if he needs it. And, by the way, don't think I don't realise how you try to nudge *me* along from time to time too.'

Dawn had now fully risen over the old battlefield still littered with the skeletons of oxen and horses as well as an occasional human one – a chilling reminder of the realities of war – most now reduced to bleached bones but some retaining shreds of dried skin, or pieces of harness and other equipment. Almost immediately trumpets blared from Hyder Ali's lines. Climbing onto a waggon to get a better view, Nicholas saw through his telescope the massed enemy cavalry beginning to move forward, slowly at first and then gathering speed as they neared the Company front lines, their triangular green banners flying and weapons extended.

The Company cannon with the gunners stripped to the waist, rhythmically firing, swabbing and reloading, swiftly knocked several horses and riders over like skittles at a market fair. A ball from a Company musket fired at maximum range hit the mount of a bearded banner bearer outdistancing his companions at the front of the charge. The horse collapsed, front legs first, throwing its rider over its head on to the muddy ground. He staggered to his feet, only to be knocked down and trampled by the horses of his onrushing comrades travelling too fast and in too close order to avoid him.

Soon the first ranks of Hyder Ali's cavalry were closing on the front line of Company infantry. Puffs of white smoke appeared from the muskets of their first rank as they fired. Their musket balls knocked down more horses and riders, but Hyder Ali's cavalry still pressed on, even through the concerted fire of the second rank of infantry. The front rank – now fighting mainly with bayonets and swords – held firm and the first Mysorean charge broke against them like waves against a rocky shore. Pursued by renewed musket fire from the Company infantry, the remaining horsemen turned away to reform, ready to renew their attack.

'They'll be back,' Coote shouted to Nicholas over the noise of the battle. 'It's time for you to join Brooks. He seems to be coping for the present but I'll be happier to know you're with him.'

Nicholas immediately mounted and within a few minutes was standing with Brooks on a hillock close to the frontline from which Brooks was directing the infantry. 'Coote asked me to join you. He thought, with you replacing Stuart, you might welcome me as a partial substitute in your old role, even if I'm obviously not as familiar with your troops.'

'I'm glad to see you,' Brooks replied. 'Though you don't know my men, I realise you know Coote better than I do and so should be able to judge his requirements well.' The two had no time for further conversation.

Almost immediately Hyder Ali's green-clad horsemen charged again, whooping and shouting, some with lances lowered and others with swords extended. The Company's infantry officers had already had their men raise and level their now reloaded muskets.

Nicholas heard one of the nearest officers shout, 'Hold your fire until they're within a hundred yards. Then let them have it!' A few men, perhaps more nervous than others, fired prematurely, but most held on, only pulling the triggers of their muskets at the ordered range. Some horsemen collapsed from the saddle. Others were thrown as their horses were hit. Yet others swerved away, either hit themselves or unable to control their frightened or wounded mounts. Perhaps a third, the most resolute, reached the Company lines where the infantrymen were again fixing bayonets. A leading Mysorean rider transfixed with his lance one of the sepoys' Hindustani sub-officers. Another cut down with a swing of his sword a young, fair-haired ensign as he was shouting orders to his men – the Mysoreans were experienced enough to go for the commanders, Nicholas thought. Nevertheless, the Company infantry were retaining their discipline. Soldiers from the second rank replaced their fallen comrades in the first as bearers carried away the wounded. Soon, the enemy cavalry were falling back again.

'Do you think we've seen the last of them?' Brooks asked Nicholas.

'Perhaps not. I suspect they may think they've weakened us both mentally and physically and will try again.'

'I'll make sure the bearers continue to bring up supplies of powder and ball and that water carriers bring up their supplies – it's thirsty work.'

A quarter of an hour passed and Nicholas began to think he'd been mistaken that the enemy cavalry would attack again. Then, to the sound of trumpets, they began to advance again, green banners still flying. However, by this time so many of their own wounded, dying or dead horses and men were lying in front of the Company lines and the muddy ground had become so churned by hooves that it seemed their attack would lose its momentum and peter out. But then from his position Nicholas saw the horsemen wheel along the line to attack at the junction between the Company's left flank and front line. He shouted a warning to Brooks who immediately told a rider to carry a message to a reserve infantry unit to move across to confront the horsemen making the incursion.

The reserve infantrymen doubled at a run towards the fighting, then crouched and fired a volley at short range, bringing down in a tangle of falling men and flying hooves most of the enemy riders who had penetrated the Company lines. The rest of the enemy cavalry turned and began galloping back, some pausing to take up behind them a wounded or unhorsed comrade.

Nicholas heard bugles sound from behind him in the Company lines. Coote had ordered a general advance by his cavalry against their retreating enemy. Nicholas saw one of the leading units swerve their mounts through the skeletons of several bullocks – clearly remnants of the Company baggage train destroyed the previous year. Suddenly a Company horseman, hit in the head by a musket ball, flung up his arms and pitched from his saddle to land on the skeleton of a bullock, some of whose bones smashed beneath him while others seemed to impale him. The rest soon caught up with the rearmost of the enemy and were hacking and slashing at them. After only a few minutes trumpets sounded in Hyder Ali's ranks and his cavalry began to disengage completely where they could and gallop hard towards the rear, making no attempt to reform as previously.

The Company cavalry at first pursued them, but soon halted. Coote again clearly wished to avoid any prospect of his cavalry becoming detached from his main body, thus risking being overwhelmed, however unlikely that prospect. Now, with Hyder Ali's army beating a retreat as they had so often done before at Porto Novo and elsewhere – conceding defeat and territory but living to fight again – Nicholas remounted and made his way back to Coote's headquarters as in front of the battle lines bearers again began collecting the wounded. Some were relatively lightly hurt, waving or shouting to comrades as they were carried to the rear, but many were covered in blood with great, gaping wounds or broken bones poking through their flesh.

Visiting the surgeons' tent a little later, Nicholas and Coote found Brigadier Stuart lying pale-faced on a makeshift bed, his left leg already amputated at mid-shin and well bandaged. 'A clean wound,' he told Coote, raising his head, 'and they got a tourniquet around it quickly so I haven't lost too much blood. There's life in me yet.' Whereas Stuart might well survive, others with stomach or abdominal wounds or shattered limbs in which cloth and dirt had become embedded probably wouldn't. A young ensign would be scarred for life by a roughly stitched sword slash from which blood was still seeping and which ran from his half-severed ear to his mouth. A metal tub full of severed arms and legs bore witness to the number of amputations the surgeons had performed with their serrated saws. Speed was key, a surgeon had told Nicholas, boasting he could amputate a leg in less than two minutes.

Coote halted by a wounded Bengali *subedar* who begged him that his savings be secured and sent to his family in Murshidabad if he died. Coote tried to reassure him his death was unlikely, but promised that, if he did indeed die, he would see to it personally that the money was safely delivered. Nicholas knew Coote *Bahadur* would be as good as his word. That was why his men loved him so much. As they left the tent and thunder heralded the onset of more monsoon rain, Coote noticed that among the bodies piled outside the entrance lay that of another infantry commander, Lieutenant Colonel George Brown of the Company Grenadiers. 'Another good man among the many we've lost today,' Coote lamented quietly to Nicholas.

As Nicholas sat with Eyre Coote by one of the campfires that evening, the old general continued in reflective mood. 'A life of soldiering has never inured me to the suffering of war. I regret how many bodies we've added today to those left on the battlefield last year.'

Nicholas nodded. 'War should only be a last resort. I too have seen enough suffering.'

'As I grow older, with fewer years left to live, each year becomes more precious to me. I've started to long to be back with my wife on my estate on the English south coast in Hampshire… to breathe the crisp air of a winter morning… feel the warm sun of a British summer on my skin, not the intense heat of a Hindustani one… even sometimes a longing for soft English rain or that of my Irish birthplace… You know, Ballantyne, I've a good mind to submit my resignation immediately to Hastings and retire before my health breaks down as I've seen happen so often to others who soldiered on too long.'

Nicholas started in surprise. It had long been obvious to him that Eyre Coote's health was not strong, but he knew that Hastings and the Company needed their best general. 'Are you sure you should contemplate retirement now, with Hyder Ali defeated but not yet crushed?'

'I'm serious in my wish to retire soon. It's something I've been thinking about for a little while. There are others who can replace me.'

'You're undervaluing yourself. No one has your combination of virtues. You've the ability to maintain strict discipline while winning and retaining the loyalty of your men. To have self-belief is important in a soldier but to inspire others to believe in you and to risk their lives for you is much more important and much less common.' Nicholas thought for a moment, then added, knowing the effect it would have on Eyre Coote who was always eager to measure himself against the – in his view unjustly – worshipped Clive, 'Not even my good friend Robert Clive could have inspired your men to achieve what they already have in this campaign. No one ever called him "Clive *Bahadur*".'

'I'm glad you think so, Ballantyne. You're probably right that it's my duty to persevere… Ascribe my sentimental longing for Britain and a peaceful life to battle weariness and no more… Now let's have a whisky and discuss how to deliver that final blow to Hyder Ali.'

18 – Vellore

Over the next days, Company scouts reported that Hyder Ali's army was heading towards the fortified town of Vellore, garrisoned since just after Clive's time by Company troops, with the probable intention of laying siege to it. Like the Company's army, Hyder Ali's movements were considerably slowed by the cumulative effects of the now declining monsoon. Landslides and fallen trees had blocked roads in places and floods, sometimes two or three feet deep, hampered progress. Coote's troops – by dint of regularly marching one or two hours a day longer – began slowly to gain on Hyder Ali.

However, early one evening a few weeks after the battle of Pollilur, two scouts who had left the fort at Vellore on foot under cover of darkness before purchasing horses and travelling by a circuitous route reached Coote's camp. They reported that advanced elements of Hyder Ali's army had now reached Vellore and were making obvious preparations to besiege it. The Company defenders had retreated in good order into the fort itself and were well provided with food and military equipment. The monsoon had replenished the fort's wells and water tanks. The garrison could hold out for a little time but, massively outnumbered, they might not be able to resist for more than a couple of weeks once the full weight of Hyder Ali's assembled forces was thrown against them.

Coote called a council of war two hours later. Just beforehand he took Nicholas aside. 'Ballantyne, I want to ask you something. I've had a number of deaths or incapacitating wounds among my senior officers recently, as you know. Now dysentery – always more prevalent during the monsoon – has set in amongst the cavalry officers. Four of the most senior are lying in their tents unable even to stagger to the latrines or to hold anything in their stomachs for more than a few minutes. The worst is Sutton, the new colonel of the 5th Bengal Horse. That's perhaps unsurprising since he only came out from Britain for the first time a couple of months ago and is obviously not at all seasoned to our climate or food. The long and short of it is that I would like you to take over from Sutton until we've relieved Vellore.'

'Of course,' Nicholas replied without hesitation.

'Thank you. A rare sign of my trust in you but don't let it go to your head! I'll announce the appointment at the council.'

This time the council meeting lasted a little longer as Coote quizzed each of his commanders in turn and in detail as to how they could help speed the column to relieve Vellore. Could infantrymen be detached to push bullock carts or gun limbers through the worst patches of mud? Could spare cavalry horses be used to augment the bullock teams? Could some stores and baggage be jettisoned, including some of the officers' own copious personal paraphernalia – 'No need for dressing tables, dressing cases, looking glasses et cetera in my army!' To each of these questions there was assent, some grudging if the expressions on several officers' faces were anything to go by.

Nicholas himself proposed that more cavalry units should be designated as scouting parties, fanning out widely in front of the army's march to ensure it was able to close in on Hyder Ali's force, being certain both of its location and of avoiding ambush. Coote quickly agreed and soon after concluded the meeting. 'Each of our small decisions today should have improved our chances of relieving those poor buggers in Vellore before they fall into Hyder Ali's hands and those of the French to face God knows what humiliation and torture.'

By early evening the next day the Company army, making good speed, was not far from the small town of Sholingur when a group of scouts galloped in to report to Coote. 'About seven miles ahead we encountered a large Mysorean force heading not towards Vellore, but this way! Or at least they were before halting and beginning to make camp for the night just beyond Sholingur.'

'Were you seen?' Coote asked.

'Almost certainly not. At first we shadowed them at a distance and then observed the camp from the brow of the hill overlooking it. One other thing, sir – through my telescope I saw the tiger standard of Hyder Ali's son, Tipu Sultan, being raised at the centre of the camp. Perhaps he's commanding, not his father.'

'What's the route like between here and where he's camped?'

'Quite good, though there's obviously some mud.'

Coote quickly dismissed the scouts with his thanks and turned to Nicholas. 'This is our opportunity to strike a decisive blow. If the scouts are right and we put together an attacking force, in the early hours of tomorrow morning we could take their column unawares at or just after first light as it begins to assemble.'

'Or even before then… The monsoon is nearly over and it's almost a full moon for us to travel by.'

Another council of war quickly put the necessary arrangements in hand for the army to set out at around three in the morning and for a strengthened force of scouts to keep watch overnight on the enemy camp. That evening, rather than accompany Coote on his usual rounds to put heart into the troops, Nicholas had officers and men of his own to go amongst. He took some time with the officers of the 5th Bengal Horse, advising several suffering from the early stages of dysentery that boiled rice water mixed with opium would help steady their bowels. Because of the number of the regiment's headquarters staff already sick, he asked each commander to designate one of his most trusted troopers to ride with him to convey messages and orders. His words to the men were as simple as Coote's. 'One more effort and we will push Hyder Ali back towards his homeland and relieve pressure on our comrades in Vellore. All I ask is that you take as much care of the man on either side of you as you do of yourselves. There is strength and victory in unity.'

Nicholas was up at two the next morning and an hour later was at the head of his cavalry regiment, waiting for Coote's signal to move off. His horse, like many around it, sensing the excitement, was tossing its head and pawing at the ground. Seeing a pale-faced tousle-haired young ensign leaning from his saddle to be sick, Nicholas rode over to him. 'Are you ill?'

'No, I don't think so. It's my first action, sir. I came out from England with Colonel Sutton. To be honest, I just feel anxious.'

'Don't worry. Anyone with an ounce of sense feels a little fearful before a battle. The bravery is in mounting up and carrying on despite it. Remember that.'

'Yes, sir.' The young man gave a wan smile.

First light was only just rising as the vanguard of Coote's troops, led by some of the same scouts who had located the Mysorean camp, approached the hill over whose brow it lay. Two other scouts who had kept watch overnight for any unusual movement in the camp joined them there. 'No sign of alerts, General, sir,' one told Coote who had ridden up on his stout black charger with Nicholas by his side. 'They're going about in a leisurely way, cooking and preparing to break camp. Their only precautions appear to be a few sentries and pickets posted within a hundred yards of the perimeter.'

'Well,' Coote said as a peacock flew down screeching from its roost in a nearby tree, 'let us serve them a breakfast to remember. If all remains quiet when we reach the hilltop that'll be our chance. Ballantyne, you'll lead the 5th Bengal Horse in a swift charge through the camp. Do as much damage and create as much confusion as you can as you ride through without getting bogged down in close-quarters fighting. Then, as the other cavalry regiments and infantry follow you down the hill in the main assault, station yourself just beyond the far perimeter of the camp to cut off as many as you can of those attempting to retreat, as they almost certainly will.'

Ten minutes later Nicholas and his men were on the brow of the hill, looking down on the still peaceful camp. Through his telescope Nicholas recognised Tipu Sultan's tiger banner but could not see that of his father. The hill, its grass bright green from the monsoon, sloped relatively gently down towards the camp but there were obstacles such as trees and a few rocks, together with irrigation and drainage ditches cutting horizontally across the hillside. Nicholas called over the messengers designated to carry his orders. 'Tell your officers to advance when I give the signal by waving my sword. Have them maintain a single front, rather than rush headlong, and in particular order them to make sure their men are aware of the ditches and take care in jumping them.' A middle-aged, red-faced officer within earshot shouted, 'You mean tell them to take the ditches as they would in a fox hunt?' Nicholas nodded, despite himself never having fox hunted.

Minutes later, the same officer was yelling, 'Tally Ho!' as the 5th Bengal Horse got into motion, pennants fluttering at their lance tips, riding line abreast down the hillside. Despite Nicholas' strictures, at least five men and horses fell when the riders failed to see a drainage ditch. Only as they neared the bottom of the hill did the camp seem to wake up to their presence, with soldiers dropping their food and rushing for their weapons. A blue-coated European officer – presumably French – appeared to be shouting at artillerymen unhitching cannon limbers from their bullock teams to hurry to get them into firing positions.

Nicholas flourished his sword again as his signal for all-out attack and kicked his own horse on. Soon his onrushing cavalry had swept aside the few pickets and sentries. Riding into the disordered camp where their enemies were still running for their weapons, Nicholas cut down a gunner who had grabbed a ramrod and was bravely trying to fight him off with it. Another European officer crouched behind a cannon limber levelled his pistol at Nicholas who immediately ducked down to his horse's neck as the ball whistled over his head. Pulling hard on his horses' reins he wheeled round, drew his own pistol and fired at the officer who at once clutched at his shoulder where his gushing blood soon began turning his blue uniform purple.

Spurring on, Nicholas saw the young ensign who had been sick as the regiment assembled trying desperately to fight off two Mysoreans. Nicholas reached him just in time before they overwhelmed him. Nicholas cut down one of the attackers who had not seen him approach with a slash to his back, opening it to the bone. The man's shriek drew the other attacker's attention to him. A tall luxuriantly moustached individual on a black horse, he took a wild sword swing at Nicholas who ducked beneath it then thrust his own sword deep into the man's exposed armpit. The Mysorean immediately collapsed onto the neck of his horse, which swerved away as he slowly slipped from his saddle, only for his foot to become caught in his mount's stirrup and for him to be dragged behind it, head bumping along the ground until the stirrup leather broke.

Looking around, Nicholas saw his men were doing well. One *risaldar*, bending from his saddle, had cut the ropes of several tents with his sword, collapsing them on to their occupants. As he watched, another who had grabbed a burning brand from a cooking fire threw it on to one of the high-wheeled artillery wagons positioned by a small group of cannon and quickly swerved away. The wagon must have contained gunpowder since moments later it exploded with a bang into a sheet of flame. Nicholas felt the heat on his face even though he was a little distance away.

The remainder of Coote's cavalry were now well into the battle in the camp and the infantry were following, running down the hill. Some determined Mysorean gunners, ignoring the fighting around them, manoeuvred a battery of rockets mounted on a bullock cart into position to fire at them. However, only half of them flew and not all these hit the infantry but some knocked over one of the leading groups of sepoys most of whom quickly got back to their feet and ran on.

Nicholas waved to those of his men who could to disengage to follow Coote's instructions and ride through the camp, ready to cut off as much as they could of any retreat. Once beyond the camp Nicholas found he had only about half his men with him. Some had been wounded, killed or unhorsed but most of those missing seemed unable – or at least in their excitement unwilling – to disengage. Ordering those around him to close formation, he and his men rode slowly back and forth along the rear portion of the camp perimeter watching for any sign of Mysorean soldiers attempting to break out. Suddenly a large group of enemy horsemen far outnumbering his own men and with Tipu Sultan's banner at its head disengaged and began to gallop out of the fight, in the process knocking over several of their own foot soldiers as well as a dozen Company grenadiers who attempted to stop them.

Waving his sword to signal his men to charge into the flank of the breakaway body, Nicholas was among the hard-galloping leaders as they crashed into the enemy horsemen, unseating several by the sheer weight of their impact. Nicholas raised his now reloaded pistol and aimed at a young green-turbaned man wearing a steel breastplate who was riding surrounded by a phalanx of guards near the banner – it must be Tipu Sultan. As he fired Nicholas' horse stumbled, spoiling his aim, and the pistol ball missed its target but hit the mount of one of Tipu Sultan's bodyguards. As it collapsed, its flailing hooves caught a second horse, causing it to rear, throwing its rider too.

Nicholas pulled his second pistol from his belt but the group was nearly a quarter of a mile away now. His men had wounded or killed twenty or so of them but most had indeed escaped including, to his great regret, the man he presumed was Tipu Sultan. Ordering his troopers to halt and regroup again, Nicholas looked back towards the heavy fighting in the camp. A large number of enemy infantry were attempting to withdraw on foot after Tipu and his squadron of cavalry. They were maintaining close formation, obeying their officers' orders to pause, reload and fire at Company troops pursuing them from the camp. One of the foremost foot soldiers suddenly spotted Nicholas and his horsemen ahead, dropped to one knee, levelled his musket at Nicholas and fired. The range was extreme and his aim poor and the musket ball whistled harmlessly by.

Tipu and his riders had escaped, but he should prevent as many as he could of these enemy infantry from joining him, Nicholas thought. 'Fifth Bengal Horse! Back towards the camp!

Stop those foot soldiers getting away!' he yelled. As the Company cavalrymen thundered down on them, the Mysoreans broke into groups. Seeing one large body veer to his left, Nicholas turned his horse towards them and signalled his men to follow. Leaning forward, pistol in his right hand and controlling his horse with his left, Nicholas picked his target – a tall, burly French officer in a blue, high-collared jacket and white breeches who had become isolated from his men. As Nicholas bore down on him, the officer halted, turned and calmly faced him.

'Throw down your weapons,' Nicholas shouted, reining in. When the man didn't respond he repeated the order in French. The officer stared at him for a moment, then replied, 'I speak your language – and better than you speak mine!' Then, with a shrug he tossed his pistol to the ground and unfastened his sword belt.

'You've made a wise decision. I accept your surrender.'

Just then one of Nicholas' cavalrymen cantered up, young face flushed and excited. 'Colonel Ballantyne – we've—' Before he could get any further, seeing Nicholas turn to the new arrival, the French officer suddenly stooped, pulled a dagger from his boot and hurled it at Nicholas. The sharp tip embedded itself in his saddle close to his groin. The attack had taken only an instant, but time enough for the Frenchman to turn and run, moving with surprising agility for such a thick-set man. Kicking his horse forward, Nicholas quickly caught up with him. Throwing himself from the saddle, he knocked the Frenchman to the ground, then, scrambling up himself, hauled the man to his feet. 'I spared your life. Why did you attack me? Have you no honour?' he demanded, his face inches from the officer's.

'Honour? What are you talking about? You should listen more carefully,' the man replied, half-winded and breathing heavily. 'You said you accepted my surrender. I never said I offered it… You were careless and arrogant in assuming you could overawe me.'

Impressed, despite himself, by the officer's defiant pedantry, Nicholas fought the impulse to swipe the smirk from his face and was glad when some moments later two more of his men rode up and he could hand over his prisoner. As he soon discovered, the 5th Bengal had taken further casualties in their attack on the enemy infantry – six troopers hit by musket balls and a seventh killed by a scimitar thrust to the belly. But they had succeeded in capturing or killing several times that number. Coote should have nothing to complain about.

'What about the groups of foot soldiers who escaped us? They can't have got far. Should we pursue them?' the young cavalryman who had first ridden up asked Nicholas.

'No. We've a more valuable target – Hyder Ali's artillery and baggage train in the camp. Fighting's still going on but his men will try to retreat with whatever they can, when they can. The more weapons and stores we deny them, the more we'll hamper their future operations.'

Kicking his horse on, Nicholas led his men the short distance back to the camp, avoiding fallen bodies and abandoned equipment. A large number of Mysoreans were indeed doggedly defending the baggage train. As two of his 5th Bengal Horse approached an ammunition wagon, a green clad artilleryman sacrificed himself by blowing it up, dismembering himself, the two Company men and their horses in the process. As he lit the fuse he had set, he shouted, 'Long live Tipu Sultan! Death to the foreign invaders!' Tipu Sultan must indeed be a charismatic leader to inspire such devoted, even fanatical loyalty, Nicholas thought, looking down and seeing that, though he had been at least a hundred feet from the explosion, he, his mount and the ground were speckled with blood and tiny fragments of flesh.

Wiping as much of the blood from himself as he could with his neck cloth, Nicholas rode into the centre of the camp where the fighting was now dying away. There he found Coote red in the face, breathing heavily and perspiring but triumphant, sitting on his now sweat-scummed black charger. 'We've done it, Ballantyne – deprived Hyder Ali and his son of much irreplaceable equipment and a good number of their best men! But I must know what is happening at Vellore. If it falls – or has fallen – to the Mysoreans, then what we've achieved today won't count for all that much. I can't afford to wait for news until I can get the column on the march again. The men are tired and we'll need two or three days to care for the wounded and to sort through all the abandoned weapons and equipment.'

'What can I do?' Nicholas asked, though he'd already guessed.

'Tomorrow take a large cavalry escort and a few of our best scouts, ride to Vellore – or as close as you can get – and see what you can find out.'

–

A pale moon was fading into the dawn sky as Nicholas, with forty of the freshest of his 5th Bengal Horse and his scouts, headed south-west out of the camp towards Vellore. The route they took lay at first through dense forests of babul trees underlain by tangles of prickly brush – difficult to penetrate and ideal for an ambush, Nicholas thought uneasily to himself. However, as they struggled through, sometimes having to dismount to slash a path, the only sound other than those they made themselves was the song of unseen birds. Nicholas was relieved when towards midday, the forests started to thin and they emerged onto more open ground and could increase their pace.

As the afternoon wore on, however, the ground became increasingly soft and muddy. Before long they were in oozing, insect-infested marshlands dotted with clumps of tall, spiky reeds and criss-crossed by streams. One was so wide it was almost a river. As Nicholas' horse, belly deep in water, picked its way across, a sudden movement among the reeds on the opposite bank caught Nicholas' eye. A long, scaly, sinuous shape was sliding into the water. 'Crocodile!' he shouted. Drawing his pistol, he aimed at the swiftly approaching V-ripple in the water. His horse had seen the crocodile as well and, just as he fired, skittered sideways throwing off his aim. Luckily, the crack of the pistol shot was enough to scare the crocodile away. As his trembling, snorting horse reached the far bank and scrambled up, Nicholas saw it swim slowly away.

Towards dusk Nicholas and his party had cleared the marshlands without further mishap. Cautiously cresting a hill a few miles further on, Nicholas found himself looking down on Vellore, set amongst bright green palms on the banks of the Palar River. Through his telescope he made out the robust granite ramparts and wide moat of the fort and a flag flying above the closed gates. At this distance he couldn't identify the flag in the fading light but the fort didn't seem to be under siege – no large encampment nearby, no batteries of cannon, none of the hundreds of soldiers that might have been expected.

Signalling his men to follow, he rode down the hill towards Vellore. As they approached some simple huts on the outskirts, few people were about. Most seemed to be staying safely in their homes. Raising his telescope to his eye again, he saw that the flag flying over the battlements of the fort was the Company's and felt a wave of relief sweep over him that the garrison had survived Hyder Ali's siege. As he drew nearer he saw that the flat ground surrounding the fort was bare, except for several half-collapsed tents, a few carts lacking one or more wheels, the corpses of two or three draught animals and piles of rubbish through which the town's dogs were nosing.

Crossing the area as darkness was falling, streaking the sky pink and purple, he noticed the embers of some cooking fires still glowing. The enemy were not long gone. Four Company grenadiers were standing sentry at the entrance to the drawbridge, which spanned the moat to what he could now see was the badly battered fort. 'I'm Colonel Ballantyne. I've come from General Coote,' he called to the sentries. 'Please take me to your commanding officer.'

'From General Coote, sir? You've taken your time! You've missed all the action!' a sergeant replied in an accent as Scottish as Nicholas' homeland.

Nicholas stood ten minutes later in the fort's main courtyard with Major Oates, the officer commanding the fort whose left arm was in a sling. 'I'm exceedingly glad to see you, Ballantyne! I was waiting to get a clearer picture before despatching messengers to try to locate Coote. As you rode up, you'll have seen we took quite a pounding.' Oates gestured with his right arm through the gloom to the battlements. 'Look at those bastions. Thick though they are, I'm not sure how much longer they could have withstood Hyder Ali's cannon. We were starting to suffer a lot of casualties – myself included, as you can see. I was hit by stone splinters while directing gunners on the battlements. But late last evening we spotted a lot of unusual movement in the enemy camp, which continued all night. I didn't send out a party to investigate in case it was a trap. But we stood to arms on the walls all night keeping watch and as the light rose we saw their leading elements were already moving out. They were soon followed by the heavy equipment and the rest of the troops. By midday they had nearly all gone. Even till you arrived, I still worried it might be a trick... but from what you say, news of Coote's victory at Sholingur must have been what forced them away.'

–

Coote was dining alone in his tent when a travel-stained Nicholas returned to his camp the following evening with the good news. 'Oates' full report is in this despatch,' he said, pulling an envelope from his satchel and laying it on the table.

'I'll read it later. Join me, Ballantyne, won't you? You must be hungry.'

After his servant had brought Nicholas some food and they were alone again, Coote took a swallow of wine and settled back in his large campaign chair. 'So Ballantyne, the news is as I'd anticipated. We've done what we set out to do – repulsed Hyder Ali's offensive. He's no longer a threat to Madras and without him, neither can be the French.'

'Hastings will be well pleased.'

'Pleasing pen pushers and bean counters is the least of my worries. But yes, he should be. I suppose I need to give him an account of what's happened.'

His words gave Nicholas the opening he had been seeking to allow him, weary as he was with warfare and eager to return to his family, to withdraw from the campaign now it was surely won. 'Much to my surprise – and perhaps to his,' Nicholas began, 'Sutton's recovered from his dysentery and, although weak, is eager to resume command of the 5th Bengal Horse. May I volunteer to take the news to Calcutta and brief Hastings?'

'That's not a bad idea…Yes, you should go. I'll miss you here, believe it or not, but I know I can rely on you to tell Hastings the unvarnished truth unlike most of those self-seeking buggers in Madras and elsewhere who might seek to aggrandise their own contribution at my expense as they relayed my message. Tell Hastings I intend to take the army west to maintain pressure on Hyder Ali. Though no longer an immediate threat to Madras, he's by no means entirely defeated. He still has the loyalty of his own troops and people and, I presume, the backing of our perennial enemies the French.'

–

The following morning, Nicholas was packed and ready to return to Madras no more than sixty miles or two days' steady ride away, accompanied by the small escort Coote had insisted he should take. Before mounting up, he walked over to the general's tent to say goodbye. Raising the flap he went in only to find an elderly orderly bent over the general who was lying on his side on the floor, a broken plate and some spilled bread next to his outflung arm. The orderly was loosening Coote's neck cloth and clothing. Then he slapped his face. 'That usually does it,' he said, looking up and seeing Nicholas. 'He fainted away on returning from his early morning tour of the perimeter. It's not the first time it's happened – and won't be the last – but he won't even allow me to speak to the surgeons about it, never mind let them bleed him.'

A moment or so later, Coote's eyes opened and he was soon sitting up on the ground, taking a sip of brandy from Nicholas' proffered flask. 'Don't look so worried, Ballantyne. It's nothing – just a bit too much exertion for an old chap. Even if you've kept your figure better than me, you're little younger than I am. You should watch yourself too.'

As Nicholas rode away from the camp, he was pleased to think he had the trust of the outwardly irascible Coote of whom he had become fond as he got to know him better. But, with the general's health so clearly failing, had he been right to persuade him in the best interests of the Company out of his intention to retire?

Part Four

The Parting of the Ways, 1781–1784

19 – Fratricide

'What are you smiling about?' Lucia asked, lying back against the pillows.

'Was I smiling? I didn't realise… It just feels so good to be back with you…' Nicholas' ship had anchored so late the previous evening that by the time his tonga had deposited him and his bags outside the Grangers' house the household was abed. The elderly night watchman had had to unlock the gates to let him in.

'I'm glad you feel as I do about Lizzie and Charles, I wasn't sure what you'd say…'

After their first embrace Lucia had told him she suspected Lizzie and Charles had reached an understanding to marry though neither had yet said anything. 'No one could accuse Charles of impetuosity,' Nicholas had replied, amused by the long time his staid cousin was taking, 'but by the same token I can scarcely doubt he'll make a steady, dependable husband.' After they'd made love, Nicholas had fallen into a deep, contented sleep, not waking until the morning light slanted in through the half-open windows. Sitting up, he stretched. 'I must send a message to Hastings at Government House… I owe it to both him and Eyre Coote to deliver the general's report quickly. But once that's over with, we can start to think about going home to Glenmire. We've been away far too long.'

'You may have to wait a day or two to see Hastings. Marian told me they were going to Alipur to inspect a new formal garden she's having laid out.'

'Have you seen much of her while I've been away?'

'Yes, she continues to call. We have some good tête-à-têtes – not just the gossip but about what's been going on behind the scenes politically in Bengal… the relationships between the high Company officials and their behaviour towards some of the neighbouring rulers… She's very astute about such things, as we women often are… much more so than you men credit us!'

'I've never doubted it. But I didn't think you were that interested in Company politics…'

'I'm not except where they might affect you. Marian has told me much you should be aware of before you see Hastings…'

Lucia's tone was suddenly so serious that Nicholas looked at her in surprise. 'Like what…?'

'Hastings seems to have acted unwisely… He needed funds for his military campaigns in the south but with the Bengal government already heavily in debt and with all the usual disagreements between the council members, he couldn't get their agreement to any proposal he made.'

'Go on.'

'According to Marian, he decided his only recourse was to "dun" – I don't think that's too strong a word – funds from Chait Singh, the Raja of Benares. His justification was what Marian called "an imprecise agreement" subject to several interpretations that the Company reached with the Raja five or six years ago when the Nawab of Oudh died and his son Asaf ud-daulah succeeded him. The agreement gave Chait Singh independence from the Nawab but turned him instead into pretty much a vassal of the Company, committed to paying them annual fees – "tribute" you might call it. However, Chait Singh wasn't good at paying. Nine months or so ago, Hastings – needing funds desperately – decided to force the matter. He headed to Benares to confront Chait Singh, taking an escort of five hundred soldiers. Marian was able to give me all the details because she accompanied her husband much of the way – so did the painter William Hodges whom Hastings wanted to portray what he anticipated would be the high ceremonial of a new and favourable Company agreement with Chait Singh.'

'I'm guessing that's not how things turned out?'

'No. About fifty or sixty miles from Benares, Hastings left Marian and the bulk of his escort behind and, not anticipating any trouble, continued with only a small number. However, when he arrived in Benares, things quickly turned sour. Chait Singh tried to put him off with what Hastings wrote to Marian were "shuffling excuses and palpable fabrications". At that point Hastings made a massive misjudgement – he ordered his men to arrest Chait Singh. Whether through a misunderstanding or not – it's unclear – the Raja's bodyguard attacked and killed most of Hastings' diminished escort. In the panic and confusion both Chait Singh and Hastings ignominiously fled Benares, each losing a great deal of their dignity in the process. Reaching safety, Hastings summoned Company reinforcements, which in subsequent weeks defeated Chait Singh's forces and occupied Benares.'

'What about the Raja?'

'He escaped, but though he took a good fortune in gold with him, he lost his throne. The Company has installed a more compliant puppet in his place, unpopular with his people, I believe, but prepared unquestioningly to pay more to the Company than ever was asked of Chait Singh. Marian joined Hastings in Benares for a while. What she saw and heard there convinced her that – although he's gained substantial revenue for the Company – the whole thing's been a dreadful and morally dubious mistake, lowering any reputation the Company has for probity and fairness...'

'From what you say I'm sure she's right...'

'I'm glad you think so, *caro*. This mess is entirely of Hastings' making... If he tries to embroil you in it you must refuse – I'm not saying that just so we can return to Glenmire, but for the sake of your conscience and your reputation...'

'I won't get involved, I promise,' Nicholas said, lying back again. Some of his satisfaction at the success of the campaign against Hyder Ali and his French allies was already fading as he pondered Hastings' actions. Where money was concerned, Hastings' moral sense sometimes deserted him – just as it had over the Rohillas nearly a decade ago. Unlike Clive, he didn't act for personal gain, but the results were no less dire. Hastings was proud of calling himself a pragmatist but what was the point of solving one problem only to create future ones? By his, to say the least, dubious tactics he had not only made an enemy of Chait Singh and most of his people but given other Hindustani rulers good cause to believe the Company was not to be trusted at the very time he needed support wherever he could find it…

'There's more…' Lucia cut into his thoughts. 'Hastings' campaign to fund his military spending also targeted the new young Nawab of Oudh, Asaf ud-daulah. The Nawab claimed – with justice, Charles says – that corrupt Company officials were already fleecing him of much of the revenue they were supposed to be collecting for him and that his treasuries were therefore bare. But Hastings saw his opportunity in a quarrel between the Nawab and his grandmother and stepmother – "the begums of Oudh", Charles calls them. Though the two women live in purdah, it seems they're no shrinking flowers. They succeeded through a variety of arrangements – again shrouded in ambiguity and many made in the Nawab's minority – in taking control of much of Oudh's wealth, while leaving the new Nawab still encumbered with his father's debts. Hastings decided to make a claim on the two women's doubtfully acquired fortunes, alleging they had collaborated with Chait Singh from behind the purdah curtain. Hastings' dispute with them is still continuing. The latest I heard is that his agents in Faizabad are trying to force the two controllers of the begums' households – middle-aged eunuchs both – to reveal where their money is. Another even more squalid imbroglio for you to keep well out of.'

'You've no need to worry. I will.'

-

It was two days before Nicholas saw Hastings and when they did meet, it wasn't at Government House but at the Grangers'. Nicholas was sitting in the library glancing through the latest issue of *The Calcutta Spy* – it included a cartoon of a leering

Hastings in bed between the two much larger bosomy begums and demanding 'surrender me your treasures' – when the door opened and a servant announced, 'The governor-general!'

A beaming Hastings strode towards him, clapped him on the shoulder and sat down. 'My secretary sent me word in Alipur that you were back. I didn't want to waste a moment in coming to see you. Well, we showed all the doubters, didn't we!'

'I suppose we did, though we were lucky.'

'They say fortune favours the brave. And don't be modest. I know from Coote's brief despatches during the campaign – he's hardly a man to give praise where it's not due or indeed to share credit – the crucial role you played.'

'I've a lengthy report from Coote for you. Once you've read it I'll do my best to fill in any gaps…'

'Excellent. Where's Coote now?'

'When I last saw him intending to continue pressing Hyder Ali and his forces as they fall back on Mysore, in the process eroding Hyder Ali's strength and resources whenever he can.'

'Let's hope he succeeds. The news of Coote's recent victories will be a huge relief to the directors and the British government in London and some consolation for the dismal reports from the American colonies.'

'What's the situation there? I've lost touch.'

'Given the months it takes any news from there to reach Calcutta, I'm hardly up to date myself but my impression is that after six years of fighting we're still no closer to snuffing the rebellion out. We might even lose…! My last specific information was that six thousand further French troops had landed in Rhode Island… But that's not my problem, thank goodness! At least we've thwarted French ambitions here.'

'I hope so for a time at least.'

'And there's more good news – superficially at least. Francis resigned and returned to England just before Christmas and good riddance! Despite all his maudlin protestations in the immediate aftermath of our duel he continued to obstruct me in every way he could.'

'What about that beautiful young mistress of his, Mrs Grand? Did she accompany him?'

'No. Don't forget Francis has a wife in Britain. His mistress returned to France with a handsome pay-off from Francis, I hear. He can certainly afford to be generous – they say he took home a fortune of over a hundred thousand pounds.'

'Why did you call his departure only superficially good news?'

'Because I'm certain he means to stir up trouble for me with the Court of Directors. As he never tired of assuring – or should I say threatening – me, he has powerful political friends in London and I think I know what the focus of his attack will be. While you were away, circumstances forced me to take certain steps to bolster the Company finances without first seeking the approval of my council...' Hastings ran a hand through what remained of his hair – surely even thinner and greyer than when Nicholas had last seen him. 'You may already have heard something about it – and if not you soon will – but...' Drawing his chair a little closer and lowering his voice, Hastings continued, 'Let me tell you what happened... and more importantly why.'

As Nicholas quietly listened everything Lucia had described – Hastings' attempts to bully Chait Singh, his ongoing campaign to extract money from the Begums of Oudh – poured out. So did Hastings' justification of actions about which, though he presented them with his usual breezy braggadocio, he clearly felt a little uneasy. Finally reaching the end of his story with a 'well, for better or for worse, that's how things stand,' Hastings sat back.

Nicholas knew Hastings wanted what he couldn't give – reassurance and approval – and that he should therefore choose his words with care. 'I understand the predicament you were in, of course. Hyder Ali was an immediate threat to Madras. He had to be dealt with. At the same time military campaigning is expensive and you needed funds to pay for it. But, to be honest, had I been here, I wouldn't – couldn't – have advised you to treat either Chait Singh or in particular the begums in the way you did or are doing. My advice now – for what it's worth – is this: tell the directors in London frankly that they can't have the profits they insist on without allowing you sufficient resources to safeguard their interests. They need to understand that the Company's position here is precarious. The war in the American colonies should be a warning to them of what may happen.'

Hastings frowned. 'That's quite a rebuke. Do you think I've been unjust…?'

'I'll answer that with another question. What would Chait Singh or the begums say if they were here with us now?'

'But they're selfish, pampered autocrats. They don't care about their people as I do for the Hindustanis the Company's responsible for. The Raja decamped with half the contents of the Benares' treasury. The Nawab of Oudh's stepmother and grandmother are simply a pair of old harpies, squeezing as much profit as they can out of monopolies they guard as jealously as crocodiles watch their eggs…'

Nicholas smiled at the image. 'That's as may be but aren't the shortcomings of their rulers matters for their own people to sort out, rather than for you, on behalf of the Company, to exploit?'

'No, that's an over simplification. The Raja in particular – until we were forced to get rid of him – and the begums had all benefited from the Company's protection and they have a duty to pay us for it. I only resorted to what you might consider illegitimate means because they wouldn't acknowledge – never mind comply with – their obligations to the Company. You won't alter my views about that! Where I can agree with you – and enthusiastically too – is over the need to convince the directors – and indeed the British government – to be more realistic about the Company's needs. My problem is how to plead the case when I'm so many thousand miles away and have so many other vital things to occupy me?'

'Appoint someone you trust to be your advocate in London – and no, I'm not suggesting myself.'

Hastings thought for a moment and then almost beamed. 'But why not? I mean it. I could create a special position for you as my envoy with all the money and privileges to go with it… You've earned it… I'd already planned to offer you any post you wanted in Calcutta…'

'Sorry to disappoint you, but before I left for Mahadji Scindia and Madras I made a promise to Lucia and to myself that it would my final mission on your behalf… I'm weary of wars and the pain they bring. I'm weary too of the moral ambiguities and compromises of Company politics… of any politics in fact. They're not for me. I believe I've helped put a stop to French ambitions in Hindustan at least for some time and that is reward enough for me. I want to go home to the cool of the hills and that's what I intend to do…'

Deflated, Hastings smiled ruefully. 'Marian told me you'd say something like that if I asked you to stay on… She also said she had every sympathy with you!'

'She's a sensible woman… Perhaps one day the two of you will find time to visit us at Glenmire.'

'Perhaps. I hope so. You've been a good friend to me and – despite some of your views about it – to the Company. Can you really detach yourself so completely from what has been such a large part of your life…? Won't you get bored…?'

Nicholas burst out laughing. 'Bored? No, I really don't think so…'

–

The following afternoon, as he sat reading on the wide veranda overlooking Martha Granger's rose garden, Nicholas had a further visitor – his cousin, Charles.

'Lucia said I'd find you out here. I'd have called sooner but I was away upcountry till yesterday. Welcome back to Calcutta! And congratulations on the campaign.' Taking a rattan chair opposite Nicholas, Charles accepted a glass of *nimbu pani* swiftly brought by one of the Grangers' well-trained staff.

'I doubt the Company has heard the last of Hyder Ali or his son. But for the moment at least the threat is over…'

As they discussed the campaign, Nicholas noticed his cousin seemed uncharacteristically distracted. Twice he asked Nicholas the same question about Eyre Coote's health and several of his other comments showed he was not attending closely to what Nicholas was saying. As their conversation finally dried up, Charles lowered his head and for some moments twisted the family signet ring on his finger round and round. Then, looking up, he said abruptly, 'Is it true you intend leaving Calcutta soon and returning to Glenmire permanently?'

'It is.'

'In that case, there's something I want… no, there's something I *must* tell you… It's this. I love your daughter and she loves me. We want to be married and we ask your blessing… I'm sorry to take you by surprise like this – learning that you'd soon be leaving convinced me I had to speak now…'

Nicholas, who had quickly divined what was coming, said, 'Taken me by surprise? No… I'm not blind – neither is Lucia. We guessed the situation quite some time ago… What puzzled us was why you were taking so long…?'

Charles took a gulp of his *nimbu pani*. 'Lizzie and I planned to tell you after you returned from Bombay – you may remember I'd just been appointed to the Revenue Board. Then all the trouble in the south blew up… Everything seemed so uncertain… You were preoccupied with planning your departure to find Scindia… It didn't seem like the right moment… Also, if I'm being honest I was relieved to find an excuse to delay…'

'But why?'

'Because I was uncertain how you and Lucia would react. I knew that when we quarrelled about the famine I lost your regard – I also sensed that Lucia only tolerated me… I've tried to atone, hoping that through dedication, hard work and rising in the Company I could regain the good opinion of you both so that you would accept me as your son-in-law…'

His cousin's conviction, even after all the years he'd known them, that succeeding in the Company was the path to winning either his or Lucia's approval caused Nicholas to suppress a smile, but there was no disputing the sincerity in Charles' voice or the anxiety in his eyes. He decided to put a swift end to Charles' doubts. 'If this is what Lizzie wants – it's her happiness above all that matters – I will happily give you both my blessing. So, I know, will Lucia. You're right – we did once have our doubts about you but you've done much to assuage them… And –' finally Nicholas allowed himself to smile '– Martha Granger will be delighted. She was the first to predict you two would wed… But now to practicalities. When do you plan to marry?'

The mingled delight and relief on Charles' face made him look almost boyish. 'With your approval in about six months – on my return from a short detachment on behalf of the Revenue Board back to Madras. We already have our eyes on a suitable house on The Esplanade.' Getting to his feet, he said, 'If I may, I'd like to go and look for Lizzie and tell her…'

'I think you'll find her in the gardens… I spotted her there a little earlier…'

Charles smiled a little sheepishly. 'She knew I'd come to speak to you, so she's been waiting there.'

The house, so tranquil just half an hour before, seemed suddenly full of festive bustle and noise. Martha – as pleased as Nicholas had predicted – decided on an impromptu celebration and sent messages summoning her husband from his warehouses and to mutual friends living close by. Lizzie dashed off notes to her closest friends and Charles to Company colleagues. As soon as Joss arrived, he ordered his *khutmagar* to fetch up bottles of his best champagne and have ice brought from the ice-house. Martha sent to the kitchens for whatever delicacies were to hand – sugared plums imported from London, ratafia biscuits, macaroons, the best grapes. Servants rushed to obey and were soon carrying huge mahogany lead-lined coolers packed with crushed ice in which nestled a considerable number of bottles into the drawing room, fast filling with guests, and corks began to pop.

'A toast!' Nicholas raised his frosted glass. 'To the future Mr and Mrs Charles Ballantyne! Long life, health and good fortune to them.'

Watching Charles' and her daughter's radiant expressions, Lucia put her arm through Nicholas'. 'I hope they'll be as happy us, *caro*... I confess I still think he's dull, but that may be my warm Mediterranean blood...'

–

Spring had returned to the Himalayan foothills when two months later Nicholas walked into his study in Glenmire. The writing materials on the rosewood desk and the book-filled shelves looked just as he had left them. It felt such a very long time since he'd last been here. But soon he would begin writing his long-planned book about the history and customs of Sikkim – a suitable occupation, he smiled to himself, for a retired gentleman in his mid-fifties.

Taking his violin case down from a shelf, he took the instrument out and examined it carefully. The polished maple back gleamed red-gold, surely deeper, richer than the day his uncle James had given it to him, saying, 'I think you should learn. Your mother had a talent.' Nicholas tautened the strings, adjusted the horsehair bow and, raising the violin to his chin, attempted a few notes. His fingers moved stiffly and he grimaced at the sound. Never mind, with time and practice the old fluency should return... Heartened, he tried again and this time was better pleased with the result.

Returning the violin to its case, Nicholas felt above all grateful to be his own master again... Was it a freedom that Hastings – constrained and beleaguered on all sides – would ever know or perhaps even welcome? At least Hastings should soon have a quieter time of it. Shortly before Nicholas, Lucia and Lizzie – happy to spend the final months before her marriage at Glenmire – had left Calcutta, reports had begun circulating that Britain and France would soon conclude a peace treaty. At the farewell dinner

Hastings and Marian had hosted for him and Lucia at Government House, they had raised their glasses to 'a coming new age of peace and prosperity in Hindustan'. If it was true about Britain and France – and if Hastings and Mahadji Scindia continued to honour their agreement – there might indeed be peace in Hindustan, something that since Nicholas had first arrived thirty years ago had never lasted very long…

Also just as Nicholas and his family were preparing to leave Calcutta, James had sent word not only that Riti was pregnant again but that he planned to take a furlough and bring his family to Glenmire. 'If Will could be with us, our family would be complete again…' Lucia had said wistfully. 'But he seems so immersed in his studies I sometimes doubt he'll ever return to Hindustan…'

It was July – full summer with the wild rose bushes blooming in the hills – before James and Riti, who because of her pregnancy had taken their journey from Delhi slowly, arrived. Nicholas, working in his study, heard the commotion and hurried outside to be quickly joined by Lucia and Lizzie. Before James and Riti dismounted, a small figure, seated on another pony with Anjuli Shastri – the woman Gilbert Cuthbertson had abused in Delhi and Riti had taken in – slid quickly to the ground and strode confidently towards the house. So this was Alexander, the three-year-old grandson Nicholas and Lucia had never seen, though Riti had sent several sketches. He was tall for his age – a true Ballantyne, Nicholas thought, but with his mother's high cheekbones and silken black hair. While Lucia picked Alexander up, Nicholas stepped forward to embrace his son and daughter-in-law. 'Welcome home.'

–

The following weeks passed as Nicholas had hoped. He and his son fished, walked and rode together in the hills. He soon learned the reason James had decided to take a furlough was the recent death of the Moghul Emperor's commander, Najaf Khan. 'He had sufficient force of character to manage the Emperor but now he's gone, I suspect Shah Alam will revert to his old ways. All the old in-fighting and factionalism Najaf Khan temporarily quashed will return and if that happens, I don't want to continue in Shah Alam's service. The question is what should I do next? Disband my cavalry unit? That's why Riti and I came to Glenmire – we need time to think what's best...'

Riti sometimes came riding with them, insisting that despite her pregnancy there was no reason why she shouldn't. Tuhin Singh visited frequently, often bringing his eleven-year-old son, Kaji, and wife, Kannika. Nicholas knew that, with most of the family gathered, Lucia was, like him, happy. She spent time with Alexander, reading him stories and showing him how to draw.

One afternoon, about six weeks after James and Riti's arrival, as Nicholas sat at work in his study, he heard rapid footsteps approaching on the wooden floorboards outside. Moments later an agitated Tuhin Singh burst in. 'What's the matter?' Nicholas asked, rising from his chair. 'Has something happened to Kannika... Kaji...?'

'No... not that, but terrible enough... It's Nokat...'

'Nokat?' Nicholas said in surprise as Tuhin Singh paced restlessly. His friend hardly ever mentioned his birthplace – a tiny state in the Himalayan foothills tucked between Nepal, Sikkim and China and too insignificant for its neighbours to bother much about. Tuhin Singh had been born the youngest son of its then Raja. His mother, a Bengali concubine, had not survived his birth. On their father's death, Tuhin Singh's two half-brothers, Sachin, the elder and the new Raja, and Ravi – sons of the Raja's principal wife, a Nepali princess, and who had always treated him with contempt, veiled during their father's lifetime – had told him he had no place in Nokat. If he remained they would not answer for his life. Forced into exile at the same age as Nicholas had been when his uncle despatched him to Hindustan, he had made his way to Calcutta. Not long after, he and Nicholas had met.

'What do you mean by "terrible enough"? A natural disaster – an earthquake… an outbreak of disease… and how d'you know about it?' Nicholas asked.

'After dark last night, an elderly man arrived exhausted at my house. He said his name was Aadesh – the vizier of Nokat. He claimed he remembered me from my boyhood but hadn't known where I was – even if I was still alive – until about five years ago when an emissary sent by the Chogyal of Sikkim to purchase yaks mentioned that a man from Nokat whose name, he thought, was Tuhin Singh and who loved horses sometimes visited the Chogyal's court. Aadesh suspected it was me. He thought little more about it until recent events in Nokat convinced him to try to find me. The emissary had told him I lived several days' ride south of Rabdentse. Even so, it took him nearly a month to locate me. To be honest, I almost wish he hadn't… He brought shocking news… Nokat is in turmoil and the people – my people – suffering and oppressed…'

'How?'

'According to Aadesh, the original cause was my half-brothers. After years of enduring what he perceived as slights by his elder brother Sachin, Ravi decided to usurp the throne. Needing troops, he made an alliance with some renegade Ghurkhas from Nepal, exiled by their own ruler. With their help he captured and occupied Bagran – Nokat's capital – and proclaimed himself Raja. His first act was to have Sachin and his two sons dragged into the palace courtyard, stripped naked and hacked to death with butchers' knives. Then he had their heads set on spikes above the palace gatehouse and their dismembered bodies exposed on the hillside as food for carrion. He forced Sachin's wife and two daughters to watch the whole grisly process, then had them strangled.'

'That's dreadful…'

'But the story doesn't end there… Nokat is hardly rich. Lacking the money to pay off his Ghurkha mercenaries, my brother has allowed them a free hand to plunder, rape and pillage in those parts of the country he suspects of disloyalty to him.

Aadesh thinks Ravi has become insane. He insists it's my duty to my dead father to put a stop to his reign of terror… He says many Nokat men have taken to the mountains and will fight for me if I come to lead them…'

Nicholas had a mass of questions but before he could ask any, his friend began again. 'In all these long years I've never harboured ambitions for the throne. I've put Nokat behind me. Latterly I've seldom thought about it. I'm happy living quietly with Kannika and my son. The last thing I want is to become embroiled in some murderous family conflict in which people may have unrealistic expectations of me… Yet Aadesh is right. It is my duty. How can I justify refusing to help, especially when I've spent years of my life aiding the Company? For better or worse, Nokat is in my blood, which the Company certainly isn't!'

The gloomy resignation in Tuhin Singh's voice reminded Nicholas so much of his uncle's reluctance to answer the Stuart Prince's call on the eve of the Jacobite Rebellion. But James had felt it was a matter of honour and that he could not refuse. Tuhin Singh clearly felt the same…

Though it was a bright day, dappled sunlight playing over the well-stacked bookshelves and comfortable old furniture filling his study, Nicholas felt a chill shadow pass over him. Despite his war-weariness and longing for a quiet, peaceful life, if this Nokat business was a matter of honour for Tuhin Singh, then it must become one for him as well. He could not let his closest friend – a man who over three decades and despite strong misgivings about the Company's activities had faced so many dangers by his side – confront this challenge alone. At least on this occasion he had no need to agonise about political compromises and moral ambiguities or the rights and wrongs of Europeans meddling in lands far from their own. Could there be a more just war than freeing Tuhin Singh's homeland from the tyranny and terror unleashed there?

'If you've decided you must go to Nokat – as I think you have – I'm coming with you.'

'No!' Tuhin Singh's tone was uncharacteristically sharp. 'You misunderstand. That's not why I'm here. I came because I wanted to tell you what had happened. I've scarcely had time to absorb the news. But I do know that before too long I will have to leave and I don't know when – or indeed – whether I'll be back. And very importantly, I wanted to ask that if anything happens to me, you and Lucia will take care of Kannika and my son…'

'Of course. You know that. But it's you who misunderstand. I wasn't asking your permission to go with you. I was telling you I'm coming. If Lucia were with us now, she'd say the same thing and you know her too well to try to change her mind… In fact of all the campaigns you and I have undertaken, this is probably the only one she'd wholeheartedly approve of…'

Tuhin Singh looked for a moment as if he was about to argue further. Then, with a faint smile, he said simply, 'Thank you!'

20 – *The Chinese Firework Seller*

As soon as Tuhin Singh left, saying he would return with Aadesh the following day, Nicholas told Lucia what had happened. She understood at once that he was honour bound to help Tuhin Singh. As Nicholas guessed he might, James insisted on accompanying him. 'I've known Tuhin Singh all my life… It was only thanks to him that when I was a child, Lucia and I weren't murdered when Siraj-ud-daulah overran Calcutta. He was wounded protecting us… I'm glad I'm here to repay him just a little, not thousands of miles away in Delhi.'

Later, alone in their bedroom, Nicholas and Lucia were each for a while lost in their own thoughts, Nicholas looking out of the window into a sky in which the stars had never seemed so bright, Lucia at her dressing table brushing out her long hair. As Nicholas went across to the fireplace to add another log to the fire – the evenings were growing ever chiller – Lucia put down her brush. '*Caro*… I think that Lizzie, Riti – if she agrees – and I should go down to Calcutta while you, James and Tuhin Singh are gone… Though their wedding will of course have to wait, Lizzie and Charles can at least see one another and Riti will have good doctors and midwives on hand.'

'It seems a good plan. At least while I'm away, I'll know you're safe.'

'I'll ask Kannika and Kaji to come with us, if they'd like to…'

'I hope Kannika agrees. Tuhin Singh asked that we take care of his family.' Coming closer, Nicholas put his hands on his wife's shoulders and together they studied their reflections in the large oval mirror on the dressing table. Lucia looked preoccupied and sad, Nicholas thought. That wasn't like her. In all their years together, through all their many partings, she'd been so strong. Though she'd always told him to be careful – 'Be sure to come safely home to me, *caro*!' – not once had her tone suggested the least doubt that he might not…

Bending, he kissed the nape of her neck. 'What's troubling you? There's something, I know. Tell me.'

'It's hard to explain… I don't understand it myself but I feel a sort of gnawing anxiety inside… as if everything we've known and loved and taken for granted might be about to be taken away and there's nothing I can do to prevent it…'

'We're getting old, you and I, that's all… We find change – and challenges – more difficult than we once did. I know I do… We both assumed that when we finally returned to Glenmire we'd lead that quiet life we so often talked about for the rest of our days… We were living it until this news broke a few hours ago. Everything altered in a flash. But as we've both learned, that's just how life is. I know Tuhin Singh feels the same. This is the last thing he wanted. I've never seen him so weighed down.'

'You're right, of course, *caro*, that this mood of mine – *presentimento* we'd say in Italian, what is it in English? – foreboding? – is because this news came without warning just when we thought our lives were settled.'

'I won't ask you not to worry. That would be foolish. But I assure you I'm too cunning and crafty an old fox not to stay safe. I promise to return to you and bring James with me… Now come to bed… we should enjoy what time we have…'

-

Over the next days Aadesh, sometimes assisted by Tuhin Singh – though he'd not seen Nokat for over thirty years – told Nicholas and James all he could about it. Nicholas built a mental picture of a small, hitherto peaceful kingdom girdled by rugged, snow-tipped mountains, with jade-green, ice-flecked rivers tumbling down from the Himalayas and rich alpine pastures grazed in spring and summer by fat-tailed sheep. White-haired, bushy-browed, stooped and leaning on a stick, Aadesh looked eighty if he was a day. Nicholas marvelled how he had survived his flight from Nokat. As he described the land he clearly loved his creased face relaxed, but when Tuhin Singh asked him about the fortress capital of Bagran from where his brother Ravi and his Ghurkha mercenaries was terrorising his people his old eyes flashed with anger. 'The officers and courtiers are too afraid to speak out. The captain of the royal bodyguard was the only one who dared, pleading with Ravi to show mercy, at least to the Rani and her daughters. Ravi erupted in fury, shouting like a madman. He accused the captain of treason and ordered his own men to fling him from the battlements. I too should have had the courage to protest. My reason for coming to find you, Tuhin Singh, was not only to help Nokat but to atone for my cowardice…'

'But will the people accept me? The fact they hate Ravi doesn't mean that they want me as their Raja.'

'They will welcome you, I promise… The blood of the royal line runs through your veins, just as in Ravi's. He has no surviving sons. With him and Sachin gone, you have every right to the throne. No one will challenge you.'

'Supporting me in principle is one thing, but what matters just now is how many will fight for me?'

'When I fled, about one hundred and fifty of Nokat's soldiers, including twenty of the royal bodyguard, had already vanished from Bagran, to Ravi's rage, I should say… He ordered a daily roll call. By now, more will have joined them – not only soldiers but villagers fleeing the Ghurkhas with their families. I think you could count on between two to three hundred to support you.'

Tuhin Singh, Nicholas and James exchanged glances. 'That's not nearly enough,' Tuhin said bluntly. 'Aadesh, you told me my brother's army numbers around eight to nine hundred in normal times. Even if more defect before we advance into Nokat, that still leaves those renegade Ghurkhas. We all know they're ferocious fighters. From what you say these particular men are so vicious not even their own rulers will tolerate them. Now my brother has allowed them into Nokat they'll be hard to dislodge…' Tuhin Singh slapped the table at which they were sitting in exasperation. 'If we can't improve our odds we may fail.'

'I agree we need more men, but from where?' James said. 'I know some of my cavalry unit would join us but I could never get them here in time.'

For a while the four men sat in silence. For all his fervour, Aadesh had an over-rosy view of how easy it would be to depose Ravi, Nicholas reflected. After all, Tuhin Singh must be largely forgotten in Nokat… Even though Ravi had no direct heir, there might be other contenders for the throne… If things went wrong, the situation might degenerate into civil war. The Nepalese might even seize the opportunity to gobble little Nokat up. But then a thought came to him, so obvious he was amazed he'd not thought of it before.

'I've not been in touch with the Chogyal since my return to Glenmire and I don't think you have, Tuhin Singh? It must be two or three years since we last met – but we should ask his help. Given how frequently the Ghurkhas raid across his borders he's likely to support any action against them. More importantly, he's always been a good friend to us and we to him…'

'What kind of help d'you mean?' James asked. 'Men, supplies, weapons…?'

'Whatever he's prepared to give us… In any case, Rabdentse is on the route to Nokat and, if the Chogyal permits it, would be a good place to sit out the winter while we prepare.'

'There's another reason it's a good plan,' Aadesh put in. 'A number of those who fled Nokat crossed into Sikkim – I encountered several on my own journey. From Rabdentse we can spread the word that there is a champion prepared to challenge Raja Ravi and ask those who are willing to join us there.'

Tuhin Singh nodded. 'Why not? What do we have to lose?'

–

Nicholas, Tuhin Singh and James watched their wives and children ride away along the drive to begin their journey down to the plains ten days later. Until the moment the small group reached a bend and began disappearing from view, Lucia looked back over her shoulder at Nicholas. At the very last moment she raised her hand in farewell.

The Ballantynes, Tuhin Singh and Aadesh set out for Rabdentse next morning. Though the journey wasn't difficult, by sunset on the fourth day as their horses wound up the hill to the fortress-palace of Rabdentse, Aadesh, swaying in the saddle, looked exhausted. Once arrived, the Chogyal soon gave them an audience in the octagonal room painted with rows of little Buddhas that Nicholas knew well.

'We've come to seek your help,' Tuhin Singh said when the formalities had been completed. 'It concerns my homeland of Nokat...'

The Chogyal listened intently as Tuhin Singh described what had happened. 'A sad, squalid business – this killing by one brother of another...' the Chogyal said when he finished. 'It happens frequently among those rulers in Hindustan whose ancestors came from the steppes – "throne or coffin", I hear they call it... Of course, I've heard something of the recent troubles in Nokat. Refugees have been arriving in Rabdentse, bringing stories of murder and destruction. Those lawless Nepalese Ghurkhas swarm wherever they scent an opportunity, like flies around dung... They are a perpetual menace to my own people. You said you wanted my help. You have it! I will do whatever I can to assist you to dislodge the murderer from the throne and destroy his Ghurkha parasites.'

–

Nicholas, James and Tuhin Singh, but without Aadesh who had developed a bad cough, met the Chogyal several times over the next few days. An old warhorse still despite his age, he insisted there would be no point setting out for Nokat until spring and that until then they should be his guests. Good as his word, the Chogyal offered two hundred and fifty of his soldiers – a number of whom Nicholas himself had trained and including some like Santem Denzongpa who'd fought with him and Tuhin Singh against the Bhutanese raiders all those years ago. Santem, now a senior commander in the Chogyal's army, greeted Nicholas and Tuhin Singh warmly. 'I will select the best and most experienced troops we can spare,' he promised.

As the first snowflakes began to fall from the pale skies above Rabdentse and the ground froze hard as iron, Tuhin Singh, the Ballantynes and Santem, drilled the Chogyal's men for the coming expedition in the fortress courtyard and on the parade ground outside. Aadesh had been right. Refugees who had fled Nokat for Rabdentse joined them. As soon as it could be arranged, Aadesh despatched messengers north and west towards Nokat to spread the news that Tuhin Singh was gathering a force to topple Ravi. By the time the snows fell in earnest, a steady stream of Nokat men had arrived, eager to reclaim their homeland from Ravi and his renegades.

'Even though, thanks to the Chogyal's generosity, our men will be quite well-equipped, I think surprise will still be our best weapon,' Tuhin Singh said to Nicholas one evening as they warmed themselves over a fire of burning logs in Tuhin Singh's room. 'But I'm worried. Even with the Nokat men who've joined us we still have only about four hundred – probably not enough to be confident of success against Ravi, assuming his remaining troops stay loyal to him, and certainly not if his Ghurkhas fight with him. We need something to give us an advantage, but hard as I've tried, I can't think of anything. It's not like taking on the Bhutanese… We can't scare them with a few barrels of gunpowder – they already have it – or with a herd of stampeding yaks…'

Gunpowder… Reaching over, Nicholas slapped Tuhin Singh on the back. 'Though you don't know it, you may just have suggested a solution. You're right that something as commonplace as gunpowder is now won't help us this time, but we could use it in a different way… Hyder Ali of Mysore uses gunpowder-propelled rockets. Why shouldn't we?'

'But we don't have any – the Chogyal certainly has none. In which case, where could we get them from? We can hardly send a polite request to Hyder Ali.'

'We can make some ourselves!'

'Easy to say. You've seen the rockets in action, but how much do you actually know about them?'

'More than you might think!' In his enthusiasm Nicholas got to his feet and began pacing. 'My cousin Charles knows quite a bit about the rockets' design – he examined one while he was in Mysore, made some sketches and even stole a part of it.'

'Your cousin stole something…?' It was Tuhin Singh's turn to smile.

'I know it seems unlikely, but he did. Suspecting – correctly as it turned out – that Hyder Ali might one day use rockets against the Company, he wanted to understand how they worked. He also thought they might have military potential for the Company. Few are better placed to advise us.'

'And of course, he'll be only too eager to please his still sometimes sceptical prospective father-in-law?' Tuhin Singh raised an eyebrow.

'Of course!'

'But do we have time to contact him? Winter's almost here.'

'We do if we act quickly – the route south will be passable for several more weeks. I'll write to Charles at once explaining why any information he can give us is so important. By now he should be back in Calcutta.'

–

By late October, twelve days after the two messengers provided by the Chogyal to carry the letter to Charles had left, the snows came in earnest. Often accompanied by shrieking winds they blanketed the land. Temperatures frequently fell so low that in the open, fingers quickly became too numb to load or fire a musket making serious military training impossible. Even within the thick-walled fortress sometimes it became so cold that water left overnight in ewers froze solid by morning and of course the high passes to Nokat remained choked with snow, as closed as any iron gates.

By late February, the snow was ceasing and by March patches of green grass poked through the softening snow around Rabdentse, followed by the first tiny flowers of spring. Farmers began releasing the livestock they had kept penned in byres beneath their dwellings through the winter months. Tuhin Singh, Nicholas and James – helped by Santem – could again be on the parade ground, practising musketry with their troops. One afternoon, while strolling with Nicholas, the sharp-sighted Tuhin Singh spotted two dark specks in the distance approaching along the road from the south. For a week or two now travellers and messengers had begun arriving at Rabdentse, but as yet there had been no sign of the two messengers despatched to Calcutta. This time, however, as the specks drew nearer, Nicholas saw it was them. One of the men handed him a thick envelope addressed in his cousin's writing. Tearing it open, Nicholas read aloud:

> *Enclosed are three detailed sketches – one of the rocket's outer casing and the combustion chamber it contains, one of the long tail needed to increase the rocket's range and accuracy, and one of the entire device. The important facts are that the outer casing should be eight to ten inches long, an inch or so in circumference and made of a very strong metal – Hyder Ali uses hammered iron. The tail should be about four-foot long. A Company engineer who studied my reports of Hyder Ali's rockets believes he's right to use bamboo for the tail because of its strength, lightness and flexibility.*

Charles then described the design of the tall metal launch stands capable of holding six or eight rockets apiece used by Hyder Ali, and how his rocketeers fired them in salvos from several stands in unison to increase their impact on the enemy.

The Chogyal placed his chief blacksmith, Pankaj Gurung – a short, strongly made man with cheeks pockmarked by small pink scars caused, Nicholas guessed, by flying fragments of hot metal – at their disposal. Making the iron metal casings seemed to present no problems. Neither did constructing the bamboo tails. Bamboo, gathered in spring and summer in the surrounding hills and valleys and used for everything from fuel to furniture, was plentiful in Rabdentse. The blacksmith also had no difficulty fashioning robust metal stands to launch the rockets.

As soon as Pankaj Gurung had made the first six rockets, Nicholas filled them with gunpowder. 'Well, let's see, shall we?' he said to Tuhin Singh as he placed the rockets carefully in the launch rack and applied a taper to the first one. With a whoosh and a fizz the rocket shot no more than fifty feet then tumbled to the ground where steam rose from the frozen earth as it burned itself out. Nicholas tried each remaining rocket in succession. Though one or two went a little further, startling some crows gathered round an icy puddle, none flew very far. Nicholas was glad he hadn't invited the Chogyal to watch their efforts.

'It must be the amount of powder we're using as propellant or there's something wrong with the gunpowder itself…' Nicholas muttered. 'Hyder Ali's rockets, for all their inaccuracies, can travel over a mile. Unless we can get it right, we're wasting our time.'

In subsequent days, as the blacksmith produced more rockets, they tried again, progressively packing the combustion chamber with more and more powder. However, even when crammed full, the results were little better. As yet another rocket wobbled unconvincingly skyward, Santem said, 'I've an idea. Before the snows set in, a Chinese merchant from Kashgar arrived here. He quite often spends the winter in Rabdentse before travelling down into Hindustan. He trades in teas and silks in the bazaar but also in Chinese fireworks, which he sells to the Chogyal's court and those in Hindustan for such festivals as *Losar*, the New Year, and the Hindu *Holi*. He might have ideas on how to improve the rockets' performance.'

Santem was right. When they visited him in the bazaar, the merchant did have some ideas. Smiling quietly, he examined one of the iron casings carefully. 'Chinese people have made rockets for military purposes for over eight hundred years – we used them to propel arrows though I admit I've never seen anything quite like this. The overall design is crude but the idea of an iron casing is clever and has possibilities. The price for my help is ten silver rupees.'

'We'll give you three times that amount if your ideas work,' Tuhin Singh said.

'We shall see,' the merchant replied. 'Now, since you tell me your need is pressing, leave me and I will begin at once.'

–

Three days later the merchant reappeared. From a large betassled bag he took a scroll of paper which he spread over a table, holding the corners down with metal weights. Then, without preamble, he said. 'There was nothing wrong with the gunpowder you're using – I tested it. The problem is with the shape and thickness of the iron casing. The circumference is too small – it needs to be doubled. It is also too thick and heavy. Your blacksmith has been too sparing with his hammering. He should reduce the thickness by one third. Finally, the inner combustion chamber must be larger by one half and be completely filled with gunpowder. Make these changes and your rockets will fly like cranes before the storm...'

Leaning over the table with the merchant, Nicholas and Tuhin Singh scrutinised his drawings – defter and infinitely more elegant than Charles'. He had also provided diagrams showing the angles at which the rockets should be fired depending on the direction and force of the wind. Tuhin Singh looked impressed. 'We'll send word as soon as the new design is ready so you can join us for the trials. We'll see if the rockets indeed fly like cranes as you promise...'

'Wait. I have a further suggestion,' the merchant said. Delving once more into his bag he produced a short length of bamboo which he held out, turning it to show one end was completely open while a thin sliver of bamboo protruded from the other. 'It's a whistle. I fit them to my fireworks so that they scream as they fly. They would make your rockets even more terrifying to your enemy… If you like the idea, I can supply as many as you need.'

'An excellent thought,' Tuhin Singh grinned. 'Thank you!'

Pankaj Gurung laboured hard, unaware of the merchant's criticisms, which Tuhin Singh and Nicholas wisely kept to themselves. Hammering the casing sufficiently thin proved taxing, but forty-eight hours later the new design was ready to be tested on the parade ground. Three rockets waited in their metal rack. Nicholas, Tuhin Singh, James and Santem watched as the merchant, who had asked to do it, lit each in turn. One after the other they soared into the distance, screeching as they went thanks to their whistles.

'You've done it!' Nicholas clapped the merchant on the shoulder. Then to Tuhin Singh he said, 'all we have to do now is make at least two hundred of them!'

21 – The Iron Gates of Bagran

As gradually the days grew warmer and longer and the first buds formed on the rhododendron trees, Tuhin Singh waited patiently until he and Aadesh judged all the indications favourable. Then, under a cloudless blue sky, the little force set out, Tuhin Singh in the lead with James and Nicholas riding together a little behind. The men from Nokat followed. Mostly farmers before they fled, Tuhin Singh had drilled them into a reasonably disciplined force. In their midst, six men carried Aadesh in a palanquin. Despite his protests that he was still fit to ride, Tuhin Singh, noticing increasing tremors in the old man's limbs, had insisted he should travel this way. The four large covered carts containing the rockets, together with three others with musket balls and barrels of gunpowder, came next. Santem Denzongpa brought up the rear, leading the Chogyal's tough troops.

After three long days of difficult travel with the Nokat men going ahead as scouts to find the way and confirm that it was free of Ravi's troops, Tuhin Singh halted the column for the night on a high plateau beside an ice-fringed lake. The ground was too frozen to bang in pegs so they had to tie the guy ropes for their felt tents to large stones, but there were sufficient leafless trees for the men swiftly to cut branches for firewood. Over the leaping flames they cooked meat from newly slaughtered sheep and goats they had driven along behind the column knowing that the food to be found along the route would be insufficient for their numbers. After they had eaten, Aadesh told Tuhin Singh that he reckoned they were less than eighty miles from Bagran and that the route would soon become easier.

The following day Tuhin Singh roused the column early. By the time the sun was high in the cloudless sky they were at a lower altitude, travelling through a steep-sided valley following a stony track, slippery with slush and melt water beside a fast-flowing shallow river. Eagles circled high above and the spring sun was warm on their faces as Nicholas rode with his son at the rear of the column.

Suddenly rocks rained down around them. One hit James' horse, which bucked and reared. Moments later, yelling attackers were running and sliding down the steep valley side. As Nicholas drew and cocked his pistol, one leapt with the agility of a mountain goat from a high ledge onto the back of Nicholas' horse, a serrated-bladed dagger in his hand. Nicholas twisted away and with one hand grasped his attacker's wrist while with the other he pushed his pistol into the man's side and fired. His assailant's warm blood soaked into Nicholas' clothing as together they fell from the horse. Quickly pulling himself from beneath his dying opponent, Nicholas struggled to his feet, only for an unseen attacker to jump on his back and grapple him to the ground again. Together the two men, struggling for advantage, rolled over and over across the stones and through the slush until they tumbled into the freezing river water.

Nicholas' opponent was strong and young and began to gain the advantage, straddling Nicholas and seeking to push his thumbs into his eye sockets. Thwarted of that, he succeeded in forcing Nicholas' head beneath the water. Suddenly remembering Lucia's foreboding as they parted, Nicholas fought back with renewed vigour, determined that that should not be their last meeting. Summoning his remaining strength, he brought his knee up twice, hard into his attacker's groin, dislodging him. Then twisting away, he grabbed a large stone from the riverbed and hit the man hard in the face with it several times, pulverising his nose and lips. His gushing blood crimsoned the icy water. Another blow to the assailant's temple and he fell back with a splash into the river.

Trying to stand, with icy, bloody water dripping from his clothes, Nicholas felt strong hands pulling him up and out of the fast-flowing water. 'Father, are you wounded?' It was James.

'No, I don't think so. This blood is from my two attackers.' Further up the column Nicholas saw Tuhin Singh with three or four of his men defending Aadesh's palanquin, which had been overturned. Shouting to James to follow, he ran towards the palanquin. Before he could reach it, Tuhin Singh had cut down one attacker with his sword and the others were turning to flee, only for two to be pulled to the ground by Nokat men and despatched. Everywhere the action was ending as quickly as it began. To the blast of a trumpet from the heights above, the remaining attackers began scrambling back up the slopes under fire from the muskets of Santem's men. Several fell, two crashing back down the slope, head over heels, smashing their heads and bodies as they fell.

'The blood's not mine,' Nicholas said seeing Tuhin Singh's expression of concern as he ran up to him, 'unlike that from the cut on your face.'

'A nick, nothing more,' Tuhin Singh replied. 'I'm more worried about Aadesh.' He pointed to the vizier who had now been carried to a raised portion of the riverbank and was being tended by two men. 'He was knocked unconscious when he fell from the palanquin – I must go and see how he is.'

Crossing to the old man with Tuhin Singh, the two Ballantynes found Aadesh attempting to sit up. He had grazes and purpling bruises all down one side of his face and was struggling to speak through bloodied split lips. He appeared to have lost at least one of his few remaining teeth. 'I'm tough… You don't get to my age without being tough.' He paused to spit out some blood. 'My skull is tough, nothing is broken. I'll be fine. Look to the more severely wounded. I just need water to clean my face and wash out my mouth.'

Realising the vizier was determined to accept no extra assistance, Tuhin Singh turned to Nicholas and James. 'The attackers were probably Ravi's men – some of his renegade Ghurkhas, by the look of them, perhaps out on a raid on settlements rather than looking for invaders. Whatever the case, we must assume he'll know now we're on our way, even if he didn't already. No surprise really – you can't hope to move as many men as we have in secrecy for long. We'll have to increase the number of sentries at night and let's increase our speed as best we can and attempt to get close to Bagran in two more days' marches.'

–

Aadesh was right. The route became easier and broader over the next day. As it did, the column occasionally passed huts, at first mainly those used by shepherds in summer when herding flocks, but then some small hamlets occupied year round. Approaching one, just after they had crossed into the territory of Nokat as Aadesh pointed out – insisting despite his injuries on climbing from his palanquin to kiss his native earth – Nicholas realised that several houses and barns were mere burned-out shells. Neither people nor animals were to be seen. Exploring behind a hut, Nicholas came upon the bodies of a woman and two children – one a baby – sprawled on the ground with their throats cut beside some newly sprouting cabbages. The woman's right hand was stretching out towards the children. Going further, Nicholas found behind a partially collapsed barn a man – presumably the father of the family, his face black and bloated – hanging like a crow from the branches of an apricot tree on which the first white blossom was just appearing.

Returning to his comrades Nicholas discovered that an elderly woman, emaciated and shivering in thin clothes, had emerged from hiding and was telling her story in a cracked voice to Tuhin Singh. 'Sir, about twenty of them came two days ago in the early morning when the village was asleep. I have no privy so I was away in the fields… well you know why… and as I was standing up, about to return, I saw them rounding up the remaining villagers – by then there were only about a dozen of us left. The rest had fled into the hills or into Sikkim, hearing the rumours of atrocities committed by Raja Ravi's men. I quickly dropped to the ground and hid behind one of the nearby bushes. From there I could hear the newcomers shouting at my neighbours to reveal where their stores were and where the women kept their precious gold dowry jewellery. Those who had some jewellery – most didn't – said nothing. Then the man who seemed to be the leader of the intruders pointed at Taxin, my nephew, and threatened to hang him if they didn't show them where it was kept.'

The woman began to weep, tears from her rheumy eyes running down her cheeks and mucous dripping from her nose. After Tuhin Singh had handed her a cloth and she had wiped her eyes and blown her nose she continued. 'Taxin tried to resist. I couldn't quite see how – I think he grabbed a knife from one of the attackers and stabbed him in the stomach. Certainly one of them collapsed. The leader began to scream and rant like a madman and well… well… they killed everyone, Taxin and his family… everyone… In my head I can still hear their screams of pain and fear… Then… then… they torched our buildings and left, taking with them our few animals… everything we possessed.' The woman stopped, her whole body convulsed in sobs and tears.

Tuhin Singh put his arm round her shoulders. 'I am determined to restore order and justice to the country of my birth or give up my life in the attempt. I will have some of my men stay to conduct funeral rites for your family and neighbours. They will make a hut fit for you to live in and leave you blankets and food.'

A little later, as they rode on, James asked Nicholas, 'Have you noticed a change in Tuhin Singh? It's as if he's already assuming the manner and mantle of a ruler.'

'Yes… I see in his eyes and his expression a growing authority… but also a melancholy consciousness of the burden he feels he must take on… We should do everything we can to help him adapt to the role fate and his birth have imposed on him.'

'Of course,' James said, 'and the first step in fulfilling our fine sentiments will be?'

'We've already taken it by coming to help depose Ravi.'

'Does it feel strange to find your own role reversed with that of Tuhin Singh? For so many years, you were the leader and he your trusted and loyal adviser and lieutenant. Now he is the prospective ruler at the head of his forces.'

'I can't deny it feels a little odd, but this is Tuhin Singh's campaign and he must be seen by all to lead, as he is well able to do. Even the least perception that he is in thrall to a European or indeed any outsider would lower the morale among his men and diminish his attraction to his people. That aside, I do feel a relief in not bearing the ultimate responsibility.'

'But I suppose often with Clive's and more recently Eyre Coote's campaigns, you were an adviser albeit a key one, not a commander.'

'True, and it's been the same with Hastings. Perhaps the big difference for me between those occasions and now is that then I was often worrying about the rights and wrongs of the Company's actions, even sometimes about its very presence in Hindustan.'

–

That evening after eating, Nicholas and James sat around one of the campfires with Tuhin Singh and Aadesh beneath a dark star-filled sky. Tuhin Singh who had been quiet throughout the meal, staring into the dancing flames, suddenly straightened up. 'Forgive me if I've been silent. I've been caught up in my thoughts. So much of my childhood has come back to me as we've entered Nokat. I recognise so much of this land. So many memories – good and bad – have flooded back… so many thoughts have been going through my mind about the future… about how I can improve things for the people of Nokat. But then I realised I shouldn't get too far ahead of myself but concentrate on the present and my immediate task of capturing Bagran and overthrowing Ravi. I'm right, Aadesh, aren't I, that Bagran is no more than fifteen miles beyond those hills?'

'Fifteen miles if you follow – as the column must – the route along the valley floor and across the floodplain – only eight or so if you take a track that you might remember not far beyond here that winds up and over the hills and across the gorge through which the Bagran River runs.'

'You're right – I do remember, and remembering has given me an idea… Even with the rockets, we don't have sufficient men to make our defeat of Ravi certain. We need a clear plan of attack and to form that we must get a thorough understanding of the terrain around Bagran and where Ravi may have deployed his forces.'

'Agreed.' Nicholas nodded. 'And so?'

'I suggest you and I take a few men along the track over the hills to look down on Bagran from above to check the position.'

'One last reminder of our old days?'

'Yes, you could put it that way. Let's depart before dawn, leaving James, Aadesh and Santem to bring our forces slowly forward. We should return by midday ready to plan our attack.'

'Will we go on foot?' Nicholas asked.

'No. I remember that the track was passable on horseback, riding in single file. Is that right, Aadesh?'

'Yes, I think so, although there may well be some remaining snow and certainly plenty of mud. You'll need to take care – there are some steep slopes.'

'We'll take that risk, won't we, Nicholas?' Tuhin Singh said, and Nicholas nodded.

Just before first light the next day Nicholas and Tuhin Singh set out on horseback accompanied by eight Nokat men, all well armed and carefully chosen by Aadesh for their knowledge of the terrain and their cool heads. Less than a mile beyond the camp the track diverged from the main one and soon narrowed as they quickly began to wind up the first of the hills. Although the approach to the summit was windswept and over bare rocky ground, there was little ice despite the sun only peeping, an orange ball, over the still dark hills. The descent was along a steep track mostly through scree. 'This reminds me of our approach towards the camp of those Bhutanese raiders ten years ago,' Nicholas said.

'Yes, although that was on foot and – if I remember rightly – I saved you from a nasty fall.'

After twenty minutes they had safely negotiated the slope on which some patches of snow still lay in hollows only for the track to start to climb again almost immediately. Picking their way past a small, still half-frozen waterfall from which rivulets of water were running across the stony path they reached the top of the second hill. Looking down, Nicholas saw far below the foaming Bagran River rushing through a narrow rock-filled gorge. 'How do we get across that?' he asked Tuhin Singh.

'Don't worry. I've already checked my memory with our guides. There's a rope and wood bridge suspended over the gorge. It's hidden from our view here by one of the folds in the hills. I'm told the point from which we can look down on Bagran is only a mile or so beyond it.'

After another half an hour they were at the bridge – a very simple affair. Thick ropes suspended from a wooden tower on each side of the gorge supported a narrow plank walkway from which a few icicles still hung. A short distance along the bridge, a plank had broken away at one side and was hanging loose over the chasm. 'It doesn't look like the bridge has been used since the thaw,' Tuhin Singh said. 'I can't see any sign of Ravi's men being stationed here to guard it.'

'Do you think we can get across?' Nicholas asked.

'Not with the horses. They're too heavy. But it should be possible on foot. The main support ropes and the hand ropes look strong enough. Only three of us need cross. The rest can remain here and mind the horses. I'll go first.'

'No, you must not. As our leader and the prospective new Raja you're irreplaceable. I will go. Besides, I'm a little lighter – you've been growing stout in your old age…'

Seeing the determined expression in Nicholas' eyes he knew of old, Tuhin Singh said no more as Nicholas moved towards the bridge and, after inspecting the ropes, stepped on to it. Holding the hand supports carefully he moved slowly forwards, testing each plank before he put his full weight onto it. The bridge began to sway under his movement. Never too fond of heights, Nicholas forced himself to keep his eyes fixed on the opposite bank rather than looking down on the racing white water forty feet below. Approaching the loose plank he took a deep breath and then, gripping the ropes firmly, took a great stride over the gap. To his relief the next plank was firm beneath his foot. Soon he was halfway across the churning chasm. Feeling more confident, he began to move more quickly, eager to reach the other side.

He was nearly across when another plank suddenly snapped beneath his front foot and fell into the water below. The bridge swayed wildly as Nicholas clung to the hand ropes and pulled his foot back. Then, after taking another deep breath he stepped across the gap. Moving ever more cautiously he reached the other side. After checking quickly that there was no sign of Ravi's men, he shouted across to Tuhin Singh over the sound of the rushing torrent, 'It's not that bad. The ropes are strong and the planks seem sound with the two obvious exceptions you can see. But only one man at a time should cross…'

Wasting no time, Tuhin Singh stepped onto the rope bridge and, moving more confidently than Nicholas, was soon across. Another man – a native of the area and one of the lightest in the group – followed to act as guide if needed. Setting out along what was now just a muddy path, the three men soon reached their destination – a small clearing on a steep hillside overlooking Bagran and the floodplain. Tuhin Singh seemed to be choking with emotion as he said to Nicholas, 'That's it. That's Bagran, my birthplace and now after all these years, my destiny.' Both men and the guide quickly dropped on to their stomachs on the muddy ground to avoid being spotted in the unlikely event any observer could make them out from such a distance.

Slightly breathless from the thin air, Nicholas took in his first view of Bagran. Protected on two sides by the same river that ran through the chasm they'd just crossed, Bagran was a small walled town, raised above the floodplain on a low hill. Long black banners fluttered from the battlements of the whitewashed fortress built into the centre of the walls over the iron-studded gates of the town. The gates were closed, but as Nicholas scanned the approaches to Bagran through his telescope he could see no forces deployed or encamped outside the walls or even any checkpoints.

'It doesn't look as though Ravi has taken any special precautions beyond closing the gates,' Nicholas said.

'Remembering him and the way he always belittled and tried to bully me, I suspect he doesn't think he need bother too much and that he can swat me away with a single blow. Well, he'll soon learn he's wrong.'

'I'm sure he will. But before we turn back, I'll sketch out how the land lies.' Replacing his telescope in the satchel slung across his chest and taking out some paper and charcoal, Nicholas quickly drew the position of the river, glinting in the light of the now risen sun, the walls and fortress, the broad track approaching Bagran, together with the location of the isolated small coppices of pine trees that would provide the only cover for Tuhin Singh's men as they approached across the desolate grey and stony floodplain. When he had finished, the three men moved quickly back along the muddy path to the rope bridge.

At Nicholas' insistence that Tuhin Singh should cross while the bridge was at its strongest, he this time went first, followed by the guide. When both were safely across, Nicholas, his heart beating more wildly than when going into battle, set foot on the walkway still swaying from the passage of the other two. All went well until he was nearly over when another plank splintered under his weight and his foot went through. As he struggled to keep his balance and his grasp on the hand ropes, he fell backwards onto the planks behind him, which cracked and creaked alarmingly beneath his body. Sweating despite the cold, he pulled himself up and, putting most of his weight on the ropes, he manoeuvred across the gap. Then with a few further steps he was across and doing his best to look calm as he rejoined his companions and they mounted up.

'Are you sure you're lighter than me?' Tuhin Singh asked.

'Any weight I have is heavy bone and muscle – a little different from that some others have gained!'

22 – *The Raja Returns*

Tuhin Singh and Nicholas rejoined the column well before midday. While they had been away, James and Santem had led their men along the valley floor to within six miles of Bagran but then, on Aadesh's advice, turned into a narrow-entranced and wooded side valley to try to keep their forces concealed from prying eyes. After Tuhin Singh and Nicholas had swallowed some hot tea and while they were still eating chapattis, they began an impromptu council of war with James, Aadesh and Santem.

Tuhin Singh spoke first, pausing occasionally to take another bite of chapatti. 'Nicholas and I successfully got to the viewpoint over Bagran despite –' Tuhin Singh smiled at James '– your father having some minor difficulties with the rope bridge over the Bagran River. We saw no sign of Ravi's men or anyone else being there since the thaw began. The dilapidated state of the bridge means we can rule out Ravi using that track to launch an attack on our rear. From the viewpoint we could see no sign of Ravi or his Ghurkhas having erected defences or stationed men outside Bagran itself. The gates were closed. We thought we could make out a couple of small cannon on the battlements. I think you said, Aadesh, that Ravi had purchased some?'

'Yes, as far as I remember four or five.'

'Nicholas, you should show the sketch you made.'

'You'll find this of particular interest, James – you too, Santem – since it gives some idea of Bagran and the lay of the land around it,' Nicholas said, pulling it out of his satchel. 'The most significant features – I think – are the pine coppices on the flood plain on the approach to Bagran. Though not that large, they're big enough to conceal quite a number of troops and our rocket carts if we wish to preserve some element of surprise in our attack.'

'As we were riding back,' Tuhin Singh took up the conversation again, 'Nicholas and I had some initial ideas about a plan of attack… We thought that just before dawn we should send a number of scouts – Nokat men, well familiar with the area – towards Bagran to confirm there are no pickets and – in the unlikely event there are – to deal with them. Then Nicholas will quickly move the rocket carts with a protecting force into the shelter of the largest coppice. Being less than a mile away from Bagran, it's well within rocket range. I'll then lead the rest of the troops towards Bagran. The horsemen will go first, each – I propose – carrying a musketeer behind him, followed by foot soldiers with scaling ladders. We can make enough from the pine trees in this valley. Then the remainder of those on foot will follow, I suggest under your command, Santem.'

'Of course,' Santem confirmed.

'As dawn comes up, I will gallop with the horsemen towards the gates. The scaling parties will follow on foot while the rest of you wait. Once past the trees, the horsemen will rein in so the musketeers can dismount and ready their weapons as if to provide covering fire for those coming behind with the ladders. Everything will suggest to the now alerted defenders that they are facing an immediate assault on the walls. But as they emerge on to the battlements and start loading their cannon, I will have a trumpet sounded – the signal for riders, musketeers and scaling parties to pull back. Then the rocket men, at Nicholas' command, will start firing their missiles. They have a longer range than any cannon Ravi is likely to possess and should create confusion and fear among the defenders who will never have seen anything like them. Only then will I signal an all-out assault.'

'Won't breaching Bagran's gates be crucial if we're to get quickly inside?' James put in. 'We could blast them down by exploding powder barrels against them.'

'I'd been thinking along those lines too,' Tuhin Singh replied, 'but placing the barrels will entail considerable danger.'

'Not if several pairs of riders each sling a barrel between their horses and gallop forward as the rockets begin to fly. Then one of each pair dismounts to position them and light their fuses. The rockets are bound to cause the defenders to keep their heads down. I'm happy to lead those placing the barrels.'

Tuhin Singh glanced at Nicholas who, despite the concerned expression on his face, nodded, then said, 'I accept your offer, James. Choose your men.'

'I can suggest where the walls might be easiest to scale. In some places they're only fourteen feet high and in one or two I know there are weaknesses – at least there were when I left,' Aadesh added quietly.

'Thank you, Aadesh. Now unless anyone has anything else to add, we should break and begin making scaling ladders, checking weapons and attend to all the usual tasks needed before a battle.'

Soon young pine trees were being felled and their slender trunks spliced and bound with stout ropes into scaling ladders. As James and Nicholas watched one of Santem's men lean a ladder against a tree and shin up to test the strength of its rungs, James said, 'I saw how worried you looked when I volunteered to lead the breaching of the gates – I do know what I'm doing, you know.'

'I understand that and that's why I said nothing. But by now you must realise how a parent feels...'

'Yes, though Alex is hardly of an age for me to have to worry about him going into battle... I will take care – and so should you, Father. You don't move quite as quickly as you once did.'

'I don't know what you mean,' Nicholas retorted smiling, while wondering whether his younger self might indeed have been more agile on the rope bridge.

-

That night Nicholas seemed to be finding it difficult to sleep, a rare thing for him even on the eve of battle. Images and thoughts of his life passed quickly through his mind – his uncle at his desk in the Scottish Highlands... Meena, James' mother, dancing voluptuously before him, before disappearing wraithlike into the ether... Robert Clive exhorting his troops at Arcot, then slumped on the ground in what Nicholas imagined was his Berkeley Square house, his throat cut... his beloved wife, Lucia, imprisoned first by pirates and afterwards in the Black Hole of Calcutta... next her eyes glowing as he made love to her... and then turning to wave as she left Glenmire for Calcutta just a few months ago.

'Father.' He suddenly felt a hand on his shoulder. It was James. 'You were shouting Lucia's name in your sleep... It's time to prepare.' Struggling to full wakefulness, Nicholas attempted to put the images out of his mind, but again couldn't help remembering Lucia's sense of foreboding... His troubled sleep was no more than the result of indigestion – anything else would be pure fantasy, he attempted to convince himself as he quickly dressed, grabbed his weapons and equipment and with James ducked out of the tent into the chill early morning air. There was only one reason that the day about to dawn would see his last battle – his wish for a peaceful life with Lucia at Glenmire. Although he had much to look back on, both good and bad, he equally had much – all good, he hoped – to look forward to.

Twenty scouts were already on horseback, their muskets across their backs, and about to depart beneath the light of a nearly full moon to check the route to Bagran was clear. After each snatching a cup of warm tea from a kettle over a fire, Nicholas and James embraced briefly before James headed towards the men with whom he would attempt to blast down the gates of Bagran. Nicholas walked quickly across to the four large eight-wheeled carts containing the rockets and their launching stands. Each cart already had its team of ten mules yoked in pairs to it, with a muleteer beside each pair and two drivers seated at the front, long whips in hand.

Nicholas lifted the covers on the carts in turn to check once again that the rockets were safely in their boxes and their launch stands ready to be lifted down. Tinder boxes to ignite the rockets were in each cart and he had more in his well-used satchel slung across his chest. Satisfied that all was as it should be, he walked over to the fifty horsemen with whom he and the rocket carts would soon follow the now departed scouts. Most were the Chogyal's men but some were from Nokat to act as guides if needed. Once they reached the pine coppice from which the rockets would be fired, half would dismount to position the rockets on their stands and fire them in salvos – something they had practised frequently.

Not far away, Nicholas could see Tuhin Singh readying his main assault force and, with Santem's help, marshalling the foot soldiers. Taking the reins from the man holding the head of his black horse, Nicholas swung himself into the saddle and rode across to Tuhin Singh. 'Well, good luck! This day will begin your new life,' he said as he leaned across and grasped Tuhin Singh's arm.

'Yes, if the gods are willing, my old friend.'

After a brief pause Nicholas said, 'Well… I think it is time for me to lead out the rocketeers.'

'Yes… I'll follow shortly with the rest of the men… May fortune go with you as always.'

'Of course.' Nicholas nodded and, pulling on the reins, turned his horse and was quickly at the head of his force as the four rocket carts creaked slowly into motion. It took nearly an hour to approach the bend beyond which Bagran lay. Rounding it to an increasing dawn chorus from the birds and with the first rays of the sun slanting over his shoulder, Nicholas had his first close sight of Bagran. With the misty early light washing out most of its colour, the walled town and its fortress seemed to float above the river and its flood plain, conjuring in Nicholas' mind images from Mallory's Arthurian legends, read so long ago in Scotland.

Urging the cart drivers to increase their pace, he and his force quickly covered the half a mile to the pine coppice from where they were to fire their missiles without any obvious sign from the battlements of Bagran of their detection. With a wave of his arm Nicholas had the designated rocketeers dismount and start erecting the rocket stands. In minutes they had assembled eight stands and positioned seven rockets on each.

By now Tuhin Singh and the main body of his men were approaching Nicholas' post. Immediately on seeing the rockets were in place, Tuhin Singh and his horsemen began to advance towards Bagran. After half a mile the riders halted so those carrying musketeers behind them could allow them to dismount. The foot soldiers carrying the scaling ladders followed a little distance behind, some breathing hard under their heavy burdens. Next Nicholas saw James ride up with the nineteen men who, with himself, would make up ten pairs to place gunpowder barrels against Bagran's iron-clad gates. His son's face was set in a determined fashion but as he saw his father he raised his hand in greeting and smiled. Then he turned aside towards the wagons from which the gunpowder barrels were being unloaded and placed in their rope cradles.

Just two or three minutes later, Tuhin Singh put his horsemen into motion again towards Bagran's iron gates while the dismounted musketeers loaded their weapons, ready to fire as soon as any defenders appeared on the walls. Nicholas quickly checked that each man deputed to light the rockets was in position and had a tinderbox ready. Soon there was every sign that the defenders were awake and alerted to the impending attack. Puffs of musket smoke erupted along the battlements and surprisingly quickly the Raja's few cannon crashed into action. Two of Tuhin Singh's horsemen collapsed from their saddles and another slumped onto his horse's neck as Tuhin Singh immediately gave the planned signal to pull back out of the enemy's range.

'Now!' Nicholas shouted and his men ignited the first salvo of rockets. All but one lit properly and flew with a whoosh and a shower of sparks towards Bagran. Five or six deviated from their intended course – one coming down in the Bagran River and others falling short. As he ordered the next salvo to be readied, Nicholas saw James and his group ride forward in pairs, each man carefully adjusting his horse's pace to that of his partner so that the gunpowder barrels were not dislodged from the cradles slung between them. All twenty men were still in their saddles and the barrels in place as the second salvo of rockets screeched over their heads. Then to his horror Nicholas saw one rider fall from his saddle, but he was soon on his feet half-running, half-staggering back out of range. His horse careered off wildly, reins dangling. His partner abandoned the barrel and turned his horse back to pull him up behind him.

'Prepare the third salvo!' Nicholas yelled to his men.

By now one of each of the nine remaining pairs carrying the gunpowder barrels had dismounted, handed the reins of his horse to his companion and, removing the barrel from its cradle, rolled it the short distance to the gates before lighting the fuse attached to it. As the third rocket salvo screamed into the sky, Nicholas could just make out through his telescope those who had placed the barrels running back, some zigzagging to put off the enemy's aim, remounting their horses and galloping back towards him. Behind them Nicholas saw a flash and heard a loud bang as the first gunpowder barrel exploded, quickly followed by what he thought were three more, then – after a short pause – another two.

As the fourth salvo roared towards Bagran, the enemy's cannon and musket fire had almost ceased. The rockets had produced the anticipated fear and confusion among the defenders, causing them to seek cover. Through his telescope Nicholas saw amid the swirling smoke one gate lying on the ground and the second hanging from a single hinge. As Nicholas commanded the firing of the fifth and last full salvo, Tuhin Singh led his horsemen and foot soldiers with their scaling ladders forward again in the actual assault. Suddenly Nicholas saw a white flash from behind the town walls near the fortress. A powerful explosion and gouts of flame followed. By great good fortune a rocket from the fifth salvo must have hit a poorly protected gunpowder store.

James and his men had now regained Nicholas' position. Reining in, James shouted, 'Father, you needn't have worried – I'm safe and so are all my men. We succeeded in blowing down the gates. Shouldn't we both now join the main assault?'

'Yes, we should.' Ordering his men to launch the remaining rockets, Nicholas mounted his black horse and kicked it on towards Bagran, closely followed by James. The last incomplete salvo of rockets screeched and whistled over their heads as they rode, making Nicholas realise how much the whistles the Chinese firework seller had suggested added to the terror created. By now many of the foot soldiers with their scaling ladders had reached the town walls. Some had already positioned them and were climbing on to the walls. In one case two defenders emerged from cover to dislodge a ladder, which fell backwards with an attacker still clinging to it.

'Let's head for the breach in the wall the explosion caused, rather than towards the gates. They're already crowded with attackers, making them a dangerous bottleneck,' Nicholas shouted to his son who nodded and pulled on his reins to follow his father. A minute or two later, they dismounted and ran towards the tumbled stones of the wall, ducking to avoid any musket balls. Reaching them, Nicholas stumbled as he scrambled after his son, just a few yards ahead of him, and with a cry fell heavily. Blood began running from a cut above his right eye.

James turned. 'Are you hit?'

'No, I caught my foot in something soft, squelchy and by its smell decaying. I fell and hit my head on a stone.'

James helped him to his feet and into the shelter of a pile of tumbled stones. 'I'll be all right once I've caught my breath,' Nicholas gasped, wiping the blood from his face with his neckerchief. 'I must have fallen over the corpse of one of the soldiers Aadesh said were caught deserting and thrown from the walls.' After a minute he stood up again. 'Let's press on.'

Without further mishap they reached the path running behind the fallen town wall and turned towards the fortress, some two hundred and fifty feet away, and the sights and sounds of fighting around it. Nicholas' head was still ringing from his fall and the sweet stench of death from the corpse he'd stepped on remained in his nostrils. As they ran they kept close to the wall from which came screams, oaths, shots and the clash of metal on metal as more and more of their men scrambled from their scaling ladders onto it. A body crashed down head first to land with a jarring crunch just in front of them. From the unnatural angle of the head his neck was broken. The *kukri* he was clutching as he fell showed he was probably a Ghurkha mercenary.

Stepping cautiously from the shelter of the wall, cocked pistol in his hand, Nicholas looked up to see one of the Chogyal's troops – face streaked with smoke and sweat – peering over. He must have thrown the man down… Recognising Nicholas, the soldier waved. Then Nicholas heard a musket shot behind the man whose face froze in the moment of his death. He tumbled slowly over the wall, landing beside the dead Ghurkha, skull shattered by his fall, exposing his pulpy pink brains.

Quickly sidestepping the two bodies, Nicholas and James hurried on, doubly careful to hug the wall. As they neared the fortress, acrid white dust hanging in the air – probably from the exploding gunpowder magazine – caught in their throats and stung their eyes. Hearing running feet behind them, Nicholas turned to see not enemy troops but about thirty of Santem's men who must also have entered Bagran over the collapsed section of wall. As they ran past, their leader shouted, 'Colonel Ballantyne, our orders are to capture the Ghurkha barracks.'

'Should we join them?' James asked Nicholas.

'No, I think there's enough of them for that task. Let's press on to the fortress.'

About twenty yards from it, they ducked behind the low stone wall of a well. The main group of Tuhin Singh's men seemed to be facing stout resistance as they pushed over the collapsed iron gates and through the narrow entrance beneath the fortress into the town. Tightly packed as they emerged, they were an easy target for enemy musketeers firing from the battlements above and from the nearby kitchen and stable buildings. As Nicholas and James watched, one man took a musket ball in the throat. Instead of falling, his body was swept along for a while, still upright, by his comrades who could scarcely raise an arm to fire a gun or wield a sword in the crush.

They took further casualties as they debouched from the entrance onto the parade ground on which several burned-out rockets lay. Then, spreading out, they began pushing the Raja's men back, first with a volley of musket fire and then with determined rushes against them, swords in hand. Some of the enemy attempted to regroup and make a stand, but most ran across the parade ground into the town. Sudden movements on the battlements of the fortress caught Nicholas' eye. An enemy fighter was levelling his musket at a group of Tuhin Singh's men intent on pursuing the Raja's retreating soldiers. Just in time, Nicholas fired his pistol, hitting the musketeer. He collapsed, dropping his musket, which fell from the battlements to land with a clatter not far from Nicholas and James, splintering its butt. Two other men appeared but as they tried to lift their wounded comrade, a shot – seemingly from somewhere behind them – felled one. Abandoning both his companions, the other ran for cover.

'If there's fighting on the roof, that must mean our men are already inside the fortress... I'm pretty sure that's where the Raja will be – and if I know him – Tuhin Singh... That's where we should go too,' Nicholas told his son. 'Look!' He pointed to the wide entrance in the fortress's back wall, one of whose tall wooden gates was dangling lopsidedly from its hinges. 'That must be the way in.'

'There might still be some defenders just inside...'

'I know. That's why, decrepit though you think me, I'm going first to check... Only follow when I give the signal!' After reloading his pistol and looking carefully around, Nicholas rose from behind the well and ran towards the doorway. Reaching it safely and entering the fortress he halted, breathing hard and blinking in the dim light. As his eyes adjusted, he saw directly ahead of him a wide stone staircase. Then from somewhere high above he caught the sound of shouting and running feet... and, yes, unmistakably shots...

Flattening himself against the wall inside the doorway, he quickly scanned the area between the fortress and the well. Satisfied the fighting had moved away, he signalled James to join him.

Then, pistol raised, he positioned himself to provide covering fire. His son, keeping low and zigzagging as he ran, was only feet away when musket balls slammed into the wall near the entrance, chipping off slivers of stone, but he made it safely. 'I've heard noises from upstairs… keep your sword and pistol ready,' Nicholas warned.

James nodded as, quickly and silently, they climbed the stairs. Some of the stone was spattered with blood. Nicholas recognised a body halfway up as one of Santem's men – he had been stabbed in the neck. Stepping carefully over his corpse as they continued upwards, he and James saw on the top step a severed hand – a ring on the little finger – lying in a puddle of blood. Clearly there'd been fierce fighting here and not so many minutes before… Reaching the landing and peering cautiously around they saw a further flight of stairs ahead, while off to their right was a large, rectangular room – the fortress's pillared main hall, Nicholas realised as they entered, weapons raised. Several bodies lay on the floor – two or three looked to be Tuhin Singh's men and the remainder the Raja's. One was clutching a wall hanging he must have grabbed and pulled down in his death throes. Then from directly above came scuffling and shouts. 'Come on,' Nicholas said to James. 'It may be nearly over but I suspect Tuhin Singh is up there on the battlements…'

Moving as quietly as they could, weapons at the ready, they ascended the second flight of stairs. As they climbed, Nicholas felt a breeze on his face. At the top a small landing led to a stone archway. Cautiously entering, Nicholas found it was four or five feet deep – the fortress's walls were thick – and led directly onto the battlements. Peering out, he saw a man in a padded yellow coat and steel breastplate. Tuhin Singh's half-brother? He was nearly as tall, though more heavily built. Blood was dripping from a slash to his left arm, which hung limp, but his posture was defiant and his right hand gripped a scimitar. By his side were five dispirited-looking but still-armed men – survivors, Nicholas, guessed, of his hard-pressed bodyguard.

'Ravi, it's over… surely enough of our people have died,' he heard Tuhin Singh shout, though from where he was standing Nicholas couldn't see him.

'My father should have had you strangled at birth, you spawn of a bazaar whore… How dare you challenge me as if you were my equal… as if you had any—' As Nicholas and James emerged onto the roof, the Raja broke off and looked around. A momentary expression of hope that they might be his supporters faded from his face almost as soon as it had appeared.

Tuhin Singh, flanked by a dozen of his own men, was, Nicholas could now see, facing the Raja some twenty feet from him. He also looked round, but then turned immediately back to his half-brother. 'My mother – as you well know – was no whore… As for my right to challenge you, blame your own crimes. You'd never have seen me again if you hadn't butchered Sachin and his family and terrorised your people, for whom it was your duty to care.'

'I've only taken what was mine, but I've been betrayed by gutless cowards.'

'You delude yourself. You're no wronged victim but a tyrant jealous of others. Your men fought bravely for you – far more bravely than you deserve – whether from loyalty or fear, I don't know. What I am certain of is that this must finish now! Surrender, Ravi.'

'Surrender? You're a fool if you expect me to step meekly aside and let you take my place.'

'You have no choice. We outnumber you. My men's muskets are raised and ready. Your companions only have swords.'

'I'll show you what nobility means…' Ravi shouted. 'It's never surrendering… never acknowledging defeat…' Suddenly throwing down his scimitar, he ran not at Tuhin Singh but towards the battlements just a few feet away. Despite his useless left arm he scrambled onto them between two crenulations and shot a look both triumphant and contemptuous at his half-brother. 'Do you think I'd ever allow you the satisfaction of having me in your power…? If I can't have what is rightfully mine, then I want nothing…' Ravi paused for a moment, then with all the power his cheeks and lips could muster directed a gob of phlegm at Tuhin Singh. 'I'll certainly not live to see you on my throne,' he yelled. Then with a defiant, 'Damn you and yours to perdition,' he turned and launched himself from the battlements.

As Tuhin Singh's men rushed to disarm the Raja's unresisting bodyguard, Tuhin Singh, Nicholas and James ran to the battlements to look down on Ravi's broken body, spread-eagled below, the parade ground beneath him crimsoning. 'It's probably for the best,' Tuhin Singh said after a few moments. 'I couldn't have let him live, but I'm glad not to have his blood on my hands… It makes me sad to think that as children Sachin, Ravi and I sometimes played up here. Whatever our youthful rivalries, I could never have imagined it would end like this.'

'Tuhin Singh?' They turned to see Santem, breathing heavily but triumphant. 'The fighting is over… The only strong resistance we met was as we came over Bagran's walls and through the gates, and much of that was the Ghurkhas. The others surrendered quickly enough when we made clear – as you ordered – that you would spare their lives. We've disarmed them all, of course, but the only ones we've locked up are the surviving Ghurkhas, including their leader, whom we captured, wounded – he's lost an eye – after a desperate fight.'

'Well done. I'll hold him hostage as a guarantee that the rest of his bandits leave Nokat immediately,' Tuhin Singh replied. 'Now, order your men to search the fortress to ensure it's secure and to check the dungeons – I suspect you'll find people there in desperate need… And then,' he smiled, 'we'll celebrate! The people too… See what we can distribute from the stores and granaries. This is a fresh beginning for us all…'

-

A week later, Nicholas entered a side room off the main hall of the fortress where an ill-at-ease seeming Tuhin Singh was standing on a low stool being prepared for his official enthronement. Two attendants were adjusting the stiff folds of his long, yellow silk coat, edged with wolf fur.

'Well, how do I look?' Tuhin Singh asked, stepping down and taking a few paces.

'Most becoming – every inch the Raja you'll soon be.'

'Thank you. I'll take that comment at face value.'

'I meant it.' Nicholas watched an attendant slide four heavy silver bangles onto his friend's wrist. The sight of his outward transformation into a ruler brought memories flooding back of all they had shared during the many years they'd known each other. 'Do you recall the very first time we met – that morning when you, Harry Ross and I went riding outside Calcutta. It didn't take me long to realise that you were a better horseman than either of us and that when we raced along the banks of the Hooghly you reined back to let Harry win.'

'I was only his steward… I was being tactful, though I don't think Harry would have minded.'

'You're right about that. And he'd have been glad you've been able to return here, to Nokat.'

'If the fever hadn't taken Harry, things might have turned out differently for us both… who knows…'

And I might never have had the truest, most loyal friend, Nicholas thought but didn't say, not wishing to embarrass either himself or Tuhin Singh.

Tuhin Singh said after a pause, 'Well, I suppose this is it… no going back now.'

'You're not having doubts, are you?'

'To be honest, I'm still not sure how I really feel about all this… Of course I'm glad to have ended the suffering Ravi caused his people, my people, in the dungeons here – women and children reduced to living skeletons, whole villages burnt on a whim and their inhabitants slaughtered. But it took Ravi's death to make me realise how completely my life is changing – and not only mine, but that of Kannika who must assume the position of my

Rani and Kaji who will rule Nokat when I'm gone... Like me they've had no choice about any of this. I worry I'm doing them a great disservice, imposing on them perhaps unwanted duties and responsibilities...'

'I think I'd feel exactly the same. But won't the most important thing to them be that you're alive! Imagine their worry over these past months... and their relief when the messengers we've sent to Calcutta bring the news that you're safe and it's over... As for Kannika, knowing her as I do, I'm sure she'll adapt to being a Rani with ease and grace... In fact, I think she's more naturally regal than you...'

Tuhin Singh's face relaxed visibly and he smiled. 'I should have known I could rely on you to insult me, even on my enthronement day!'

Hearing trumpets sound, Nicholas slapped his friend on the back. 'It sounds like it's about to begin. I'd better go and take my place with James. Good luck and don't trip over that robe of yours...'

Nicholas stood by his son's side in the great hall where a week ago corpses had lain. Now the walls were hung with embroidered yellow silk panels, thick rugs covered the stone floor and courtiers and soldiers, some with their wounds from the recent fighting bandaged, and including Santem Denzongpa and his officers, lined the room. In the centre, facing Nicholas and James, stood a high-backed carved rosewood chair with feet depicting eagles gripping serpents in their talons – the royal throne of Nokat. The eagles, Tuhin Singh had told Nicholas, symbolised how the ruler would always overcome evil.

Before long, to the reverberating blare of ram's horns, Tuhin Singh entered, followed by Aadesh and an attendant carrying a cushion on which rested a silver chaplet set with turquoises. When Tuhin Singh had seated himself, Aadesh took the chaplet, raised it high then placed it on his head, proclaiming, 'We, the people of Nokat, greet our new Raja! May your reign be long and auspicious!' Taking three steps backwards he bowed low as a cheer rose from those watching. For a brief moment Tuhin Singh's eyes met those of Nicholas. Then one by one a line of men approached to kiss the ring on their new ruler's finger and swear allegiance.

Watching the scene, Nicholas' satisfaction at how things had worked out for Tuhin Singh was tinged with melancholy. How often would they meet in the future? Though their friendship would endure, inevitably their years of close comradeship were ending… But they had been good years, very good years, and he would always have their memory… Now he must leave Tuhin Singh to face his new responsibilities here in Nokat. As for himself and James – glancing at his son he saw he too looked reflective – it was time to return as quickly as possible to their families and embark on the more settled times he hoped awaited all the Ballantynes.

23 – Bloodless as Ivory

The sun – a colourless disc in a shimmering aureole of silver – had barely risen as Nicholas and James cantered south along the Hooghly. Mist hung low over the river as spectral fishermen cast their nets from their boats and egrets probed among the reeds. The familiar sights meant their long journey was almost over.

They had first accompanied Santem Denzongpa and his men back to Rabdentse where, despite his now failing health, the Chogyal had listened closely to their account of events in Nokat. Letters from their wives awaited them at the Chogyal's palace. Eagerly opening Riti's, James learned that, as well as a son, he now had a daughter – named Isha, as they had agreed if the child was a girl. Both mother and baby were flourishing. Lucia's letter also talked about the new arrival – 'I've never seen such a greedy baby' – but beneath her brisk tone, pride and happiness in their new granddaughter were obvious. So too was her anxiety to know that they were all safe. Her letter had crossed with Nicholas' from Bagran so by now she should know all was well. They should soon reach the bungalow she had rented on Marian Hastings' advice on the banks of the Hooghly, five miles from Calcutta, and she would again be in his arms.

The sprawling white-stuccoed building set back from the river that Lucia had described appeared ahead. Despite the early hour, the entrance gates were open and a carriage and a pair stood near the porticoed front door. Who could be calling so early, Nicholas wondered. He and James had barely dismounted before the door opened, Lucia appeared and he quickly realised this was not to be the joyous reunion he had pictured. Lucia's face was gaunt and her eyes pink as she came towards them.

'Thank God you're back.' Lucia threw her arms around Nicholas' neck.

'What is it? Is the baby all right?' James asked. But before Lucia could reply, Riti, new daughter in her arms and Alexander tugging at her knee, appeared in the doorway. As James ran towards them, Nicholas held Lucia tight, feeling her whole body shaking. '*Cara*, what's happened?'

'It's Lizzie… Before you left, I sensed something terrible would happen while you were away – that's why I felt so afraid for you… but I never thought my *presentimento* meant anything like this…'

'Lucia, please… You must explain.'

She disengaged from him, brushing away tears with the back of her hand. 'I'm sorry… Seeing you again after so long made me lose control… Lizzie's very ill… Four days ago Martha took her to a fête champêtre. That night Lizzie complained of a terrible headache – by morning she could scarcely open her eyes and soon she became delirious. I got the Grangers to send their physician, Doctor Bennet – he's with her now.'

'What does he say?'

'That he's not sure he can save her. Nicholas… It's my fault. If only I'd stayed with Lizzie at Glenmire this would never have happened.'

James, who had taken Riti and their children inside, rejoined them. 'Riti tells me the doctor's trying everything he can think of.'

'Yes – cold compresses… hot compresses… bleeding… but nothing seems to help… She recognises no one, not me… not Charles… no one…' Lucia began to sob. 'I feel so helpless…'

'We mustn't give up hope,' Nicholas said as much to himself as to Lucia. 'Take me to her…'

The bedrooms in the large, rambling bungalow were set around a courtyard where four jacaranda trees were in bloom, their purple-blue flowers scenting the air. Although the double doors were wide open and a *punkah* swung back and forth, the atmosphere in Lizzie's sickroom was stuffy. As Nicholas entered, the doctor – an elderly man with his sleeves rolled up – and Anjuli Shastri were leaning over his daughter. Lizzie's hair was cropped short like a boy's and her face was waxy with sweat. When Doctor Bennet tried to press a pad of cloth to her forehead she twisted away.

'Lizzie...' As the doctor moved a little to make room for him, Nicholas knelt by the bed and took her right hand. 'It's me... your father...' He scanned her face for any sign of recognition but found none in her dilated eyes.

The doctor again attempted to apply to Lizzie's forehead the pad, which by its pungent smell was soaked in camphor. 'I've tried the best remedies I know – syrup of rhubarb and cloves steeped in spirits... compresses of vinegar and camphor, as you can see... and I've bled her several times,' Bennet said. 'Nothing as yet has lowered her fever, but we mustn't lose heart. Your daughter is young and has a strong constitution...'

After some minutes, Nicholas stood up, oppressed like Lucia by a feeling of helplessness. A parent's greatest desire was to protect their child yet he could do nothing... This was worse than watching James ride into battle... Going outside into the courtyard with Lucia, he again held her close, stroking her hair. Lizzie's condition conjured memories of Harry Ross but much more powerfully and painfully of Meena, his first wife, James' mother. She too caught a fever like this and had died in his arms in Madras. He had carried her body to the funeral pyre he and Tuhin Singh had built on the beach, feeling sorrow beyond anything he had known before. And now such grief might be about to overwhelm him again.

During the next few hours, Nicholas divided his time between the courtyard and Lizzie's bedside where Lucia had taken up residence in a rattan chair. Their daughter didn't seem to be getting any worse but her condition wasn't improving either. Though Doctor Bennet said little, Nicholas read frustration and concern on his face. As dusk gathered, feeling weary, he stretched out on a string *charpoy* beneath one of the jacarandas just outside the room. Through the open doors he could watch the shadowy figures of the doctor and Anjuli, lit by oil lamps, moving quietly about their work.

He looked up at the darkening sky as first one star then a second – surely Canopus? – appeared. In Delhi, Emperor Shah Alam had told him a Hindustani sage, Agastya, had named Canopus the 'cleanser of the waters' because its rising signalled the calming of the Indian Ocean. If only it could bring tranquillity to his family, Nicholas mused, trying to shut out the thoughts of human mortality crowding in on him.

'Nicholas…'

Lucia, hair tumbling loose over her shoulders, looked down at him.

'What is it? What's happened?'

'The fever's ebbing… Lizzie recognised me… Come quickly.'

As Nicholas and Lucia entered the sickroom, Lizzie turned her head to look at them and said faintly 'Father! Is that really you? You've returned…'

Taking her hand, this time Nicholas felt a responsive pressure. 'Yes, I'm back.'

'I'm confused… I've been having such disturbing dreams… That you were far away and in danger.'

'I'm safe. So are James and Tuhin Singh.'

'It felt so real…'

'You've been ill. There's nothing for you to worry about, I promise.'

Lizzie managed a faint smile. A few moments later her eyes closed and, as she began to sleep, her breathing seemed to Nicholas to become more regular, less hectic.

Lizzie's condition improved so much over the next few days that Doctor Bennet decided even his daily visits were no longer necessary. As Nicholas' anxiety ebbed he found some relaxation talking to Charles who called every afternoon to see Lizzie. Lucia had told him how distraught Charles had been when Lizzie fell ill – 'I saw a different side to him. He became so emotional he could almost have been Italian…' Now Lizzie was recovering, Charles was his usual composed self again and keen to know about Nokat. 'I'm glad my information about the rockets was useful,' he said as they strolled in the courtyard early one evening. 'Whatever the case, Hyder Ali won't be needing his rockets any more…'

'Why?'

Charles looked surprised. 'He's dead. Haven't you heard?'

'No – don't forget how remote Nokat is. Did he die in battle?'

'Nothing so glorious. Although the usual wild rumours of poison are flying about, according to reliable reports he died from some kind of malignant growth on his back. Tipu Sultan's succeeded him as ruler of Mysore, so little will change. In Tipu's eyes, perhaps even more than in his father's, the Company and the devil are one and the same.'

'No let up for Eyre Coote then…'

'Coote? He's dead as well. You *have* been out of touch. He died four months after Hyder Ali of an apoplectic seizure in Madras.'

Nicholas took some moments to absorb that the ebullient, abrasive general he'd known so long was no more. 'I'm sorry,' he said at last. 'Coote could be difficult – infuriating sometimes – but I respected him. He was a good commander and a courageous one. I knew he hadn't been in good health for some time – while I was with him in the south he had a seizure… He even contemplated resigning and returning to Britain. I persuaded him not to because I knew how much the Company depended on him to blunt Hyder Ali's ambitions. Perhaps I was wrong to press him to put the Company's best interests before his own…'

'Aren't you flattering yourself to believe you had that much influence over such a stubborn man? If Eyre Coote had been truly determined to resign his post, I think he'd have done it and damned the consequences and anyone who criticised him.'

After Charles had left, Nicholas reflected on their conversation. His cousin could have reminded him of some of their previous discussions – more correctly arguments – about ends not justifying means. In this case, the end had been victory for the Company and his means had been exploiting Coote's personal vanity and jealousy of Clive to dissuade him to the detriment of his health from resigning. Despite what his cousin had said, he couldn't feel entirely blameless that Coote had not lived to go home.

The following day brought a letter from Hastings congratulating Nicholas on Lizzie's recovery and adding, *I would very much like to see you. Though I realise you might not wish to visit Government House at present, may I call on you tomorrow? Name a time and I will be there.* Nicholas immediately replied assuring him he would be welcome. Guessing the pragmatic Hastings would have more to say beyond courtesies, however heartfelt, about Lizzie's recovery, he awaited him with some curiosity.

Hastings arrived at the appointed time – midday. Nicholas was alone in the room he had chosen for a study when he was ushered in. 'It's good to see you!' Hastings said, gripping Nicholas' hand, then taking a chair. 'How's Lizzie? Your cousin says she's doing well.'

'Yes – improving every day, though the doctor warns her full recovery will take time.'

Hastings nodded. 'I sympathise. God knows, I love Hindustan but not its diseases… You know Marian's gone home on the *Atlas*? I've always worried the Hindustani climate was too much for her and we decided it was for the best.'

'Lucia told me. She misses Marian. She was one of the few women in Calcutta she felt at ease with.'

'I may soon follow her home.'

Nicholas stared at him in surprise. 'What do you mean? You're not quitting Hindustan, are you?'

'Maybe… I don't know yet… Things only seem to get more difficult here. However much I achieve, for every step I take forward, it feels like I'm pushed two back. The home government mulishly refuses to acknowledge the huge complexities of my task as governor-general. Instead of granting me the freedoms I need, the damned fools have limited my authority – and the Company's freedom of action – even further. Our beloved new

Prime Minister Pitt has forced an act through Parliament establishing a Board of Control to which the Company – including me as governor-general – must answer. It leaves me all the responsibility but even less real power.'

'It's not like you to give up – or do anything rash. You didn't resign when forced to accept a council that could outvote you… Shouldn't you at least wait to see how things develop…?'

'And this advice from you – the man who out of hand refused power and position to be rid of their attendant complexities and compromises and to return to a quiet life at Glenmire?' Hastings smiled. 'We're neither of us young any more. Why shouldn't I say "a plague on all your contending houses", resign and lead a peaceful life with Marian in England? I'm wealthy enough to achieve one of my greatest ambitions, which is to buy back the Hastings family estate, Daylesford. I could lead the life of a leisured country gentleman just as well as you…'

'I know. I'm just not convinced it's in your character to succumb to the slings and arrows of outrageous fortune – or even to dither Hamlet-like about doing so!'

'Perhaps,' Hastings laughed. 'But to be serious, I've not told you the worst of it. I suspected that once back in Britain, Philip Francis might make trouble for me and he certainly has. Thanks to his silver-tongued lies and vindictiveness – as well as his many friends in Parliament – I'm being pilloried day after day in the press.'

'What are you accused of?'

'Everything and anything you can think of… exceeding my powers by agreeing that damned treaty with the Nawab of Oudh that enabled him to annex Rohilkhand with the help of Company troops… deposing the Raja of Benares for not honouring his obligation to pay towards the campaign against Hyder Ali… my treatment of those old harpies the begums of Oudh… enriching myself through supposed corrupt practices… I'm even charged with judicial murder for failing to reprieve Nandakumar, a man convicted of forgery – unjustly, my opponents claim, which is another lie – and condemned to hang. It's said I didn't pardon him out of spite because Nandakumar once faked evidence of corruption against me at Francis' behest! How can I defend myself properly against this sea of lies if I'm not there in person?' Hastings drew his hand across his thin face.

'All I can advise is don't act impetuously out of anger or frustration but only after careful, calm consideration – hardly novel advice, I'm afraid.' What more could he say, Nicholas wondered. Hastings seemed genuinely upset and aggrieved, but it wasn't for him to encourage him to stay or go – only he could decide that…

Hastings seemed to read his mind. 'I'm sorry, Nicholas. I'm being unfair, especially when you've problems of your own. It's just that with Marian gone you're one of the few people I can talk to… or trust… I needed to unburden myself to someone…'

Before Nicholas could reply, the *khutmagar* entered abruptly without knocking. 'Sir,' he said to Nicholas, 'Mrs Ballantyne asks you to come at once.'

'What is it?' Nicholas asked, rising immediately.

'Your daughter.'

Hurrying to the sickroom, Nicholas saw Lucia trying to hold Lizzie as she tossed about. Hearing Nicholas behind her, Lucia looked round. 'She was sleeping peacefully – I was reading in my chair – but then I heard her cry out and now she seems to be relapsing into delirium again…'

'I'll send for Doctor Bennet at once.' With a quick anxious look at his daughter's face, once more waxen and sweat-beaded, Nicholas returned to the courtyard to find Hastings there. 'Lizzie's fever has returned – the doctor warned us it might… Excuse me. I need to get a message to him immediately,' Nicholas said.

'Can I suggest something? I employ a herbalist – Lal Seth – at Alipur to tend the physic garden Marian planted. He's a student of Ayurvedic texts and an expert in Hindustani pharmacopoeia. Marian swore by the remedies he made her when she was ill. He might be of use as well as your doctor. Should I send for him? Alipur's closer than Calcutta.' Barely able to take in what Hastings was saying, Nicholas simply nodded, then hurried off to despatch a message summoning Doctor Bennet.

Lal Seth – short, stout, young and bespectacled – arrived first. Lucia took him at once to Lizzie's bedside where, instructing Anjuli Shastri to hold Lizzie's head still, he rolled back her eyelids, then inspected her tongue. Next he felt her pulse. When he was finished, he turned to Lucia and Nicholas. 'I think I can help… It's fortunate Governor-General Hastings summoned me when he did. Another few hours and it might have been too late. I'm glad you did not rely on those doctors of yours with their bleedings, cuppings and purgings… quite wrong for this case. They would only weaken her further. Now please have a brazier of burning charcoals brought to the courtyard so I can have a constant supply of boiling water.'

While the brazier was fetched and water boiled in an iron pot set over it, Lal Seth settled himself beneath one of the jacarandas and spread out a large square of chintz. On it he arranged a brass pestle and mortar that he took from his bag, together with a small bundle swathed in white cotton. As he unwrapped it, Nicholas saw it contained a bunch of tiny purple flowers. 'I picked them in the garden at Alipur before I left. They're called "*tulsi*" – "holy basil" in English – and reduce fever and cleanse the body,' Lal Seth explained.

'Sir. A message from the city.' It was the *khutmagar* again, with a note from Doctor Bennet's assistant saying the doctor had been called away from Calcutta and could not attend Lizzie before the following morning. Until then the assistant advised bathing the patient in cold water and administering laudanum. Nicholas screwed up the note. Should he ride into Calcutta to fetch another doctor? That would take time… In the sickroom he had a quick whispered conversation with Lucia but she looked up at him distractedly. 'Do what you think best…' she said, before returning her attention to Lizzie. Back in the courtyard, Nicholas found Lal Seth carefully stripping the flowers from their stems. His methodical way of working, his air of quiet assurance, decided

Nicholas. He and Lucia would trust him… Time would tell if they were right…

Lal Seth tossed the purple petals into his mortar and crushed them into a lavender-coloured paste with his pestle. Then, scraping the paste into a large clay cup, he slowly added boiling water, stirring the mixture with a small silver spoon, now and then tasting it. 'Good,' he said at last to Nicholas. 'We can begin.'

Carrying the cup into the sickroom, Lal Seth said to Anjuli Shastri, 'Hold her head back, please.' To Nicholas, standing by Anjuli, he said, 'Take your daughter's shoulders and keep her steady.' Going round to the other side of the bed, Lal Seth bent over Lizzie and held the cup to her lips. She struggled so that some of the purple liquid was lost, trickling down her already sweat-sodden white night gown. From a pocket, Lal Seth produced a long-spouted silver funnel. As he gently pushed the spout's end between her lips, Lizzie struggled afresh but Nicholas managed to keep her sufficiently still for Lal Seth to insert it far enough to start trickling in the infusion. Persistent, patient and skilful, after ten minutes he had managed to make her swallow at least half the liquid.

And so the process continued. As the day wore on, James and Charles, who arrived from Calcutta, waited anxiously in the courtyard as Lal Seth mixed infusion after infusion, each time increasing the potency. To Nicholas' anguish the treatment seemed to be having little effect. As dusk fell, in the sickroom he watched Lal Seth administer yet another dose, but the sight of Lizzie continuing to toss and turn beneath sweat-drenched sheets, face bloodless as ivory, was too much. He went back outside and, avoiding Charles and James – what was there to say to comfort any of them? – sat on the *charpoy* and closed his eyes.

A few moments later, he felt a hand on his shoulder. It was Lal Seth. 'The infusions are over… soon we will know. I am hopeful, but you should be with your wife and daughter.' Nicholas nodded and returned to sit beside Lucia. Lal Seth stationed himself at the end of the bed and fixed his eyes on his patient's face. As the minutes passed and they watched and waited, Lizzie lay eyes closed, chest rising and falling alarmingly fast as more and more sweat poured off her. Suddenly her eyes opened wide and she struggled to sit up. She tried to speak but her words made no sense. Then, just as abruptly, she went limp and fell back against the pillows.

Lucia gasped and a chill gripped Nicholas' heart. But then he heard Lal Seth say, 'See how quietly she's breathing now… The *tulsi* has done its work. Your daughter will live.'

And so it proved.

Epilogue

Six weeks later, in his study in the bungalow on the banks of the Hooghly, Nicholas glanced at his pocket watch – nearly three, the hour at which Charles usually called to visit Lizzie who was now virtually recovered. Sure enough, he soon heard a carriage draw up outside – Charles was ever punctual – and then light steps as his daughter ran to greet him.

Adjusting the glasses he was finding increasingly necessary, Nicholas settled down to his oft-postponed work on a history of Sikkim. He had planned to consult the Chogyal – the books and manuscripts in Calcutta's libraries said little about the origins of the Chogyal's dynasty – but news had reached him just a month before of the Chogyal's death. His book would have to be a posthumous tribute.

Nicholas was starting work on drawing a map showing Sikkim's western border with Nepal when to his surprise Charles entered. 'I thought I should tell you at once. It's been announced this morning that Hastings has resigned. He says he's ready to defend himself before Parliament if need be against the charges levelled against him by his opponents and sails for Britain next week on the *Barrington*.'

Nicholas took off his glasses and laid them on the desk. 'Hastings told me Phillip Francis was orchestrating accusations against him and that he might return home but, to be honest, I didn't think he'd actually do it.'

'From what I heard, one of the things that clinched it was a report that that villain Gilbert Cuthbertson – you remember him from Delhi, don't you? – is claiming he was forced out of the

Company because he'd found evidence that Hastings was taking bribes… He says he's given his friend Francis written proof. You and I both know that's a damned lie – Cuthbertson's the one who's corrupt. That's clear as day. But of course Francis and his friends like Burke and that playwright Sheridan have seized on it with glee. Hastings seems to think the only way to save his reputation is to confront his enemies in person.'

When Charles had left, Nicholas sat back in his chair. Through the French windows that opened on to a patch of lawn he could see his grandson, Alexander, playing on the coarse yellowing grass with his pet mongoose under the watchful eye of Anjuli Shastri who was sitting beside Isha in her wicker cot in the shade of a neem tree. But for some moments Nicholas saw not the children but the spare, wiry figure of Hastings as he had been in the early years, brimming with quiet confidence and unassailable self-belief. Later, doubts and anxieties had crowded in on him, yet he still had the courage and determination to face down his critics. Though he and Hastings had by no means always agreed, of two things he was certain. For all the errors pragmatism, opportunism and expediency had drawn him into, Hastings was far from being the most corrupt, venal or self-serving of the Company's senior officials. He cared much more than most about Hindustan and its peoples and valued their cultures. Time would tell whether Hastings ultimately vindicated himself, but knowing his determination, somehow Nicholas didn't doubt it.

As for himself, he too had grown to love Hindustan but in a different way from Hastings, who perhaps saw the country through the lens of his own aims, ambitions and achievements. Nowhere else – not even the faraway Scottish Highlands where he'd once thought to live his whole life – could ever be home to him now. The realisation of how much he owed Hindustan made him all the more glad that – as Hastings had gently mocked him – he had rejected the Company with all its prizes and pitfalls. 'Wars and rumours of wars', as the Bible put it, had drawn him back in for a while but he'd always tried to act for the best. He may not have always succeeded but then what man could ever claim honestly to have done so? Above all, he'd helped defeat French ambitions in Hindustan and thereby probably prevented widespread conflict. That at least seemed an achievement he could be proud of when – God willing – in a few weeks he and Lucia returned at last to Glenmire to grow old there together.

But what did the future hold for Hindustan and its peoples and indeed for the further generations of Ballantynes? Alexander and Isha and any children born to Lizzie and Charles, who would marry soon? Could Hindustan ever be to them what it had been to him? Of course not. Nothing stayed the same… In any case, unlike him, Hindustan was their true not their adopted home. Putting away his half-finished map, Nicholas rose a little stiffly and went outside into the sunlight to join his grandson.

Historical Note

Although some characters are fictional, as indicated in the cast list, this novel is based around historical fact, of which some is outlined below.

The East India Company

The East India Company (also known as the English or British East India Company) was founded in 1600. When Robert Clive arrived in India in 1744 and Warren Hastings in 1750 it was Britain's largest and most important trading company. The Court of Directors, which comprised twenty-four stockholding members under a chairman and deputy chairman, managed its activities from East India House in Leadenhall Street in London and accrued great wealth for themselves and their investors. The directors, some of whom were Members of Parliament, maintained a close relationship with the British government, to which the Company made loans.

The centres of Company activity in India were three settlements – the presidencies of Calcutta (Kolkata), Madras (Chennai) and Bombay (Mumbai). Here Company trading was conducted within a hierarchy. At the bottom were the 'writers' – the junior rank at which men joined the Company – then 'factors', then junior merchants, then senior merchants. At each settlement, a president (or governor) and council guided and monitored Company activities and reported back to London.

The settlement in Madras in southern India, based around Fort St George and established in 1640, was the oldest of the three. In the mid-eighteenth century Madras was the wealthiest town on the Coromandel Coast with a population of four hundred Europeans and forty thousand local people. The Company acquired Bombay in 1668, following the marriage of the Portuguese princess Catherine of Braganza to Charles II of England, bringing a dowry that included the deep-water port. Charles rented Bombay to the Company for just ten pounds of gold a year and it quickly supplanted Surat as the Company's main establishment on India's west coast. In 1690, Company employee Job Charnock identified the then village of Kalikata in Bengal as a suitable site for what became known to the British as Calcutta. Fort William was completed in the very early years of the eighteenth century and rebuilt in the years after the 1757 Plassey campaign when the buildings around it were cleared and the maidan was laid out.

During the period covered in *Fortune's Heir* the East India Company's main purpose was to trade and to produce dividends for its shareholders. Its directors in London had little wish to spend money on administering territory, only desiring to secure trade advantages in India and to eliminate its main European trading rival France and thus to produce a profitable monopoly of trade with the subcontinent. However, in the years after Plassey, with French interests much diminished, this policy had begun to change, particularly in Bengal, initially under the influence of Robert Clive, where the Nawab of Bengal had become a virtual vassal of the Company.

The three presidencies were initially independent of each other. They enjoyed a great deal of autonomy from London due not least to the long time it took – four to six months – to sail from India to Britain, which meant that it took up to a year to send a report to the directors in London and in turn to receive their instructions with regard to it. In 1774, with the Company facing financial difficulties, under a new Act of Parliament the post of governor-general was introduced to oversee all Company activities in India. Warren Hastings, already governor in Calcutta, was appointed to the post at the lavish salary of £25,000 (some

£4 million today) plus expenses. At the same time, the new governor-general was given a council of directors in Calcutta who could veto his actions.

Throughout the period of this book, the number of Britons in India was very small. The population of all the Company's establishments was overwhelmingly Indian. In particular, few British women were in India. The years of the 'fishing fleet' of women arriving in India to seek husbands, were still to come.

The East India Company armies

To protect its activities the Company recruited its own infantry, cavalry and artillery troops from local populations. These sepoys were equipped with modern weapons, officered by Britons and comparatively well paid compared to their peers. Over time the Company introduced some all-European regiments. Sometimes British Army regiments were sent to India to serve alongside Company troops, particularly during times of conflict with other European powers. They were often referred to as 'HM's Regiments' or 'Royal regiments'. In all the campaigns described in the book, the Company's armies consisted mainly of Indian troops.

Military campaigns

The military campaigns and battles described in the book nearly all happened, although in many cases the detail of the action is imagined. There are three exceptions – the engagement in chapter ten between the Moghul Emperor's troops, the Rohillas and the Sikhs, which is, however, typical of the many between these three protagonists; the short campaign against the Bhutanese bandits in the prologue; and the fictional Tuhin Singh retaking power in his fictional fief of Nokat at the end of the book.

The Moghul Empire and the Indian subcontinent in the mid-eighteenth century

Aurangzeb, the last of the six great Moghul Emperors – each the subject of one of the books of the Empire of the Moghul series – died in 1707. He had spent much of his life campaigning in the Deccan and southern India. A strict Muslim, his religious policies had divided the people of his empire. He had alienated the powerful martial Rajput leaders, major supporters of his predecessors. After his death, the Moghul Empire had begun its slow decline and disintegration – a fact underlined when in 1739 Nadir Shah of Persia sacked Delhi and stole the fabulous Peacock Throne, which had been created to showcase the best gems of Emperor Shah Jahan. It was never seen again. Though the Moghul Emperors still exercised some control in the north through their vassals, in the south their suzerainty over powerful vassals such as the Nizams of Hyderabad had withered. The resulting vacuum encouraged jostling for power between local rulers such as those of the Marathas, the Sikhs and the Jats and gave European rivals like the British and the French the chance to intervene in hopes of winning trading and other concessions.

During the action of this book, the Moghul Emperor was Shah Alam II. He was brought up in comfortable semi-captivity in the Red Fort in Delhi. After the murder of his father, Alamgir II, in 1759, he became Emperor. Defeated with other Indian allies at the Battle of Buxar by the East India Company, he became a virtual pensioner of the Company, living quietly in Allahabad writing good poetry and enjoying the pleasures of the haram. In return he legalised the Company's position in Bengal, giving them tax-raising powers. He returned to his capital, Delhi, in 1772, restored to power with the help of the Maratha leader Mahadji Scindia. Although tensions developed with the Marathas, Shah Alam's Persian commander-in-chief, Najaf Khan, (1723–1782) helped him retake control of considerable territory in northern India in frequent wars with, among others, the Rohillas, the Sikhs and the Jats. In 1788, the Rohilla leader Ghulam Qadir seized Delhi and enraged at his failure to find treasure had Shah Alam blinded. The Marathas under Mahadji Scindia defeated the Rohillas again and Shah Alam lived on under their protection until their defeat by the East India Company in 1804–1805 whereupon he again became a pensioner of the British until his death in 1806.

In the period of the book, the peoples of the Indian subcontinent were at least as diverse and disparate in terms of spoken language, script, religion and culture as those of Europe at the time.

The 1745 Jacobite Rebellion and the emergence of parliamentary power

The rebellion – which was the cause of the fictional Nicholas Ballantyne going to India – began when Prince Charles Edward Stuart – 'Bonnie Prince Charlie' – landed in Scotland's western isles and called on the Highland clan chiefs to support his bid to take the throne for the Stuarts from his cousin, the Hanoverian King George II. (The last Stuart king, James II, had been deposed some fifty years previously.) Many Highland chiefs like Cameron of Lochiel felt they could not, out of honour, refuse the prince's appeal even though they suspected his campaign would fail. Others, in particular the Campbells, supported George II.

At first the prince's campaign prospered. With the help of troops drawn from the Scottish clans, he defeated government forces and seized Edinburgh. However, the troops promised by King Louis XV of France failed to arrive and as the prince led his army south into England, the lack of popular support for him became obvious to the Highland chiefs who, when the army reached Derby, some 120 miles from London, insisted on a withdrawal back to Scotland.

As one commentator wrote, 'No one is afraid of a rebellion that runs away.' As the Highland army retreated to Scotland, the government despatched troops under George II's son, the Duke of Cumberland, north to Scotland to destroy the Jacobite threat. The final confrontation came on 16 April 1746 at the

Battle of Culloden near Inverness, the last battle ever fought on British soil. There the prince's army was defeated by Cumberland and his men and Charles forced into hiding until a French ship arrived to carry him to safety. There was no such rescue for many of his supporters. The estates of clan chiefs were confiscated, some Jacobite supporters were executed, more imprisoned, and Cumberland's troops drove many ordinary clansmen and their families from their humble homes. Many of the dispossessed emigrated to North America.

Political and religious differences played a significant part in the Jacobite Rebellion. The Stuart kings had in general believed like Kings Louis XIV and XV of France in the 'Divine Right of Kings' to rule, make and change laws and impose taxes as they wished, unfettered by the views of those they ruled, as expressed in Parliament and elsewhere. Many Britons found such behaviour anachronistic and unsustainable and the desire to entrench the rights of Parliament was key to the placing of the Hanoverian George I, father of George II, on the British throne in 1714 with significant agreed restrictions on his powers. Thereafter, the British Parliamentary system began to develop with Robert Walpole becoming the first Prime Minister in 1721.

By the 1770s under King George III (1738–1820), the power of the British Parliament was becoming paramount. The movement speeded up when the king became subject in 1786 to recurrent bouts of mental illness. From 1770 to 1782, the British prime minster was Lord North, a Tory. It was under his administration that the British fought and lost the American War of Independence (1775–1783). As a consequence of their support for the American colonists, France went to war with Britain from 1778 to 1783.

With the Jacobite Rebellion disappearing into history, tensions between Hanoverian Protestants and Stuart Catholics and those between English, Irish and Scots were lessening. Scotsmen formed a greater number of East India Company employees than their proportion of the British population might have suggested.

Warren Hastings was born in December 1732. His mother died days after giving birth to him. His clergyman father deserted his family and fled to Barbados. Hastings was first brought up by his grandfather – a bankrupt, during whose life the family estate, Daylesford, in their hands since the thirteenth century, had to be sold. Hastings was initially sent to a village charity school for orphans. However, at the age of eight he was rescued by his uncle who arranged for his schooling at the famous Westminster School in London where he excelled. On his uncle's death, Hastings had to leave school and in January 1750 set sail for India to join the East India Company in Calcutta.

Hastings' career prospered in the years before Clive's victory at Plassey. He became fluent in Urdu and Bengali and learned Persian. He married in 1756 and had two children, both of whom died in childhood. His wife, Mary, died in 1759.

Hastings played a role in the East India Company's intrigues in the early years of Mir Jafar's rule as Nawab of Bengal and in 1761 became a junior member of the Company council in Calcutta. He himself traded on his own behalf but became a target of other senior figures whose corruption he did not share. He sold up and left for Britain a wealthy man in 1764. Back in Britain he went through his wealth in a recklessly extravagant manner. He was therefore glad that his proposal to rejoin the Company was accepted and in 1769 he went to Madras as a member of the Company council there. In 1771 he was appointed governor of Bengal and in 1774 governor-general overseeing all the Company affairs in India.

Hastings' historical career as governor-general is as described in this novel. He opposed corruption among Company officials, overhauled the administration and centred it in Calcutta. He indeed agreed a treaty with the Nawab of Oudh in return for a substantial sum to help restore Company finances, which allowed the Nawab to call on Company forces to annex Rohilkhand, which he did.

Hastings in general followed a policy of maintaining stability in India including the preservation of the Moghul Emperor as a titular authority. He opposed the efforts of Company officials in Bombay to secure power in the Maratha Confederacy for the pretender Ragoba. Despite Hastings' opposition, the Bombay Company went ahead and supported Ragoba and he and the Company forces were defeated by the Marathas led by Mahadji Scindia. Hastings then concluded peace treaties with Scindia, which meant that the Maratha Confederacy did not support Hyder Ali of Mysore's attacks on the East India Company in Madras which were repulsed over a long campaign by the forces of General Eyre Coote.

At this time, Hastings deposed the Raja of Benares, Chait Singh, who would not contribute to the East India Company's war chest against Hyder Ali as Hastings believed he should. He also attempted to secure money from the begums of Oudh to replenish Company coffers.

Hastings was often at odds with his council and exactly as depicted in this book fought a duel with one of the members, Philip Francis, in which Francis was wounded.

On his voyage out to Madras in 1769 Hastings began an affair with the twenty-two-year-old Anna Maria Apollonia Chapuset, born in 1747, from a French Huguenot family, who was travelling with her impoverished husband, Baron Karl von Imhoff, a soldier and painter of miniatures. When they reached Madras she and her compliant husband moved into Hastings' house – an arrangement that continued when Hastings was appointed to Calcutta. With a bribe of £1000, he persuaded the baron to return to Europe to seek a divorce. This did not arrive until 1777, when Hastings married the baroness. He remained devoted to her for the rest of his life.

Hastings is generally regarded as having taken an enlightened approach to colonial administration compared to his contemporaries and to have had a genuine regard for India and its culture. He sponsored a compilation of Hindu law and the production of a grammar of the Bengal language. He also sponsored a translation of the Hindu *Bhagavad-Gita*.

On Hastings' return to England in 1785 following further disagreements with his council, he was able to repurchase the family estate of Daylesford. However, in 1788 he was impeached before the UK Parliament for his behaviour in regard to the treaty with the Nawab of Oudh and the annexation of Rohilkhand, his deposition of the Raja of Benares Chait Singh, his attempts to seize the fortunes of the begums of Oudh and for his failure to pardon Nandakumar who had faked evidence of corruption against him and passed it to Francis and then, sometime later, been sentenced to death for an unrelated forgery – forgery was a capital offence – and executed.

The impeachment trial lasted until 1795 when Hastings was acquitted. He lived thereafter quietly but in considerable luxury in Daylesford until his death in August 1818. He and the baroness had two children who did not survive infancy. She outlived him, dying aged ninety in 1837.

Mahadji Scindia

Scindia (1730–1794) was a major leader of the Maratha Confederacy and the ruler of Ujjain. He restored Shah Alam II to his throne in Delhi in 1771. He defeated the attempt by officials of the East India Company in Bombay to support Ragoba as the head of the Maratha Confederacy. After a protracted series of negotiations he agreed the Treaty of Salbai with Hastings under which the Company agreed to the Marathas regaining certain territories and acquiring others. In return, Scindia kept the Marathas out of Hyder Ali's war against the Company. The treaty produced twenty years of relative peace between the Company and the Maratha Confederacy. Scindia also further expanded Maratha territories and made the Marathas the dominant power in central and northern India.

Hyder Ali

Hyder Ali was born some time around 1722, the son of an officer of Punjabi origin in the Mysorean army. An excellent tactician and commander, he made swift progress in the army and in 1762 deposed the Raja of Mysore. As the state's new ruler he considerably increased its territories. He fought many wars including against the Marathas and the East India Company. His first with the Company ended in virtual stalemate in 1769. In the second, he inflicted serious defeats on the Company forces, in particular at the Battle of Pollilur in September 1780, and threatened Madras. Company troops, hastily brought together under Eyre Coote, eventually defeated him at the Battle of Porto Novo in July 1781, and later in the same year at the second Battle of Pollilur and another battle at Sholingur.

Although apparently illiterate, Hyder Ali studied military tactics, bought modern weapons for his troops – mainly from the French – and drilled them into a disciplined fighting force. He employed French officers in his army, in particular for his artillery. He oversaw the development of the famous Mysore rockets. Mounted on carts for transport they were a major innovation. He also established a Mysorean navy. He died on campaign in December 1782 from a malignant growth on his back. He was succeeded by his equally famous son, Tipu Sultan, who had long commanded parts of his father's armies.

Eyre Coote

Eyre Coote was born in Ireland in 1726, the son of a Protestant clergyman. He joined the army and fought on the Hanoverian side in the Jacobite Rebellion. In 1756–1757, he was a key commander in the East India Company's victory under Robert Clive in the Plassey campaign. A bluff, mettlesome character, he developed a rivalry with Clive with whom he quarrelled and for whom ever afterwards he preserved a considerable dislike.

After other successful campaigns in sou... defeated French forces at the battle of Wandiwash in ... elsewhere, he returned to Britain, but was back in Bengal in 1769. He quarrelled with the Company administration and after two years again returned to Britain where he became a Member of Parliament. He went back to India once more in 1779, leaving his wife at home on his estate in Hampshire on England's south coast. He became the commander of the Company's forces in India, who were being hard pressed by Hyder Ali in southern India. In a protracted campaign he defeated Hyder Ali at Porto Novo, the second Battle of Pollilur and at Sholingur (all in 1781).

Although becoming increasingly ill, Coote was persuaded to remain in command and died in Madras of a stroke while still on active service, in April 1783. Popular with his troops for his care for them, they called him 'Coote *Bahadur*', 'Great Coote'. In his autobiography, the American general and secretary of state Colin Powell claims direct descent from Coote's identically named nephew, Eyre Coote, while the latter was serving as governor-general of Jamaica.

Points on specific chapters

In some cases time scales have been changed and some events omitted or simplified to fit within the ambit of the book.

Prologue

Phuntsog Namgyal became Chogyal of Sikkim, a kingdom founded by his dynasty in the seventeenth century, in 1733. During his reign, Sikkim was often in conflict with both Nepal and Bhutan.

The Archaeological Survey of India (ASI) have been working to restore the palace and monastery complex of Rabdentse, which have been declared a monument of national importance.

…o settle in Nova Scotia lasted only from …wnership of the territory was for many years …en the English and the French. However, by the …e 1745 Jacobite Rebellion, Nova Scotia had been in Bi…n hands for a while and many Highlanders fled there. Many more Scots followed during the infamous Highland Clearances of the eighteenth and nineteenth centuries – between 1770 and 1815, nearly fifteen thousand settled there.

Chapter Two

The Revenue Board was set up by Hastings early in his governorship to reduce scope for corruption in tax collection. At that time he also established a postal service, surveys of roads and rivers and currency reforms.

Hastings' first wife was Mary Buchanan. After her death – and before meeting the Baroness von Imhoff – he is said to have had an affair with Jane Austen's aunt, Philadelphia Hancock. In 1761, Philadelphia, whose marriage had been childless until then, gave birth to a daughter, Elizabeth. Hastings was her godfather and settled large sums on 'Eliza' – an important figure in Jane Austen's life and almost beyond doubt Hastings' illegitimate daughter.

Hastings was indeed warned in similar words to those quoted that an attempt might be made to poison him.

The French *voluptueuse* referred to by Lucia is Jeanne Dupleix, a French agent and wife of the Marquis Dupleix, governor-general of French territories in Hindustan, who in the previous book, *Fortune's Soldier* attempted to seduce Nicholas.

The infamous Bengal famine lasted from 1770 until 1774. Murshidabad was among the worst affected areas. Estimates of the number who died as a result of the famine vary but between five and ten million people probably perished.

Chapter Three

Hastings' comments that the Company was no longer a golden goose accurately reflect the situation he faced. In 1772 a Parliamentary committee discovered the Company's total financial obligations amounted to over £9 million but that its assets were worth less than £5 million.

Chapter Four

Shuja ud-daulah, Nawab of Oudh, was, as described, renowned for his physical strength and the astonishing feats with which he demonstrated it.

Hastings did indeed build more granaries after the Bengal famine.

Chapter Five

By the period of this book, almost half the writers employed by the Company were Scots. By the 1790s Scots accounted for over 10 per cent of the Company's officials, over 50 per cent of its British soldiers and nearly 70 per cent of its officers.

Robert Clive committed suicide in November 1774 in his house in London's Berkeley Square as described. Lady Clive was the former Margaret Maskelyne who features in *Fortune's Soldier*.

The first English-language newspaper in Calcutta – as opposed to gossip sheets – was the *Bengal Gazette* produced by Irish-born printer James Augustus Hicky from January 1780 as 'a weekly political and commercial paper open to all parties but influenced by none'. It was followed by the *India Gazette*, *Bengal Journal*, *Oriental Magazine* and *Calcutta Journal*.

The details of the Bogle/Hamilton expedition to Tibet, including the text of the letter the Panchen Lama sent to Hastings and the latter's interest in polyandry, are factual. George Bogle indeed required medical attention for syphilis on his return. Hastings sent a copy of Bogle's journal describing his expedition to Samuel Johnson whom he had got to know in England. Having read Johnson's account of his journey to the Hebrides he thought Johnson might enjoy it.

Chapter Six

The Baroness von Imhoff was renowned in Calcutta for wearing the latest European styles and clearly aroused some envy. One woman wrote waspishly 'as a foreigner she may be excused from not strictly conforming to our fashions'. Her extravagance prompted complaints that she drove up seamstresses' and milliners' charges by grossly overpaying. One of her outfits – a black satin bodice and skirt edged with pearls and with diamond buttons – was estimated even then as worth an incredible £25,000.

The Moghul Emperor Aurangzeb indeed invited in the Rohillas.

Sikh Guru Tegh Bahadur was murdered in 1675.

Chapter Seven

The Amber Fort, near Jaipur, remains one of the loveliest fortress-palaces of Rajasthan and indeed has a *Suraj Pol*, 'Sun Gate'. Raja Prithvi Singh II was the ruler of Amber at the time. His comments to Nicholas reflect the Rajputs' once close ties to the Moghuls, including through marriage – the Moghuls had a substantial amount of Rajput blood in their veins. These ties existed until the reign of the strict Muslim Emperor Aurangzeb.

Hyder Ali was renowned for his innovative use of rockets in combat. They could indeed be launched from mobile batteries moved from place to place by teams of Mysore's famous oxen and sparked British interest in rocket technology. In the early nineteenth-century Britain, William Congreve studied Mysorean rocket cases while developing what became known as 'Congreve rockets' used in the Napoleonic wars.

Chapter Eight

The Salimgarh, first built in 1546, is today a museum in the care of the Archaeological Survey of India (ASI).

Sir Thomas Roe was the first English ambassador to the Moghul court, arriving in 1614, and became a drinking companion of Emperor Jahangir. During his time at the Moghul court, Roe observed the growing influence over political affairs of Nur Mahal (also known as Nur Jahan), Jahangir's empress and the aunt of Mumtaz Mahal for whom the Taj Mahal would be built.

Chapter Nine

The family of Najaf Khan fled their Persian homeland after Nadir Shah displaced the Safavid dynasty. He did suffer recurrent bouts of illness and died relatively young in 1782.

Chapter Ten

Pousta – an opium concoction that over time destroyed the brain – was used quite frequently by the Moghuls to neutralise rebellious family members they baulked at executing outright.

Zabita Khan, the Rohilla chieftain, died in 1785. An additional reason – apart from not finding enough treasure – why his son and successor, Ghulam Qadir, blinded Emperor Shah Alam was that the Emperor had castrated Ghulam Qadir in the late 1770s after capturing him.

Chapter Eleven

Philip Francis' affair with the young and beautiful Catherine Noel Grand was a *cause célèbre* in Calcutta.

Chapter Twelve

Hastings somewhat intriguingly described Lieutenant-Colonel Thomas Goddard, Leslie's second-in-command, as 'lively and enterprising, sensible, and the very reverse of the sordid disposition and morose and disgusting manners of his predecessor'.

After acquiring Bombay, the British built the castle using local blue stone and red laterite stone from the south on the site of a manor house that had belonged to a Portuguese nobleman, Garcia de Orta. The remains of the castle are still sometimes called the Casa da Orta.

Chapter Thirteen

The Company forces led by Egerton and Carnac in support of Ragoba were surrounded and overwhelmed by Marathas some sixteen miles from Poona after abandoning some of their equipment as described.

Chapter Fourteen

Coote's comment that 'Acts that proclaim confidence and determination are the only way to overcome danger. Everything else is defeatism!' are his actual words.

The duel between Warren Hastings and Philip Francis took place on 17 August 1780 and is well documented in letters and contemporary accounts, including Francis' misfirings, their comments to one another and how Hastings sent Francis his personal physician from Calcutta. Hastings in fact wrote three letters to Marian – two on the day of the duel and another on the following day. In the latter he wrote, 'You must not be angry; perhaps it is best that what has passed has passed, and it may be productive of future good.'

Chapter Fifteen

The description of the forces sent to Madras under Coote and Pearse is accurate.

Though Nicholas' meeting with Scindia is of course fictitious there was a real danger to the Company of the Marathas and Hyder Ali making common cause against it.

Chapter Sixteen

Before the disaster at the first Battle of Pollilur, Baillie and Munro, as Scots, wrote to each other in Gaelic in case their messages fell into enemy hands.

Chapter Seventeen

Today, a memorial at Pollilur still commemorates Lieutenant-Colonel George Brown.

Chapter Nineteen

After his return to Britain, Francis entered parliament and became a vigorous member of the movement seeking to abolish slavery.

After later returning to France, the beautiful Mrs Grand became first a courtesan, then mistress and later wife of Napoleon's foreign minister Talleyrand.

It was claimed during Hastings' impeachment that the Company 'waterboarded' the eunuchs to try to force them to reveal where the begums of Oudh had hidden their hoard.

Chapter Twenty-Four

Hastings' critics drew attention to the fact that Hastings' friend and former schoolmate at Westminster school Elijah Impey presided over Nandakumar's trial for forgery before the Supreme Court.

Hastings was indeed interested in Hindustan's flora. He planted his garden at Alipur with 'curious and valuable exotics from all quarters' as the basis for a systematic study.

Unlike many of his time, Hastings already foresaw the end of the British in Hindustan, predicting a time 'when the British dominion in India shall have long ceased to exist, and when the sources which it once wielded of wealth and power are lost to remembrance'.